Beyond the Eyes

Edition May 2012

Acknowledgments

This book is dedicated to my wonderful husband and best friend Kevin Ford. There are no words that can express how grateful I am for your support and encouragement. I love you, always and forever.

I'd like to thank the wonderful and talented Valentina Cano for her support and friendship. It means the world to me.

Thank you, Dad and Mom Wilhelm for believing in me. I love you both.

Thank you, Lisa Damerst, for your help. I greatly appreciate it.

I want to give a special shout-out to my cover artist, Stephanie Bibb who did a terrific job on my cover and is a pleasure to work with. Thanks, Stephanie. www.sbibbphoto.com

Thank you, Chase Nottingham, for editing this manuscript. I appreciate your help more than I can say. You're awesome.

Thanks to Amy Siders and her team for formatting this manuscript and answering all of my questions. You guys rock.

I would like to acknowledge Joe Ford. Even though he left this earth in 1999, I know if he were still here, he'd be cheering me on. I miss you, Joe.

And last, but certainly not least, I want to thank you, the reader. Yeah, you. Thank you from the bottom of my heart and every inch of my being, for reading this first book in the series. Without your support, my book would be sitting on a shelf collecting dust, sad and lonely. I hope you enjoy it.

Yea, though I walk through the valley of the shadow of death,
I will fear no evil.

Psalm 23:4

Beyond the Eyes

REBEKKAH FORD

Chapter One
Premonition

I never thought I would die at the age of seventeen, so when I received the death message, I was a little freaked out.

It happened on a Friday, late afternoon in March, at my favorite hangout spot–a coffeehouse called Café Nation. Routinely, my friends and I went to Café Nation to sit around, drink coffee, and bullshit about mindless, but entertaining crap. It was a way to decompress and forget about things for a while, like the biology essay due on Monday, or the SAT that was creeping up on us. Café Nation was a place where we could just be ourselves and not have to worry about some adults scrutinizing us because we didn't fit the wholesome, apple pie a la mode ideology crap we'd heard them talk about. Not that I didn't respect adults, I totally did. I just wished the ones who judged us so harshly would extend the same courtesy.

Anyway, Matt and I were sitting at our usual table in the far corner of the café, and he was talking nonstop in his caffeinated babble. The silver hoop protruding from his bottom lip seemed to flap a million miles an hour.

I eyed the five empty espresso cups scattered in front of him, hoping he wouldn't order another one. His jacked-up energy exhausted me.

"The Bible was written by man, not God," he said, going off on one of his religious tangents. Again. He paused, and a devious smile formed on his lips, as if he knew a secret he wasn't willing to share. "The people who wrote it knew what they were doing."

I loved history, and Matt was a genius when came to it, but lately we'd been having the same conversations about religion and humanity, and I was tired of it. I had no interest in mocking other people's beliefs. I mean, I wouldn't want people to mock mine, or me for that matter, which I was painfully aware could easily happen if they'd found out my secret.

"Most people don't know what the hell is really going on, and they're easily manipulated, and …"

I tuned him out and thought about what I was going to do on spring break. I'd love to go to Scotland or Ireland. But then again, that would totally suck ass to be crammed in a seat for like ten hours or however long it took to get there. I wondered how much a first class ticket would cost. I took a sip of my latte, tasting the warm, sweet vanilla against my tongue, and that was when it happened.

The voice spoke.

Normally, I would have ignored it like I always did, but it said my name, which it had never done before. And then a harsh grinding noise erupted.

I glanced at Matt who continued on babbling, then my frantic eyes searched the café for any hint of acknowledgment to the voice I'd just heard.

There were a couple skaters sitting on the brown patchwork couch across the room, animatedly talking. The rest of the café was filled with hippies, Goths, and people in suits.

Of course they hadn't heard it. What was I thinking? It wasn't like anybody had before.

Then the ghostly voice spoke again, startling me. I flinched, and stared at the dark wood grain on the table as the voice repeated the same cryptic words:

"*The arms of death are opening up to you. The name Paige Reed falls from its lips. Tears of sorrow will be shed, bringing you closer to your destiny.*"

"Paige, what's wrong?" Matt's voice sounded distant, like it was tailing the wind from a faraway canyon.

And then my ears rang in a high-pitched noise that was totally annoying. A squealing pig combined with a tiny bell was what it sounded like.

What the hell?

I blinked and jabbed a finger in my ear, wiggling it. Matt was watching me, and when I looked at him, something flickered in his eyes, like a lightning bolt in the clear blue sky. I wasn't sure what it was, though, because he looked away.

Dropping my hands into my lap, I stared at my fingers as the ringing began to fade. I could feel Matt's questioning eyes on me. He was waiting for an answer.

My heart pounded.

Nobody knew I'd been receiving cryptic premonitions from a ghostly voice for years. Not even Carrie or Tree (his real name was Jack, but we called him Tree because he was tall and had a bitchin' Mohawk), my two best friends in the whole world knew. I wished I could tell them, but my fear of them seeing me as a freak prevented me from doing so. So I had to play it cool with Matt, and mask the sudden terror I felt with indifference, an act I had performed many times.

The coffee grinder stopped, and the café resumed its natural hum of chattering patrons.

I slowly breathed in the fresh yummy smell of coffee and shrugged. "Oh, it's nothing. I was just distracted by a disturbing thought."

Matt leaned forward. I kept a straight face, trying not to waver under his gaze. "What disturbing thought was that?" His words were slow but alive with interest, and his eyes bore into mine as if he were trying to lift the answer out of my mind. It was kind of spooky, but then again, I was a little spooked out.

"Oh, it's nothing really," I repeated, looking away to avoid his scrutiny, but out the corner of my eye I saw him glowering at me. He ran his fingers through his thick dark hair and grunted.

Great. Now I pissed him off. It was bad enough I had a premonition in front of him, and even worse it had to do with me, and I didn't know what the hell it meant.

I scanned the café seeking a diversion and saw Ashley at the counter with one of her leg-puppies beside her. She was the cliché of a head varsity cheerleader: blonde, athletic, and snobby. I mean, she was so full of herself it made a person want to throw up. Seriously.

"I think Ken should grow some balls and tell Barbie to piss off," Matt said after Ashley waved an accusing finger in Darren's (leg-puppy) face, then stomped off to a table beside a window. I looked at him, not realizing he had been watching as well, and he had a sardonic smirk on his face. "But the dumb jock prefers to be whipped, instead of a real man who wouldn't put up with her shit." He stuck his hand out toward Darren and continued. "If this is a prelude to what men are going to become in the future, the human race is much more slow-witted than I thought."

"That's kind of harsh," I said, and he shrugged like he didn't give a crap. I frowned and saw Carrie entering the café. She smiled and waved. Her black hair now had dark red tips that touched her shoulders, and she wore a vintage Cure T-shirt with Robert Smith's face poking out of her black cargo jacket.

"Do you like it?" She swung her hair from side to side.

"It looks really good on you." I forced a smile, trying my best not to allow my rattled emotions show. But her attention was focused on Matt instead. And when he nodded in approval, she lit up like a Christmas tree. I had to suppress an eye roll. I mean, yeah, she had the hots for him (it was so obvious), but she could at least be more dignified about it.

She snatched a lock of my hair and held it up to hers. "I wanted the tips to be the same color as your hair, and I think it's pretty close to it."

"So, Carrie, I'll pick you up at nine tonight, and then we'll pick Paige up." Matt rose from his seat, not interested in sitting through a conversation about hair color.

I had totally forgotten about going to The Lion's Den and really wasn't in the mood to go. What I really wanted to do was try to figure out my premonition before something bad happened. But then again, maybe being around friends would do me some good. And maybe, if I was lucky, it would take away this knot in my stomach. But truthfully, I wasn't a lucky person.

As we were leaving, Ashley gave us a disgusted look. I ignored her like always, but Matt couldn't pass up the opportunity to be rude. He leaned behind Darren and wiggled his tongue at her. Ashley's mouth dropped, clearly surprised at Matt's bold move. Carrie and I exchanged humorous looks. We pushed past Matt. Carrie grabbed his hand, pulling him with us out the door into the gray, cloudy world. The air had a dank, fishy smell that caused me to wrinkle my nose.

"Did you see the look on her face?" Carrie said, giggling.

Laughing, I nodded. That was one of the fun things about Matt. He had no inhibitions.

Matt smiled and pointed at the window where Ashley sat. "She deserved it, especially with the way she treats Paige."

Right then, a thought occurred to me. What if antagonizing her wasn't such a good idea. I mean, for the past six months, Ashley had been nothing but rude to me, and I still didn't know why. It wasn't like I had ever done anything to her. And yeah, she had been rude to Carrie as well, but for some reason I was her favorite target.

"Maybe you shouldn't have done that," I said, the raspy part of my voice cracking. It always did that when I was worried, scared, or upset, and I hated it.

They looked at me like I'd grown another head.

"Paige, have you forgotten about the whole Zack situation, and the shit she said about you?" Carrie reminded me.

"No," I said. How could I forget? Ashley had told everybody I was such a loser that my own mother didn't want to be around me. Then Zack came up to me at the beginning of class and said he couldn't go out with me because he had to wash his jock strap. My gut twisted when the vision of Ashley and some of my classmates snickering, entered my mind. I had been totally humiliated and wanted to die right there. That night, I'd cried myself to sleep because what she'd said about my mother had slammed me pretty hard.

Carrie pointed a sharp finger at me. "So don't you go feeling bad for her. She doesn't deserve your guilt, and don't forget about the shit she said about me too." She pressed her hands into her hips and glared at me.

"You're right," I admitted, heading across the street, leaving the rows of shops behind, "but she's never been mean to you, Matt, so what's your excuse?"

He kicked a rock. It bounced off the curb into a gutter. "It's simple. I just don't like her."

Carrie laughed as if it was the funniest thing she had ever heard. "You're too funny." She bumped her hip against Matt, totally crushing on him. I wondered if they'd end up dating. I hated feeling like a third wheel and was already starting to feel like one. Thank God we reached my car first.

Almost two years ago on my sixteenth birthday, Mom had bought me a black 1991 Morris Mini Rover. It was her way of telling me she loves me and buying off her own guilt for not being around like a normal mom, which was fine with me. I mean, this car totally rocked, and I wasn't about to begrudge her intentions behind it.

"I'll see you guys later." I stepped inside my car, breathing in the vanilla aroma wafting off my Hello Kitty sachet. I flicked it with my finger, and it spun beneath the mirror.

I sat there for a few minutes, watching them walk across the lawn of the courthouse square. The purplish-gray sky and the skeletal black trees around the white courthouse reminded me of a Tim Burton movie. And as I sat there pondering over my premonition, a distinct feeling of being watched came over me. It wasn't Carrie or Matt. I'd seen them like a minute ago wave good-bye to each other and head in opposite directions. I twisted in my seat and peered out the back window. The street lamps popped on, casting a yellow glow across the zebra-striped crosswalk. A couple with two young kids going inside Tasty Cone were the only people around.

They weren't watching me.

"Stop being paranoid," I told myself, backing out onto the street. But then I caught a glimpse of somebody darting behind the courthouse, and my heart sank.

I panicked, thinking about the premonition again, wondering if somebody was going to murder me. I mean, it did say the arms of death were opening up to me. So were the arms of death some psycho killer who wanted to torture me? But what about the tears of sorrow bringing me closer to my destiny? That didn't make sense. If some dude was going to kill me, how could that bring me closer to my destiny?

On the way home, my mind conjured up scenarios of how somebody would try to kill me. When I finally reached the gray and white bungalow style house nestled among cathedral trees, I was home.With a shaky hand I pushed the garage door button. It gave off a loud rattling sound as it slowly crept up, unnerving me. Finally, it jerked to a stop–metal grinding against metal. I parked the car and bolted inside the house. I quickly turned the lights on and stopped in the hallway that divided the kitchen from the living room. The brown couches and matching recliner appeared undisturbed. Beside the flat screen TV was the remote, where I'd left it this morning. I glanced in the kitchen. All four chairs were tucked neatly under the table, and my coffee mug sat on the counter beside the sink. I breathed in the familiar scent of cinnamon and nutmeg while I listened for any movement in the house.

Silence.

But then I thought I heard a clattering noise outside the front window. I hurried over to it and peeked out the curtains. The street was deserted, except for a cat walking toward the house. Breathing a sigh of relief, I sat on the couch, dropping my head into my hands.

"This isn't like you," I mumbled to the floor. "You need to get a grip on yourself and forget about these stupid fears."

Yeah, I must try. But damn it. Something wasn't right. I could feel it in my bones, and it had to do with me. *Why*? Why couldn't I be like a normal teenager? What had I ever done to deserve this? Tears collected in my eyes. Taking a deep breath, I ran my fingers through my hair, telling myself again, I must try to forget about it and act like a normal teenager. With determination, I set out to do just that, ignoring the constant gnawing in the back of my brain.

***

A car horn blared outside. I adjusted my black pleated mini dress, and stepped into my black Mary Jane platform shoes, loving that it boosted my height another inch to five-four. I threw on a dark purple-hooded sweater coat over my dress and lifted my hair up, allowing it to fall down my back.

"You can do this, Paige," I said to the round-faced image in the full-length mirror. My dark red hair sparkled from the glitter product I had put in earlier. I tried to smile to take away the pinch in my mouth. "You've been ignoring these premonitions for years. You can at least forget about this one for a while."

The horn blared again, but this time with much more urgency.

"I'm coming," I hollered, rushing out my room, smacking the light switch off.

Downstairs, I grabbed my keys and backpack purse off the kitchen table. I flipped the porch light on and stepped outside. The gray and black stray cat I'd seen earlier was sitting on the porch step, staring at Matt's jeep. His tail twitched and danced around like he was aggravated. When I walked by him, he leaped off the step, following me to the edge of the lawn. And then my ears began to ring again. I sighed and hopped in Matt's jeep.

Carrie peeked around the front seat, her eyes gleaming in the dark. "Was that your cat?"

I dropped my keys in my purse, trying to ignore the ringing, and shook my head. "I think he's a stray." Matt's jeep smelled like sweaty feet, so I rolled the window down to let some air in.

Cursing under his breath, Matt flipped through radio stations, trying to find a worthy song to listen to. His cd player was broken, forcing him to rely on the radio instead. He stopped on a country song, and we all groaned in unison. Carrie and I looked at each other and shuddered.

"I hope this damn thing doesn't just get country stations. If it does, I'll be pissed," he said, turning the knob again. "*Yes*! Here's a kick ass song." He nodded his head to the beat. Carrie turned around in her seat, and I sat back, grateful I wasn't alone, and the ringing had stopped.

***

"Wow. This place is really busy tonight," Carrie said, glancing around the crowded parking lot. She pulled the cuffs of her red waistcoat over her hands and shivered against the frigid air. It looked like she had a black lace-up corset underneath it. No wonder she was cold, but at least her long black skirt covered her legs, although the metal zipper that ran up the side of it was probably cold against her skin. I was suddenly thankful I had decided to wear my sweater coat.

"Of course it's busy." Matt stepped between us and placed a hand on our shoulder. "What else are people going to do in good old Astoria besides clubbing and bar hopping?" He lifted his shoulders when we looked at him, as if to say, "Am I right?"

Astoria, Oregon was a city of ten-thousand people on the Columbia River. I loved Astoria. I loved the tall evergreen and spruce trees, the mountains, the river, the forest, and that it was just a few miles from the Pacific Ocean. Astoria was our home.

I flashed him an alluring smile. "I can think of a few things."

Carrie giggled. "You're bad."

Matt stepped ahead of us and turned around, walking backwards. "Yeah, they're either doing this"–he made a round circle with his right hand and stuck his left index finger in and out in a rapid motion–"or they're doing this"–he made a fist with his right hand and jabbed it back and forth near his crotch–"but either way, they're having fun." He tilted his head to the side; his red and blue spikes shined beneath the yellow glow of the street lamps. Grinning, he waggled his eyebrows.

Carrie and I burst out in laughter.

Up ahead stood The Lion's Den, dark and menacing, with its fake fog pouring out of the round stone entrance in waves. Bright red and orange lights flashed inside its mouth to the beat of the alternative music we now heard. The ancient brick building held several bars inside the length of it, but The Lion's Den was dead center and alcohol free.

Matt turned around and sprinted toward the entrance. "C'mon, they're playing my favorite song." He waved over his shoulder.

The place smelled like wood cleaner and leather and was packed with teenagers. Most of them I knew and were friends with. I spotted Tree right away, on the dance floor across the room, jerking his head to the rhythm of the music, spurts of red and orange lights flashed across his black Mohawk. He saw us and waved.

Carrie pointed to Matt, and we laughed. He looked like he was doing a war dance. Some of the kids joined in, mimicking his moves, reminding me of aborigines. Tree was breaking away from the crowd, heading our way.

"Hey," Tree said, practically yelling over the loud music, totally checking Carrie out.

"Hi, Tree," Carrie said, her eyes still on Matt. "How are you?"

He shifted his weight back and forth. "Good, but these combat boots are hurting my feet." His Mohawk was bone-straight and as tall as my forearm. When he looked at his foot, I saw a fake tattoo of a skull and crossbones on the side of his head. It looked totally awesome. "I guess I should've broken them in first," he added.

Carrie tore her eyes away from Matt, and they widened when she dropped her gaze to his feet. "Those are cool boots! Where did you get them?"

Tree smiled. "I ordered them from Cheaper Than Dirt."

"Cool." She turned to me as if Tree wasn't even there. "Let's go dance."

"We should go get a locker first," I told her, disappointed she blew Tree off.

"There's an empty one next to mine," Tree said. "I'll show you."

I knew Carrie wanted to dance with Matt, so I offered to take her stuff and get us a locker. Tree stood there, staring after her, his face baring his hurt feelings. I hated seeing him like that and made a mental note to talk to Carrie about it. Tree was our best friend and just because she had the hots for Matt, didn't give her the right to treat Tree that way. I mean, I loved Carrie, but sometimes I wanted to knock some sense into her.

"What's the locker number beside yours that's empty?" I asked him when we reached the counter. The kid behind it looked no older than fourteen. His blond hair was spiked up in all different directions, and he wore black eyeliner–thick around his dark eyes.

"It's number fifty-five," Tree told the kid.

The kid searched through a row of keys on a huge round key ring until he found the right one. I gave him two dollars as he handed me the key, and then we went to the lockers on the back wall beside the entrance. I took my sweater off when I spotted the large white number fifty-five on black metal. Tree opened his locker and grabbed his stuff.

"Are you leaving?" I didn't want him to go like this–bummed and depressed.

"Yeah, my feet hurt, and I've been here for a while already." He glanced over at Carrie dancing with Matt, and then his eyes fell back on mine. They were full of the same disappointment I'd felt earlier, and I wanted to make him feel better.

"Don't go," I said. "You can dance with me. Maybe she'll get jealous and realize she still likes you." It was difficult talking to him like this. We had to strain our voices over the music, and I found myself wanting to be in a quieter place.

He shook his head while putting on his leather trench coat and scrunched up his face. "I don't think so. I know Matt is your friend, but I think he's a douche bag." He paused. "And if he ever hurts Carrie," he added, his face now clouded with anger, "I'll beat his ass."

The hostility in his voice surprised me, causing my heart to flutter with jealousy. I mean, nobody cared enough about me to act that way. I looked away, gripped by loneliness.

He placed his hands on my shoulders. "I'd beat his ass if he hurts you too," he said.

I squinted at him and laughed. "You'd use any excuse to beat his ass."

"Yup." He grinned. "Have fun, Ms. Reed. My little fairy."

"Okay, bye." I watched him throw one more glance in Carrie's direction before heading outside. He towered over a group of kids coming in. All five of them stopped to stare at him, and I couldn't blame them. He did look like he belonged in a punk band somewhere in Europe.

"Are you going to join us?" Carrie asked, tugging on my arm.

"Yeah, but I need to talk to you about Tree," I said, still feeling bad for him.

"Okay, but later." She took my hand, towing me behind her.

As we made our way through the crowd of moving bodies, my ears started to ring again. Okay, this was seriously getting on my last nerve, but then I reminded myself I was here to have fun and began swaying my hips when we reached Matt. My body automatically moved inside a bubble of energetic sound waves–free and unencumbered. I was no longer the freak, with a mother who showed up when she wanted to and a father who had died when I was four. None of that stuff mattered, because in that moment I was one with the music and the pulsing lights. And as each song changed into pure techno melodies, I became more entranced, closing my eyes, swaying my body to the beat of the music, entering my own world.

Then something strange happened. The people around me were now far below me, and I was tethered to a silver cord attached to my dancing body. I wasn't scared though, and found myself enjoying this sense of release. I had no worries. Even when I thought about the premonition, the fear I'd felt toward it earlier didn't touch me. Probably since I knew I wasn't dead. I mean, hey, the silver cord remained attached to my body, so I was good, right?

As I took in my surroundings, a guy wearing a long black coat caught my attention. He was on the high platform overlooking the floor with his hands gripping the black railing. His hood concealed his face, but he appeared to be watching the people down below.

My eyes swept over the crowd and rested on Matt standing there staring intently on my swaying body. He took a step closer and leaned forward.

Was he sniffing me?

He looked up, searching for something.

At that exact moment, the hooded guy jumped off the platform, over the black railing, and ran to the dance floor. And then Matt's eyes locked onto mine. They were pale and glowing.

I shuddered.

The silvery cord rippled, and then yanked me toward my body, as if I was a balloon being pulled down by an eager child's grasp. Everything rushed before me: the tables, the crowd of moving heads, and my own head, moving in a figure eight along with my body. I closed my eyes, and collided into a hard, confining surface, and that was the last thing I could remember.

Chapter Two
Confusion

"Is Paige going to be okay?" Carrie asked.

"Carrie?" I tried to say but couldn't.

What the hell?

For a second I wondered if this could be a dream. But I sensed Carrie and another presence near me, so it couldn't be. I was lying on something soft–a couch maybe–and the air smelled like tobacco.

I willed myself to move.

Nothing.

I couldn't even move one stupid finger.

Crap.

And then a male voice told her I'd be fine, and something cold and damp was placed on my forehead. I tried to recall what happened, but my mind was all foggy. All I could remember was going to The Lion's Den with Carrie and Matt and talking to Tree.

"Do you know if she ate something tonight?" the mystery guy's soft voice asked.

"No," Carrie said, unsure. She paused for a minute. "Why?" Her voice came from across the room and even though my eyes were closed, I knew her well enough to know she had a questioning look on her face, and she was looking at this guy for an answer. "Do you think that's the reason why she passed out?"

"I think it could be," he said next to me.

Who is this guy? I thought, and at the same time wondered if I did eat this evening, but then Carrie captured my attention by asking him if he was new in town. For some odd reason, the sound of his voice comforted me, and I wanted to listen to it some more.

"Yes. I moved here from Seattle three months ago."

"Are you from Seattle?"

"No. I'm actually from Missouri."

"Oh … So what brought you here?"

All of a sudden the pig-squealing-tiny-bell-sound exploded in my ears, and the door opened.

"Carrie, is Paige okay?" Matt asked above the tide of thumping music.

When I heard Matt's voice, everything came back to me in quick flickering images: the look he gave me when we were having coffee, Carrie pulling me on the dance floor, hovering in the air, seeing that hooded guy, watching myself dance, and Matt's eyes glowing.

My heart pounded in my ears, and the words from my premonition leaked into my conscious mind. My body shook as a cold feeling came over me that I might be dying. *Oh. God. Please. I don't want to die!*

"What's wrong with Paige?" Carrie shrieked.

"You need to leave," the guy barked at Matt, surprising me because I didn't understand why he'd say that to him. I mean, Matt just wanted to know if I was okay, so what was his problem?

"Don't tell me what to do," Matt said, sharp and defensive.

"Look. She'll be waking up soon. Can you get her a protein drink from the juice bar." It wasn't a question, but a harsh command.

Jeez, what was with this guy?

"Fine … By the way. What's your name?"

"Nathan Caswell."

"Well, Nathan Caswell, I'll be right back." Matt spat out each word like they were poison on his lips. I could feel the hostility in his words as if they had slapped me in the face.

The door slammed and the ringing in my ears abruptly quit. I stopped shaking and tried to open my eyes as the heaviness in my body began to lift.

Carrie sounded both shocked and nervous. "You really pissed him off."

"He'll get over it," Nathan murmured.

I could feel him kneeling beside me, his hand next to my side, pushing down on the cushion.

Slowly my eyes opened to a pair of dark blue eyes that were full of concern. I blinked a couple times, and saw relief cross his boyish face. His short brown hair had blond tips that stood on top of his head in '80s skater fashion, and he still had his jacket on. I wondered if he was cold.

He was cute, and I couldn't understand why he'd be concerned about me. A warm smile formed on his face, and for the first time in my life something fluttered inside my chest.

"Paige, you're awake." Carrie bumped Nathan aside. "I was so scared." Tears glistened in her brown eyes. She took my hand. Her palm was all sweaty, and I had to resist the urge to pull my hand away and wipe it off. "But Nathan knew what to do. He picked you up and brought you here to the employee lounge. The night supervisor said it was okay, but I think it was because he thought you might sue him and--"

I lifted my hand. "Hold on a minute." I pushed myself to a sitting position. The damp washrag fell off my forehead onto my lap, soaking through my dress, the wet coldness pressing against my thighs. I stared at it stupidly until Carrie picked it up and tossed it across the room into the metal sink. "Thanks," I said, touching the wet spot in my lap.

Nathan handed me a towel and bent down next to Carrie. His hand rested on the arm of the couch next to my shoulder, his face inches from mine. He looked at me, searching for any hint of discomfort. My stomach flipped.

"How are you feeling?"

I dropped my gaze, patting my lap with the towel. "I think I'm okay, but I do feel weak, and my head is foggy."

"Matt's getting you a protein drink," Carrie said. She stuck her hand out. "I'll take that for you."

I handed her the towel and turned to Nathan, and I swear the energy between us crackled. Or was I imagining it? I didn't know. But I was getting annoyed with myself for allowing a cute guy to affect me like this. Was I that pathetic? "And thank you for everything."

"Anytime," he said with a half-smile, dazzling me.

"I'm going to get our stuff and see what's taking Matt so long," Carrie announced.

I glanced at her and realized I wasn't breathing. Inconspicuously, I exhaled a lung full of air, feeling ridiculous. What the hell was wrong with me?

Carrie stepped beside Nathan and thrust her hand in my face. "I need the locker key." Her eyes darted between Nathan and me, and I knew she sensed how he was making me feel by the strange look on her face and the slight curve in her red lips. We shared a look two girlfriends exchanged when one of them didn't want the other to blab about something.

Nathan wandered over to the door as if the black paint and the silver knob suddenly fascinated him. Carrie hitched her thumb at him, screwing her face up. I lifted my shoulders and glanced down. Reaching into the front of my dress, I pulled a brass key out of my bra. The locker number was etched into it. I handed it over to Carrie and narrowed my eyes when an impish smile crossed her face. She turned to Nathan.

"Make sure she doesn't get up. She tends to be stubborn, and I--"

"Hey. I'm not *that* stubborn." I glared at her back, irritated she said that. It was bad enough I was experiencing strong emotions toward a guy I just met, but now she had to embarrass me in front of him. I gritted my teeth.

"Anyway," she said, ignoring my outburst, but I saw her jerking her thumb at me, nodding, and Nathan smiling, "I think Paige should drink the protein smoothie before we leave. So make sure she stays where she's at."

"Don't worry. I will," Nathan said, sounding amused.

"I don't need a babysitter, Carrie," I said under my breath, staring at my fingers, wishing she'd keep her trap shut and get our stuff already. I couldn't believe she had said that.

She turned. "Paige, you've been taking care of yourself almost your whole life, and I know you don't need a babysitter, but for once please allow somebody to take care of you."

As she said that, the room tilted at an odd angle, and I could feel the energy draining out of me. I blinked several times to fight against it. My temples throbbed and red blotches crossed my vision.

Carrie's eyes bugged out between the sharp black panels that kept flashing in front of me. "What's wrong, Paige?" Her scared voice rang out. "You're so pale."

"I … I … I don't know," I said, still blinking, rubbing my temples.

Nathan rushed to my side and told Carrie to get my drink and to hurry. He mumbled something about needing a vending machine in here and kneeled beside me. He had that concern look on his face again.

I wanted to tell him I was okay, so he didn't feel stuck with me, but the heaviness in my tongue prevented me from doing so. I closed my eyes. The fear of passing out again and never waking up entered my mind, and for some reason I thought about my father, missing him. But I wasn't ready to join him in the afterlife. In fact, I wanted it the other way around. If he were alive, Mom would be home working in town instead of as a traveling nurse, and we'd all be together. We'd be a family. Our house would be filled with love and laughter instead of silence. But that would never happen.

I felt truly alone.

"You're going to be all right, Paige," Nathan whispered, tenderly brushing a tear off my cheek, making my heart race. "Please don't cry."

I opened my eyes, thankful the room was no longer tilting, but embarrassed about my tears, and how he was making me feel. I cleared my throat. "I'm sorry. I usually don't cry in front of people." I glanced at him and looked away, my cheeks burning.

I wiped the tears off my face and sniffed in shame. It was just my luck I'd cry in front of the cutest guy ever.

"There's nothing to be sorry about." He lifted his hand to my face, then dropped it.

Carrie burst through the door with a Styrofoam cup in her hand. "Here you go, Paige." She handed it to me, and I immediately drank the fruity mango smoothie. The coldness slid down my throat and into my chest, freezing it. I shivered. It tasted yummy and fueled the energy back into my body. "I gave Matt the key so he can get our stuff. He said there was a huge line and that's what took so long." She was too distracted to notice I'd been crying.

"Is he taking you two home?" Nathan asked, rising to his feet.

I nodded with the straw still in my mouth and thought I saw disapproval in his eyes.

"Yeah, why?" Carrie asked, sounding defensive.

He shrugged. "I was just wondering."

"Thanks for getting me this." I lifted the cup to Carrie, as if I was toasting her.

"You're welcome." She smiled. "You look a lot better."

I stuck the straw back in my mouth and moved it around, making loud sucking noises as it grabbed every last drop. With a satisfied look, Carrie threw the container in the trash.

"I was thinking maybe I should stay at your house tonight," she told me.

Nathan's brow furrowed. "Aren't your parents home?"

I opened my mouth to answer him, but Carrie beat me to it.

"Paige's father is dead, and her mom's job takes her away from home. So to answer your question … No, Paige's *parent* is not home, but she has a gun and is not afraid to use it."

"Carrie!" I exclaimed, shocked at her behavior. What the hell was her problem?

"Are you mad at me?" Nathan asked Carrie while I looked at him and thought about how tall he was. He had to be six-foot one, putting him a couple inches taller than Matt.

"No," Carrie said. "It's just Matt is in a bad mood because he's pissed off at you."

"Um, Carrie, I hate to tell you this, but Matt was pissed off earlier too," I said. "He's been moody all day." I stole a glimpse at Nathan. He had his arms tight across his chest, appearing deep in thought.

God, he was frickin' cute.

I rubbed my forehead, silently telling myself to quit thinking those thoughts. Yeah, Nathan was totally hot, but drooling over him wasn't cool. Besides, he could do way better than me.

She jerked her head back, her forehead creasing. "I don't remember him being moody."

"Well, when we were having coffee earlier, before you showed up, he got mad at me, and on the way here he was irritated with his stereo."

"Why would he be mad at you?" Nathan asked in alarm.

"Because I wouldn't tell him what I was thinking," I replied, not wanting to say the real reason. I looked away, self-conscious about what I truly was. A *freak.*

Right then, Matt walked in with our stuff in his arms, and my ears squealed into a high pitched ringing sound again. Standing up, I jabbed a finger in my right ear and wiggled it.

Nathan moved to my side as Matt and I exchanged looks. For the first time since I woke up, I thought about Matt's eyes. He raised his hand, and I thought maybe what I had seen was an illusion created by the lights in the club. That had to be it. I mean, nobody's eyes could glow like that on their own, right?

"Are you okay?" Nathan asked.

"Yeah, my ears are just ringing," I said, catching the startled look on his face before he looked away.

An overweight guy with black disheveled hair entered the room. His earlobes had round gages in them, and his chubby face was decorated with metal studs and hoops. He immediately came over to me, told me his name was Derek, the night supervisor, and asked how I was doing. Beads of sweat clung to his broad forehead, and I wondered if Carrie was right about him thinking I would sue him.

"I feel much better," I told him, intentionally making my voice sound reassuring as I pulled my finger out of my ear.

"That's good to hear," he said with a nervous smile, and continued while Carrie handed me my stuff. "I have tickets I want to give you guys to see a band that's going to be playing here in two weeks." He retrieved four tickets from his back pocket and handed one to each of us.

"Which band is that?" Matt asked.

"Alchemy, and they kick ass." Derek grinned. "They play techno-metal. And believe me, you guys are going to love them. I think they're going to revolutionize the music industry."

After we thanked Derek, we followed him out into the club down a long, narrow hall with black, round speakers poking out of the red walls. Nathan stayed by my side while we walked behind the three of them, his arm close to mine. I tried not to focus on that fact. Instead, my mind sank into deep thoughts about everything that happened tonight, including how weird it was a guy I hardly knew could stir feelings in me I'd never felt before. I even had felt an electrical charge between us, which made me wonder if he felt it too. Or if he felt anything at all. Maybe I shouldn't be thinking this stuff. It all seemed so silly. Nutty even. But regardless of how premature my feelings were, I couldn't stop my mind from wheeling over them.

Teenage hormones.

Yeah, that was it. That was my problem. It had to be. Not to mention, primordially speaking, I was at that ripe age to reproduce, and Nathan would be the perfect candidate for that. He was cute with a strong, powerful body…

I mentally shook myself, feeling ridiculous. What was wrong with me?

"Do you mind if I take you home?" Nathan asked, giving me a sideways glance, startling me out of my mental chatter. He was close enough to where I could hear him above the music. His voice sounded husky. "I know Carrie is going to spend the night, but Matt can take her to get her stuff and drop her off at your house."

I thought about spending more time with him, and my pulse soared as if somebody slammed my veins with a dose of liquid excitement. I pretended to ponder it while I told myself I needed to live a little and have some fun. I deserved that, right?

"Well, I usually don't allow somebody who I just met take me home, but you are an exception," I said in a teasing tone of voice. I couldn't help it. I had to flirt with him.

He bent his head down and peeked at me. "Is that a yes then?" He was totally flirting back.

I smiled and wondered if I was treading dangerous water to allow somebody to affect me like this, but I felt too compelled by him to care. I nodded. When he mirrored my smile, I bit my bottom lip and looked away.

The club was still packed. Some were standing around in groups while others danced to the loud industrial music. Red and orange lights pulsed to the beat, flashing the dancers. I shifted my gaze to the juice bar on the far wall. There was a line, which told me Matt wasn't lying to Carrie.

Craning my neck, I looked up at the platform. There were people sitting at the tables and others dancing next to the black railing. An image of a hooded guy jumping over the railing entered my mind. But the platform was too high for somebody to do that without seriously hurting himself or dying for that matter. And who was that guy, and how could he have jumped off that platform? And why did I have an out-of-body experience? Why had I passed out? What was happening to me?

Once outside, Nathan hung back beside the club while I told Carrie and Matt about him taking me home. There were clubbers hanging outside the bars laughing and smoking. Their loud voices floated over to us from across the street, along with the music.

"Are you sure about this?" Matt's distrustful eyes strayed over to Nathan.

I playfully slapped his arm. "Stop that. He's a nice guy."

"No, he's not. He's a *dick!*" he said, half-yelling.

For some reason his scornful words offended me, and I didn't like the hateful look on his face. He didn't even know Nathan and needed to get over his pissy mood.

I squared my shoulders and faced him. In my peripheral vision I saw Nathan watching us, taking a step forward. "He is *not* a dick," I said, glaring at him. "I'm sure he didn't mean to piss you off."

"Paige is right," Carrie interceded. "He was very sweet to her."

"But you don't even *know* him," he argued. "And now you're going to let him take you home?" He flung his hands up and blew out an exasperated sigh.

"He's harmless, and I think he likes her." Carrie winked at me and a burning sensation filled my cheeks. "And besides," she continued, "you're dropping me off at her house later, so I think she's going to be just fine."

He raised his hands in defeat, his face twisted in annoyance. "All right, let's go." He grabbed her hand, spinning her around.

Carrie glanced over her shoulder at me and grinned.

"Have fun," I said, knowing this was what she had hoped for.

"Matt is still pissed at me, huh?" Nathan asked, stepping beside me.

I shrugged. "He'll get over it. He's just being a brat." *More like an ass monkey.*

As we walked to his car, I gazed at the dark sky. The bright stars reminded me of sparkling diamonds against black satin, and the yellow moon was equally beautiful with white, misty clouds skirting it. And while I marveled over its mystical wonder, an intense feeling of change came over me, the kind of change that transported Dorothy from a black and white world into a world of brilliant color. It was a bizarre, but undeniable feeling to say the least.

"Are you and Matt good friends?" Nathan asked, breaking the brief silence between us.

"Yeah, we are," I said, "But when we were kids, we weren't. He used to be mean and hateful, but then he moved to Seattle and just moved back three months ago, now he's like a totally different person." I glanced at him. He appeared deep in thought, staring at the ground. "Why?"

"Did your ears ever ring like that before?"

"No, not until today."

We stopped in front of a black extended cab Ford truck. I turned to him in surprise.

"Is this your truck?"

The corner of his mouth lifted (I loved how his mouth did that, like it was part of his persona). "It is. Why?" He opened the passenger door, and I hopped in. Sitting back, I pulled the seatbelt over me, clicking it into place, breathing in the smell of the soft leather seats. I loved the smell. It reminded me of my father's leather jacket.

"You just don't seem like a truck person," I told him when he slid behind the wheel.

"Why is that?" He paused. "Before you answer that, I need to know where you live."

"Oh, that would help." Hot blood flooded my cheeks.

I gave him the directions to my house and said he seemed more like a 1965 Ford Mustang type, which impressed him since he used to own one. When he told me that, I shot him a weird look, like *yeah, sure you did.* I knew guys tend to lie about stuff like that in order to appear cool, but he sounded honest when he told me he really did own one, and he had the pictures to prove it. So when I asked him what happened to it, and he told me it got totaled in a car accident, I amazed myself that I actually believed him. I mean, if it were anybody else, I wouldn't have. But I could tell he was being completely honest with me.

I thought how strange that was since I just met him, and I sat there mulling over it, while he continued to tell me he was more of a truck type of person anyway. He grew up on a farm in Missouri, and the truck was sort of nostalgic to him.

"What was it like growing up on a farm?" I pictured him, all hot and sweaty (shirtless, of course), working out in the field and sighed at that pleasant vision.

"It was wonderful. I wish every kid could grow up that way."

"Why is that?"

"Because it helps build confidence and teaches you self reliance and endurance, and you learn so much about nature to where you feel a connection with it." He looked at me like he wasn't sure if he should continue. "I know this might sound a bit crazy, but it can be spiritual. Does that make sense?"

"It makes perfect sense," I said, touched by his openness, realizing as I stared out the window into the darkness, how comfortable I felt around him.

A long silence fell between us, and the trees were getting thicker along the shoulder of the road. To my dissatisfaction, I'd soon be home. But I didn't want to leave him yet and wondered if I'd ever see him again. I was enjoying his company and wanted to know more about him. I decided to ask another question in hope it would prolong my time with him.

"Can I ask you something?"

"Absolutely," he said.

"How old are you?"

"I'm nineteen … How old are you?" His eyes held mine, and I looked away, ashamed to tell him because I didn't want him to think of me as a kid. I decided to play it off like it was nothing.

"I'm seventeen, but in a couple months I'll be eighteen." We were approaching my house, and I pointed to it. "There's my place."

"I figured that," he said in good humor. "There are only three houses in this little secluded area, and one with a porch light on."

He parked at the curb and turned the ignition off, which made my heart beat a little faster. Not because I feared he would harm me. If he wanted to do that, he would have done it already. I think it was the anxiety of him possibly blowing me off because of my age. But then again, if that were the case, he would have dropped me off and bailed. So maybe it was the anticipation of spending more time with him. Honestly, I didn't really know.

He shifted in his seat, facing me. "Are you okay?"

"Yeah, why?"

"You got quiet all of a sudden. I just thought maybe we could talk for a few more minutes. That is, if you don't mind?"

"I don't mind," I said, wondering what he wanted to talk about.

"Can I ask what you were thinking about a minute ago?" His voice was soft and curious.

I glanced out the side window. The stray cat was sitting on the porch, looking in our direction. It looked like he nodded, as if prompting me to answer Nathan's question. I blinked and shook my head, thinking I must be out of my mind. I turned to Nathan before my eyes played more tricks.

"I was wondering if my age bothers you."

"Not at all," he answered. "You're going to be eighteen in a couple months anyway." He looked down, then peered at me through his lashes. "Unless, your mom would mind."

I couldn't believe it. He didn't mind my age. But he was so hot and could have anybody. Yeah, I'd been told I was hot, but whatever. The people who had said that, were horny teenage boys who would say anything to get in a girl's pants.

So just to see what he'd say I told him my mom wouldn't mind, but she'd want to meet him.

"That's fine."

"So, you want to see me again?" I tried to sound indifferent and hoped I'd pulled it off, but really my insides were shaking.

He leaned forward; his eyes fixed on mine. When he spoke, his words were genuine and heartfelt. "Oh yes." There was no doubt in those two words. My insides shook again, but not from nerves this time. He leaned back, his gaze still on mine. "When can I see you again?"

"Is tomorrow at two okay? We can go to the river walk and walk along the waterfront."

After the last word escaped my lips, I cringed inwardly at how eager I sounded. *Great going, Paige. If you keep it up, he's going to think you're some desperate, psycho chick.*

"Sounds good to me." I think he smiled, but wasn't sure because he stepped out of the truck before I could catch his reaction. He opened my door, and I picked my purse off the floor, thanking him for the ride home.

The air had a thick rain smell to it, and sure enough, when we reached my front door, it started raining.

The stray cat had disappeared.

"What are you looking for?"

"Oh, sorry. I was looking for a stray cat that showed up at my house earlier. I saw him on the porch when we pulled up, but now he's gone. I was just wondering where he went."

"Is today the first time you've seen him?" Nathan asked, a note of anxiety in his voice.

"Yeah. He was here when I got home this evening. I'm guessing somebody didn't want him." I hated to think somebody would do that, but whatever. I'd take care of him.

"What did he look like?" His troubled eyes latched onto mine, confusing me. I couldn't understand why he'd get upset over a cat. It was a cat for God's sake.

"He was black and gray. Why?"

His face appeared tense now.

"What did the cat do when Matt and Carrie showed up?"

"Nothing really, he just followed me to the edge of the lawn." My eyebrows pulled together, and I couldn't help but make a face. I mean, seriously. What was his problem? Why was he acting this way?

"Why are you so interested in this cat?"

His gaze drifted to the ground, then back to me. "Just curious, that's all," he said, but yet he still had a troubled look on his face, and I knew he wasn't telling me everything.

"I'll see you tomorrow." I pulled my keys out of my purse and unlocked the door. "Thanks again for everything," I said, rearranging my face to hide my disappointment in him not being up front with me.

He frowned. "Did I say something wrong?"

"I'm just tired," I said. "Carrie is going to be here soon anyway."

"Well, I'll see you tomorrow then." He paused beneath the edge of the roof, flipped his hood up, and went down the steps into the sheeting rain. He turned and lifted his hand in a bye gesture. Rain thumped on his hood, glancing off it.

I waved good-bye, and dashed inside the house, more perplexed than I had been all night.

Chapter Three
Suspicion

My mind was whirling. Big time. I mean, seriously, tonight had to be like the weirdest night of my entire life. Not only did I have an out-of-body experience, but now I knew that was Nathan on the platform. But how did he jump off of it without hurting himself? It didn't make sense. And Matt's eyes totally freaked me out, but thankfully I found a logical explanation for that. But then came Nathan's bizarre behavior regarding the cat. What was that all about?

I changed into my sweats as those thoughts and questions kept parading through my mind. Then the thought about me dying joined those thoughts like a freak joining a circus of other freaks, and I got caught in the memory of my first premonition. A memory I went to great lengths to avoid:

I was four-years-old, coloring a picture of The Little Mermaid at the table in our Spanish tile kitchen. I thought she looked like me except my long hair was darker, and my eyes were dark green instead of blue. I decided to turn her into me and ran into my father's arms that night, clutching the picture in my hand and gave it to him. He hoisted me into his arms, kissed my cheek and told me he loved it.

And then I heard the voice say, "*He's going to leave you because he loves you, and it's his choice.*"

I leaned back and stared at my father's smiling face, thinking he whispered it into my ear, but then the voice repeated itself, terrifying me. I threw my arms around his neck and clung to him, crying not to leave me.

"What's wrong with Paige?" Mom asked, rushing over to me while he rubbed my back, trying to calm me. I continued to cling to him, wrapping my legs tighter around his waist.

"I don't know," he said. He sat in the chair with me until I cried myself to sleep.

About a month later, a female police officer came to our house. The next thing I knew, Mom fell to the floor, sobbing, pounding the hardwood with her fists. I ran to her, not understanding what had happened. She crushed me to her chest and wailed my daddy was gone. At that very second, I thought about the voice and bawled. If my daddy truly loved me, he would have never left, but he chose to. The voice told me so. The voice that wouldn't go away and now targeted me.

The memory snapped. My throat felt raw and stung with tears. I sat on the floor and cried in my hands. The premonition I'd had today was similar to my first one. It repeated itself and sounded dark and final. Granted, the one about my father didn't directly speak about death, but it didn't have to because I knew even at the age of four what it meant.

Gripping my bed, I pulled myself up. I thought about my father, and a sob coughed out of me. Slapping a hand over my mouth, I went into the bathroom and splashed cold water on my face. Carrie would to be here soon, and I didn't want her to see me like this. I had to think this premonition through and stop thinking about my father.

Back in my room, I dumped the clothes I had worn tonight into the laundry hamper and began dissecting my premonition. I remembered reading about dream interpretations. If you dreamed about death, it meant a change would occur in your life. Maybe my premonition meant change. I mean, after meeting Nathan, I knew my life would be different. And now that I thought about it, it made complete sense because Nathan evoked feelings in me like no other. But the rest of it didn't make sense, and the feelings that had accompanied it were a blend of horror and sadness.

I didn't know and was tired of analyzing it, so I thought about something fun. Nathan. *But why did he act so strangely about the cat?* My thoughts reverted back to his bizarre behavior. I went downstairs to wait for Carrie and took the orange and white afghan from the old wooden trunk in the living room. Sitting on the couch, I held it to my nose, breathing in the cedar smell, and wrapped it over my shoulders.

Maybe he was superstitious and saw the cat as an omen. But why wouldn't he tell me? Unless, he didn't want me to think of him as a weirdo.

I guess I would have to ask him about it tomorrow.

It was getting late, and I thought maybe Carrie had changed her mind about staying over, but then I heard a loud rhythmic thumping noise outside. The windows began to vibrate, and I knew it was Matt playing the bass in his jeep too loud. I threw the afghan off and went to the door. I hated when he did that, but Carrie thought it was cool, which meant everything must have gone well tonight. I just wished he wouldn't do it–I glanced at the clock on the wall–at one in the *frickin'* morning.

When I opened the door, Carrie confronted me with a huge grin on her face. Beads of water were dripping off her hair from the rain, but she didn't seem to care. She floated in with her backpack slung over her shoulder.

"I'm sorry I'm late," she chirped. "But when we left my house, Matt and I went to the park and sat in his jeep and talked for a while."

I took her coat and hung it in the closet next to the front door, and then I went to the bathroom to get her a towel. When I was back in the living room, she dropped her backpack and flopped on the couch, letting out a contented sigh.

I handed her the towel and sat next to her, covering us with the afghan, nudging her arm with my elbow. "So tell me what happened."

She looked at me as she dried her hair, her face glowing. "He kissed me." She bit her bottom lip and nodded when my mouth dropped in surprise. "In the park and before I got out of the jeep. It was so awesome."

"That's great, Carrie!" I forced myself to sound enthusiastic and even hugged her, but all I could think about was what Tree had told me earlier. And truthfully, I'd rather see her with Tree. They totally belonged together. I just knew it by the way they acted when they were together. But of course, I wasn't going to tell her that. I knew Carrie well enough to know she would date whomever she wanted regardless of what other people said or thought. And even though we were best friends, I knew she wouldn't listen to me either.

"Yeah. And let me tell ya"–she grabbed my arm–"the boy can kiss." She let go and placed her fingers on her lips. She had a far away look in her eyes, like she was reliving the moment.

I thought about Nathan and wondered what it would be like to kiss him. The very thought of his lips touching mine made me breathless. Was that how Matt made Carrie feel? I had to know.

"Tell me what happens when you're around Matt and he touches you."

Her eyes shifted to mine, and she let out a dramatic sigh. "I feel all giddy inside, like going to Disneyland."

I made a face. "That's a weird analogy."

"I don't know how to explain it," she said, and then paused. "All I can say is, I have fun when I'm with him."

"So, he excites you in the same way as an amusement park?" I tried not to sound patronizing and hoped she didn't take it that way.

She smiled and nodded.

"Do you feel drawn to him, like there's a magnetic energy?"

The corner of her mouth pulled down, and she touched it. "Hmm, kind of, I guess." She thought about it some more. "But it's more of a hyper kind of energy, like I know I'm going to have fun when I'm with him."

I settled myself deeper into the plush brown cushions to get more comfortable.

"Okay, but what about when he touches you? How does it make your body feel?"

She stretched her arms out as she spoke and had a dreamy look on her face. "He makes my body all bubbly."

I did my mental comparisons and realized what she felt for Matt wasn't the same as how I felt for Nathan. But I'd just met Nathan, and Carrie and I have known Matt most of our lives. So how could I feel such strong emotions for a person I hardly knew and felt so comfortable around? How could that be possible? God, I was confused.

"What happened with Nathan? Did he kiss you?" She puckered her lips and made kissing sounds.

I frowned and shook my head.

"But he wanted to," she said, like she knew something I didn't know.

"How do you know?" My heart raced at the thought of Nathan wanting to kiss me.

"Because of the way he looked at you." She paused, and a slow smile crossed her face. "And I saw the way you looked at him."

I knew she was right. At least, on my part, but I wasn't sure if the feelings were mutual.

"But we just met, so how could that be? What if it's my teenage hormones messing with me?" I thought I'd throw that one out there to see what she would say about my theory.

She snorted. "Teenage hormones. Good one, Paige."

I snatched the towel from her and smacked her arm with it. She tried to get it from me, but I threw it across the room. It bounced off the arm of the recliner and landed on the floor.

"I'm serious," I said. "How else can you explain it?"

Her lips were quivering from trying not to laugh. When I rolled my eyes, she held a hand up and cleared her throat through the giggles that had escaped her lips.

"Sorry." She took a deep breath. I glared at her, daring her to giggle again. "I'll admit," she continued, "Nathan is smoking hot. I mean, who wouldn't want to tap that ass? She made a tapping gesture with her fingers.

"Carrie!" My face was flaming.

She laughed, and I couldn't help but laugh with her.

"But honestly, Paige," she said, shifting to serious mode, "there's something between the two of you that has nothing to do with *hormones.*" She made air quotes. "I think you might be soul mates."

Now I snorted. "Yeah, right. Why would you think that?"

"Because you've never acted this way toward another guy before."

"But don't you think that's kind of weird?" I tried to find a logical explanation for how I felt toward Nathan and hoped she'd give me an answer other than *soul mates*. So lame.

"No, because the way I feel about it is you two might have just met here in the physical plane, but maybe your spirits"–she poked my chest–"have known each other for eternity."

I blinked at her, stunned at this revelation of hers. The possibility of what she said made me want to weep because I'd always thought I'd never be truly loved and even had resigned myself to a lonely existence. But to be honest, I was scared to believe it. I mean, how could somebody truly love me? I was a freak. And yeah, I knew there were people who had premonitions–blah, blah, blah. But their premonitions weren't spoken to them or cryptic like mine was. And if I were to tell anybody about them, they'd throw me in a padded room. No thanks.

"What about Tree?" I blurted.

She looked down and fiddled with the afghan. "What about him?"

"You used to be crazy about him, and you two were getting close, but when Matt came into the picture all that changed. I mean, honestly, you really hurt Tree's feelings tonight."

"I didn't mean to," she said, her voice filled with regret. "I still care about him, but he tends to be too serious and right now I just want to have fun."

I nodded, suppressing a yawn. "I understand, but please think of Tree's feelings and try not to blow him off. He is our best friend."

"I will," she promised, and we yawned together. "I think we should go to bed."

Knowing this conversation about Tree was over, I pushed the afghan off us.

Carrie put the towel away while I checked the locks on the doors and turned off all the lights. And when I followed her upstairs into the spare bedroom, I told her I had a date with Nathan tomorrow.

"Are you serious?" she squealed.

I grinned and bobbed my head.

"See. I told you he likes you. And he's *so* cute too," she gushed. "You'll have to give me all the details."

"I will," I said, still grinning.

She unzipped her backpack and pulled her flannel pajamas out. They were black with little pink skulls and cross bones all over. The skulls had bows on top of their heads. She headed to the bathroom, towing her stuff with her while I waited on the bed, wondering what tomorrow would to be like with Nathan. I lifted my hand and touched my cheek where his finger had earlier, feeling an explosion of warmth inside my chest. What would it be like if he were to kiss me? My stomach did another silly flip.

"What time is your date tomorrow?" Carrie asked, now in her pajamas, interrupting my thoughts.

I breathed out, making an effort not to think about Nathan touching me. "He's picking me up at two, and we're going to the waterfront."

She crawled in bed and slipped under the covers, peering at me with sleepy eyes and blinked hard. "That will be nice." She yawned and closed her eyes.

I headed out the door, turning the light off. "Goodnight, Carrie, I'll see you in the morning." She looked like a little glow bug cocooned inside the brown comforter.

"Goodnight, Paige. Oh, by the way," she said, already half asleep, "I think that stray cat has adopted you."

I hesitated and turned around. "Wh-why is that?"

"Because he was in front of your door when I got here."

"What did he do?" *I'm sounding like Nathan now.*

"Nothing ... Well, this is crazy, but it looked like he nodded at me, and then he let me by and left. I thought cats didn't like water, but I guess the rain doesn't bother this one."

"Maybe," I whispered and wondered if she would remember telling me this in the morning. Her words, *"he let me by,"* stood out in my mind like bright neon. Why would she word it that way? And the nodding thing, I didn't know what to think. I went to my own bed and settled underneath the covers, but before I could think about it any further, I fell asleep.

***

The next morning I awoke to the smell of bacon and eggs and for a second thought Mom was home, but then remembered Carrie had slept over. I squinted at the clock on my night stand.

Holy Cow! It was almost 10:30!

I couldn't believe how late I'd slept and threw the covers off, wondering how long Carrie had been awake. Hopping out of bed, I thought about Nathan as I crossed the hall to the bathroom. What was he doing at this very second?

A few minutes later, I stared at myself in the mirror and groaned. My face looked paler than normal. I splashed some cold water on it and pinched my cheeks in a poor attempt to bring color to them. It didn't work. I grimaced at my ghostly image while running a brush through my tangled hair. I decided to pull it up into a messy bun until I took a shower and told my growling stomach I'd feed it in a minute.

"What a wonderful surprise," I said, entering the kitchen. Carrie was pouring coffee into two mugs and adding cream to them. "When did you get up?"

She handed me my coffee. "Oh, about an hour ago. I went to check on you, and you were dead asleep, and I didn't want to wake you. How are you feeling by the way?" She picked up a couple plates off the counter with bacon and egg sandwiches on them. "I hope you don't mind," she added when she saw me looking at the breakfast. "I was hungry and thought you needed some real food."

"Not at all," I said, scraping a chair against the tile floor and sitting down, "my house is your house, and I appreciate you doing this. And you're right. I do need to eat. I feel okay, just hungry." I took a bite and chewed slowly. The bacon and egg flavor popped delightfully against my taste buds. "Mmmmmm, this is awesome Carrie. Thank you."

"You're welcome," she said in a garbled voice. She tried to smile, but her mouth was too full. She looked like a chipmunk storing food in her cheeks.

I laughed. "You must be hungry too."

She nodded and took a sip of her coffee. "I am." She set her coffee mug down and picked up her sandwich. "Oh, your mom called. She said she'll be here on Monday for a few days."

I shifted in my seat, eyeing her warily. "Did you tell her what happened last night?"

"No, I didn't. I told her you were sick, so I stayed the night to make sure you were okay." She paused and smiled. "She said you're lucky to have such a good friend and thanked me for being there for you."

"I am lucky," I said. "You're the best."

"I told her about Nathan."

I was in the middle of swallowing my coffee and sucked half of it down.

"You did?" I said in between coughs. I couldn't believe she told Mom about Nathan. I mean, Nathan and I just met. It wasn't like we were a couple. And yeah, it would be cool if we ended up dating, and there was that hope somehow things would work out and he did turn out to be the one. But I didn't want to get roped into a conversation about it with Mom. That would be too weird. Besides, she lost that privilege with me a long time ago.

"Sorry. I didn't mean to make you choke. But yes, I told her." She waved a hand in the air. "It's no big deal. She's happy you're seeing somebody, and she wants to meet him."

I imagined Mom talking to Nathan. She'd drill him with questions, of course, but after she got to know him, I was certain she'd like him. But to be honest, a part of me still couldn't believe this was happening to me, and I had my doubts. I mean, why would Nathan want me? I was damaged goods. I wasn't even good enough to have my own mother want to be around me. So why would he be interested in me? Unless, the whole soul mate thing was true, and we were meant to be together. Or, simply, we were just meant to be together. I liked that theory much better because if soul mates were true then a person could be searching for a soul mate a lifetime and may never find him or her. Just the thought of that made me sad. But then again, maybe everybody had more than one soul mate. Maybe your soul mate could even be your best friend, like Carrie and Tree were mine.

Carrie took our plates to the sink, and I loaded the dishwasher. The silverware clinked as I threw them in the holder.

"You know, I think you'd make a good roommate," I said, giving her a sideways glance.

"I don't know. I can be neurotic." There was a playful warning in her voice.

"I have a freaky side nobody knows about," I challenged, grinning.

She turned and leaned against the counter.

"Really? And when did we become best friends?" She arched an eyebrow.

"Ahhh, in kindergarten," I said, closing the lid with my foot.

"And now you're telling me this? Unless, you're talking about only dating two guys in your entire life and never going all the way," she teased. "You didn't even go all the way with Brayden." She shot me a look as if I committed a crime against humanity.

Brayden was our other best friend who moved to California two years ago. We dated for about two years, and when his mom told him they were moving, it hammered us. We'd decided not to pursue a long distance relationship and had shed many tears over it.

I stuck my tongue out. "Well, I live vicariously through you."

"Not anymore, because now you *have* Nathan," she said.

I grabbed the dish towel and threw it at her. "Shut up. I don't *have* Nathan."

She laughed and threw it back at me. "Not yet, but you will *have* him any time you want."

I rolled my eyes. "Whatever."

She walked by me and flipped around. Her eyes were wide, hands beside her face, fingers wiggling. "You bewitched him, Paige, and now he's under your spell."

I laughed and playfully shoved her shoulder. "Yeah right, you goof."

Rubbing her shoulder, she stuck her bottom lip out like a pouting child. "You mean girl," she said in a baby voice. "I no play with you anymore."

"You're a brat," I said, still laughing.

Her face broke into a smile, and she winked. "I'm going to go take a shower." She skipped out of the room, and I stared after her, hoping she was right about Nathan.

***

My heart rate accelerated when it dawned on me I had a half hour before my date with Nathan. The thought of being alone with him made me excited and a bit edgy, and I restlessly roamed the house, not knowing what to do with myself.

Insecure thoughts plagued me, like what if he changed his mind and never shows? Or, was I pretty enough for somebody like him?

"What's wrong?" Carrie asked when she got off the phone with Matt.

I stood in front of her. "Do I look okay?" I felt bloated and fat and wasn't sure if my outfit looked good on me. I swear I could feel the bacon and egg sandwich on my hips now.

"You look fine," she reassured. "That sage green sweater goes good with the color of your hair." She pulled some lip gloss out of her pocket and applied it to her lips.

I yanked the hood over my head. "Does it look good like this?"

"It looks good either way, but I like it better down." She smacked her lips together and pocketed her lip gloss. Her lips looked all shining and glittery.

I pushed the hood off and ran my fingers through my hair. "Do I look fat?"

She sighed. "No, you couldn't look fat even if you tried."

"I feel fat," I complained, flopping on the couch beside her.

"You're not, so stop worrying. You look great."

I decided to tell her about Nathan acting weird about the cat, and afterwards she shrugged like it was no big deal, coming up with the same reasoning I'd had. Superstitious. She made me feel a lot better about it and that maybe I had conjured up a bunch of nonsense. And then I thought about the platform.

"Before I passed out last night, did you see Nathan beside me?"

She thought about it for a minute. "No, but I was too busy dancing with the people around us to notice. But he was right there when you fell, so he had to be dancing next to us."

"Maybe," I murmured, but I wasn't convinced. I knew what I saw.

A car horn beeped outside, and I immediately jumped to my feet, startled.

"That's my mom." Carrie jerked her backpack off the floor. "I can tell by the sound of the horn." She gave me a quick hug. The strawberry scent off her lip gloss filled my nostrils. "I'll talk to you later. And don't worry. Everything will be fine."

My heart galloped. And in a split second it takes a hummingbird to flap its wings, I wondered if Nathan and I were destined to be together, and in that same time span, I shut that thought out of my mind.

Carrie stepped outside, but before she closed the door, she popped her head back in.

"Nathan is here."

"He is?" My eyes darted around the room like a mouse in a room full of cats. I tried to steady my heart by breathing through my nose and out my mouth, telling myself there was nothing to be scared or nervous about.

"*Really?"* A soft voice in my head said. *"Have you forgotten he makes you want to do things to him you've never wanted to do to another guy?"* I touched my forehead and told the voice to shut up.

"He's walking up the lawn," she informed me, enjoying herself. She raised her eyebrows. "Enjoy *having* Nathan tonight," she said, using her porn voice.

My finger went to my lips. "Be quiet. He's going to hear you."

She closed the door, and I heard her say hi to him.

Oh no! I hope he didn't hear what she just said. I touched my burning face and rushed to the gilded wall mirror.

Dark red.

This wasn't good. I had to do something quick to get rid of the redness in my face. I thought of something sad. My father. And then there was a tapping knock at the door.

I took a deep breath and opened the door, attempting to sound cheerful when I said hi. I couldn't help but notice how Nathan's tan sweater hugged his muscular frame perfectly, and how it created that fluttering sensation in my chest again.

"Hi," he said with a bright smile, but then narrowed his eyes in such a way that told me he knew something was wrong. *Great.* This was so not how I wanted to start our date.

"Come in. I need to get my stuff." I stepped aside, trying not to focus on the feelings he stirred in me, or the sadness I had awakened inside myself.

"What's wrong?"

Crap.

I didn't want to unload on him, especially on our first date. But when I saw the way he was looking at me, with genuine concern, I had to.

"I was thinking about my father," I said, swallowing back the sorrow.

He took a step closer to me. "Do you want to talk about it?" He lifted his hand as if he was going to touch my face, but then dropped it.

"Not really." I turned away, feeling like an idiot.

"I think you're going to need your rain jacket." He stood by the door, watching me, and nodded when he saw the look on my face.

"That sucks. I was hoping it wouldn't rain today." I pulled my rain coat out of the closet. He took it from me, and when I gave him a strange look, he lifted it by the shoulders, the open side facing me and shook it. I made a tsk sound, rolled my eyes, and turned around. "Duh. Sorry," I said, feeling the heat in my cheeks. He must really think I was an idiot now.

"That's perfectly all right." He slipped the coat on me. "Can I talk to you about something?" He looked at me, and his shoulders sagged. I could tell something was bothering him by the sudden awkwardness in the air.

My chest throbbed as thoughts raced about what could be wrong: Did he change his mind about our date? Maybe when he went home last night he realized I was too young for him, and he could date somebody way better than me.

"I want to apologize for my behavior last night with the cat. I didn't mean to upset you." He took my hand and sandwiched it between his. "I never want to see you hurt, and I hope you believe me when I say that."

His sincerity threw me. I glanced at his hands holding mine and back to his face. And this was totally wacky, but as I gazed into the deep blue sea of his eyes, I felt a strong connection with him. And in that brief moment I realized this was what I was feeling last night when we were together. Regardless, I still wanted to know why he reacted the way he had last night. I placed my hand on top of his and asked.

He lifted my hand to his lips and kissed it. A rush of raw, untamed energy went through my body that was unfamiliar to me, causing me to bite my bottom lip.

"Many years ago, a stray cat just like that one showed up at my door step, and I thought maybe it was the same one." He released my hand, and we stepped outside.

Low and heavy clouds covered the endless gray sky, and the smell of rain still hung in the air. With the barren black trees around us and no soul in sight, it seemed like we stepped into a futuristic wasteland.

"So, you thought this was the same cat you saw in Missouri?" I asked when we were in the truck.

"I know it sounds crazy," he said, sticking the key in the ignition, "but yes I did."

"That's okay. There are things about me you might think is crazy."

"I don't think so," he said. "But I'd like to know everything about you."

"Well, I'll tell you what. I'll tell you about me, if you tell me about you."

He smiled. "You have yourself a deal Ms… What's your last name?"

"Reed."

"Ms. Reed." His smile deepened, and I smiled with him.

We began talking about the minor, inconsequential things about ourselves, such as what type of movies and music we liked. And when we reached the waterfront and strolled along on the river walk, we were still immersed in that same conversation, both laughing at his silly childhood stories as four young girls skated passed us on roller blades.

"Your three brothers sound like a riot," I said. "Where are they right now?"

Nathan looked away, and I wondered if I said something wrong. But then he looked at me and said they were dead and so were his parents, stunning me. My heart immediately went out to him, but instead of asking him what happened–which I really wanted to do–I told him I was sorry. I know losing my father was the worst thing that had ever happened to me, but to lose your whole family … I couldn't even imagine what that would be like.

"It's okay," he said.

I decided to change the subject to brighten the mood and asked if he was in school or had a job, questions I knew Mom would ask me sooner or later. He told me he went to college in Seattle and then sold some land he owned, so he didn't need a job. I told him I didn't have a job either–even though I wanted one–but Mom told me school was more important. Then I went on about Carrie teasing me about being spoiled because she had to work a couple times a week at her mom's antique store, but I did volunteer my help when they needed it.

"When did you and Carrie become best friends?" he asked, interlacing his fingers with mine.

Our hands felt perfect together and natural. The warmth of his hand in mine flooded through my blood stream, and inside my head I did a happy Snoopy dance as I watched a commercial fishing vessel go by. In the distance a freighter navigated the foggy river and one of the smaller boats blew its horn.

"We started hanging out in kindergarten," I said.

"That's a long time."

"It is. We've been through a lot."

"I have a friend like Carrie. His name is Anwar."

That's an unusual name. I wondered what nationality he was.

"He's African," he said, reading my face. "He helped us on the farm and became a part of our family. He's in Kenya right now, but he'll be visiting me soon."

"I'd like to meet him," I said, thinking it would be cool to meet an African.

He squeezed my hand. "I'm sure you will, but don't let his size intimidate you. He's a gentle soul."

I thought about Tree being six-foot five. "How tall is Anwar?"

"He's almost seven feet."

"Holy cow! I bet he's going to think I'm an elf."

He laughed. "No, he's going to see you as you are, which is the most beautiful girl in the world."

We stopped and the people walking passed us seemed to fade away. When he pushed the hair off my face and softly glided his fingers down the side of my neck, beneath the collar of my coat, I shivered. His fingers trailed back to my cheek, stopping at the temple, and his thumb slowly skimmed across my lips. My heart was racing.

A burning desire rushed through parts of my body, a desire I'd never experienced before. A desire to be with him and to feel his touch. I parted my lips, and his breathing slowed as he closed his eyes. When he opened them, they appeared a little brighter. And then he spoke in a deep, husky voice that softened my bones.

"I know this may seem absurd since we just met last night, but I feel something between us I've never felt before." He paused and gazed into my face. "I'd like to see you again."

For a second I stared blankly at him until my mind was able to process what he'd said.

He wants to go out with me again.

"I'd like that," I said, my heart still racing.

He smiled, bent his head down and kissed me.

At first, his lips were gentle, but when I moved my body closer and parted my lips, he responded. His mouth moved in harmony with mine.

He was an amazing kisser, and my stomach did a continuous flip as our kiss grew deeper, tongues connecting. His fingers found their way into my hair, and I hooked my arms around his neck, standing on my tiptoes, wishing I was taller. His hand drifted to the small of my back, lightly pressing on it. My body molded with his, and I shivered again. Then a male voice shouted from across the river. I jumped back, and spun around.

"Get a room!" A young blond-haired guy shouted from the deck of his boat. He smiled and waved, sticking his thumb up. Flushing, I waved back and turned to Nathan, reveling in the way my whole body tingled and how the pressure of his lips lingered on mine.

"I hope I wasn't being too forward, but I couldn't resist my feelings for you any longer," he said, peeking at me from beneath his lashes, the corner of his mouth curling when I moved toward him.

I took his hand. "What you did was fine because I feel the same way about you."

He tilted his head to the side and had an adorable smile on his face. "I was hoping you'd say that."

"Yeah, well, I wasn't planning to," I said truthfully, "but you kissed it out of me." I picked up a stone and skipped it across the river, thinking how earth shattering that kiss had been. In fact, I wanted to do it again, and again, and again.

"Why weren't you going to tell me?" He sounded bothered by this.

"Because we just met and it seemed crazy for me to feel the way I do toward you. And I wasn't sure if you felt the same way, even though Carrie told me you did."

"Carrie is pretty perceptive, isn't she?"

"Sometimes she is, but never with her own life, which is unfortunate."

"Is she dating Matt?"

A couple kids went by on skateboards. The wheels clicked against the uneven stones, and they were complaining about not having a skate park here.

"Yeah, but I'm not sure how much Matt likes her. I'll have to ask him when I'm alone with him."

Nathan stopped, and a cold hardness crested over him, like thick ice over a gentle river. He turned to me, his face now serious. "Listen, Paige, I don't want to seem overbearing but you need to trust me on this."

"What?" The nervousness in his voice confused me.

He hung his head, sighed, and peered at me. "There's no better way to put this without sounding like a Neanderthal, but I don't want you alone with Matt."

I knew they didn't like each other, but Matt was my friend, and nobody was going to dictate to me on whom my friends were, even if it was Nathan. I crossed my arms over my chest and asked him why, crushed he would ask this of me.

"Because there's something in him I don't like, and I'm afraid he's going to hurt you."

"Carrie is alone with him, and she's fine. In fact, he kissed her twice yesterday," I said, tapping my foot, feeling an invisible wall being placed between us. He frowned and looked up as if asking for help from above, but then I realized it was because it started to rain.

Everybody around us rushed to the nearby shops for shelter, but I stayed rooted in my spot, not caring my hair and face were getting wet.

He grabbed my hand. "C'mon, you're going to get soaked if we stay here."

I gritted my teeth. "Fine."

I followed him to Shiver Me Timbers, a seafood restaurant that looked like a pirate ship from the inside. I always thought about the pirate captain Squint Eye Jack who came to the Oregon coast and did battle with Spanish galleons in the early 1600s, whenever I ate here. There were privacy booths in the back, and we sat there, away from the rowdiness of the other customers. The wooden plank walls had portholes for windows. Behind the glass were live fishes swimming back and forth, and the place smelled like fried seafood.

Nathan and I didn't say much to each other until after our waiter–a young, redheaded, freckled face guy, dressed in a pirate outfit–took our order and gave us our drinks.

"Please don't be mad at me. I just want you safe," Nathan said, reaching across the table, touching my fingers.

I glanced at our hands, forcing myself to focus on the issue instead of how he made me feel. "I'm not mad at you. I'm irritated because I don't understand why you think Matt would hurt me. He's alone with Carrie, and she's fine."

"Yes, but you're different," he said without hesitation.

I eyed him suspiciously. "What do you mean *I'm* different?" I withdrew my hand and took a drink of my Dr Pepper, knowing he was holding something back. I mean, he totally displayed the same signs as my mom when I'd ask her about my father: shifting in the chair, not answering right away, then ultimately avoiding my question.

He leaned forward, an intense expression on his face. "Do you trust me?"

I hated to admit it because it seemed foolish, but I couldn't deny what we had between us.

But still, he wasn't making sense, and I wanted to know why he had a problem with me hanging out with Matt and why he thought I wasn't the same as Carrie. He acted like Matt would hurt me, which was totally crazy.

"Yeah, I do," I finally said, "but please don't answer a question with a question."

He dropped his gaze, then lifted it back on me, his eyes now guarded. "I can't answer that question, Paige."

My hands gripped the edge of the table. "Why?"

"I have to figure some things out first."

I ground my teeth and blurted, "You're just like the damn premonitions I get. *Cryptic!*" After the words escaped my lips, I became mortified. That was a deep secret I planned on taking to my grave, and now I blew it. "I'm going to the restroom." I jumped out of the booth and half ran to the restroom, nearly knocking over a waiter with a tray full of food.

I lingered in the empty restroom for a while, trying not to cry. If Nathan wanted to kick me to the curb right now … Well, who could blame him? I was a freak and so frickin' stupid to think I could have a normal relationship and be able to hide this secret. I should have never gone on this date. What was I thinking?

But I knew what I was thinking.

I wanted to be with him. But it didn't matter anymore. I totally screwed up. I told myself to get it together, and if I was destined to be alone, so be it. But as soon as that thought entered my mind, the wind knocked right out of me, causing me to latch onto the white counter.

I felt pathetic because I shouldn't be feeling this way toward somebody I hardly knew. It was nonsensical, but I couldn't help it.

God, I was a mess.

I splashed cold water on my face and dried it with a brown paper towel.

I stared at my dark green eyes in the mirror. They looked round and sad. "Get it together, Paige," I whispered. "Your father and Brayden left you completely brokenhearted. Do you really want to go for a third?" My bottom lip quivered. No, I couldn't go through that again because it would most likely destroy me.

I wiped my cheeks off with the heel of my palm and took a couple deep breaths. Maybe it was best this way.

Yeah, maybe.

Maybe subconsciously I wanted Nathan to know I had premonitions so it would be an easy excuse for me not to see him again. I mean, we just met yesterday, and I shouldn't be feeling such powerful emotions toward him already, right? I thought about the soul mate thing, but then quickly blew it off. Soul mates, we were meant to be together, or whatever, it didn't matter. I couldn't see him because A.) He knew my secret and B.) I liked him way too much and wasn't willing to take the chance of possibly getting burned by him.

On that note, I straightened my back, threw the wet towel in the trash can and walked out. With my head held high, feigning a confidence that said: I'm an independent person who doesn't mind being alone for the rest of my life, I marched between a row of tables and as I did so, a high-pitched ringing sound went off in my ears, like yesterday. I wondered why it was happening again and if it had anything to do with the premonition. But when I neared a dimly lit booth and glanced at a pale, dark-haired guy, my whole facade fell by the wayside.

He looked like a heroin addict–skinny, and gaunt, but that wasn't why I paused at his table. I paused because he sneered at me with disdain and mouthed my name, stunning me. Then I saw a yellow laser beam flash across his dark iris in a swiping motion. Horror ran through me. I rushed past his table, hearing his menacing laughter behind me. I shot a look over my shoulder, and he stood in the aisle, turning in the opposite direction, still laughing.

When I rounded the corner, I ran into Nathan. He caught me by the shoulders. I swear the world had shifted me into its fun house, and I wanted to pound my way out, like what my heart was trying to do to my chest.

"Are you okay?" he asked. "I was getting worried about you." He took a closer look at my face. "Why do you look so frightened?"

I hesitated on the words that desperately wanted to come out of my mouth while quickly weighing whether to tell him or not. Pressing my lips together, I took his hand and pulled him over to our table where our food was waiting.

"I'm sorry I took so long," I said, still seeing that guy's face in my mind. "And I'm okay, you just scared me," I added, telling myself I wasn't completely lying to him since he did scare me.

He wrapped his arms around me. "You're shaking. Here, sit and eat." I slid into the booth. "The food is still warm. The waiter just brought it out." He glanced at me from across the table, but didn't say anything.

I took a drink and forced myself to eat my catfish. I wasn't hungry and seriously freaked out about that guy, but at least having my mouth full gave me some time to collect my thoughts. And Nathan was clearly being patient with me, more patient than I deserved, while we ate in silence.

The premonition I had the day before kept replaying in my mind and that guy's laughter echoed inside my skull. I lifted my eyes and caught Nathan's. I looked away, unable to answer his silent questions.

What would I tell him? That some scary dude knew my name; that I saw a beam of light flash across his eyes; and that he might want to kill me? And what would I tell Nathan if he were to ask me why I felt that way and if I was sure he said my name and saw what I'd seen in his eyes? I knew exactly what I'd do. I'd tell him the truth.

But seriously, if he were to look at me like a nutcase who belonged in an institution, I wouldn't be able to handle it. I'd already exposed my freakish nature to him, so there was no way in hell I would tell him. This was my problem, not his, and I had to deal with it on my own. I didn't know how because I didn't understand any of it, but I had no other options. I clasped my shaking hands in my lap and tried not to think about it.

Once outside, I was thankful the rain had finally quit, but a thick fog covered the docks and the edge of the river, and the cold air bit at my face. I stuck my hands in my pockets and walked beside Nathan. I was nervous about telling him I didn't want to see him again, because really it was a flat out lie. I was also afraid of what might come out of my mouth. I mean, honestly, it would be just my luck to unintentionally shoot my mouth off about that guy in the restaurant, and Nathan didn't need to know that. He needed to just move on with his life and date a normal girl.

"Please don't shut me out, Paige," he said when we were in the truck. "If you're worried about what you said earlier, don't be. It hasn't changed the way I feel about you, and I would like to know more about it." He slipped his hand in mine. "I want to know everything about you."

Surprised at what he said, I glanced down at his hand in mine. It felt so right to be here like this, to tell him everything. My decision to never see him again wavered. But then I reminded myself of the probability of opening myself up, and then losing him. Nathan deserved better, I told myself. And so, I gathered what strength I had, and released his hand.

Reluctantly, I looked at him, ordering myself not to cry. "I don't think we should see each other again." When his face fell, I looked away and stared at my lap.

"What?" He paused to take a deep breath. "Why would you say that?" He sounded genuinely upset, which made it much harder on me.

I continued to stare at my lap. "We just met, and I don't think it's a good idea. It's just too much. I can't take it." Words tumbled out of my mouth that I could hardly catch. I sounded like a blabbering idiot. But it didn't matter anymore how I came across to him because whatever was between us had to end. I crossed my arms over my chest and turned away from him. "Please take me home."

He touched my shoulder. "Don't I have a say in this?"

I pressed my forehead to the cold glass on the side window and closed my eyes. Why was he making this so hard? Something wet rolled down my face. I sniffed, wishing I could be the kind of girl a guy like Nathan ended up with, but I wasn't. Hell, I didn't even want kids. Yeah, I loved kids, but I only wanted to be responsible for myself, not for another life. And if anybody should be reproducing in this world, it should be Nathan.

"Paige?"

A choked whisper came out of me. "Nathan. Please. I can't."

He gently squeezed my shoulder. "Listen to me. I know we just met yesterday, but you can't deny there's something between us. If you want to take it slow, I'm good with that. Just please give it a chance."

I needed to think and set all emotions aside. I was a logical person. I mean, there was no doubt there was something between us, and what if he was the *one*? Sure, I thought he deserved somebody better, but that wasn't my decision, right? And what if I did shut him out of my life and regretted it later? But then again, what if I gave myself completely over to him, and then he left me? Was I willing to take that chance? I didn't know.

"I need some time to think about it," I finally said, turning to him. I saw a hint of relief cross his face, but I could tell that wasn't exactly what he wanted me to say.

He peeked at me. "How much time do you want me to give you?"

I shrugged, and gave him a weak smile. I wasn't really sure how much time I needed. All I knew was I had to protect myself from getting emotionally shattered.

He reached into the glove compartment and pulled out a piece of paper and pen. He used his knee to write something. He tossed the pen back into the glove compartment and snapped it shut.

"Here's my cell phone number." He folded the paper in half and handed it to me. "Call me anytime."

I nodded and stuffed it into the side pocket of my purse while he drove out of the parking lot.

I turned to him, watching him closely. "Can I ask you something?"

"Of course, you can ask me anything," he said.

"Were you on the platform last night watching me?" I thought I saw the corner of his mouth twitch, but wasn't sure by the angle of his face.

"Yes, I was."

"Did you jump off of it right before I passed out?"

He stared at the road and tapped his thumb on the steering wheel. I took that as a yes, but then he said, "Paige, that platform is too high for a human to jump off. And when you fell, I was right beside you." He glanced at me. "Why?"

I shrugged. "I was just wondering." I shifted in my seat and looked out the window, watching the dark forest along the side of the road flash by. For some reason, Nathan skated around my question, and my gut feeling told me there had to be more to what he just said, however, he made a good point about the platform being too high. So maybe I was reading too much into his actions.

I thought about Matt's glowing eyes and reminded myself about the logical explanation I came up with. But with this guy tonight, I couldn't think of a logical explanation for what I saw. I stopped myself right there, knowing where this train of thought would lead to. I didn't need to go there with Nathan around me. So for the rest of the way home, I occupied my mind by counting each tree we passed.

When we reached my house and stepped out of his truck, I pointed to the cat sitting on the porch. "See. There he is."

"Was he here earlier today?"

"No, but look at him now. It's like he's waiting for me. I wonder if I should give him a can of tuna?"

"I'm sure he eats well out here," Nathan said. "And besides, you don't want to invite every critter in the forest to your house."

"Oh yeah, I didn't think about that."

He smiled. "That's a sweet thought though."

We climbed the steps to the porch and the cat went straight to Nathan, rubbing his legs. He reached down to pet it with an idle smile.

"Is that the cat you were thinking about last night?" There was no way a cat could travel all the way from Missouri to Oregon on its own. But it seemed like he knew Nathan and was even purring when I went to pet him.

Nathan patted the cat's side. "I think he's just being friendly."

I fumbled with my keys until I found the right one and unlocked the door. I flip the porch light on to get a better look. His face and paws were black, but he had a gray body with a strange black mark on it. I knelt next to him.

"Did you see this?" My eyes found Nathan's. "It looks like he has a huge star on his back, but it's bent over his sides." I smoothed out his fur to show Nathan.

"He's a special cat," he said, but the timbre in his voice was saying something more I didn't get.

A gust of cold air blew through the porch, swaying the trees around the house, blowing my hair back. I pushed myself off the ground, and watched the cat wander off the porch, disappearing into the trees.

I felt awkward all of a sudden, standing there with Nathan. My eyes kept straying to his lips, and I couldn't stop thinking about that earth shattering kiss we had earlier.

I so wanted to kiss him.

I looked up and realized he caught me staring at his lips. The corner of his mouth curled, and my longing to kiss him was mirrored in his eyes. He was about half a yard away, and although a cool breeze was nipping at my face, my cheeks felt hot.

Aw, screw it.

As if we read each other's minds, we closed the gap. He cupped my face in his strong hands and pressed his lips to mine. My lips were hot against his, my tongue darting in. Something in me sparked. It was hot and electric. I'd never in my whole life felt like this before, not even with

Brayden. I kissed him harder, hungry for more, but then he jerked back, and covered his eyes with the tips of his fingers.

"What's wrong?" I pushed my hair out of my face, trying to steady my breathing. I noticed he was panting as well.

He turned away from me. "I think the breeze blew something in my eyes."

"I have some drops for them in the house. Do you want some?" I gestured toward the front door.

He stepped off the porch and moved into the shadow of the trees, still rubbing his eyes. "No. I'm fine." He dropped his fingers and squinted at me.

I could barely see his face and wondered if he was really okay. I was about to insist on him coming in the house so I could take a closer look, but he spoke first.

"I know you want some time to think, but can you start doing that thinking on Monday? I'd really like to take you to breakfast tomorrow."

What was one more day with him going to hurt? And then I could have the whole week to decide on what to do.

"Okay. What time?"

"How about 9:30?" He sounded pleased, which added a little boost to my dwindling confidence on relationships.

"Yeah, sure," I said, even though I wasn't usually up that early on weekends. I would definitely have to set my alarm clock.

Despite my reservations and everything that had happened at the restaurant, I found myself looking forward to tomorrow. I didn't know what the future was going to bring, but as I waved good-bye to him, I felt a new high. I couldn't help but smile, thinking maybe things might finally be going my way.

Maybe.

Chapter Four
Torn

The next morning, pale light streamed through the crack in my cream-colored curtains, waking me before my alarm went off. I hit the switch to beat the beeping noise and flopped back on my fluffy pillow. The breaking dawn threw sunbeams across the room, kissing the lilac wall, making it glow.

I glanced around, loving the antique furniture, thanks to Carrie's mom's generosity. It was almost like you had stepped back into a simpler time. Almost. Except for my computer was like a big black dot in the corner of a beautiful Victorian painting. But that was okay. Sometimes necessity outranked the things we preferred, like pretending to live in a different era.

I hopped out of bed, went to the bathroom, and then headed to the kitchen to make some coffee. I was virtually useless without it in the morning. And it had to be strong, not that weak, diluted crap a lot of people drank. My mom was one of them. Colored water is what I called it.

A few minutes later the phone rang.

"Hello."

"Paige, it's Mom."

"Hi, I was just thinking about you. Carrie told me you're coming home tomorrow."

"I was, but there's been a change of plans."

This wasn't unusual for her, but I still really wanted to see her. I folded my arms on the counter and rested my head on them.

"I'm sorry, honey, but the flu is going around here, and they're short handed at the hospital."

"I understand." I should have known she'd bail out on me.

"I knew you would. You're such a good daughter. How are your grades?"

"You should know. You can pull them up on your computer, or call my teachers."

"I know, but I want to hear it from you."

That's right, whatever you want is all that matters.

"Are you still there?"

"My grades are perfect like always," I grumbled.

She sighed into the phone. "I know you're angry with me, but I'm doing the best I can. Things are the way they are for a reason."

"I know."

"Carrie told me about a boy you're dating," she said, changing the subject.

"Yeah." I snickered. She was going to crap if she ever did meet Nathan because he was far from being a boy.

"Please do yourself a favor, honey."

"What's that?"

"I know you're almost eighteen, and it's none of my business, but if you're going to have sex, please use protection. I know you're already on birth control to help regulate your periods. At least, I hope that's the only reason why you're on it, and--"

"Mom," I said, horrified. "I'm still a virgin. Okay? And I already know about that stuff, so don't worry." Silently, I hoped she'd drop the subject. I so didn't want to go there with her.

"Oh, that's good to hear. I just don't want you to get pregnant at such a young age, because you still have a whole life ahead of you."

"I agree." I knew she meant well, but she was seriously getting on my nerves.

"Listen. My break is over. I have to run. I love you. I'll talk to you soon."

"I love you too."

I hung up the phone and finished making the coffee. This was the story of my life, my mom breaking plans. She used to work at the hospital here in town, until two years ago when she discovered she could make a lot more money being a traveling nurse. She then started taking jobs within a half day drive to where we live, so she could still be nearby and have weekends off. But as soon as I got my driver's license and car, she accepted jobs farther away, and would stay gone for months at a time. I was used to it now, but even though I tried not to let it bother me, it still did. I mean, I was her daughter, why wouldn't she want to be around me?

I thought about my father and the few pictures we had of him, thanks to Mom. When I was younger, I'd ask Mom why we didn't have pictures of Daddy in the house, and she told me it was too painful for her. She wouldn't tell me where they were and when I persisted, her eyes would fill with tears, and she'd leave the room. But one day, when I was bored and alone, I decided to look for the pictures. I had a feeling they were in the attic since Mom wasn't that inventive, and after searching for a while, I found a square Christmas tin in a box of trinkets. I rocked it back and forth and felt something sliding inside it.

My throat tightened.

I sat on a wooden crate, ignoring the thick coat of dust covering it. My fingers shook as I pried the lid off with my fingernails, not sure what would be inside, and when I popped the lid off, my heart just about jumped out of my chest.

I found the pictures.

There were only three, which made me angry that Mom had kept so few of Dad.

The first one was of a young guy smiling, with his hands above his head and a small child in the air.

A sob escaped my lips.

He was throwing me in the air and had an expression of pure joy on his face. I stared at it for a while until a tear fell on top of his face. I quickly wiped it off and set it aside, determined to keep it.

The next photo was of Mom and Dad. They were standing in front of a huge waterfall, somewhere tropical, smiling.

And the last was only of my dad, sitting on a Triumph motorcycle, looking like James Dean in his leather jacket, dark sunglasses, and his tousled auburn hair. He had a charming smile, and I could see why he captured Mom's heart.

I took that picture as well and put back the one of my parents. She could keep that one, but the others were mine. I had told myself if she ever found out, I'd tell her keeping them from me was wrong and she couldn't have them back.

Those two photos were now stashed in an antique jewelry box Carrie's mom had given me on my birthday one year. It had a false bottom, and that was where I kept them, just in case Mom decided to snoop in my room. And from time to time, I pulled them out when I wanted to have a good cry.

Now, as I got dressed, I wondered if there were more stuff of his Mom had kept from me. I did search the entire house and found nothing. But strangely, my dad's existence always seemed like a mystery to me. I never understood why Mom never wanted to talk about him, and the only thing she ever said was they were very much in love, he was a wonderful, doting father, and we meant the world to him. And when it came to his family, well, he had none. He grew up in foster homes in Phoenix and met Mom at ASU, where they became college sweethearts. But that was all I knew, which was so unfair.

After deciding on wearing a white hooded sweater and brown cargo pants, I pulled my hair into a loose braid, then applied make-up to give my face some color. I went downstairs to wait for Nathan while I finished my coffee.

The house reminded me of a cave with everything shut–dark and confining. I went to the front window and pulled back the curtains. Where sunlight had slanted in from the east earlier, the window framed a gray cloudy sky. A thick fog crept out of the black forest, like fingers through steel bars. Little eddies of dirt and leaves whirled in the desolate street, and the trees were swaying. I imagined the wind carrying a biting chill. I hugged myself, pining for Nathan's warmth instead of mine.

The acute silence pressed down upon me. It was as if the world had been abandoned, not only by the sun, but by humans as well, all but one.

Me.

And then I saw that guy's face in my mind, and in its reflection, I saw several things in systematic order: the sneer on his gaunt, pale face, mouthing my name, and the beam of light swiping across his black eyes. I had no idea how he knew my name, why he looked at me like that, and why his eyes did that? And I stood there for a while contemplating it.

But there were no answers, just a cold feeling in the pit of my stomach. I wondered if I should tell Nathan, but quickly decided against it. He knew enough about me and didn't need to know this. Maybe someday I'd tell him, but not now. What happened last night would have to be filed away in my repository with the rest of my unanswered questions.

Nathan's truck pulled up in front of the house, and my heart lurched in excitement. I hurried to the door and flung it open, astonished to see him there because he wasn't even out of his truck a few seconds ago.

"Hi," he said, smiling.

Without thinking, I pulled him in the house and somehow ended up in his arms. I didn't want to let go, and he smelled so good, like wood smoke in cold mountain air. I was beginning to question my decision to take some time away from him to think.

"I could stay like this forever." I sighed against his orange hooded sweatshirt.

"Fine with me," he said. "But eventually one of us is going to have to go… You know."

"Go pee, or take a dump. Is that what you were implying?"

He laughed, and pulled back to look at me. "Yes, but I'm not one to speak of such filth in front of a lady," he said in a British accent.

I pushed his arm back. "Get out. I'm not a lady, so you can speak filthy words to me, because I will do the opposite of what Polonius said to Laertes, which is I will not give thought to thy tongue with trivial words."

He raised his eyebrows in surprise. "You read Shakespeare?"

I pursed my lips and pompously lifted my chin. "But of course."

The corner of his mouth curled. "You amaze me."

"Because I read Shakespeare?"

"Because not only are you beautiful, you're intelligent, and you are you." He cradled my face in his cool hands and brushed his soft lips against mine.

I pressed my mouth to his, feeling a fire ignite inside my belly. Our tongues connected and moved in synchronicity. I softly moaned in response to the heat and intensity of his deep kiss and slid my hand under his sweatshirt. His skin was smooth, tight against hard muscles.

He immediately stepped back and looked away. I could hear him breathing through his nose like he did yesterday.

"I'm sorry, but we must not do that yet." His voice was deep with frustration.

"It's okay. I want to," I said, still feeling the heat between us. "We don't have to go all the way," I added, and remembered what Carrie had said, I could *have* Nathan whenever I wanted to. *I guess she was wrong about that.*

His eyes flicked to my lips, then to my face, and they appeared to be getting a little brighter. There was an internal battle going on inside him, and I knew if I pushed a little further, he'd cave. But when I reached out to touch him, he turned his back. I sucked in a sharp breath. I didn't mean to, but I wasn't expecting rejection. I dropped my hand and stared at his slouched shoulders, swallowing back the tears.

"I'm sorry, Paige. I can't do this right now," he said, still frustrated.

"Don't you want me?" My voice was barely audible.

"That's the problem," he said through clenched teeth. "I want you *too* much."

"Then I don't--"

"Understand," he said, finishing my sentence. "I know, but I promise in time you will. But for now, we need to try and refrain from kissing like that because I don't think I can stop myself next time." His voice was low with forced constraint.

"You know, I appreciate you being honorable and all, but it's my decision too. You can't just make the decision for both of us." My annoyance shook each word.

A laugh barked out of him.

"What's so funny?" I crossed my arms over my chest and glared.

"Carrie was right. You are stubborn." He turned and some of the brightness and desire he felt lingered in his eyes, but there was also humor in them, which pissed me off.

I squished my face up. "Whatever." I couldn't believe he was using my stubbornness against me.

He looked down and pinched the bridge of his nose. "Can you *please* be patient with me?" He lifted his gaze, his expression strained.

"All right," I said, feeling bad now because he looked genuinely upset.

"I promise, we'll have that moment, but for now, we should be good," he said, placing his hands on my shoulders, lightly squeezing them.

I didn't say anything.

He kissed my forehead and asked where I wanted to go eat. I had totally forgotten about breakfast, but now that he mentioned it, I was hungry. "Do you like pancakes?"

He lowered his eyelids and peeked at me. "Of course."

He was so damn cute. I wanted to grab him. Oh, but we had to *be good*. That was how the hormonal side of me thought, but the other side of me thought it was sweet he was being a gentleman.

"There's this place downtown called Pancake Heaven, and they have any kind of pancake you can think of. And they're yummy." I patted my belly for emphasis.

"Then Pancake Heaven it is." He stepped aside and swept his arm in the air toward the door, ushering me forward with a stately bow. "After you, madame," he said in a silly French accent.

"Why thank you, sir. Be sure to have Jeffrey pull the Rolls Royce around," I said, using a British voice, walking past him to get my jacket and purse. "But do let me pay."

He took my jacket and slipped it on me. "No," he objected, back to his normal, sexy voice. "I invited you, so it's my treat."

"Fine," I said, stepping outside. "Then I'll get the tip."

He shook his head and smiled mischievously.

***

Pancake Heaven was crowded, but we managed to get a table beside a window. Unfortunately though, a screaming toddler in a highchair sat across the aisle from us and another one kept whining in the next table over about wanting more chocolate milk.

I threw Nathan an apologetic look from across the table. "I'm sorry. I forgot it gets this busy on a Sunday."

He bit into his pecan pancakes. "That's okay. It's worth it," he said after swallowing. "This is outstanding." He stabbed a triangle piece covered in dripping syrup. "Here, you should try it." He held the fork up and fed it to me.

The taste of buttery pecan syrup awakened every taste bud I had with pleasure, and for an added bonus, there were pieces of pecans inside.

"Mmmmm. I'll have to get that next time." I glanced at my plate, the classic buttermilk kind covered in whip cream and strawberries. *So boring.*

Suddenly, a pacifier whizzed passed my face, making me flinch. It smacked the window and fell into Nathan's hand.

"You're quick," I said, impressed.

He smiled. "I would have been quicker, but I still had the fork in my hand."

"I'm sorry." A young woman appeared, looking frazzled with her dark hair poking out of her short ponytail in tiny mountains around her head. She blushed when her eyes fell on Nathan.

"No problem." He handed her the pacifier, making her blush even deeper.

She went back to her table, and her child wailed. She picked him up and left.

"Do you think you'll ever want one of those?" Nathan nodded toward the screaming toddler, taking another bite.

I chewed my pancakes and shook my head. "No," I said, taking a drink of my orange juice. "I love kids, but they're a huge responsibility, and the only person I want to be responsible for is myself." I paused to watch his reaction. "I hope that doesn't seem selfish of me," I added when I couldn't read his expression.

"Not at all." He hesitated, his eyes measuring my face in a way that told me he wasn't fully convinced. "But are you sure? You might change your mind later."

"Nathan, I'm sure," I said. "When I was a little girl, I didn't play with dolls. Instead, I was outside playing BB gun wars with the boys. In fact, I still have my Red Ryder rifle." I loved Reddy. We had lots of fun together, and I never shot my eye out.

He stared at me and shook his head. "See. You never cease to amaze me."

"She does have that affect on people," a familiar voice said from behind him.

We looked up, and there was Tree, Mohawk and all.

"Hi, Tree," I said, smiling. He was wearing a Sex Pistols sweatshirt and black jeans. I introduced them, and Tree shook Nathan's hand. "Hey, Tree, tell Nathan about our BB gun wars."

He laughed and bent down in front of Nathan. "See this scar right here?" He pointed to the dot-size indentation in the center of his forehead. "Paige did that to me when we were twelve."

Nathan looked at me in surprise. "You did that?"

Tree and I laughed.

"Guilty as charged," I said, remembering the day I marked him for life.

"You should have seen her," Tree animatedly told him. "She stuck leaves and branches in her clothes and hair, to camouflage herself. I was directly in her line of sight and didn't even see she was there. Then, POW!"–he slapped his forehead–"I was done for."

All three of us laughed.

"Well, nice meeting you, Nathan," he said still laughing. "My family is here, and I have to get back."

"Likewise," Nathan said.

"I'll see you in class tomorrow," I told him.

"I'll be there," Tree answered over his shoulder.

After we finished our breakfast, I tried to be quick about putting a tip on the table, but Nathan beat me to it. He grinned triumphantly. I made a face and stuck my tongue out.

When we stepped outside, I told Nathan I wanted to show him Carrie's mom's store, which was a block away. I've always envied Carrie for her tight-knit family. Even when they ragged on her, because it was never about stupid crap, like clean your room. No, her parents were totally cool, and her mom's antique shop was awesome, and I knew Nathan would love it as much as I did.

He stood in front of me, blocking the breeze. "It's chilly out here. Maybe we should take my truck." He inclined his head toward the parking lot.

"No, it's not that far. We can walk." My hand encircled his wrist.

He frowned. "Are you sure?"

I pulled him forward. "I'm not a china doll," I said.

"That's right." He laughed. "You're my sniper chick. I better watch what I say. Otherwise, you might pop a cap on my ass."

I playfully punched his arm. "That was a long time ago."

"Who taught you how to shoot a gun?"

"I taught myself. When I saw the movie 'A Christmas Story,' I was bound and determined to get a rifle like that. At first, Mom was like totally against it, but she finally gave in. I then read books about firearm safety and watched movies. When I got my Red Ryder, I practiced in the woods behind my house with pop cans. Mom wasn't thrilled about it. She wanted me to be like a normal girl and play with dolls, but that's just not who I am."

"You know, each day with you, is like opening a new and better present," he said. "I know I keep saying this, but you truly amaze me."

"I don't know." I shook my head, deflecting his compliments. "If I were that amazing, my mom would be around more." I could hear the sadness in my voice and hated it.

Nathan gently squeezed my hand. "She just doesn't know who--"

A red sports car screeched around a corner down the road, speeding toward us, and my ears were ringing in that high-pitched sound again. I released Nathan's hand and jammed my fingers in my ears. The car slowed as it approached us. I gasped when I saw the guy from the restaurant hang his head out the window. He had a ghastly smile on his face. Who the hell was this guy and what did he want? Nathan pushed me behind him, and when I peeked around his side, I saw the guy mouthing my name again. He let out a dark, hollow laugh, and I shrank in back of Nathan.

He turned to me when the car disappeared down the road. "Do you have a pen and a piece of paper in your purse?"

"Uh, yeah." I handed them to him, and he quickly wrote the license plate number down.

My legs wobbled. I began to crumble to the ground, but he caught me in time, sat me on the sidewalk, and settled next to me. I didn't realize I was shaking until he embraced me. I rested against his chest, feeling safe in his arms.

"I think I should take you home." His voice was deep with worry.

I pulled back, yanked the pen from him, and shoved it in my purse. The last place I wanted to be right now was home, and I'd be damned if I was going to allow my fears take control over me.

"No. I need to be around people. Okay?"

"Okay, but I need to ask you something." He placed his hands on my shoulders. "That guy in the car, have you ever seen him before?"

I nodded, and all the color drained from his face. "Last night, in the restaurant when I was coming back from the restroom, before I ran into you."

"That's why you were shaking," he whispered, putting the pieces together. I didn't need to reply, he saw something in my face that confirmed it. "What happened?"

"He did the same thing he did now, except ..." I trailed off and looked away, not wanting to relive that horrifying moment but could still see it in my mind.

"Except what?" He took my face in his hands. "This is important, Paige. Please tell me."

I stared at him and one emotion after another flashed across his face: anxiety, anger, determination, and... Love?

"His eyes," I whispered. "I saw a beam of light swipe across his irises."

Nathan hung his head. "Did your ears ring just now?"

"Yeah, but how did you know?"

He looked up, his face still without color. "Because you had your fingers in your ears, like you did the other--" And then something occurred to him, and his face became whiter.

"What?" I said, getting more nervous now. Why was he acting this way?

"Have you ever seen Matt's eyes like that?"

I didn't answer right away, but when my mind caught up to his question, I bristled. I mean, Matt was my friend, and Nathan needed to back off. Never once have I ever felt threatened by Matt, and so what his eyes glowed at The Lion's Den. The lights in the club were what caused it, unlike with this guy where I couldn't explain why his eyes had done that. "You know, your dislike for Matt is getting old," I snapped, fed up with this whole Matt issue.

He sighed heavily, and ran a hand through his hair. "I know what Matt *is*," he said, frustrated. "But I need to know if you saw the same thing in Matt's eyes as you saw in this guy's."

"Why? And what do you mean you *know* what Matt is?" I stood and walked away, but he caught my wrist and turned me around, a pleading expression entered his face.

"Please, Paige. Don't walk away from me."

My vision blurred. "Then tell me what's going on." I didn't understand any of this, and he did, but yet he wasn't confiding in me. He knew my secret about having premonitions. So why couldn't he trust me enough to tell me why in the hell he was acting this way? I should have never agreed on this second date.

He reached for the tears on my face, but I smacked his hand away. When I saw the hurt in his eyes, I clapped a hand over my mouth to stifle a sob.

"Please, don't do this," he whispered.

"If you won't tell me what's going on," I cried, "then what's the point in continuing this relationship?" I could barely breathe and held my stomach, knowing what I might be giving up. But I also knew I couldn't be with somebody who would hide things from me, even if it was Nathan.

"I promise, soon you'll understand." He moved forward, but I raised my hand and took a step back. I knew if I allowed him to touch me, I'd give in.

He stopped, his face anguished.

"It's always later with you, and it's not fair to me," I choked between tears, pointing at myself. "*Me*. Nathan. Why can't you think about me and my feelings?" I couldn't believe this was happening, and it looked like he couldn't believe it either. I mean, he looked so sad and upset, but yet he didn't care enough to clue me in on what was really going on.

"I am. I'm thinking about both of us."

"No, you're not. You're just thinking about yourself."

"Paige, you're shaking. Let me ..." He moved forward again, his arms open.

I turned away. "No, just go, Nathan."

"I need to take you home." His voice cracked.

"That's not your concern anymore," I said, and then ran to the antique store, crying the whole way.

Chapter Five
Heartache

Carrie had spent the night at my house, and I told her almost everything about what happened between Nathan and me. Quite simply, he wouldn't open up to me. Of course, she thought I should give him a chance and even went as far as to say he was in love with me. I didn't know about that. I mean, we'd just met and the whole love-at-first-sight thing seemed kind of silly to me. However, if I were to be completely honest with myself, I'd have to say I was the one falling in love with him, and felt a connection between us I'd never felt with anyone else before. But that didn't matter because it was over. And that night was the first night I'd cried myself to sleep over somebody other than my father.

***

"Hey, Carrie. Hey, Paige," Matt called out from across the lawn at our high school. He jogged to us, and my ears began to ring. I stuck my fingers in my ears, not understanding why they rang whenever he came around, just like with that guy in the restaurant. What the hell was going on?

When he reached us, he picked Carrie up and hugged her. My stomach twisted into a knot. I tilted my face to the cloudy sky, trying not to think about Nathan's arms around me.

"What's wrong, Paige?" Matt asked when we headed toward the red brick building.

"Paige broke up with Nathan," Carrie informed him, and I caught her giving him a warning look to be nice.

"Well, we need to cheer you up then," he said to me, looking a little *too* happy. I felt like kicking him just to get that damned smile off his face. "Let's go do something fun after school."

"I don't think so," I said, pulling my finger out of my ear when the ringing stopped.

We maneuvered our way through a crowd of students into the building and went to our lockers. The halls were buzzing with chatter of what people were going to do on spring break. A couple of boys were wrestling across from me, slamming each other against the lockers. A crowd formed around them, some cheering, some making bets, others laughing.

Ignoring them, I opened my locker, grabbed my stuff and slammed it shut. Carrie and I had first period together, and I was looking forward to occupying my mind with school work, hoping it would distract me.

"Can you do me a favor?" Carrie asked on the way to class.

"Sure. What?" I knew she screwed something up by the sheepish look on her face.

"I need to do a book report on Jane Austen's, *Pride and Prejudice*, and I know you've read it."

"Yeah. Why? You want me to do your book report?"

"No, but can you write an outline for me, so I don't have to read it?"

"Okay, but you're missing out on a good story," I told her.

"Thanks, Paige." She smiled and skipped beside me.

"When do you want me to do it?"

She stopped skipping, her smile faded. She glanced at the pea-green door that led into our classroom. I knew the bell was going to ring any minute, but I stood there with my backpack slung over my shoulder, gripping the strap, waiting for her reply.

"Right now," she said, ducking her head.

"Now!" My shrill voice leapt out. "Carrie, why didn't you ask me earlier?" Two girls who were down the hall turned to look at me, but I ignored them and stared at Carrie in disbelief.

"I forgot. I'm sorry. But I had so much fun with Matt over the weekend, I spaced it." Her brown eyes were begging me to forgive her irresponsibility.

"Fine. I'll do it this hour, but I want to hear what you and Matt did Saturday."

"I'll tell you all about it later," she said, hooking her arm through mine.

We entered the classroom right when the bell went off and took our usual seats in the back. Ashley sat a couple seats in front of us talking to one of her disciples. When she saw me, she raised her voice.

"--So for spring break, my *mom* is taking us to a health spa in California for a *mother* and *daughter* weekend. *My* mom loves spending time with *me,* and *we* have so much fun *together.*" She shot me a nasty grin, and then looked at Carrie.

Carrie held her middle finger up and moved it up and down her cheek, staring back at her. Ashley stuck her nose in the air, turned around, and flicked her blonde hair off her shoulder.

"Bitch," Carrie whispered.

"You're terrible." I snickered. "But that's why you're my best friend."

She winked at me.

Mrs. Hong came in and told us to be quiet and do our work. Most of the kids did what she said, but some were still chatting.

"Ms. Johnson and Ms. Brown, if you girls don't have anything to do, I have plenty of work to give you," Mrs. Hong told them–a tiny four-eleven Asian woman who carried herself like a general.

"We have lots of work to do," Jordan Brown's timid voice told her.

"Then get busy," Mrs. Hong snapped.

They opened their books and didn't say another word.

The hour went by quickly. Before I knew it, the bell was ringing. I handed Carrie the outline. She thanked me, and then dashed off to her next class.

When I entered my English class, I saw Tree in the back with his foot on the desk he always saved for me. He removed it when he saw me walking down the aisle toward him.

"How's my little fairy doing?" he asked.

I shrugged and sat down, dropping my backpack on the floor, harder than I intended. Why couldn't I get a frickin' break in this life? I must have been an asshole in a previous life and was paying for it in this one. I glanced at Tree. He was frowning.

"What's the matter?"

"I don't want to talk about it." I unzipped my backpack and retrieved my English book. He reached over and squeezed my shoulder.

"Hey," he said, his voice soft with reassurance. "If it's about Nathan, don't worry."

Just hearing Nathan's name spoken out loud made me want to cry, but I asked him why anyway, curious to know why he would say that. I mean, it was obvious Nathan had changed his mind about us. I guess I couldn't blame him because of what he now knew about me. But the look on Tree's face told me he saw it differently, which created a faint flutter of hope inside my chest.

"Because he's crazy about you. When I saw him yesterday, I could tell right away. So, whatever happened between you two, I'm sure will work out."

"I don't know," I mumbled.

He sat back, his face filled with self-assurance. "Well, I do, and I could tell he's a good guy, and I like him."

"He has your approval then?" I raised my eyebrows in mock surprise.

He folded his arms across his chest and nodded. "Yup."

"You know, he doesn't like Matt."

He pointed at me and grinned. "Now I like him even better."

Mr. Russo called the class to attention. Every time I looked at him, I couldn't help but think of The Count from Sesame Street, and imagined him counting numbers and laughing (ha, ha, ha). I wasn't the only one though. Other kids thought the same thing and actually called him The Count behind his back.

We had a whole hour devoted to Hemingway and his works. At the end of class, Mr. Russo told us we had to write an essay on one of Hemingway's books. It would be part of our final grade for the year. He warned us if he could tell we hadn't read it, points would be docked off our grade. The whole class groaned in unison.

The bell rang, and we gathered our stuff.

"Have you read any of his books?" Tree asked me on the way to my locker.

I sighed. "Not you too?"

He stared at me like I spoke a language he didn't understand.

"I just did an outline for Carrie on a book she was supposed have read," I said, catching the spark in his eyes at the mention of Carrie's name before he looked away.

"How is Carrie?" he asked when we reached my locker.

"She's good."

He raised a questionable brow and waited for me to elaborate.

Hiding things from Tree wasn't an easy task. In fact, the times I'd received premonitions when we were together, I had to come up with a lame ass excuse when he'd question the distant look on my face. And believe me, it was a tricky thing.

I snatched my biology book and banged my locker shut. "She's dating Matt now," I reluctantly said. "But it's not serious," I quickly added when his face crumbled.

"I don't know what she sees in that monkey spank," he said.

We headed to my next class, wading through the chattering students choking the halls and stairs. Tree remained by my side, deep in thought. When we reached my Biology class, I pulled him aside.

"She's not in love with him," I told him.

He licked his lips, and a glimmer of hope entered his eyes. "Really?"

I nodded. "She's just with him to have fun. So don't give up on her."

He smiled. "I'll see ya later, Paige."

***

Biology class dragged on forever, but I was grateful to have my mind occupied. I figured that was one hour in my day I didn't have to struggle with. One hour down, ten to go, before I could go to sleep. As long as I kept my mind occupied, I should be good. I decided to immerse myself in my school work since we were getting our assignments for our final grades today, thinking that would be perfect. I could devote my time to that and worry about what to do later.

After class I found Carrie waiting at my locker, bright and cheery. I tried to assimilate her mood, but couldn't.

I was a hopeless case.

"Matt and I are going off campus for lunch. Do you want to come with us?"

My ears were ringing again, and I saw Matt walking toward us. He waved, and Carrie motioned for him to hurry up.

"No. I think I'm going to stay and get something at the snack bar." The ringing in my ears annoyed me, and I still didn't understand why they rang when Matt came around and with that other guy too. And why did it quit after a few minutes of being around Matt? I felt like screaming.

"Oh, c'mon, Paige." Carrie wrapped an arm around my shoulders. "I think you need to try to have some fun."

"Maybe some other time." I shrugged her arm off, wanting to escape.

Matt came up behind her and tickled her sides. She squealed and jumped around, pushing on his chest with both hands. He stood there laughing at her weak attempt to push him backwards. I thought about Nathan teasing me about being his sniper chick and wanted to weep.

"Are you coming with us, Paige?" he asked, grabbing Carrie's hands, pinning her back against him while she struggled to break free. His sky-blue eyes were intently on mine, as if he was trying to compel me. Something in my gut stirred.

"No, but I'll catch you two later." I pushed past them before they could object.

As I waited in line at the snack bar, debating whether to eat or not, I felt a tap on my shoulder. Looking behind me, my gaze went up to Tree's face.

"Do you want to sit with me?"

After I paid for my chef salad and Dr Pepper, he took my tray. I followed him to an empty table, glad we were alone. I wasn't in the mood to be around anybody else but Tree.

"Where's your sidekick?" he asked. "You two always eat lunch together."

I picked at my salad. "She's with Matt." I glanced up to him scowling at the table. "They invited me along but I didn't feel like going off campus."

"I heard you fainted the other night," he said.

"Yeah, I did, but Nathan ..." I took a deep breath and ran my fingers through my hair. "I had an emotional weekend to say the least." I so didn't want to go there.

He nodded, knowing not to press the issue. He took a drink of his Coke, then bit into his brownie.

"Hi, Tree. Hi, Paige," Sam shouted from across the cafeteria.

Sam came toward us, dressed almost identically to Tree, in a black leather trench coat that hung past his arms. He looked like a little kid playing dress-up. A thin piece of blond hair was drooping out of place from his Mohawk.

"Here comes your 'mini me,'" I whispered to Tree.

The corners of his mouth curled, raising the brownie crumbs that clung to them.

"I think he has an idol of you he sticks on an altar in his bedroom," I persisted.

"Very funny, Paige," he said, trying not to laugh, licking at the corners of his mouth.

"I heard what happened to you, Paige. How are you feeling?" Sam asked.

I smiled politely at him while I played with the tab on my Dr Pepper.

"Fine, thanks."

His admiring eyes fell on Tree. I covered my mouth, hiding my smile. Tree kicked my foot underneath the table and squinted at me. Sam didn't catch on; he was too busy looking at Tree's ear.

"That's sick." He pointed at the little silver dude hanging onto the side of Tree's ear. "Where did you get your ear cuff?"

Tree made an effort not to look at Sam by picking pieces off of his brownie and popping them into his mouth. "I don't remember. I think my brother got it for me when he was in Germany."

"I wonder if I could order it online," Sam mumbled.

I stifled a giggle, and Tree made a face at me. It felt good being around him, and I couldn't help but find humor in Tree's wanna-be doppelganger standing next to him.

"Shit. I have to go. I'll see ya later," Sam said, looking at the clock on the wall.

Tree smashed his Coke can with his hand, making a loud crinkling sound. "Later."

"Bye, Sam." I waved, and then leaned across the table. "Do you think he knew we were laughing at him?"

Tree shook his head. "I don't think so." He looked at my salad. "You didn't eat much."

"I'm not hungry." I pushed it aside and frowned. "I hope I didn't hurt his feelings."

He rolled his eyes and flicked crumbs at me. "Sam and his feelings will be just fine."

"Oh, I have read some of Hemingway's books," I blurted, answering his question from earlier, taking pieces of shredded cheese off my salad and flicking them at him.

"That's great." He smiled. "Can you tell me about one you have read?"

"I will, but you need to read it though." I took a drink of my Dr Pepper and watched the hope in his face transform into a pleading look. It was the same look he used to give me when we were kids. And despite how bitchin' he looked, the little boy inside him emerged in his facial features. He became ten again, and my heart warmed to the memories of us being kids together, staring wars and all.

"Tree, if you don't read the book, Mr. Russo is going to be able to tell. You heard what he said." Despite Tree's lack of literary knowledge, he was smart, and I didn't want him in trouble.

The muscles in his face bunched up, like a kid being told he had to eat liver. "I know, but that stuff is so boring to me, and if I try to read it I'll fall asleep."

An idea came to me. "I'll tell you what. I'll go to a used bookstore and buy one of his books and highlight what you need to know. Then you can take that information and write your essay on it." *That will totally work.*

"Great idea." He beamed.

"I'll go today after school and buy the book, and I'll highlight what you need to know tonight." I was benefitting from this as well because it would give me another thing to do.

"You don't need to do it today," he said, sounding guilty.

"It's no problem. I planned on doing all my school work this week anyway."

"Paige, it's going to be okay. Things will work out. You don't have to use your school work to--" Sympathy now took over his guilt, stabbing at my heart.

I raised my hand. "You know me too well, but I need to do this to help cope with things. Besides, once it's out of the way, I won't have to worry about school work for the rest of the year." At least something positive would come out of my misery.

The bell rang. Tree took my tray and threw the contents on it in the trash, along with his.

"I'll give you the book tomorrow. Unless, you want me to stop by your house tonight to give it to you."

"I won't be home." He flashed me a guilty look. "I have to work at my dad's garage after school. We're rebuilding an engine."

"That's fine. I'll bring it to school then," my voice squeaked, as if to say "no worries."

He kissed me on the cheek before going up the stairs to his next class.

My last class for the day was history. I saved Matt a seat. But when class started, and there was no sign of him, I wondered if he ditched for the rest of the day. Until ten minutes later when he entered in the middle of Mr. Harrin's lecture, and my ears were ringing.

Mr. Harrin's pale-blue vulture eyes shifted to Matt. "It's nice of you to grace us with your presence, Mr. Schall."

All heads turned to Matt.

"Sorry," Matt said, rubbing his belly, making a sick face. "I ate some Mexican food and was detained for a while." He took the empty seat next to me.

Soft laughter rumbled throughout the room.

"So, if it starts to smell like boiled eggs over here, you'll know why."

The laughter broke free. A couple of girls across the room shot him a disgusted look. I couldn't help but snicker. Matt was totally playing it up, and our teacher wasn't amused.

Steve who sat behind Matt raised his hand. "Can I sit somewhere else?"

"No, Mr. Hass. You will remain where you are," Mr. Harrin said through tight lips.

"But I'm in the line of fire," Steve complained.

More laughter.

In his Gestapo style, with his back straight, shoulders back, Mr. Harrin approached Matt's desk. "Mr. Schall, we were just talking about the bubonic plague. If you can answer the following questions correctly, I'll forget about your insubordination. But, if you can't, then you will have detention for the rest of the week."

I think we all held our breaths because the silence became deafening. Mr. Harrin looked down his nose at Matt.

"Lay it on me," Matt said with a cocky smile.

Mr. Harrin returned his cocky smile and asked, "What was the bubonic plague also known as?"

"The black death." Matt smirked, slinging his arm behind the chair.

"Where did it originate?"

"Central Asia."

"How many lives did it claim?"

"On record, close to two-hundred million."

I glanced around the room. All eyes were glued on Matt, shocked and impressed.

"What year did it become a pandemic?"

"1328," Matt answered. "And during that time a third of the population died."

Mr. Harrin responded with a sharp nod, his cold eyes thawing. He patted Matt on the shoulder. "You're forgiven, Mr. Schall." He went to the front of the class and continued with his lecture.

"You rock. That was totally awesome," I whispered to Matt when Mr.

Harrin turned to the blackboard; my ears were no longer ringing.

He snorted with indignation. "Those were bullshit questions and a waste of my time."

"Yeah, well, I wish I knew as much as you did."

He stared at me in an odd way, like he knew a secret. "Maybe someday you will."

I held his eyes with mine and thought I saw something flickering beyond them, but he looked away before I could be sure. Then the ghostly spoke:

"Black in the day. Black as night. They love human flesh, but it must be just right."

The hair on the back of my neck prickled. I peeked at Matt, and he was glaring at Mr. Harrin. My eyes fell on my open textbook to a picture representing the people who were afflicted with the plague. Was this message talking about the plague? And why was I having another premonition? They never came this close together. I wanted to throw my book across the room and scream, but instead I wrote down our assignment and bolted out the room when the bell rang. I couldn't deal with this anymore and was on the verge of flipping out.

"Hey, wait up," Matt called above the herd of rushing students.

I stopped and waited, even though I wanted to get the hell out of there.

"What's the matter?" he asked, shifting his books in his arms.

"Nothing. I just have a lot of work to do," I said in a rush, my heart racing.

"Are you mad at me for going out with Carrie?" He moved closer to me.

I shook my head and frantically looked around.

"Do you want to meet us at Café Nation at four?" He stepped into my space.

"No. Tell Carrie I'll talk to her later." I spun and bailed.

***

At Betty's Used Books, I purchased Hemingway's, *A Farewell To Arms* in a paperback. I hoped, Tree might take a liking to this story. Maybe even bring some culture into his life. And then I admitted the only culture Tree had in his life was speaking German and eating Chinese and Mexican food, which would probably be the extent of it. Not to mention the only things he read were car and guitar magazines. Oh, and he had a huge collection of comic books.

Stepping outside into the cold wind, I hurried to my car, not liking the looks of the clouds whipping across the dark amber sky. I wanted to get home before it turned ugly, but then felt the weight of somebody's eyes on my back. I stopped and turned. My hair flew in front of my face. I swiped it back, looking about. Debris swept the street, swirling around me, but nothing else caught my attention. I quickly entered my car and peeled out of the parking lot, liking the sound of the tires squealing against the damp asphalt.

When I got home, I immediately went to work. A fierce wind rattled the windows, and a rumble broke just above the roof. I kept my mind busy by highlighting the book for Tree, not wanting to think about anything else but that. I pretty much knew the story, so it didn't take me long to do. Afterwards, I turned the TV on. A continuous beeping filled the room with a robotic voice warning of a serious thunderstorm for my county.

Damn, if only Nathan …

Cutting that thought off, I redirected my mind on my own essay. It was easy, and I had the rough draft done before bedtime. The lights flickered at the same time the phone rang. Closing my notebook, I rose from the kitchen table and went to the phone. With a pounding heart, I looked at caller I.D. and picked it up.

"Hi, Carrie," I said, taking slow breaths to calm my heart.

A flash of white light sparked through the sliding glass window in the kitchen. Then a loud boom shook the house. The lights flickered again. I snatched a flashlight from a bottom cupboard in the kitchen and place it on the table next to my schoolwork.

"Are you mad at me?" she asked point blank.

"No, I just need some time to myself." I moved over to the window and watched Mother Nature's strobe stab through the dark forest. For a brief second, I thought I saw a face poking out from behind a tree. It looked like Nathan, but when I took a closer look, there was nothing there.

"Promise."

"I swear. I'm not mad at you." I yanked the curtains across the window and scolded myself for being so pathetic. I mean, seriously, I had to force myself not to think about Nathan, and now I was having hallucinations of him. How sad was that?

"Good, because I was worried when Matt said you'd talk to me later, and you didn't call."

"It's all good," I said.

The rain thrashed across the windows, followed by a *ding, ding, ding* sound. Hail.

Carrie stayed on the phone with me until the storm died, probably because she knew how I hated to be alone in a thunderstorm. She told me all about her date with Matt and that they made out for hours in his jeep. But before we hung up, she became quiet. I braced myself for the inevitable question.

"Have you heard from Nathan?"

"No."

"He'll call. He's probably just giving you some space."

"I don't know, Carrie, but I don't want to talk about it."

"I understand. But if you do, I'm here for you."

"I know and appreciate it. I'll talk to you tomorrow."

"Okay. Have sweet dreams."

"You do the same."

I hung up the phone, feeling myself spiraling downward. I knew I had to do something quick before the loneliness in my heart consumed me. I decided on taking a shower, thinking the hot water would calm me, but I soon discovered it was a lost cause when the thoughts I'd been suppressing all day began circling me like a pack of hungry wolves. Cruelly, my mind reminded me of Nathan's arms around me, the touch of his lips on mine, that fire he ignited inside me, the overwhelming electricity we had between us, and how perfect we were together.

And now, despite what Nathan and I had between us, he was out of my life. And yeah, I could call him, but he did reject me the other day and wouldn't go to "second base." Not to mention he didn't even care enough to open up to me, so what was the point?

He didn't care enough.

The realization of that punched a hole in my gut, and I sat in the middle of the tub hunched over, my broken sobs echoing off the ceramic tile. The hot water sprayed over my shaking body, joining the tears pouring off my face. But the tears weren't only reserved for Nathan, they were for my father and Brayden as well. My heart ached for them, and I missed them like crazy. And so I stayed hunched over in the tub until the water turned ice cold, and I had no choice but to get out.

***

The next four days came and went in a blur. Tree was happy to get the book I highlighted for him and tried to cheer me up. He even sang the silly songs we used to chant when we were little. I couldn't help but laugh and play along. Carrie joined in, remembering the lyrics herself. During that brief period, it was like we stepped back in time. We were no longer young adults struggling to make sense out of our lives. Instead, we were living in the moment, three best friends not caring how dorky we sounded in a cafeteria full of people.

But they weren't only my best friends. They were my family as well, and the only ones in my life–besides Brayden, but he wasn't around anymore–who had always been there for me and vice versa. And honestly, if it wasn't for them, I'd probably still be in bed.

My ears continued to ring when Matt came around, which drove me crazy. I tried to politely avoid hanging out with him, but the more I declined his invitations, the more he persisted. I finally gave in and suggested hanging out on Friday night, but he told me he had other plans, so I was off the hook. Carrie had plans too. Her aunt arrived in town, and she had family obligations. Tree was also busy. One of his dad's employees had been sick all week with the flu, and his dad needed his help in the garage.

My mom called me on Wednesday, and told me she had the next four days off, but a friend of hers offered to take her to Vegas, and of course, she decided to do that instead of coming home. That stung me pretty hard, but I forced myself to sound happy because I didn't want her to come home out of guilt. She did say she'd make it up to me, but whatever. She was more like a fleeting ghost in my life than a mother anyway.

The cat remained outside my house every day, and I was always happy to see him. A couple times I tried to lure him inside, but he wasn't interested, however, he did allow me to pet him, and we were becoming friends.

Now that it was Friday evening, I didn't know what to do with myself. It was spring break, and I already finished my schoolwork for the semester, cleaned the house, and did laundry. I thought maybe tomorrow, Carrie and I could see a movie and hangout at the mall, but what was I going to do until then?

As I stood in the livingroom, pondering whether to channel surf or read a book, I heard a vehicle outside, and then a bright light flooded through the front window, sweeping across the room. Looking out the window, I saw the cat sitting at the edge of the lawn, staring at a pair of taillights disappearing down the road. I squinted, but couldn't tell what type of vehicle it was. Somebody probably got lost and went down my street to turn around, I reasoned, while admiring the sky that was turning a beautiful violet color. I looked up, and high above the trees hung the yellow moon, a glowing orb, becoming God to its star children. I imagined Nathan's truck pulling up like it had last Sunday and rested my forehead on the cold glass. My heart throbbed with the ache of missing him, followed by my father and Brayden.

Bursting into tears, I ran upstairs to my room, fighting the urge to throw myself on the bed and cry myself to death. I paced around my room instead, with my clawed hands woven in my hair, trying not to give into this gut-wrenching sadness that seemed to be squeezing the life out of me.

I slid my hands down my face, blowing air through my fingers, and before I realized what I was doing, I found myself rushing to my car. I didn't care if somebody was watching me–a feeling I had all week–or about the two premonitions I recently had, or if that guy was stalking me. All I knew at this point was, if I stayed in this house tonight, I'd go frickin' crazy.

I aimlessly drove around for a while, trying to figure out where to go. I thought about Café Nation, but I didn't feel like going to a familiar place. Really I just wanted to disappear for a while, and go where nobody knew me. But where could that be? Then a thought occurred to me, and I made a sharp turn off a dirt road near downtown. There was a seedy bar in an old, shabby building a few miles away that allowed teenagers and would be perfect for my agenda.

I parked next to a street lamp in the far corner of the parking lot, not caring how dangerous this might be, and stepped out of my car. Bright stars lit the dark sky like fireflies, and the moon hung full and proud above me. A sharp, smoky smell filled my nostrils, reminding me of a campfire. Somebody must have been burning leaves in the woods nearby. But as I neared the bar, the smell transformed into beer and cigarettes. Laughter and music spilled out the open door. When I walked in, a couple young guys turned and smiled at me. They were gross and creepy looking. I almost walked out, but held my chin up instead.

"Hi," the sandy blond one said, winking his lazy eye at me. "Are you here alone?"

"No. I'm waiting for someone," I lied, looking away, hoping he'd get the hint.

A middle-aged, overweight guy, who smelled like fried chicken bumped into me, but I recovered my footing before I fell. He didn't even stop to say he was sorry. *Asshole.*

"You better watch it, honey. A little thing like you might get trampled here," the blond guy said, his eyes lingering on my face, making my skin crawl.

"I'm fine," I said, turning away. I hurried to the pool tables and could feel his gaze on my back, which made me wonder what I would do if he were to force himself on me. I'd scream and kick him, but that would be the best I could do. I shot a nervous glance over my shoulder and breathed a sigh of relief when I saw him leave with his friend. Thank God.

The sharp sound of billiard balls breaking, caught my attention. A frizzy, blonde chick with dark roots showing, stood there with a pool stick in her hand. Her acid wash jeans bulged at her hips and thighs, and her black Harley shirt barely hid her flabby potbelly. *Did she even own a mirror?* She could be attractive with the right clothes and a trip to the beauty salon, but I guess the dark-haired biker looking dude with the mullet found her appealing. They were obviously together, and when he bent over the pool table to make a shot, she grabbed his ass. The white ball leaped over another, right off the table. A deep, gurgling sound escaped her lips–laughter.

I moved through the haze of smoke, trying not to bump into anyone, to the back of the bar near a corridor. There was a lot of hooting and hollering and beer bottles clinking. I took a couple steps back, hoping nobody would turn their attention on me. Eighties music played over the loud speakers, and I thought about Tree (he loved playing '80s music on his electric guitar). If he knew about me coming here alone, he'd rip me a new one. But I didn't care because right now, I'd do just about anything to forget about my life.

I rested against the edge of the wall, feeling awkward in this grubby place. But despite my uneasiness, I stayed and watched the people for a while, wondering what type of lives they had. I bet most of them had parents who loved them, and knew where their place in life was, unlike me, the freak-of-nature. I stared at my shoes, telling myself to forget about this stuff and not to dwell on it.

And then a high-pitched ringing sound went off in my ears. In the time it took me to look up, catch a glimpse of a robust man with curly brown hair enter the bar, and a guy call out, "Hey, Romulus," to him, somebody seized my wrist, and pulled me into the dark corridor. A gentle hand covered my mouth, pulling my back against him.

"Shhhhh. Don't make a sound," the soft voice said. I knew that voice and had been longing to hear it for almost a week now. He moved me behind him, still holding my wrist, and peeked around the corner. "I don't think he saw you," he said. I strained my eyes to see his face, but it was clothed in darkness. "C'mon,"–he took my hand–"we need to get out of here."

He led me to a door at the end of the long corridor. We slipped out into the frigid night, and with his hand still in mine, we hurried to the parking lot. When we reached my car, we stopped. He dropped my hand and faced me.

A warm pressure pushed to the top of my cheeks, straight around my eyes, spilling its way out in a slow, watery fashion. I blinked a couple times to clear my vision. He had on the same jacket he wore the first night we met and was still unbelievably cute, but discontent masked his face. When he fixed his eyes on mine, I could see the sadness and longing in the depths of them.

"Nathan, I--"

He held a hand up, and I covered my mouth, feeling the tears trail down my cheeks. I had no idea what he was going to say, but I was more than willing to listen just to hear the sound of his voice.

"I'll tell you everything you want to know, but I need to get some things off my chest first." He stepped forward, closer to me, and the butterflies in my chest reemerged from their slumber.

"I'm a wreck without you, Paige," he said. "I can't eat … I can't sleep … Sometimes I can't even breathe. You're all I think about." He bent his head and closed his eyes. Rubbing his temples with his fingertips, he continued in a low, woeful voice. "This week has been the worse week of my entire existence." He dropped his hands, his deep blue eyes capturing mine. I opened my mouth, but he raised a finger. "Please, let me finish. I need to get this out."

I nodded and wiped the tears off my cheek.

"I didn't mean to hurt you. I was afraid if I were to confide in you, I'd scare you off." He paused and took a disturbing breath. "I made a huge mistake because I lost you … I want another chance … I'll do whatever it takes to keep us together." We both stepped forward, closing the gap between us. He held my face in his cool hands. His eyes were smoldering with passion. "It's always been you, Paige. I've waited my whole life for you. You're the air I breathe, my heart and soul. Without you, I'm in hell."

"I feel the same way," I whispered.

He lowered his face, his soft lips on mine, but then he pushed me aside. I stumbled against my car, bewildered, until I saw what was happening.

Chapter Six
Answers

Nathan had Romulus by the throat. I gasped and clapped a hand over my mouth. Romulus' eyes were bulging out of their sockets. Wet choking sounds came out of his open mouth, his face turning shades of red and purple.

Omigod! Nathan was going to kill him.

"Nathan!" I screamed.

He whipped his head around, and I winced at the murderous look on his face. He caught my reaction, blinked, and threw him over three cars. My mouth dropped at how far he flew, landing on an old pickup. He slid off, and charged at Nathan. He threw punches, but Nathan's hands moved and blocked them with ease. I stood in awe, watching his movements blurring before my eyes. Romulus was fast too, but not nearly as fast or strong as Nathan. He threw another punch at Nathan, but Nathan ducked and did a roundhouse kick, slamming a foot into Romulus' face, sending him sprawling backwards onto the asphalt.

"Paige, move away from the car," Nathan called out, snatching him by the collar of his denim jacket, yanking his wrist behind his back, holding them in a vise grip.

I did what he said, and he threw him on top of the hood with a loud thud, smashing his face into it. With his other hand, Nathan gripped the back of Romulus' neck, pinning him. He bellowed a deep, throaty laugh, his colorless eyes locking onto mine. His bloody lips turned into a sneer, and he hissed through broken teeth.

Icy blood flooded my veins. His white eyes totally freaked me out, and I wondered how they changed like that. I took a couple cautious steps back, intimidated by the hatred I saw in them. I mean, why would he want to hurt me? I'd never done anything bad to anybody, and I always went out of my way not to offend or hurt a soul.

Nathan applied added pressure. "You will stay away from her!" he said through clenched teeth, surprising me with how angry he sounded.

When Romulus spoke, my stomach twisted. His deep voice lashed out with harsh words that sounded similar to the Latin I'd heard when I went to an old Catholic mass with Carrie. It also reminded me of *The Exorcist* when the priest spoke to the entity inside the little girl.

Holy crap!

Was there a demon inside this guy?

My heart and lungs froze. I stumbled backwards into the car behind me, feeling myself fading into a gray, swirling cloud.

"Breathe, Paige," Nathan's rough voice ordered. My gaze shifted to Nathan. "Breathe," he repeated. His anxious eyes and commanding voice jolted me into opening my mouth and breathing in large quantities of air.

Romulus said my name and spit out something in the Latin-sounding language, laughing maniacally.

I didn't know what he said, but Nathan seemed to understand it, and the expression on his face turned lethal. He grabbed a fistful of hair, yanked back, and bent low so his lips were next to Romulus' ear. Nathan spoke rapidly.

Whatever Nathan said made Romulus scream in horror. And then Nathan did something that totally flabbergasted me. He placed his palm on Romulus' forehead, and in a strong and powerful voice, he chanted an incantation in Latin. Romulus thrashed his body about, but Nathan's strength overwhelmed him. He wailed an agonizing screech that echoed all around us. I covered my ears. A cold gust of wind blew passed me, brushing against my cheek, lifting the hair off my shoulder. I shivered, and hugged my arms tightly around myself, unable to tear my eyes away from the body that now lay limp on the hood of my car.

Nathan looked up, still holding him down. "Are you okay?"

I moved my lips to respond, but no words came out. I wanted to say, "Um, hel-lo. I just witnessed you casting a demon out of some dude and saw how fast and strong you are. What the hell are you?" But I didn't.

Nathan slung the guy over his shoulder. "Stay here. I'll be right back."

Then he disappeared. But before I could try to rationalize the events, I was in his arms, shaking. He held me and whispered soothing words into my ear. Even though I had no idea how he could do those things or what he was, I felt warm and safe in his arms.

"I'll tell you everything you want to know," he said, gazing into my face. "But we need to get out of here. Do you think you can drive home?"

I nodded. Could I even remember how to drive? With my mind so disoriented, I wondered if I could.

He kissed my forehead. "I'll follow you."

He opened my car door, and I slid behind the wheel, allowing him to pull the seatbelt over me, snapping it into place. I took his hand. He bent down, placing his other hand on my knee.

"What are you?" I couldn't help it. I had to ask him.

The corner of his mouth lifted, and he shook his head. "I'm not a monster, Paige. In fact, I'm far from it. I promise you though, I'll answer that question later, but there are things I need to tell you first."

"Okay, but why didn't my ears ring when that guy snuck up behind me?"

He reached up and cupped the side of my face. I leaned into his hand, loving the feel of his touch. He studied my face for a long moment, tenderly moving his thumb across my cheek, sparking those fiery feelings in me.

"Because during our passionate moments, that ability we have becomes ineffective. It's as if our feelings for each other disconnects that capability, making us more vulnerable to them."

"Your ears ring too?" I asked in astonishment, catching the "we" part.

He nodded, and in his eyes I could see there was more he needed to tell me. I opened my mouth to ask another question, but he placed a finger over my lips.

"Let's talk more about this at your house. All right?"

I nodded.

"Wait for me before you turn on Commercial Street."

"I will." I instructed myself to put the key in the ignition and to turn it.

He gave me a quick kiss. "I'll see you shortly," he said, then vanished.

"You can do this," I whispered. "Just stay calm and pay attention."

***

On the way home I kept glancing in the rearview mirror, comforted to see Nathan's truck behind me. I felt safe with him and knew I'd be okay as long as we were together. My mind tried to process everything, but it was like a thousand emotions and questions strung together. I decided to treat it like a complicated math problem. There had to be a formula. I just needed to figure it out. It started with my first premonition, the one talking about death. But death meant change, and my life definitely had changed since then. And then I had an out-of-body experience and saw Matt's eyes glowing.

Omigod! Was there a demon inside of Matt? Was that why Nathan didn't want me to be alone with him? It had to be the reason. But Matt was my friend. And yeah, I saw his eyes glow, and my ears rang when he was around me, but why would a demon possess him?

I thought about the other day in history class when I had the last premonition. I thought at the time it might have something to do with the plague, but now it seemed to tie into this somehow. I recited the premonition in my head, but then my mind shifted back on Matt trying to persuade me to hang out with him. A haunting, cold feeling came over me when I recalled the weird look he gave me in history class. But the thing was I'd been hanging around him for months, and he'd never been hateful or mean toward me.

My mind skipped to the guy in the restaurant and on the way to Carrie's mom's store. Was there a demon inside of him too? The characteristics he'd displayed were the same as the guy in the bar. But why would demons be after me?

All those thoughts were exploding inside my head, so when I reached my house, I sighed with relief, knowing my questions would soon be answered. I pulled into the garage, and when I went outside to meet Nathan, he was already there.

"Can I ask you something?" He embraced me.

"Sure." I wrapped my arms around him, not caring if a nuke went off at that moment.

"I hope this doesn't sound too presumptuous, but if it's all right, I'd like to stay the night."

"I prefer you did," I answered, my stomach flipping with the thought of being with him all night. Hell, he could stay with me every night if he wanted to.

He leaned next to my ear. "I was hoping you'd say that." His warm breath blew against my skin. I shivered. Yeah, every night with me would be just fine.

Something rubbed against my leg. I looked down, meeting shiny green cat eyes.

"Hi, Mr. Kitty," I said, finally coming up with a name for him.

Nathan took my hand, and we went inside. I turned lights on while he hung our jackets in the closet. When I glanced at him, my mouth dropped. I knew Nathan had muscles, but wow. I mean, this was the first time I'd ever seen him in a short sleeve shirt, and man was he smoking hot. His arms were perfect, just like everything else about him, and in that brief moment I imagined them around my body. I quickly looked away before he caught me drooling over him. I headed for the kitchen.

"Do you want something to drink?"

"Here, let me." He followed me into the kitchen, and in one sweeping motion, he lifted me into his arms.

"What are you doing?" I laughed, liking that I felt small and protected.

He sat me on the couch and smiled, but it was weak. He looked worried.

"I want you to relax." He took my shoes off and went back to the kitchen.

"The glasses are in the cupboard next to the fridge," I told him. "And there's some sweet tea in the fridge." It felt kind of weird being waited on, and I had to force myself to stay put.

The sound of ice cubes dropping in the glasses told me he had it under control. A minute later, he handed me my glass.

"Thanks." I set the glass on the coffee table.

"You're welcome." He sat next to me and took a drink. "This is good tea. It reminds me of my mom's."

I stared at my lap, not knowing where to begin. I had all these questions to ask, but now my mind went totally blank, like white noise on a tv screen with no reception.

Nathan remained silent and drank his tea, waiting for me to speak. The only sound in the room were the ice cubes clinking. He was being incredibly patient with me, somehow knowing when I needed my space. But I didn't know where to begin, so I blurted the first thought that came to mind:

"Did that guy have a demon inside of him?"

He turned to me. "No, it was a dark spirit." My forehead wrinkled, and he continued. “They sometimes fashion themselves as demons because they know humans have been instilled with the ideology demons exist, and it scares them. But in truth, they don’t exist. At least, not in the way history has taught them.”

Confusion clouded my mind. “I don’t understand.”

He gave me a small patient smile and said we were spiritual beings who had free will, and all of us had the choice on how we wanted to create ourselves and what paths we wanted to take. Some would decide to turn dark and not cross over to the next plane of existence. But I couldn’t understand why anybody wouldn’t want to. I mean, heaven or wherever we go was supposed to be an awesome place. Why would somebody turn away from that? And he told me for a number of reasons: anger, selfishness, hedonism, ego.

“But there are spirits who are good that linger in this world too, right?” I asked.

“Absolutely. And eventually those spirits cross over with no problem. Once they’re ready that is.”

“But dark spirits don’t?”

His face turned dismal. “No, they reject any help offered to them.”

I wondered what would compel them to want to stay here, and asked him what their purpose was, and when he told me to inhabit humans when they wanted to and to claim earth as their own, I suddenly became cold and shook. He scooted next to me and placed his arms around my shoulders while he continued to tell me they saw earth as their personal amusement park and felt entitled to it.

“Can dark spirits inhabit any human?” I thought about one inside me, and a violent shudder went through me. He pulled me closer to him.

“Here’s the thing, Paige. There are humans born without a soul. They walk among us every day. These humans are the ones who commit atrocities with no remorse. Whether it’s physical or mental, it’s still the same. And when you look into their eyes, there’s nothing beyond them because the human shell is vacant.”

I got up, snatched the afghan from the trunk, and curled back into his arms. He moved it over my shoulders and said they could inhabit humans who had a soul, but they had to be invited in.

That made me feel better, but then I thought about Matt, and how we became friends when he moved back here from Seattle. I also thought about his eyes, and the premonition I had the other day. I decided to tell Nathan about Matt. After I was finished, he turned me around. He looked frantic, like he caught me about to drink a vial of poison.

"Matt has a dark, ancient spirit inside him. The oldest I've ever seen, and you need to stay away from him." He paused. "Matt's eyes glowed like that because of how old the spirit is. You see, the young ones are still acclimating to the human vessel, so you'll see that beam of light swipe across their eyes instead of the whole eye glowing, like Matt's does."

My mind struggled to absorb every word that came out of his mouth, including Matt having a dark spirit inhabiting him. Now I knew why Matt was such a mean and hateful kid. He had no soul. My blood seemed to be coagulating into ice from the terror running through my veins because I'd been hanging out with this dark spirit for like three months now, and … Carrie was dating him!

I took a drink to get rid of my cotton mouth, and kept my face neutral under Nathan's watchful eyes. But by the look on his face I wondered if he thought maybe I would fall apart, or run away. He was almost right. Part of me did want to run and not look back because the things he told me weren't a part of this box we lived in. What he had said broke down those cardboard walls, to where I was no longer boxed in and confined to a reality some people clung too. A reality to where they didn't have to do or think beyond what others told them. A reality where one found, comfort in complacency, and doing whatever needed to be done to get through their daily life. I had willingly participated in that reality, but not anymore, not with what I knew now. I couldn't run away, even if I wanted to. But Carrie could.

"Will he hurt Carrie?"

"I don't think so. He has no reason to."

"You don't *think* so," I said, worried now. "Nathan, Carrie is my family. If she's in any danger, I'll do whatever I have to do to get her away from it. Even if that means confronting what's inside Matt." There was no way I would back down from this. My face hardened.

He placed his hands on my shoulders and locked his eyes onto mine. "Listen to me," he said, his firm voice matching my stubbornness. "You *cannot* be alone with Matt. And if I have to, I'll stop you."

A short laugh escaped my lips. "You can't stop me."

The corner of his mouth curled, and he raised his eyebrows. "Try me."

I lifted my chin. "Don't underestimate me."

Worry now crossed his face. "I'm serious, Paige. You may be risking your life being alone with him. I'd take care of him myself, but he's too old for me to do that. So stay away from him."

"Why?" I asked, my chin still raised.

He ran a hand through his hair and sighed. "Because I've noticed, he's interested in you. There's something unique about you, and he knows it." He looked disturbed, and I gulped. "During this past week, when I knew you were safe, I found out some of them can see a powerful light within you, but they're not sure what it is. They're just going by what the 'old one' in Matt has told them."

"You know, I don't understand any of this," I said in frustration. "And I want to know now what's going on." I still didn't get what this had to do with me. I was a nobody.

He nodded. "All right, but if I'm going too fast, or you don't understand something, interrupt me, and I'll explain it to you. But I'm only going to tell you what you need to know right now. I don't want to overwhelm you."

"I have no idea what you're talking about, but okay."

He hesitated and drew in a deep breath.

For a moment I didn't think he was going to tell me. He looked scared in a way, like I would reject him afterwards. But then he spoke in a fast but clear voice, and I focused on his words to keep up.

"People like me can cast dark spirits out of a human, but they're not gone for good. It just hurls them out, and they can't enter another one until they recover from the excruciating pain it causes them and regain their energy. Sometimes, they never enter a human again."

"So, you're like a Catholic priest who can cast spirits out?"

He shook his head. "Catholic priests don't really get rid of the spirit. The spirit just leaves after it's finished toying with the people around it, gets bored, and finds another vessel. However, I do have to say, there are a few Catholic priests who are like me and can exorcize them."

"But what does this have to do with me? I don't know how to cast spirits out. And why do my ears ring when they come near me?" The panic I felt came out shrill in my voice.

"I'm going to answer your questions, but first I need to explain myself to you," he said. "That night at The Lion's Den, I already knew the dark spirit in Matt was interested in you. When he walked into the backroom, your reaction alarmed me. I knew it had to do with him, but I couldn't understand how you picked up on it. Then you stuck a finger in your ear, and it took everything I had to compose myself because I never suspected this would happen to you. And then you mentioned the cat, and I panicked. But when I saw the way you were looking at me, like I was out of my head, I knew I had to get a grip on myself. I didn't want my bizarre behavior to jeopardize my chance with you. But my thoughts were reeling to say the least, and on the way home I called Anwar to ask him about it, and he confirm--"

I raised my hands. "Wait a minute." I scooted to the edge of the couch and faced him. "What does the cat have to do with any of this, and what do you mean when you said you never suspected this would happen to me?" My eyes narrowed.

His face fell. "I'm sorry I didn't tell you this earlier, but at the time, I wasn't sure how to. But the cat is an exalted soul who is a house protector for those mortals who are destined to observe and protect humanity from the dark energies that want to engulf it." He paused, like he wasn't sure whether to continue or not. He cradled my face in his hands, his eyes pouring into mine. "The cat is also a marker for immortality."

"Excuse me?" I didn't think I heard him right. Immortality? That was stuff of fiction. I had the sudden urge to laugh hysterically, but rolled my eyes instead.

"Paige, I'm serious," he said, his gaze steady on me. "I wouldn't joke about this. You have a choice here, and it's one only you can make." His expression turned sorrowful, and a painful ache trembled through my heart.

"What choice?" My vision blurred, and I blinked to clear it.

His eyes shifted on my tears, and he moved his thumbs over my wet cheeks. "I'm sorry," he said. "I told myself not to get upset in front of you. It's not right for me to burden you with my emotions."

I was worried now, feeling a sense of impending doom, and the grief on Nathan's face crushed me.

"What's the choice Nathan? Why are you so upset?"

"You have the choice of becoming immortal or staying human. And I'm upset because if you stay human you're going to die. The dark spirits will eventually kill you, and right now your life is in danger." He looked down and shook his head. "I'm sorry for being selfish. I don't want to influence your decision."

"Wait a minute," I said, still trying to wrap my head around this. "You're telling me immortality *is* true? And I have a choice to live forever here on earth, or having to look over my shoulder each day and possibly dying young?"

He nodded, his eyes holding mine.

I threw the afghan off me and jumped to my feet.

"I'm sorry," I said, half laughing. "I believe everything you told me without a doubt, but the immortality part … Come on, you got to be *frickin'* kidding me."

He stood up. "Really? You think immortality isn't true?"

I laughed. "Yeah, I do."

His lips turned into a mischievous smile. "Can a human do this?"

He disappeared, and before I could take a second breath, he was back with a knife in his hand, stunning me. He took my hand and led me to the kitchen, then stuck his wrist out.

"Wh-what are you doing?" I asked, but then realized exactly what he was going to do when he raised the knife blade. I grabbed his wrist. "Don't do it."

"Move your hand. I want you to see this."

"No, I won't!" He was insane. Why would he do such a thing to himself, or to me?

"Please, trust me, Paige." The blade still hovered over his wrist. "I'll be okay. I promise." He flashed me an encouraging smile.

"Fine." I released my hand. "But if you die, I'm killing myself, and then I'll find you and kick your ass." I would too. I'd kick his ass for eternity.

He laughed, and with one swift swipe of the blade, he cut a deep gash in his wrist. The skin separated. Dark gooey blood gushed onto the tile floor. I went to get some towels, but he snatched my arm.

"Watch," he said.

The sight of all that blood made me lightheaded, but I continued to watch. To my amazement the bleeding stopped, and his skin pulled together, sealing the wound shut. Within minutes, his wrist looked normal. There wasn't a scratch or a scar where he had sliced it. I couldn't believe it. This was frickin' crazy! Was my reality just a damned lie all along?

Grinning, he proudly drew himself up. "Can a human do those things?"

The room pitched and rolled. My knees buckled, but Nathan caught me. The next thing I knew, I was lying on the couch. I closed my eyes and felt something cold and damp being placed on my forehead.

Nathan was immortal. But how could that be? And now I could be immortal too. All of this didn't seem real, like being trapped in a vivid dream.

At that moment, it became too much for my mind to process, and as a precautionary defense against a possible melt down, it shut all those thoughts out.

"Are you still with me?" Nathan asked, his voice deep.

I opened my eyes. The room had stopped spinning, and Nathan was on his knees beside me. I lifted my fingers and traced the line of his round face and square jaw, every perfect part of it. He looked down when I brushed my fingers over the top of his eyelids, to his cheek, and then his lips. I traced the bow on his lip, around to his bottom lip. His chest rose and fell faster, and my quick breaths could be heard in the silence. In that moment, I didn't care about what I now knew, or what was going to happen. I just wanted to be with him. I rested my hand on the side of his neck. He looked at me, and his dark blue eyes were extraordinarily bright, unlike the last time when it was too subtle to even question it. But now, the radiance in them jumped out at me from beneath his lashes.

"Why do your eyes change like that?" I whispered, moving my hand down his neck, feeling an uncontrollable desire swallowing me, making me a part of it.

"Because I want you," he said in a low, fierce voice. His eyes shone with an intense yearning that made the ache to feel his touch unendurable.

I grabbed the washcloth off my forehead and threw it behind me, then seized his shirt, pulling him forward. I wasn't usually this aggressive, but the fire inside my belly became too great to ignore.

"Wait." He locked his arms above my head, his eyes still bright.

In one swift move, he had me cradled in his arms. I locked my hands around his neck and pressed my lips to his. Our tongues connected, touching in a slow, seductive manner. My stomach did a continuous flip as our passionate kiss grew into hunger. I pulled him deeper into the kiss. A soft groan rumbled out of him, and then warm air brushed against my face. Nathan broke our kiss. I looked up, and he was glancing around the upstairs hallway. I pointed to my room where the bright moonlight spilled through the window. Nathan's lips found mine again. He lowered me to the bed, encapsulating us inside the moon's white light. I pulled his shirt over his head while he unbuttoned my sweater. Sitting up, I yanked it off, and threw it across the room.

He caressed my cheek. "I love you."

"I love you too," I whispered, running my fingers down his muscular chest. He had the body of a champion gladiator who could take on two lions at once. It was breathtaking.

He leaned forward, slowly pushing me down. His hand held my wrists above my head while our lips reunited in passion and abandonment. A low, deep moan erupted from me when his other hand snaked beneath my white lace camisole, pushing it above my breasts, exposing them, causing my breathing to become unsteady. An electrical heat shot through me. Then his lips found their way to my neck, trailing down it, his hand gently moving down my stomach.

"Are you okay?" he whispered a while later.

I smiled and nodded. "Just keep doing what you're doing," I whispered breathlessly.

His lips found mine again.

And for the next two hours, nothing existed but him and me.

Chapter Seven
Nathan's Story

I think I died and went to heaven. Seriously. I mean, here I was lying in Nathan's arms in the middle of the night, running my hand across his muscular chest, marveling at how it gleamed in the moonlight. I was also enthralled by Nathan's flesh joining with mine, melded together like a beautifully crafted sonnet. I sighed, enjoying how relaxed my body felt.

Since I felt so good, I decided this was the best time to tell Nathan all about my premonitions and how they came to me in an audio form. I explained the voice didn't come from inside my head, it was like outside the very edge of it. It made me kind of nervous talking about it because I didn't want him to think of me as a freak. But when he assured me he'd never think of me in that fashion, my heart completely melted. He was like the most wonderful person in the world, and the first person in my life I could truly be myself with. It also felt good to share this secret with somebody, to actually talk about it, knowing I wouldn't be ridiculed for it.

But when he asked me about my first premonition, I clammed up. I didn't want to go there. However, I knew I'd eventually have to, so I swallowed the lump in my throat and told him. As I did so, I thought about my dad choosing to leave me and could feel the tears forming. I mean, if he really loved me he wouldn't have left, right?

I rested my arm against my eyes to hide my tears from Nathan, but he must have sensed it because he leaned over me and gingerly wiped them off my face.

"I believe your father loved you very much," he said.

That did it. I covered my face with my hands and sobbed like a little girl. Nathan gathered me in his arms, and I rolled on my side, pressing myself against him. Snot was creeping out my nose, so I went to the bathroom to clean up. I took a couple deep breaths and placed a cold washrag on my face. Afterwards, I went back into the bedroom and crawled back into bed. Before Nathan could say anything about what had just happened (so embarrassing), I told him about the last premonition I had in history class.

"It was talking about the dark spirits," he considered. "They love being in the flesh because they can partake in its desires. And it must be just right because they can't enter just anyone. It's warning you about them."

"You're right," I replied because what he said made sense. "When I heard it, we were studying about the plague which made me wonder if it had to do with the premonition I had."

His soft lips touched my cheek. "I can see why."

I thought about Matt, and how he knew all of Mr. Harrin's questions, and how envious I was on his historical knowledge. Now I knew why. It wasn't Matt that knew, but an ancient spirit dwelling inside him who had lived through those times.

A part of me struggled with that concept, even though I knew it to be true. And another part of me hungered for his knowledge since he knew things even our greatest historians were clueless about. I then wondered if he would hurt me, if he had the chance. Honestly, I wasn't sure. I mean, he had numerous opportunities to do so, but hadn't.

But why was he dating Carrie?

I could try and break them up, but Carrie would see right through me, so that wasn't an option. I grimaced at the thought Carrie was dating a dark spirit who totally scammed us, and I hated I couldn't tell her about it. I guess I could keep a watchful eye on them, and if it came down to it, I'd confront the dark spirit, regardless of what Nathan said.

"What are you thinking?"

I didn't want to tell him, so I decided to ask him about a thought that had been hovering around in my mind–the thought of when he became immortal and how it happened. It still boggled my mind immortality existed, and I could now become immortal.

He pulled his arm from under me and propped himself on his elbow. With his free hand, he stroked my cheeked.

"I became immortal in 1856."

I sat up. "1856!" I quickly did the math. If he was nineteen when he became immortal, then his actual age would be ... "That makes you one-hundred and seventy-five-years-old!" My shrill voice rang out.

He smiled, amused by my reaction. "That's right." But then his amusement ran away from his face when he saw something in my eyes that troubled him. "Does that bother you?"

He sounded concerned, so I quickly answered, "No. It just trips me out. I mean, what did you do for all those years?"

He relaxed and opened his mouth to answer.

"Wait," I blurted before he could reply. "First I want to know how you became immortal, and will it be the same for me?" I really wanted to know this and hoped it didn't involved neck biting and drinking blood. I had a weak tolerance for blood.

We scooted down in the bed, and I settled myself back in his arms. His voice became low and distant when he spoke:

"The same cat on your doorstep came to mine. At first I didn't think much of it because stray cats sometimes wander onto our farm, but after a while I noticed a difference in this one. He would stay in our front yard or on the porch, like a guard dog. Then I saw the strange mark on his back, like you did."

"Did your ears start to ring like mine?"

"Yes, and to answer your earlier question, your ears ring to let you know a dark spirit is nearby, but they have to be within a certain range to trigger it."

"How many immortals are there in this world?" I wondered if I had ever met one and hadn't even known it.

"I'm not sure, but I know quite a few. Anwar is one of them."

"But didn't he help your family on the farm?" I thought about the 1800s, and him living on a farm in Missouri. Back then there were slave holders. Was his family one of them?

"He did, but he wasn't our slave. My parents didn't believe in slavery, and they treated Anwar like another member of our family. My parents were wonderful people, and so were my brothers. They would have loved you, and you them." I could hear the sadness in his voice.

"You miss them, huh?"

He stared at the ceiling, and his voice dropped to a high whisper, each word spiked with longing. "There's not a day goes by I don't think about them in one form or another."

"You were lucky to have a family like that. I've always been envious of people like you."

"Yes, on the one hand I was very fortunate, but on the other hand, one of the hardest things I had to do was exile myself from their lives."

My heart sank. The thought never occurred to me if I were to become immortal I'd never see Carrie or Tree again. Just the very thought of it made me want to weep. And to think he had to do that with his family.

"I'm sorry you had to go through that," I said.

"My father knew, but I'll tell you about him some other time."

"Finish telling me about the immortal part." I wanted to respect his space as much as he respected mine and hoped this would derail his thoughts from his family.

He went on to tell me Anwar was already immortal when he started working for them a month before the cat appeared. He had tracked down some dark spirits around their area, and as he was observing them from afar, he saw some guys beating on Nathan's brother and saved his life. In gratitude, Nathan's father offered him a job and a place to stay. Anwar accepted and was instantly folded into the family. I thought about the people back then, how they probably hated Nathan's family for treating Anwar like an equal, but Nathan said they were ignorant about it. People just assumed Anwar was a well-behaved slave.

He continued and said he and Anwar became good friends and spent a lot of time together. When the cat showed up, his ears began to ring, and a few nights later, Anwar explained everything to him.

"Did you believe him?" I thought about my reaction and wondered if his were the same.

He shook his head. "I thought it was a joke. I told him I didn't believe in his superstitions, or the voodoo the slaves around town talked about. So I ignored it, until one night when we were in town, a dark spirit attacked me. He caught me off guard with his strength and swiftness. The next thing I knew, he had a knife blade to my throat, but then Anwar stepped in and yanked him off me. Anwar's strength and agility fascinated me. When he'd cast the spirit out, I could no longer turn a deaf ear to him."

He looked away, remembering that time in his life, and when I asked him what happened after that, he looked at me, his eyes shining in the bright moonlight.

"I had the same choice you have now, and I chose immortality because I wasn't ready to die. And I always had this insatiable need to be something outside the perimeters of conventional thought. I never knew what it was until that night.

"A few nights later, I went to the guesthouse my father provided Anwar, and by the light of the kerosene lamps, he gave me immortality."

I sat up and hugged the pillow. "But, how?" An image of Anwar biting his neck popped in my head, churning my stomach. I really hoped it didn't involved blood.

He stared at me for a long moment, and I covered my mouth, knowing by the hesitant look on his face that it did. *Ugh!*

"I'm sorry," he said. "I don't mean to put you in suspense, but it may gross you out, so I'm just going to say it." He took a deep breath and spoke fast. "What I'm going to tell you cannot be done to just anyone. You have to be chosen. Otherwise, it won't work. But the chosen one has to be bled out, which is quite gruesome. Seconds after the body dies, the immortal takes his blood and introduces it to the dead human's open wound, draining some of his own blood into it. The body then regenerates itself into immortality."

I hugged my queasy stomach, trying not to retch at the mental visual of being bled out and how painful it would be. I lay back down and pulled my knees to my chest, swallowing against the sickness threatening to spew forth.

"Are you okay?" Nathan asked, his arm around my shoulder.

"I don't think I can do it," I whispered. "The blood. The pain."

"It doesn't hurt much." His voice was calm and reassuring. "Honestly, I think it's the fear of pain that makes it worse than what it really is."

"Yeah, whatever," I said, feeling tired all of a sudden. Everything that happened tonight was finally catching up with me, and my brain wanted to go into sleeping mode. It was like somebody flipped an exhaustion switch inside me, overriding my sickness and fear.

"I'm serious. It's not that bad, and I'm not saying so to ease your mind. It's the truth. It goes by quick. Before you know it, it'll be over." He fell silent, and I began to drift off, but then he spoke again. "Oh, by the way. I took care of the guy."

I turned over, alert now. "What guy?"

He looked at me like he couldn't believe I didn't know who he was talking about, and then it dawned on me. A rush of an anxiety shot through my veins.

"You know. The guy--"

"What did you do?" A vision of him pounding that guy to a bloody pulp entered my mind.

"I tracked him into a deserted alley. I was in a foul mood, knowing what he could do to you, and he knew your name." He paused for a minute. "I forced him to tell me what he knew, and before I cast him out, he told me what I had told you earlier about some of them seeing a light inside you and don't like it. He also told me the 'old one' holds great interest in you."

He saw me trembling and wrapped his arms back around me. My groggy mind shifted on the premonition I had at Café Nation.

Maybe I misinterpreted it. But my life had changed dramatically since then. However, now I knew there might be a chance I could die, and who would try to kill me and why.

I really didn't know what my premonition meant though, and at that point my brain and body were telling me they had enough. I closed my eyes and surrendered. Whatever worries and concerns I had would have to wait until tomorrow. I fell asleep in Nathan's arms, and for the first time in my life I felt truly loved and wanted.

***

The next morning, I awoke still in Nathan's arms and caught him staring at the ceiling. He looked at me and smiled. Okay, I was definitely in heaven now.

"Good morning, beautiful," he said, kissing my cheek.

I returned his smile and tried not to breathe on him.

"Good morning." I yawned in the crook of my arm. "What time is it?"

"Almost noon."

I covered my face and groaned. "I need to brush my teeth and take a shower."

My stomach growled. It always did that when I was hungry, which was so embarrassing.

He placed his hand on it. "And eat too."

I thought about what we could eat. Bread and peanut butter were our only options. I had planned on going to the grocery store, but totally spaced it after Mom bailed on me. And with everything that was going on, food wasn't a priority. I think I even lost like five pounds.

"Um, I can make us peanut butter toast."

He pretended to ponder it. "Hmmm, peanut butter toast."

"I'm sorry, but that's all I have," I said, my cheeks burning.

He traced his finger down the length of my cheek. "I'll tell you what. You go take your shower, and I'll stop at the deli and get us something to eat. By the time you're done, I'll be back."

I squinted at him. "But don't you need to take a shower too?"

"Do I smell bad?" he joked, sniffing himself.

"No." I laughed.

"We'll go to my house after we eat. I'll shower then."

"You're going to take me to your house?" My voice was raised in surprise.

He placed his hand on my cheek. "You're my life now, and I want you in every part of it."

My breath caught in my throat. He really meant it. He really, honest to God, meant it.

I covered his hand with mine. "I would like that."

"I love you," he whispered.

He leaned to kiss me, but I stopped him. He moved his head back and looked at me in question.

"I love you too, but I really need to brush my teeth." My mouth tasted like a fairy squatted over it and took a dump.

He smiled. "Okay. So what do you want me to get?"

I stepped out of bed, still wearing my lace camisole and matching boy shorts. His gaze moved seductively across my body, and then he reached to grab my arm. I jumped back and wagged a finger at him. His eyes were brightening, which created a warm stirring sensation in my belly.

"Not now. I feel really gross." A slow smile crept on my lips. He was so cute with his blond tip hair sticking up, and that ornery look on his face.

"You are far from being gross. In fact"–his eyes moved up and down my body–"I think you're the most gorgeous, sexy girl who ever walked the earth."

I wrapped my arms around myself, blushing. "I'm going to take a shower," I said, changing the subject. "Get me a croissant veggie sandwich, light on the mayo, and no avocados."

He sat on the edge of the bed while putting his black jeans on. He glanced over his shoulder, his eyes back to normal. "Is that it?"

"Oh yeah, pepper jack cheese or American. The money is in my purse downstairs."

"Oh, no." He slipped his T-shirt over his head. "I'm paying for it."

I headed to the bathroom. "Fine, but I'm taking you out to dinner tonight then." There was no room for argument in my voice. I was paying for dinner. End of story.

"Fair enough," he called out. "I'll see you soon."

***

The phone was ringing. I finished tying my shoes, and hurried down the stairs. Jumping off the last step, I turned into the kitchen. I picked up the phone, noticing the white tile floor was wiped clean. I silently thanked Nathan for getting rid of the bloody mess.

It was Carrie, at home doing the family thing–bored–I told her about me running into Nathan last night and how he bared his feelings to me.

"I'm so happy for you, Paige," she squealed. "I told you he's in love with you. You two are *so* meant to be together."

I laughed. "Yeah, you were right. Guess what?"

"What?"

"He spent the night last night." I twirled in a circle, slapping a hand over my heart, and sighed.

"Omigod! Did you two?" She paused. A door closed with a heavy thunk.

"We did," I said. "And it was the most erotic and beautiful experience I've ever had or imagined." Just thinking about it made me all hot and sweaty. I plopped on the couch and wiggled to shake it off.

"Eroootic." She stretched the word. "I love that word." I could hear the smile in her voice.

I laughed, but then stopped, thinking about the "old one." "Don't tell Matt."

"I won't. We're going out tonight," she said.

"How is he when you're with him?" I asked, trying to hide the caution in my voice. The thought of her being alone with him seriously bothered me.

"He's so funny. And like I told you before. He's a great kisser."

I cringed, and had the sudden urge to tell her whom she was really kissing, but I knew I could never tell her about any of this.

A door slammed outside.

"I think Nathan is back."

"Okay, but I want the details of your deflowering."

I laughed. "You're such a dork. But I will later."

I hung up the phone and looked out the front window, surprised to see bags of food and a gallon of milk dangling from Nathan's hands. He saw me, lifted his hands, and grinned. I waved, and rushed outside to help.

A bright ray of sunlight had broken through the thick, gray clouds, streaming down into the forest, like a portal from heaven. I wondered what it would be like to stand inside it. Would I get a glimpse of heaven?

"Hand me some of those bags." I tried to take them.

He shook his head. "I got these. There's three more in the backseat if you want to get those." The muscles in his arms were bulging from the weight of the groceries.

"Nathan, you didn't have to do this," I said, touched by his thoughtfulness.

"I know, but I wanted to." He leaned over and kissed me.

"You're sweet, and I appreciate it." I opened the door for him, then went to get the rest of the groceries. Mr. Kitty came out from behind the house and followed me to the truck. I bent to pet him. "You know," I said, "I consider you my friend, and I know you have things to do, but whatever I decide, I hope you won't be completely out of my life." He rubbed against my knee, purring.

A few minutes later I was in the kitchen, putting the food away. Nathan helped and kept asking me where to put things. It felt natural to be with him like this, and I found myself smiling.

"I ran into Tree at the deli," he said.

My head was in the refrigerator, arranging everything.

"Really? What's he up to?"

"He's working for his dad today and stopped by to pick up some lunch. I really like him. He reminds me a lot of my older brother Thomas."

I threw some ice cubes in a couple glasses, and poured us some tea.

"How does he remind you of Thomas?" I opened the blue plastic container, pleased to see red potato salad with it. "This looks yummy. Thank you."

"My pleasure," he said, and took a bite of his sandwich. A minute later he continued. "Tree is a hard worker like Thomas. He's also, honest and reliable. He's the type of person who would give you the shirt off his back."

I smiled in agreement. "He is a wonderful person. He's like a brother to me. Last week, he did everything he could to make me smile."

"He came into the deli after me and wasn't shy to tell me I made a big mistake letting you go."

My fork fell into the potato salad, and I stared at him in disbelief. There was an amused gleam in his eyes. "He said that to you?" I pictured Tree, bitchin' as he looked, standing over Nathan, laying into him. I mean, Tree could just about intimidate anyone. Not only was he frickin' tall, but he was German, with a sturdy build.

"He did." Nathan grinned and shook his head. "I'll tell you what. If I were human, I wouldn't want him sore at me."

"What did you say?"

"I told him I was a wreck without you, and we're back together."

"Then what happened?" I took a drink of my tea, mentally visualizing the scene.

"He was happy to hear it. He said he likes me, but if I break your heart, he's going to break my face."

Tea sprayed out my mouth, almost tagging Nathan. He jerked his head back and laughed.

"I can't believe he said that to you," I said, wiping my mouth.

"Yes, well, I told him he doesn't have to worry since I plan to be with you forever. He shook my hand. He's a cool guy, and I like he looks out for you."

"He is a cool guy." *The best.*

"I told him you had no food in the house, and I wanted to buy you some, so I asked him what you liked."

"Ah, I wondered how you ended up buying all the foods I liked. You're pretty slick."

A slow, devious smirk appeared on his face, and my heart skipped a couple beats. "When I have to be," he said.

***

A while later, we were in Nathan's truck, heading to his house. I still had no idea where he lived, and was taken aback when we drove along the coastline. The jagged cone-shaped rocks jetted from the misty ocean in the far distance, like a mythical sea serpent's horns. Beyond that, a high double-peaked mountain stood majestic above the hills. Evening was encroaching upon us, and the dark gray sky added to the ghostly scenery.

Nathan turned on a narrow paved road, lined with spruce trees, piquing my curiosity. I'd never really thought about where he lived, but now I began to wonder.

"We're almost there," he said, having fun with me not knowing.

He turned left, onto a dirt path that was between a row of trees at the base of a mountain. It snaked upwards for about half a mile. Rocks crunched beneath the tires. He turned onto another dirt road, that led through the mouth of the forest. The thick woods gradually thinned, eventually opening up into a huge clearing. Lights automatically came on around an A-frame house constructed of wood and stone. The house had a broad outdoor deck that hugged its girth, and the tall tinted windows covered the entire front, reflecting Nathan's truck and the forest back at us. A stone chimney poked out of the roof, like a spire in an old gothic church. For a second I thought we magically entered Mother Goose land.

I was in total awe.

Wide-eyed, I turned to him. "This is where you live?"

"Do you like it?" He kept a straight face, but his lips were twitching, fighting a smile. I could tell he enjoyed my reaction.

I looked at him as if he were insane. "Are you kidding me? I frickin' love it!"

He couldn't contain his smile any longer. "C'mon, I'll show you inside."

He dashed out of the truck, and before I had the seatbelt off, he opened my door. I took his hand, and as we approached his house, I noticed how good we looked together in the glass. It was an arrogant thought, but so what?

When we stepped inside, I breathed in the heady smell of pine, savoring the aroma. Nathan hugged his arms around me from behind, and rested his chin on top of my head while I looked around in wonderment.

The first thing that captured my eyes was a rustic staircase that spiraled up to a wide-open loft, fashioned into a library with books adorning the whole back wall. A couch and a couple matching chairs in a deep, burgundy color, were grouped together in an intimate half circle near the books. Across from them, on the far wall, stood a mahogany desk with a laptop computer and a tall chair tucked inside its nook. The wooden railings bordering the room with its perfect scroll design, looked handmade.

The rest of the house was equally breathtaking with its stone fireplace, soaring ceilings, U-shaped kitchen and rich trappings. It was a place of intellect and comfort, a place I could lose myself in for quite awhile.

After Nathan gave me the tour, he told me to make myself at home while he took a shower. I decided to check out his library and found a lot of old books on philosophy and religion. I had my hand on *PLATO Complete Works* when I spotted a leather bound book sticking out two shelves above it. Reaching up, I pulled it down. The brown cover was blank, but when I opened it to the first page, a hand-drawn picture of two interlaced triangles within a circle with weird symbols between the gaps filled the page.

With interest, I sat on the couch and flipped to the next page. There was another hand-drawn picture, but of an upright star inside a circle.

A pentagram.

I knew what that was from doing research on my premonitions. It symbolized the four elements: earth, air, water, and fire. And the upright star represented our spirit while the circle meant eternity.

On top of the next page–written in perfect black calligraphy–it said: The Seal of Solomon. Beneath it was a carefully drawn picture of two rings. One had the two interlaced triangles on it, and the next had the pentagram. But there were four jewels drawn on each ring next to the symbols. Spooky.

"Paige," Nathan called from downstairs.

"I'm up here." I didn't move and kept the book open.

Within seconds he was standing in front of me, looking incredibly cute, wearing a dark blue sweater that complimented his eyes. He tilted his head to see what book I had.

"What's The Seal of Solomon?" I pointed at the page.

His eyes darted to the book, then to me. An expression of shock and humor crossed his face. He hung his head and shook it.

"What's so funny?"

He lifted his head halfway, the humor now in his partly squinted eyes. "I planned on telling you about this, but not for a long while since you have a lot to think about right now. And I think it's comical you discovered something of vast importance to my kind, the dark spirits, and to a handful of humans on your first visit here."

I scooted to the edge of the couch, excitement surging through me. I loved a good historical mystery. "Okay, you have to tell me now, or I'll have to torture you."

His head snapped up. "Oh, really," he said with a wicked grin. "And how would you do that?"

I said the first thing that came to mind:

"I'll confront the 'old one.'"

His face instantly became hard.

"That's not funny, Paige. He could kill you, so you better not even--"

"Nathan," I said, "it's all right."

"No, it's not," he said harshly. "I don't want you to even entertain the idea of confronting him. He knows you've been marked, and your life is already in danger."

"He didn't see Mr. Kitty," I pointed out. "That night when he picked me up, he was too busy messing with his stereo to notice."

"That doesn't matter. Remember, what that dark spirit told me?"

My voice rose in frustration. "Yeah, but why hasn't he tried killing me then?" My words came out shrill, but I didn't care. This was a stupid argument.

He ran a hand through his hair and sat next to me, his eyes eager for me to get his point.

"For one, those two dark spirits *were* going to kill you. And two, he's interested in you for some reason, so he's hanging back for now."

My heart raced at the thought of those two dark spirits Nathan took care of. It didn't hit me until now they wanted to kill me.

He leaned forward, his arms on his knees. "I hate to say this, but I'm glad you're scared because it tells me I'm getting through to you on how serious this is."

I blinked in surprise. "How do you know I'm scared?"

He pointed to my chest. "I can hear your heart." And when he saw the baffled look on my face, he continued. "Extreme hearing is one of the many gifts of immortality."

"What other gifts are there?" Now I was intrigued. It never occurred to me to ask him if he had any other preternatural abilities other than speed, agility, and strength.

"Extreme eyesight and a sharper mind. You'll find out if you decide to become immortal, which you need to make that decision soon."

I moved closer to him, our legs touching. "What if I asked you to do it tonight?"

"I'd tell you to have Anwar do it. I've never done it before, and I don't trust anybody else."

"But I want you to do it," I said, hearing the whine in my voice.

"I'm sorry, but I will not risk losing you."

I didn't want to talk about this anymore and asked again about the book in my lap.

"The Seal of Solomon," he began, taking the book, running his fingers over the pictures, "was or is a magical signet ring, which gives the person who wears it the power to control the dark spirits. Legend calls them demons, but they're really dark spirits masquerading as demons. There are two pictures of different rings here because we're not sure which one it is. We do know it's made out of part brass and part iron and has four jewels."

"So whoever gets a hold of the ring can control the dark spirits?"

"Yes. That's why we're trying to find it, so we can destroy it. But the good thing is, the ring is ineffective without the incantations, which are lost and can't be found without the ring."

"Do the dark spirits want the ring destroyed too?"

He closed the book and stuck it back on the shelf.

"They say they do, but we don't trust them. Imagine if a dark spirit in human form possessed the ring and found the incantations. He or she would be able to control all the other dark spirits."

"How do you know if this ring even exists?" The hairs on my arms stood up, and I hoped he'd say it didn't exist, even though my gut was saying otherwise.

"To be honest, we don't know, but we have reason to believe through documentation and research that there's a possibility it does." He sat next to me and held my hand. "We can't afford to let something like this go. Even if in the end we find out it's just a legend."

"I understand," I said. "But who is Solomon?"

"Solomon ruled Israel from about 968 to 928 B.C. and there's a legend a temple he erected was actually built by the dark spirits he controlled."

"That's freaky." A chill skittered up my spine when an image of dark spirits building a temple filled my mind. I shivered.

"It is, but we don't know if it's true. So it's up to us to figure out the truth. And if there is a ring, to find and destroy it."

"How many years have you searched for the ring?"

He touched his chest. "Me, personally, off and on since I've been immortal." He stood, and I followed him downstairs. "Anwar has done a lot of research on it but hasn't found anything except for legends about Solomon," he added.

"Does Anwar think what the dark spirits think about me?"

We stepped outside. The bright yellow moon shimmered in the black sky, and the chirping sound of crickets surrounded us. The crisp air had a clean smell to it, and the cool breeze felt good on my face.

"Yes, he does." Nathan opened the door for me, and I threw him a doubtful look. He continued when he got behind the wheel. "And he's going to be here as soon as he can get away from what he's doing now."

I asked him what he was doing and wondered if he really did believe that about me, then why wasn't he here? Nathan glanced at me and said Anwar was in Kenya when he came across a dark spirit and followed him to England. This dark spirit might be leading a terrorist cell which could be planning on blowing up the British Embassy.

I curled an arm around my rolling stomach, remembering 911. I was little when it happened, but could still recall the horror and devastation of that day.

"Why doesn't he cast this spirit out?" My hand fluttered to my forehead when a wave of nausea hit me. I wiped the dampness off. Gross.

"He will, but right now there's a nest of them, so he has to ambush each one individually. Once he takes care of that, he'll be here."

We were on the coastline now. The moonlight glistened off the black water–a glittery gold tail, trailing along the oily surface. In the distance were a couple fishing vessels looking like they were heading to port. I pushed on the side window button, opening it part way, allowing the cool, salty air in. I closed my eyes and inhaled through my nose, hoping to settle my stomach. Nathan touched my arm. I looked at him and could see the concern in his eyes.

"Are you okay?"

"Yeah," I said, not wanting him to worry. "But you know what?"

"What?"

"I think you should go help Anwar." I couldn't believe what just came out of my mouth. Why would I say that when the very thought of him not being in my life made me want to bawl? But I knew why. Protecting the innocent was more important than my happiness.

He shook his head in fierce disagreement. "No way. I'm not leaving you, and Anwar understands." His jaw was adamantly set, telling me there was no room for debate.

I decided to change the subject and asked him where we were going. The tightness in his face broke, and he smiled.

"You said you wanted to take me out to dinner, so we're going to a burger joint."

I frowned. "I can afford to take us to a better place than that. You don't have to settle for fast food." I was a little insulted and would much rather go somewhere else.

"I'm not," he said.

"You swear?" I scrutinized his face, not really believing him.

"Yes. I have a serious craving for those sweet onion rings at Burger World."

"Okay then, Burger World it is."

***

Burger World turned out to be loud and chaotic–toddlers running around, babies crying, kids throwing fries at each other–so I was more than ready to leave when Nathan asked me. He thanked me for dinner and apologized for picking a rowdy place. I said that was fine and suggested we go to Café Nation. On Saturday nights, they had live poetry readings. I thought maybe we could check it out and have a cup of coffee.

When we got there, I was pleased to see my usual corner table available, solitary from the rest of the tables, and steered Nathan to it.

"I'll get us our drinks," he said when I sat down. "What do you want?"

"A vanilla latte would be great."

He smiled. "I'll be right back."

I sat in the chair and relaxed. A blond guy with dreadlocks placed a microphone stand in the center of the room. He tapped it. A sound like nails on a chalkboard erupted. Red-faced, the guy quickly adjusted it until the sound went away. I looked around and noticed the place was half-full with all different types of people, none of them I knew though.

Nathan was standing in line waiting, looking the other way, but as soon as my ears rang, his head snapped in my direction.

He heard it too.

And then I saw Matt and Carrie coming toward me. Carrie cheerfully waved while Matt jerked his chin up. I glanced at Nathan. His eyes were trained on Matt. Matt didn't seem to be aware of him, and then a thought occurred to me. Did the "old one" know about Nathan? I stared at Matt, my heart thudding against my rib cage. I mean, the dude wasn't really Matt, and that just freaked me out.

"Hi, Paige," Carrie said, taking the chair beside me. "Are you here alone?" She glanced around the room and spotted Nathan, answering her own question. She turned to me. "He's so cute." She paused and slowly licked her lips. "And erotic," she said in a low voice.

Despite myself, I giggled and elbowed her arm. "Shhhh, you're not supposed to say anything," I whispered.

She leaned her head next to me. "I didn't. Matt doesn't even know you two are back together," she said out the corner of her mouth.

As Carrie said that, Matt sat across from me, staring at my ears. They were still ringing, but last week I took on the habit of ignoring it, which I was now grateful for.

"Hi, Paige," he said, his gaze on me now. "I'm sorry I couldn't hang out with you last night, but if you want, tomorrow night we could go do something."

"Paige already has plans with me." Nathan's voice was deep with a connotation that said, *back off.* He handed me my latte and sat on the other side of me, his eyes never straying from Matt.

Matt acted like he didn't hear him. "That's fine. We could do it another time," he said only to me. The corners of his mouth twitched into a slow smile, giving me the creeps.

I held his eyes with mine, telling myself not to think about the spirit who was really talking to me, but my heart was still thudding. "Sure. I'll let you know."

Nathan put his arm protectively around my shoulders. "Don't hold your breath," he said, staring Matt down. "I'll be occupying most of her time."

Matt smirked and leaned forward, resting his elbows on the table. "Most of the time is the key word here"–he tapped his fingertip on the table–"and since you can't be her shadow 24-7 that will give us the opportunity to spend some much needed quality time together." He leaned back, challenging Nathan. I knew then the "old one" knew who Nathan was and shuddered at the fact this spirit wanted to be alone with me.

Nathan's body became rigid, his anger rolling off him. I rubbed his thigh, hoping it'd calm him down and clear the air that was thick with testosterone. Thank God for Carrie.

Carrie's eyes darted between Nathan and Matt, her face tight with irritation. "The two of you need to chill out. I know you don't like each other, but that doesn't mean you have to ruin our night"–she pointed to me, and then to herself–"And if you continue with this macho bullshit, Paige and I will leave."

A smile crossed my face. I tucked my lips in and turned to Carrie. Her eyes fell on mine, and they widened. She covered her mouth, hiding her own smile. I loved how blunt Carrie could be.

Matt rose from the table. "I'm going to get us some coffee. Do you want your usual?" he asked Carrie.

She nodded, still hiding her smile.

"Hello, everybody," a hippy looking girl said. "My name is Bree, and my poem is called, 'I'm Just a Used Piece of Gum.'"

Carrie and I shared a look and snickered. Nathan, on the other hand, was glaring at Matt. I squeezed his knee and whispered to forget about it. He glanced at me and sighed, turning his attention on the hippy chick. She was wearing a long, flowing gypsy skirt, and her mousey brown hair was in small tangled braids that hung down her back.

Bree held the microphone, and the room fell silent. A few people walked in, but they paused beside the door to listen. The diamond stud in her nose twinkled in the dull light.

"Jackson was his name. He became my world." She dropped her voice and touched her chest, observing the room. "I was in love with him and delighted when he said I was his girl. We had a lot of fun together and shared the same interest." She paused, then raised her voice. "Or, so I thought. But after I gave myself to him, I later found out he was sleeping with another girl whom I call a *skanky* crotch."

People around the room laughed, including us. Matt gave Carrie her coffee, laughing as well.

Bree raised her voice even higher. "I'm just a used piece of gum. That's all I was to him. A piece of gum that he chewed and spit out." She spat at the floor in disgust, then lowered her voice. "He broke my heart, and I may never be able to trust another guy again." She paused, then raised her voice once more. "The other day my friend Hannah said to me, 'Bree, Jackson doesn't just like girls … He also likes men.' I couldn't believe it, but in her face there was no doubt. I was a used piece a gum that he spit out." Her voice dropped to a high whisper. "Just a few hours ago he came to my house wanting me back. But I told him I'm not his used piece of gum, not anymore. He asked me why won't I take him back." She raised her fist and pulsed it in the air and yelled, "Because you're a man whore!"

Everybody clapped.

She put the mic back. "Thank you." She crossed the room to the guy with the dreadlocks, lounging on the patchwork couch. He raised his coffee cup and smiled at her.

Matt slung his arm over the back of the chair and turned to Nathan. "Are you a man whore?" His voice was antagonizing.

Nathan shook his head in disbelief and blinked. He leaned forward. "What was that?"

"You're being an asshole," Carrie said, glaring at Matt.

People in the room were laughing and visiting with each other while several cappuccino machines were running, muffling the chattering. I watched as a long line formed in front of the counter, and bit my lip when a powerful ache threaded through my stomach. I shivered and broke into a cold sweat. But before I could say anything, Matt continued with his stick poking.

He touched Carrie's arm. "No, I'm not. I'm only looking out for Paige." He looked at me and winked.

Carrie pulled her arm away. "How's that?"

Nathan's eyes were tight on Matt, his bright red ears signaling the anger inside of him.

"Because Nathan is older than we are, and I want to know how many girls he took to bed. I think Paige needs to be aware that if she ends up sleeping with *him*"–he stuck his hand out at Nathan–"how many other people she'll be sleeping with."

Nathan shot out of his chair, knocking it backwards with a loud bang. He went to lunge at Matt, but I managed to grab his hand in time. He looked down at me with blazing eyes. I didn't know what he saw on my face, but they suddenly became disturbed.

He knelt beside me, placing his hand on my forehead. Carrie hopped out of her chair and moved close to my side. Nathan's cold hand felt wonderful against my hot skin. I grimaced when a sharp pain ripped through my stomach.

"What's wrong?" Carrie asked.

I looked up and saw Matt talking to a blonde-haired girl behind the counter.

"You're burning up," Nathan said, moving his cold hands on my cheeks.

"I don't feel good," I groaned. My head fell forward, and my arm flung to my stomach as another piercing pain went through it. I bent over, groaning again, cursing at myself for eating that damned burger.

Carrie touched my forehead. "You feel like a furnace."

"If that's the case, you better go break the fever before it's too late," Matt said behind me, in a flat tone of voice.

"Get away from her," Nathan hissed.

"I was just going to give her some water." Matt reached over Carrie's shoulder and placed the glass on the table.

"I'm taking you home." Nathan stuck his arm beneath my knees, and before I could protest, he was already heading for the door with me in his arms.

A few people stopped us to ask if everything was okay. I hid my face in Nathan's chest while he told them I was sick. Carrie and Matt followed us outside, and she told me if I needed anything to let her know. I gave her a weak nod, and then flinched when another sharp pain ripped through my stomach. Nathan held me tighter, rushing across the street past a group of rubber-necking people.

"How are you doing?" he asked.

"Not so good," I moaned. I couldn't believe how awful I felt.

He opened the truck door and carefully placed me in the seat. I lay in a fetal position, clutching my stomach. In no time, we were pulling out of the parking lot. Nathan rested his hand on the side of my face.

"Does anything else hurt?" He was worried. I could hear it in his voice.

"My head and body." I closed my eyes when he stopped at a red light. "But I don't feel nauseous." The pain in my stomach came in violent waves, causing me to curl into myself.

"You're running a high fever, and that concerns me."

I didn't say anything, and we remained quiet the rest of the way home. All I wanted to do was crawl into bed, pull the covers over me, and try to sleep it off. But unfortunately that wasn't what happened.

Chapter Eight
Sickness

Nathan carried me to my bedroom, even though I told him I could walk.

Yeah, I felt like crap, and my whole body throbbed, not to mention a mad butcher was having fun with my stomach, but I wasn't some damned invalid who couldn't take care of herself. I'd been independent most of my life, and though I appreciated his attentiveness, I wasn't as delicate as he thought. All I wanted to do was pop a few Tylenols and sleep, but he wouldn't hear of it.

When we entered my room, he turned the light on, then carefully placed me on the bed. But when I moved to get up–my arms still around my stomach–he stopped me and asked where I was going.

"I'm going to the bathroom. I have to pee and change my clothes," I said.

"Tell me where your clothes are, and I'll take you to the bathroom."

Now he was going too far.

"I can do this myself."

He backed off when he heard the growl in my voice and asked me if I had any vinegar in the house. I told him underneath the kitchen sink and shuffled to my dresser like an old lady bent in half.

"Do me a favor and grab a pair of old socks."

"What for?" I looked up, and he was gone. "Whatever," I grumbled, getting a pair of socks, pajama bottoms, and a T-shirt from my dresser drawer.

A few minutes later while attempting to brush my teeth, I looked in the mirror and became horrified at the corpse like image looking back at me. My green eyes were dull, almost lifeless, and my already pale skin appeared paler than usual. I looked like death girl. I groaned and took two capsules of Tylenol. Now I understood Nathan's behavior, and all my irritations vanished. If I were in his position, I'd be acting the same way.

When I stepped into my room, I got a strong whiff of vinegar and wrinkled my nose. Nathan was sitting on the edge of the bed with his sleeves rolled up and a mixing bowl beside him on the night stand. He helped me into bed, pulled my socks off, then placed his hand on my forehead, and frowned. He turned back to the bowl, submerging the socks in the water.

"What are you doing?" I hope he didn't expect me to wear those wet, smelly socks.

"I filled this bowl with half vinegar and half water," he answered, sloshing the socks around. "I'm going to put these on your feet and tie a plastic bag over them."

"I don't want to wear those socks," I said as I watched him wring them out. The sound of water pouring back into the bowl seemed to bounce off the walls. He turned, facing me. I scooted to the other side of the bed, giving him a wary look.

"Trust me, Paige," he said with a crooked smile. "My mother used to do this when my brothers and I were struck with fever, and it worked every time."

I eyed him suspiciously and then relented when I realized his intentions were genuine and he wasn't messing with me. I scooted back to him. He cupped my foot in his hand and slipped the sock on. I scrunched up my face.

"I know," he said, sounding apologetic. "I used to hate it too."

After he tied the plastic freezer bags around my ankles, he took his shoes off and climbed in bed with me, taking me into his arms. I rested my face against his chest, breathing him in, his natural smell becoming my personal aroma therapy. For a long while we didn't speak, but then he broke the silence.

"Can I ask you something?"

"Sure."

"Why aren't there any pictures of your father in this house?"

I wasn't expecting him to ask that, but I quickly recovered. "My mom says it's too painful for her." My contempt dripped off of each word. "And besides, there's nothing but a few pictures left of him. She hid them in the attic without telling me."

"That's odd," he said. "You would think she'd want you to know everything about him."

"You would *think,* but there's very little she's told me about him." I paused. "At least I have a couple pictures of him I found. She doesn't know I have them." A part of me reveled in defying her, and in the fact I found something she didn't want me to find. I mean, seriously, she was in the wrong, and I didn't feel one bit bad about it.

"Do you think there's more stuff of his she's hiding?" He paused. "And what about his family?" he wondered aloud. "Don't you have contact with them?"

"My father grew up in foster homes in Phoenix. He met my mom at ASU. That's all I know, and I've already searched this house and found nothing else."

"Have you tried talking to your mom's family about him?"

"My mom is an only child. Her mother died when she was a teenager, which devastated her and her father. My grandfather became an alcoholic and was unbearable to be around. Mom left as soon as she could and never turned back. He never even met my father … or me for that matter. And to be honest, we don't even know if he's still alive. He said some horrible things to her that still makes her cry, and I've learned not to bring him up in conversation."

Inside myself were empty holes. Whenever I saw kids with their grandparents or thought of what could've been, those holes ached, like they hurt now as I spoke to Nathan about my grandfather.

"I'm sorry," he said. "I know this is difficult for you to talk about. I wouldn't have brought it up if there wasn't a reason behind it."

"What's your reason?" Pain clawed through my stomach, but I bit down on my tongue, not wanting to distract him from what he was about to say.

"Before I tell you. How did your father die?"

"We lived in Phoenix. He was found dead in an abandoned warehouse. Apparently he fell off of a scaffold and broke his neck."

"What did your father do for a living?"

"He was a contractor."

"Were there any witnesses?"

"No, not to my knowledge. Some kids found him the next morning. Their dog led them to him."

Nathan didn't respond. I propped myself on the pillow, still feeling like crap, but not caring. I could tell he was debating something, making me more curious by the second. "What is it?"

His face turned somber. "I'm sorry. I should have waited to talk to you about this, but I sense an urgency." He took a deep breath. "I think your father was murdered."

Instantly, everything in the room warped around me, and a zinging noise filled my head. For years I'd secretly pondered this very issue, but never came up with a motive. I even planned on going to Phoenix after graduation to check it out. This of course was before I met Nathan.

But nobody knew about it. I would've told Carrie, but if he was murdered, I didn't want her involved. So I kept it to myself. Now, Nathan brought this very idea to the surface, shocking me into a mixed state of relief and anxiety.

"Wh-why would you think that?" I stammered.

He shrugged. "It's a gut feeling, and I think we should check into it. Maybe search this house again."

Without a word, I settled back into his arms, mentally thanking the universe for bringing him to me. Because all my life I'd been alone, but now I had Nathan, my personal guide, carrying a torch, and leading the way through the dark caverns of my untouched world.

Feeling cold all of a sudden, I pulled the covers tighter around me. Nathan hugged me closer and placed his hand on my forehead. I could tell the fever was coming back from the heat creeping up my neck, but I didn't want him to move.

"You're starting to feel warm again. Maybe I should get up and--"

I placed my finger over his lips. "Not now. Stay." I draped my leg over him to emphasize what I wanted.

He kissed my finger, and reached to turn the light off, upsetting my comfortable position. But before I could complain, he arranged me back as before. I sighed in contentment and closed my eyes.

***

They're chasing me through the forest, dark ghostly figures with elongated mouths opened wide, their screeching sounds echoing off the trees. The moon is full and bright, casting its light upon the fog I'm stumbling through. They're catching up to me now, wailing my name and chanting harsh words in Latin. I glance over my shoulder and one is upon me, knocking me into a pile of leaves and broken branches. The rest of them catch up and circle like vultures. Their piercing laughter shoots through the top of the trees, shaking them like a violent windstorm. The one that knocked me down moves closer and repeats something in Latin. His dark energy is closing in on me. I begin to suffocate.

"Paige! Paige! Baby, wake up!"

Did he just call me baby? In the far recesses of my mind that question presented itself, waking me from that horrid dream. I bolted up into his arms, gasping for air, feeling the cold, wet socks on my feet again.

"It's okay. I got you." Nathan's hand moved in circles on my back. "Take slow, deep breaths. You need to calm your heart." He was struggling to keep his voice steady, but I could hear the fear he felt because it left a speck of its tarnish on each word he spoke.

Finally, I was able to catch my breath, but I continued to shake as those words the dark spirit had repeated to me played in my head like a broken record. I decided to try to say them out loud:

"Vos ero pessum ire."

Nathan's hand stopped in the middle of my back, his body stiffening.

"What did you say?"

I repeated it.

"Where did you hear that?" He sounded disturbed, which made my stomach clench.

The green numbers on my alarm clock, was the only light in the dark room. I didn't like it, but his arms remained securely around me, which made me feel safe. I took a deep breath and told him my dream.

"What was he saying to me?" I wanted to know, regardless of how bad it might be.

His voice sounded rough. "It means you will be destroyed."

"Oh." My mind went blank, numb even, hindering my thoughts for a moment.

"I think we need to keep a low profile until Anwar gets here," he said.

"Okay, but remember Alchemy is playing at The Lion's Den on Friday, and I still have to go to school." I hoped he wasn't suggesting for me to hide in this house because I wouldn't.

"You should be fine at school, as long as you're not alone, but I don't know about seeing Alchemy." He shuddered.

I pressed my face against his shoulder, tightening my arms around him. He felt cold and was making swallowing noises as if he were guzzling water.

"What's wrong?"

Cupping my face in his hands, he rested his forehead on mine. "You scared the shit out of me," he whispered. "I thought you were on the verge of going into a cardiac arrest." He sucked in some air, cleared his throat, and pulled back. "You're still warm. How do you feel?"

I shrugged. "The same, but my stomach doesn't ache like it did." I wiggled my toes inside the damp socks. "When did you wet these socks again?"

"About an hour after you fell asleep." We settled back under the covers, and he took me into his arms. "I was being careful not to wake you."

I snuggled against his chest. "I didn't feel anything at all, so I must have been in a deep sleep."

"You were, but then you started moaning and thrashing about, and your breathing became extremely erratic. I tried to calm you, but couldn't …" He trailed off, inhaling and exhaling before continuing. "Jesus Christ, Paige, you scared me. If I were to lose you …" He fell silent.

I didn't like seeing him like this and knew what I needed to say to make him feel better, but I also knew I would have to mean it. But was I willing to say good-bye to my two best friends and my mother? And was I willing to live an immortal life in an unstable world full of hate and pain?

But then I thought about death. If I were to stay mortal and die, I'd lose Nathan. And if I saw what the dark spirits were doing in their quest to claim earth as their own, knowing I could have helped prevented it, I'd never forgive myself. But on the other hand, if I were to become immortal, Nathan and I could be together for eternity and team up against the dark spirits. I also could live through all the changes in this world, chronicle it, and have the opportunity to travel the world. I'd be free from the restrictions placed on humans. And with Carrie, Tree, and Mom, I might be able to pull off seeing them for at least ten more years. I looked young for my age anyway.

I knew without a doubt what to do. It had been there all along, sitting quietly in the back of my brain, waiting for me to come to terms with it. Most mortals wouldn't have thought twice about it. But this was a huge decision, one that almost didn't seem real. I think that was why it hadn't dominated my thoughts because of me having a hard time grasping the reality of it. But within my core being, I knew what I had to do.

"I have something to tell you," I said.

He looked at me.

"I want to be immortal."

"Are you sure?"

"I want to be with you for eternity, and if I were to die, heaven wouldn't be heaven without you."

He kissed me. Despite feeling sick, I wanted desperately to pull him on top of me, to feel his weight, but my body felt too weak to attempt it, and then I thought about what Matt said earlier.

"You don't know how happy this makes me to hear you say that," he told me. "I'll call Anwar tomorrow to tell him your decision."

"I still want you to do it." I pouted. "I know you're worried you'll screw up, but I trust you." I know this was a sick thought, but I wanted Nathan's blood inside my body.

He shook his head. "That is one-hundred percent out of the question. You may trust me, but I don't trust myself. And like I said earlier, I've never done it before and if I were to lose you." He paused and shook his head again. "It's too horrible to even think about."

"We'll have Anwar do it then," I said, "but I want you there to hold my hand." The whole process of becoming immortal terrified me. I mean, seriously, being cut open and bled out would scare the crap out of anybody.

He lifted my hand and kissed it. "Of course I will."

"Can I ask you a question?" I wanted to change the subject before my mind started visualizing the whole bloody act.

"Absolutely," he said, cheerfully.

"How many girls have you slept with?"

"I was wondering how long it would take you to bring that up." There was a hint of amusement in his tone I didn't like, and a sickening jealous feeling came over me when he became silent. I wanted to cry, even though I knew it was silly for me to feel that way. But the question still played out in my mind:

Did he sleep with so many girls that he must stop to count them all in his head?

He encircled his arm around me. "I hope you're not presuming I'm counting my conquests in my head," he said, playfully.

"Get out of my head. This is serious. I want to know," I snapped.

"You were actually thinking that?" He sounded both surprised and hurt.

"Nathan. Please answer the *frickin'* question." Why won't he answer the damned question? This wasn't a joke to me.

He sighed. "This may sound cheesy to you, but it's the truth. I've had many women, but none of them meant anything to me." He propped himself up on his elbow, resting his cheek on his palm, and gently pushed the hair away from my face. He looked so serious, yet his eyes were full of passion. His hand stopped at the corner of my jaw, his thumb making lazy circles around my cheek, sending my pulse racing. "Last night, was the first night I've ever made love to anybody. It was the most extraordinary, ethereal experience I've ever had."

That made me feel a lot better, and then I thought about what I told Carrie and snickered, ruining this romantic moment.

"What's so funny?"

"I thought last night was a bit erotic myself."

He flopped over on his back, bouncing the bed. "It was, but let's not talk or think about that right now."

"I agree, but I don't want to go to sleep. How about we go downstairs and watch a movie. Unless, you're tired." Truthfully, I was too scared to go to sleep.

He sat up. "I'm fine." He touched my forehead. "Your fever seems to be under control."

I pushed the covers off, but before I could sit up, he already had me in his arms, heading downstairs.

Chapter Nine
Tree's Visit

I remained sick for the next five days. The fever would come and go, but at one point it raged so high Nathan was beside himself with worry. The only option he had–besides taking me to the hospital–was the one I fought against as hard as going to the hospital. The one that sucked ass.

But he wouldn't give into my pleas, not this time. Instead, he turned into a madman on a mission. So when he came back from the store with several large bags of ice and dumped them into the tub, I did the most childish thing I could ever have done in his presence. I locked myself in my room and prayed he'd forget about this whole thing. I didn't like the sock thing much, but I'd take that over being submerged into a tub full of ice water.

I sat in the corner of my room with a blanket draped over my head. Evening was approaching and the trees outside my window swayed, casting shadows across my lavender walls. I could hear rain splatter against the windows as I listened hard for Nathan's footsteps.

When I heard them coming toward my room, I pulled the blanket tighter around me, feeling like I was five again. The sound of the doorknob turning made me gasp. I grasped my knees, resting my chin on them.

"Open the door, Paige," Nathan said. "This isn't funny. We need to break your fever." He turned the knob again, harder this time.

I didn't answer and thought maybe if I stayed quiet he'd give up and let me be.

"I'm going to give you one more opportunity to open this door. If you don't, I'm coming in." His voice had a hard edge to it, slicing through my hope he'd leave me alone.

I scanned the room for a place to hide. The bed sat too low to the floor, so I crawled as fast as I could to the closet, dragging the blanket with me. Quietly, I closed the white shutter doors. I settled myself in the corner. There were tall bags of clothes I've been meaning to take to the Good Will. I stacked them in front of me, pulling the blanket back over me. I knew this was an immature thing to do, but at that moment I didn't care.

The knob wiggled and clicked.

"I guess I'm coming in on my own." Still not amused.

He turned the knob again and bore his weight against the door. A splintering sound cracked through the room. The door flung open, hitting the wall with a loud bang. I peeked out of the blanket. His shadow moved between the closet door's wooden slats. Holding my breath, I crouched under the blanket again.

"You can't hide from me." His voice sang out next to the closet. "Because you've forgotten one thing." He opened the door. "I can hear your heart, and right now it's racing."

He tossed the bags out of the way, like they were made of Styrofoam. I flipped the blanket off as he was reaching for me. Our eyes locked. With a slight smile, he shook his head, but behind that smile stood a stubbornness I'd never seen in him before.

"Please don't," I begged, pushing his hands away, bracing my bare feet against his stomach. "I hate to be cold."

"I'm doing this for your own good," he replied. "Believe me, if it weren't necessary, I wouldn't do it."

In one quick move, he snatched my hands and dragged me out, then slung me over his shoulder. I continued begging him and even tried bargaining with him, but he ignored me. When we entered the bathroom, he stopped in front of the tub.

"I'm doing this because I love you, and I hope you don't hate me."

"Please, Nathan!" I screamed.

But it was too late. He placed me in the icy tub and held the bottom half of my body down, preventing me from jumping out. I inhaled sharply and howled as soon as the ice water touched my skin, piercing every nerve ending from my shoulders down to my toes, like sharp razor blades. I struggled to get out, but it was pointless. He was too strong, and my pajamas clung heavily against my skin. My howls turned into whimpers and half cries. When I glanced at him, he had a tortured look on his face.

Within minutes, my whole body became numb, and my teeth were clacking together. I thought if I stayed in here much longer, parts of my body would fall off. But thankfully, Nathan stood and helped me out of the tub. He handed me a couple towels and left me alone.

After that horrible incident, my fever became controllable and finally went away. I forgave Nathan, and he remained by my side, taking care of me. When I wasn't sleeping, we watched movies, or talked about things that were normal–anything to forget about what lay ahead of us.

One night, when we were both bored of watching movies, he read *Macbeth* to me. With my head in his lap I listened to his captivating voice read in a convincing Scottish accent all the way through, saying each line as if he were performing the play. And when he got to the witches' part, he changed his voice to sound like scratchy, withered old hags, making me burst out in laughter.

Afterwards, while we were talking, we heard a car door slam outside. Nathan peered out the window and told me Tree was here.

"Hi, Tree," Nathan said, opening the door.

Tree returned the greeting and came in holding a white paper sack–his Mohawk brushed the top of the door frame. When he saw me sitting on the couch, he smiled and raised the sack.

"I heard you were sick, so I brought you some blueberry cheesecake ice cream."

My face lit up. "You're so sweet. Thank you."

"I'll put it in the freezer for later." Nathan took the sack and left the room.

"I ran into Carrie at the convenience store," Tree said, sitting in the recliner. "She told me what happened the other night at Café Nation and you've been sick."

Nathan sat next to me, his arm naturally draping over my shoulder.

I frowned. "Yeah, Matt was being an ass."

Tree leaned forward and smirked. "He was being his usual self then?"

Nathan laughed and nodded. "The guy is a piece of work."

"More like a piece of shit, if you ask me." Tree sat back, resting his ankle on his knee. His eyebrows knitted. "I just wish Carrie could see it."

"Well, Carrie wasn't too happy with him. So maybe she'll change her mind about him," I said, even though I knew she was still dating him.

Doubt clouded his face. "I don't know. She told me she was mad at him until he promised he'd call you and apologize for his behavior."

Oh crap! I still hadn't told Nathan that Matt called a couple days ago when he went home to get his clothes. I'd been meaning to, but kept putting it off. He was going to be pissed.

I looked down and fumbled with my fingers in my lap.

"He hasn't called here," Nathan replied.

I glanced up and caught Tree frowning at me. He knew me too well, but I knew him just as well, and I knew he was going to throw me under the bus. And I knew why. He didn't trust Matt and out of respect for Nathan. I shifted in my seat, giving him a look to keep quiet, but he slowly shook his head.

"He did call. Paige just didn't tell you," he said.

Nathan removed his arm from my shoulders and turned to me. "Is that true?"

I glared at Tree, and he flipped his palms up in innocence. He would pay for this, I vowed to myself.

"Um, well," I said, running my fingers through my hair. "Yeah, he did."

"When?"

"When you went to get your clothes." I peeked at him. His face was like stone, his eyes filled with disapproval.

"That was three days ago. When were you planning on telling me this?"

"Well, that day, but everything became normal," I began, trying to tell him in a way that he understood, hoping Tree wouldn't catch on. "And then the subject of what's ahead never came up, and I didn't want to ruin the nice time we were having." I could feel Tree staring at me, but I ignored him, refusing to stumble under his scrutiny.

"Regardless, you should have told me," Nathan said, annoyed.

"I'm sorry." I touched his face, feeling it soften beneath my hand.

"Okay," he said. "But next time I want to know right away." His eyes were steady on mine with a severity that told me he would let this one pass, but if it happened again, he would seriously be pissed.

"All right. I promise." I dropped my hand back into my lap, relieved I was off the hook and this conversation had ended.

"What did he say?"

Damn it. Why won't he let this go? I glanced at Tree and made a face at him when I saw the amusement in his eyes. I didn't like him siding with Nathan, and how he enjoyed watching me squirm.

I took a deep breath and faced Nathan.

"He said he was sorry, and he misses me. He also doesn't like you monopolizing all of my time. He admitted he's jealous and that's why he acted the way he did the other night. He told me besides Carrie, I was one of his best friends, and he would like to hangout with me." I said this all in a rush, anxious to get it out and over with.

"He doesn't care about Carrie," Tree huffed, pounding the arm of the recliner with his fist.

Nathan became tense again. "What did you tell him?"

"I told him I'd let him know," I said.

Nathan smashed his lips together and scowled at the floor.

Tree sat up and grinned at me. "I talked to Brayden last night. He told me to tell you hi." He waggled his eyebrows.

Aw, crap.

Nathan's attention instantly snapped on Tree. "Who's Brayden?"

"He's one of our best friends, but moved to California a couple years ago," I told him.

Tree shot me a wicked look. I flushed, knowing what he was going to say.

"Brayden and Paige used to make out *a lot*. In fact, every time I talk to him, he asks me about her."

That took me by surprise, but it didn't matter. I was with Nathan and completely in love with him. Nobody could ever compare to him, not even Brayden.

"Is that so?" Nathan said, and to my secret pleasure, I saw jealousy cross his face. "Well, you can tell him she's taken now." His arm went around my shoulders.

"I already did," Tree answered. "And he's pretty bummed about it. I think he's still in love with her."

Just then, "Born to Be Wild" blasted from the recliner. Tree pulled his cell phone out of his coat pocket and rose. It was his dad calling. He programmed that song into his phone so when his dad called, he knew who it was. He shoved it back into his pocket.

"Aren't you going to answer it?" I asked, following him to the door.

"No. I'll see him in a few minutes."

"Thanks again for the ice cream and stopping by." I hugged his waist.

"I have to make sure my little fairy friend is okay," he said, hugging me back.

"Nice to see you again," Nathan said.

Tree was halfway out the door when he stopped. "Are you still going to see Alchemy play this Friday?"

I looked at Nathan, hoping he'd say yes.

"Probably. Why?"

"Because I'm going, and if Matt gives either one of you any shit, I have your back."

Nathan smiled. "I appreciate it. And the same goes for you."

Tree returned his smile. "See ya there."

***

By Friday I felt back to normal. Carrie called me a few times during the week, complaining about spending most of her spring break working at her mom's store. I asked her if she'd been hanging out with Matt, and she said only once since the night at Café Nation. They went to the movies and made out in his jeep. I asked her about Friday night, if she and Matt were still planning on going to see Alchemy play. She told me they were. I told her we were too and Tree would be there as well. I also informed her Tree and Nathan was becoming good friends, which silenced her for a minute because we used to talk about how cool it would be to have boyfriends that were best friends like us. And then she had to go.

My mom also called. I told her I'd been sick for days, but I felt fine now. She asked me about Nathan, and I told her we were still dating and how sweet he was. She was looking forward to meeting him, which would be around Easter time. I wasn't holding my breath on that one though.

Nathan got a hold of Anwar and found out he was in the thick of things and wouldn't be here anytime soon. Nathan reminded me about us keeping a low profile until he got here. I gave him a complacent nod, but truthfully, I wasn't planning on being holed up in this house until then. So I was happy when he told Tree we would be going to see Alchemy play.

After my nap and a cup of coffee, I went behind Nathan–he was sitting at the kitchen table, catching up on world events on his laptop–and slipped my arms around him. I looked over his shoulder at the computer screen. An article on a sleeper terror cell in the United Kingdom caught my attention. Apparently, a radical planted a car bomb in London, but it failed to go off.

I wondered out loud if this was the same person Anwar was tracking.

"I don't know," Nathan said, rubbing my forearm. "But I think these failed car bomb attacks are coordinated for a purpose."

I rested my chin on his shoulder, staring at the picture on the screen of parked cars and people walking in downtown London. "Why do you think that?" I asked.

"Because they like to toy with people's emotions by instilling fear into them. It's a game to them to watch humans give up their freedoms for a sense of security. It makes them feel omnipotent."

"I can see that, but what about the bombs that do go off and kill people?"

"It's the same thing. They're just playing chess with these failed attacks."

"Does a dark spirit reside in all terrorists?"

"No, but the ones who have a soul have the propensity to turn dark when they die. But then again, it's not for me to judge. I'm just going by my own experiences on the matter. But the leaders I've come across had a dark spirit residing in them."

"The one Anwar is tracking down. He's the leader, right?"

"He thinks so."

I kissed his cheek. "Do you wish you were there helping him?"

He moved his head back and looked at me. "I'm not leaving you." His voice was firm and resolute. For some reason his reaction made that burning desire in my belly swell.

I lowered my lips to his, and he pulled me onto his lap, giving me slow, lingering kisses at first, flipping my stomach like he always did. But when his fingers knotted inside my hair, his kisses became more intense and passionate. My lips and tongue followed, eager for more. With thick, uneven breaths, I tugged on his shirt. He cradled me in his arms and carried me to my room.

And then the world around us melted away into an Elysium, in the fading light of my room, in a tangle of arms and legs. I shook beneath him, feeling a feverish energy charging the air. It encapsulated us in a thick cloud of unspoken desires and pleasures. I knew he felt it too, by the way he touched me and moved. By the way his quicken breaths kept in time with mine. And by the way he looked at me and said he loved me with pure honesty. I held his face in front of mine and told him I loved him too, and I was his for as long as he wanted me.

He lowered his face, his lips next to my ear, and whispered, "Then it will be for eternity."

Chapter Ten
The Lion's Den

After I took a shower and got dressed, I checked myself out in the mirror, bending to make sure my red tartan miniskirt wasn't too short. It wasn't. I pulled on my tights, and stepped into my black platform Mary Janes. My fishnet shirt clung against the black lace beneath it, enhancing my figure. As for my hair, I decided to put the sides halfway up in a silver barrette with a Celtic knot design. I frowned at my pale face, but after I applied some makeup, I became satisfied with the results. Add a little glitter, and I was ready to go.

Nathan was in the bathroom getting ready, and as I left my room, I heard a thumping noise coming from outside. I stopped in the doorway to listen. The window in my room began to vibrate. Without thinking, I ran downstairs, flung the front door open, and stepped out into the night.

The white waning moon illuminated the clouds inside its huge ring of light, keeping the darkness outside its circular barrier. I hugged myself against the chill in the air, watching the tail lights of Matt's jeep disappear down the street. A silhouette of a cat sat at the edge of the lawn, staring after it. I wondered what Matt wanted, while questioning my own motives for rushing outside.

Why would I do that? Was it out of curiosity? Or, because I still found it hard to believe the truth about him, and I came out here like I would before any of this stuff happened, to greet a friend?

Something touched my shoulder, making me jump.

"Sorry. I didn't mean to startle you," Nathan said. He placed his arm around my waist. "What are you doing out here?"

Mr. Kitty rubbed against my leg. I bent to pet him, thinking he was my little four-legged protector. I wondered why the dark spirits avoided the area he was in. I rose and asked Nathan.

He jerked his head, looking about. "Why? Did you see one?" He moved in front of me, his body stiff and protective.

I placed my hand in his and pulled him to the house. The front door was open, and the light from the living room spilled out onto the porch. Mr. Kitty followed us to the door and laid beside it. He crossed his black paws in front of him and closed his eyes.

"Are you going to answer my question?" Nathan asked when I closed the door.

I turned and couldn't help but admire how smoking hot he looked. He had on a long black jacket with a copper nail head o-ring closure and three copper buttons going up each tight cuff and black jeans tucked into laced-up boots. And when I looked up, I was pleased he kept his hair the same with its blond tips sticking up on top. But I noticed an impatience growing in his eyes, and realized I hadn't answered his question.

"Oh, sorry," I said, exhaling the air out of my lungs. "Matt just drove by."

He crossed his arms over his chest.

Uh-oh. That didn't look good. I mean, the way he narrowed his eyes at me, with his lips now in a tight line, told me he wasn't a happy camper. I searched for a good excuse but couldn't come up with one. Avoiding his accusing stare, I busied myself by going into the kitchen to get my keys and purse. He followed me without saying a word, but when I headed to the front door, he grabbed my arm and turned me around. I looked up and saw something on his face I'd never seen since we'd been together.

Anger.

For the first time, he was angry at me. I mean, really pissed. Beyond that rage, I could see hurt. A sharp pricking sensation developed at the corner of my eyes. When he spoke, I dropped them, not wanting him to see my face or think of me as one of those girls who cried to get out of trouble with her boyfriend.

"Did you know it was Matt before you went outside?" His tone was flat, lifeless.

I nodded at the floor.

"Why did you go outside without me?"

I swallowed hard and tried to keep my voice steady. "I wasn't thinking. When I heard the bass in his jeep playing, I went outside like I always do. It was a natural response I think."

"Don't you care about me?" Now the hurt stepped forward in his voice.

I looked at him, blinking back the tears. "More than anything," I whispered. "Why would you ask me that?"

His hand covered his face. "I can not bear to see such woes of the heart in the eyes of my beloved," he mumbled to himself, speaking in a way I've never heard him speak before.

"What?"

He looked at me. When he spoke, his voice took on a pleading tone. "Don't you understand? By risking your life, you're risking destroying us." He gently brushed my tears away and leveled his face with mine. "If something were to happen to you, my heart and soul would be decimated."

"I feel the same way." I sniffed. "I don't ever want to live without you." And I didn't. If he weren't in my life, I'd be totally crushed.

"Then promise me you won't be careless with your life." His gaze was steady on mine, searching for the answer before it came into existence upon my lips. And when he saw it, the tension in his face lifted.

"I promise."

He kissed me. "I love you."

"I love you too."

The corner of his mouth tilted. "Now we should go have some fun, but first I have to tell you something."

My heart slipped. Was he still upset with me? He didn't appear to be. The tension that surrounded him a few minutes ago was gone, and he seemed relaxed. But when he took a couple steps back, slowly drinking in my entire body, my worries left me. I noticed the admiring look on his face changed into a hungry desire. I stopped breathing.

"I have to say you look incredible tonight."

When his eyes fell upon mine, they were bright with excitement. I bit my lip, not knowing how to respond to a comment that had never been made to me, so I dispelled it by reflecting his words at him. A playful argument followed on who looked hotter, until I finally changed the subject.

"Why does a dark spirit avoid entering the area Mr. Kitty is in?" I asked, slipping my arms into my black leather jacket.

"Because his energy is pure and has never been tainted," Nathan said, opening the front door. "What dwells inside the cat is the light of creation, or God if you want to put it into religious terms. The dark spirits don't want to go near such a light in fear they may become trapped inside it." He followed me outside. "Does that make sense to you?"

Mr. Kitty was still sleeping beside the door with his nose nuzzled against his stomach.

"It does. And you know what?"

"What?"

"I love him." I smiled.

He opened the passenger door. "You do?" He sounded amused.

I nodded, still smiling as I hopped in the truck.

"Do you know his name?" I asked when he got behind the wheel.

"No, but Anwar might," he said.

"How old is Anwar?"

He looked at me and grinned. "Over six-hundred."

My mouth dropped. "Holy crap!" That just totally blew me away.

He laughed. "I've learned a lot from him, and since he's so old he can cast the spirit out of Matt."

"I can't wait to meet him." A bubble of excitement rose inside me as I thought about all the things he had seen throughout history and wondered what he could tell me about it.

We were quiet for the rest of the way to The Lion's Den, entangled in our own wandering thoughts. I stared out the window, watching the trees pass along the shoulder of the road. A couple of does stepped out of the woods, but we passed them before they reached the street. Then the forest gave away to concrete and eventually buildings. We were almost there. I rested my head against the seat, hoping there would be no trouble tonight.

***

When we entered through the foggy stone archway to The Lion's Den, we were confronted by a large guy with purple and black bed-head hair. He stood beside the huge claw mark ingrained in the round wooden door, taking people's tickets. He wore a silver hoop in the side of his nose and brow. Thick black liner rimmed his hazel eyes. Nathan handed him our tickets. I noticed the guy was checking me out. Blushing, I smiled at him.

He returned my smile and waved us on. "Enjoy yourselves. They just made their introductions and should be starting soon."

We thanked him and went inside where I was completely amazed at the club's dark, gothic transformation. It totally rocked.

"Check that out." I pointed to the elevated pipe organ on the back of the stage, looming above the band members like a devil over his minions.

"Wicked," Nathan said as we went to get our lockers.

The round stage was lined with gray broken stones and enclosed in a thick, metal fence. Inside looked like a graveyard with tombstones and fog blanketing the entire floor. There were spider webs hanging off the two keyboards that stood at each end of the stage. And the two large amps were encased in a mausoleum type structure. The four band members were all guys, each one looked like he belonged to an underground world of vampires, zombies, and mad hatters.

I glanced around for Carrie and Tree, but didn't see them in the sea of faces. I did see quite a few of my classmates, including a couple jocks, which astonished me because most of them called this place The *Loser's* Den, preferring country to this type of music.

As we were putting our stuff in the locker, my ears rang in that high-pitched sound I was now accustomed to. Nathan and I turned our heads to the entrance and saw Carrie and Matt handing over their tickets. Matt said something to Carrie, making her laugh. Nathan stepped in front of me, turning his back on them.

"Remember to keep your wits about you," he told me. "I don't know why he stopped by your house, but I don't like it."

"I think he likes to antagonize you since he knows who you are," I commented.

He frowned. "I think he does, but I don't care. He can't get to you through me, and he knows it. I'm sure it vexes him, so you're probably right."

I noticed Tree waving at us, indicating a spot next to him on the dance floor. At the same time the mad hatter looking guy grasped the microphone.

"Is everybody ready to have their auditory nerves destroyed?" he called in a deep, haunting voice. His ice-blue eyes were wide with a promise to release us from our shells.

"Yeah!" The crowd screamed, bobbing their heads, throwing their arms in the air.

Nathan and I wove our way through them to an open space next to Tree. I looked for Carrie and spotted her across the dance floor, glaring at Kylee, an Asian girl in our class, standing next to Tree. Matt had his attention on the zombie behind the keyboard, so he didn't see me watching him.

"Are you ready to be polluted by darkness, and then purified through magic?"

Another round of screaming exploded.

"We are Alchemy. A paradox in our own right." He took the microphone off the stand and stomped around the front of the stage, working the crowd. "We will submerge you into darkness, only to bring you up shiny and new through the magical waves of sound."

For some reason the talk about being submerged into darkness frightened me. I clutched Nathan's hand. He was staring at Matt, but when he felt my fingers intertwine with his, he kissed them.

The lights darkened. A big puff of white smoke blew from behind the organ, making me jump. Red and orange lights flashed around us, pulsing with the beat of the electric keyboards. I took a couple breaths to calm myself.

"This song is called 'Resurrection!'" The mad hatter hollered.

Everybody started dancing when he broke into song. Nathan placed my hand on his shoulder. He had a playful expression on his face, daring me to make the next move. I slid my hand down his chest, swaying my hips to the floor while his eyes held mine with an intimacy only we shared.

When the electric drums began to beat faster, and the techno sounds of the keyboard echoed around us, I threw my hands above my head, moving my body to the beat of the music.

Taking my hand, Nathan twirled me around, pressing my back against him. With his arms around my waist, we gyrated to the thumping beat of the electric drums. He twirled me, facing him, and we continued to swing in time with the music.

We danced like that through their first four sets of songs. When the singer announced they'd be back in twenty minutes with another set, we followed Tree and Kylee to the juice bar.

"They totally rock!" Tree said, wiping the sweat off his forehead as we stepped behind a huge line of people who were animatedly talking in excited voices.

"At first I couldn't understand why they called themselves Alchemy, but now it makes perfect sense," Kylee said. "They turn something dark into something magical, like turning lead to gold. That's why their music starts out dark, then changes into beautiful melodies."

An image of a dark, ghostly figure standing in a doorway between good and evil entered my mind. Behind him was darkness, but laid before him was a bright, beautiful world full of peace and love. All he had to do was to step over the threshold to bring back his magical essence, but he turned his back on that world, choosing darkness instead.

Pushing that depressing thought aside, I turned to Nathan.

"Can you get me a peach-mango protein drink?"

"Sure." He paused, then tilted his head to the side, regarding me. "Why?"

"I need to go to the restroom."

"I'll come with you."

I glanced around, spotting Matt and Carrie on the platform talking to a group of people. A spasm of guilt pierced my heart for not hanging out with Carrie tonight. I frowned, promising myself I'd talk to her before we left. I didn't want her to think I'd been avoiding her.

I jerked my chin toward the platform. "You don't have to."

He looked at them while bending his head next to mine. "I think I should still go with you." His voice was deep and rough. I knew if I didn't make a quick exit, he'd shadow me, which was something I didn't want or felt I needed.

"I'll be fine." I kissed him before he could disagree. "I'll be back in a few minutes." I hurried off, hearing Tree asking Nathan where I was going.

After I did my business, I found myself alone in the restroom. Out of curiosity, I looked to see if there were any feet in the stalls. There were none. *That's odd.* A few minutes ago there were people packed in here. Maybe the band was about to start its next set and everybody rushed out to get a good spot on the floor, I considered, sticking my soapy hands beneath the faucet, rubbing them together in the warm water. I wondered if Nathan was freaking out by now. I hated to worry him, but in my defense, I didn't know how busy it would be in here.

As I dried my hands, my ears began to ring. The door flew open, bouncing off the wall like a rubber ball.

My stomach dropped.

I stood there paralyzed by the trash can as a husky, dark-haired butch girl walked in. Her black eyes locked onto mine, a beam of light swiped across them.

Oh, crap.

How in the hell was I going to get out of this one? Running or fighting her wasn't an option. Her strength and speed alone would overpower me. Think, Paige.

Wait.

Nathan told me earlier to keep my wits about me. Maybe I could outsmart her.

"So, you're the girl some of my brothers and sisters are whispering about," she said, sizing me up like a piece of cattle she wanted to buy.

"I don't know what you're talking about." I kept my voice firm and leveled, playing dumb. But she made a face, clearly not falling for it.

Despite her bulk, her movements had a feline quality that carried her to me. She stared mockingly at me. The beam of light swiped across her iris again. Her eyes wobbled back and forth in her head until they landed where my hands were clutching the trash can.

"Liar!" she half shouted in my face, making me flinch.

My heart was slamming against my chest, but I refused to back down. If she was going to kill me, fine, but I'd fight her till the very end. And yeah, she was way stronger, but so what? I'd rather die standing than cowering on my knees and could probably whack her a good one before she killed me. But hopefully it wouldn't come to that. I had to stick to my plan.

I released the trash can and stood erect. "What do you want?"

She took a step closer and crossed her tattoo arms over her chest. "You're a little spitfire, Ms. Paige *Reed*." She said my last name as if it was the foulest word in the world, her eyes flashing with hatred.

I blinked a couple times, as if she slapped me across the face, dumbfounded she knew my name, like the guy in the restaurant did.

"But I like that about you," she continued. "The brazenness that is."

I hugged my arms. "What do you want?"

Her thin lips turned into a hideous grin. "I want to make you a deal."

"What?" I said, bewildered. At first I didn't think I heard her right, but when her face turned serious, and she said it again, I became speechless. Why would a dark spirit want to make a deal with me?

"I want you to find the ring and give it to me."

"What ring?" My brows furrowed. What the hell was she talking about?

She looked at me as if I were a disgusting insect. "I'm sure your superhero boyfriend out there told you about The Seal of Solomon."

My heart sank. I covered my mouth. *Omigod.*

Her eyes turned to slits, and the tone of her voice rose to a pitchy, spine-numbing sound. "That's right. I had a feeling you knew about that." She looked pleased with herself.

"Why do you think I'm the one who can find it?"

"Many reasons," she said. "We know you've been marked for immortality and have–*abilities*. We also know the 'old one' can snap your neck like a baby bird, but he won't. Hell, we all can for that matter." She let out a peal of laughter that ricocheted off the black tile walls, turning my blood to ice.

"Why won't he?" I asked, despite my fear.

She leaned forward, moving her face around mine like a snake ready to strike. I stepped back into the trash can. It made a loud knocking sound against the wall. She reached out and flicked a lock of hair off my shoulder.

"Because he likes you, and you're an enigma he's determined to figure out. I personally think he wants you to become immortal, so he can see what you can do."

"What's the deal?" I asked, willing myself not to shake under her stare.

She clapped her hands together. "The deal is this. When you find the ring, you give it to me. If you promise to do that, I'll let you live, and you can become immortal."

Summoning every bit of courage I had, I decided to play along to see how far I could get her to talk. Pretending to ponder it, I placed a finger on my lips. A slow smile crossed her cruel face.

I scratched the side of my head. "Do I have to find it while I'm mortal? Because I don't think I can. I still have to go to school, and I might die before I find the ring."

"No, you do need to be immortal. Otherwise, you probably would die. No. Take that back." She waved a hand in the air, her face turning vicious, threatening. "You *will* die."

"Is that why the 'old one' hasn't killed me?"

Her heartless eyes moved suspiciously across my face, and then she answered:

"One of the reasons I think."

"What about the ones who want to kill me?"

"They don't like you because you're a threat to them."

"But what if they kill me before I become immortal? If they do that, I won't be able to find the ring and give it to you." I tried to appear relaxed, but in my head I was screaming for Nathan, wondering where the hell he could be and why nobody was coming into the restroom.

"I'll see if I can get them to leave you alone." She was getting excited at the prospect of obtaining the ring.

"Can I think about it?" I swear my heart was going to bust out of my chest. I mean, the spiteful look that was on her face, made me wonder if I made a mistake asking her that. "I need to make sure I can find it," I quickly added.

She glared while she considered my request. I debated whether I should try to make a run for it, but she was blocking my view of the door.

"I'll give you six weeks," she finally said, "to think about it and do some research, since I have reasons to believe you won't become immortal until after then. And I'll *know* if you lie to me, so don't *even* think about tricking me because I'll *kill* you." She paused, cocked her head to the side, and slowly ran a finger across her chin. Her eyes latched onto mine–black ice, reflecting a putrid being full of malice and self-righteousness. "If you agree, then change your mind once you become immortal, I'll find and shackle you away from those you love until you succumb to my demands."

I shuddered.

Her face knotted into ugly pleasure.

"That's right. You should be shaking in your little Mary Janes. Because if you cross me, I *will* hunt you down, then kill or torture you."

"But why do you think me of all people can find it?" I asked, my voice shaking.

She let out a long, boring yawn. "Because I believe your father might have known where it was. For years I didn't think so, but now I think he did know *something*. It's too bad he died before we could find anything out. The poor *bastard* should have accepted immortality."

As soon as she mentioned my father, hot tears stung my cheeks.

"What are you babbling about? My father had nothing to do with this," I spat.

She shook her head. "Dear child, you need to do some research on your father. Why don't you ask Anwar about it? Or, maybe even your boyfriend. He might know."

Just then, Carrie burst through the door, stressed. The dark spirit looked at her admiringly before strolling out with an arrogance that frightened me.

"Are you okay?" Carrie asked. "Nathan told me to get to you fast."

I buried my face in my hands and broke down, still feeling the dark spirit's hostility, along with the bite from her venomous words. I couldn't believe this was happening to me and what she had said about my father.

Carrie hugged me. "What happened? Did that girl say something to you?"

I held onto Carrie and bawled on her shoulder. All I could think about was my father and the possibility he had the choice of becoming immortal but didn't take it. Why hadn't he?

"Do you want me to kick her ass? I think I can take her. I'll just use some of Tree's Power Ranger moves." She stepped back and acted like Tree did when we were kids, jumping up and down, twirling in the air, making karate chops, kicking her foot up.

Despite the ache in my heart and tears, I half giggled at her silliness, trying to do those moves in her fitted black dress, her skull and crossbones suspenders slipping off her shoulders.

She stopped and smiled. "I knew that would make you laugh."

I went to the stall to get some toilet paper and blew my nose.

"I'm sorry if it seemed like I'd been avoiding you tonight." I threw the toilet paper into the trash can. "That wasn't my intention."

"I know that now," she said, pulling her suspenders over her shoulders.

I headed to the door, but she stopped me. The freckles around her nose bunched together.

"What is it?" I knew something happened by the anxious expression on her face.

"Tree, Matt, and Nathan got into a fight, and it's a mess out there."

"Oh, no!" I turned to the door, but she clasped my arm.

"Wait. Let me tell you what happened before you go storming out there."

Sighing, I tapped my foot, grasping my elbows.

"I went to talk to Tree," she said in a rush, "and Matt went with me. Well, Nathan was about to go look for you, but then Matt had to open his big mouth."

My eyes widened. "Are you serious? What did he say?"

She placed her hands on her hips. "He told Nathan by the way you were dancing with him, he could tell you're now another mark on his bedpost."

I gaped at her. "He said that?"

She nodded, her face covered in disgust. "Yes, he did. That *dumb fuck*."

"What happened? Did Nathan hit him?" I thought about how hard Nathan could hit, and imagined Matt's face shattered into tiny pieces.

Carrie shook her head. "No. Tree grabbed him by the waist, threw him on the floor, and wailed on him." She animatedly demonstrated Tree's moves.

"Seriously?" I couldn't believe Tree actually did that.

"Yes, but then Matt got the upper hand and hammered Tree. I never realized how strong and quick Matt was. But then Nathan jumped in and yanked Matt off of Tree. He threw Matt across the room like a rag doll. Everybody got out of the way when the fight started, so when Nathan threw Matt, he landed at the other end of the club by the stairs to the platform. I thought Matt was strong, but Nathan had him beat by a long shot," she said with an impressed smile.

"Then what happened? Is Tree okay? What is everybody saying?" My mind spun.

"The vampire dude in the band saw everything, and stood up for Tree and Nathan when security came. So they're not in trouble."

"Thank God. But what about Tree?" I hoped Tree was okay.

"He has a bloody nose, but he's fine. And everybody is talking about you."

"Me?"my voice squeaked.

"Yeah. They're saying Matt should have never said that to Nathan. They think it's cool how Tree and Nathan defended you like that."

I covered my face and groaned. "Now it's going to be all over school." This totally sucked. I hated being the center of attention. Why was this happening to me?

"Yeah, well, Nathan is really worried about you, but can't do anything because security is detaining him and Tree for questioning, so he told me to get you."

"But I thought you said everything is fine, and they're not in trouble."

"They're not, but they still need to question them. Matt didn't even press charges," she added.

"But Matt started it," I said, wanting to punch him myself.

She shrugged and shook her head. "That doesn't matter. Tree attacked him first."

I flexed my hands in irritation. "Please tell me you're not going to still date him."

She raised her hands. "Oh no, I'm through with him. He crossed the line tonight."

I gave a sigh of relief. That was one less thing I had to worry about now, and one good thing that happened tonight.

"So, what did the girl say to you?" she asked when I turned to leave.

I stared at her, her face becoming one big blur. My throat tightened. "Um, she …" I couldn't tell her what actually happened, so I told her the harmless part, the part bothering me the most. "She knows something about my father, but won't tell me."

"But how could she know about your father?" She was just as perplexed as me.

I wiped my cheeks with the back of my hand. "I don't know, but I don't want to talk about it right now. I need to see how Nathan and Tree are doing. I'm sure Nathan is jumping out of his skin right now."

"You're right. He was already doing that earlier," Carrie said.

We stepped out into the club and dodged the people standing in groups, talking about what happened. Even though they were too busy talking among themselves to notice me, I kept my head down to avoid being seen.

"Why isn't the band playing right now?" I asked Carrie. The band members were standing on the stage in a tight circle. They were probably talking about the same thing everybody else seemed to be chatting about. The fight my dumb ass caused.

Her gaze followed mine. "They're waiting until everything gets cleared up before they start their next set."

This was all my fault. If only I had danced like everybody else, none of this would have happened. I mean, honestly, I gave Matt the ammunition to piss Nathan off, and he used it. But then Tree had to get involved, shifting the attention off of a band, struggling to make it into the music industry, onto a fight I could have prevented. God, I felt guilty. And yeah, I was sure Matt would have eventually made another stupid comment to Nathan, like he had the other night, but I wished it wasn't under those circumstances, all because of how I danced. I should have realized how inappropriate my moves were. I ruined everything.

As we walked around a group of people, I saw Nathan sitting on the leather bench near the front entrance, his elbows on his bouncing knees, his head bent as if in prayer. Tree was sitting beside him, his nose stuffed with cotton, talking to the security guard standing to his left.

When we approached them, Nathan's head snapped up. Relief flooded his face, but then he took a closer look at me. Jumping to his feet, he immediately embraced me. It felt good to be in his arms.

His hand went to the back of my head, stroking it. "Paige?"

I shook, thinking about the dark spirit in the restroom and all the things she said to me. I tried not to think about my father in fear of crying again. This wasn't the time or place to do that, and I didn't want to make things worse. I knew if I allowed the tears to flow, I wouldn't be able to stop them this time.

"Mr. Caswell," a bored voice said from behind me. "We need your signature on this form." When Nathan didn't move, he impatiently cleared his throat.

Nathan's chest heaved against mine, an annoyed sigh escaping his lips. He reluctantly released his arms, and went over to the beefy, blond security guard. I stepped in front of Tree.

Carrie was sitting next to him with her hand on his knee. I took that as a good sign.

"How are you?" I scrutinized the round red mark on his right cheek bone.

"I'm great." He inclined his head to Carrie and smiled.

I nodded, and looked over at Nathan. He was holding a brown clipboard in his hands, reading the form. I then realized Kylee wasn't around.

"Where's Kylee?"

"She went home," Tree said. "She's mad about the fight and told me I needed to grow up." He pushed air through his lips and rolled his eyes.

I placed a hand on my hip. How dare she talk to Tree like that. "Well, I'll talk to her on Monday and--"

"You won't have to," Carrie said. "I already told her like it is." She had a proud smile on her face. I imagined she said more to Kylee than a few choice words.

Tree curled his arm around Carrie and grinned. "She defended my honor."

I smiled, thinking how cute and perfect they were together. Carrie's face was glowing, and Tree was in heaven. To him this was his best night ever. He got to hit Matt and get his girl back.

"If I see her, I'm still going to talk to her though," I said, "and by the way, thanks for defending *my* honor."

Tree waved a hand like it was no big deal. "He had it coming to him a long time ago, and he shouldn't be talking about you like that anyway." He paused. "Carrie told me about the girl in the restroom who knows something about your father." I caught Carrie sticking her elbow in his side before my eyes fell to the floor. "Sorry. I'm just curious," he added. "But how could she know about your father? That was almost fourteen years ago."

I heard Carrie say something to him in a harsh whisper, but I didn't catch what she said. It sounded like she told him to shut up, not now. I couldn't tell though, but I did everything in my power not to cry, which included mentally chanting: *don't cry, don't cry, don't cry.*

"Yeah, she did," I confirmed, staring at my feet. "But I really don't want to talk about it." I lifted my head and bit my bottom lip.

"I'm sorry, Paige," Tree quickly said when he saw the look on my face.

I glanced at Nathan at the same time he glanced at me. The frustration and anxiety he felt showed in his face. He turned his head to the security guard, appearing interested by nodding, and then ran a hand through his hair, sneaking a peek back at me.

"I'm going to go outside and wait for Nathan," I told them.

"Do you want me to come with you?" Carrie asked.

"No," I said when she started to rise. "I need to be alone for a few minutes."

"I'm really sorry," Tree apologized again. "Sometimes I have a foot-in-mouth disease."

"That's okay. Just remind him to get our stuff before he leaves."

"We won't have to. It looks like he's getting it right now." Carrie pointed past me.

I turned and saw Nathan walking toward the lockers. I thought how frustrating it would be to have to act human at a time when you really wanted to use your speed to hurry things up.

My superhero boyfriend, faster than a speeding bullet, or pretty damned close to it.

My superhero boyfriend. That was what the dark spirit called him, and told me to ask him and Anwar about my father. She seemed confident Anwar knew things about my father, but did Nathan?

I swallowed against the thickness growing in my throat.

"Then tell him I'll be outside," I said to their guilty faces, feeling everything closing in on me at once. What if Nathan knew things about my father all along, but hid them from me?

I rushed outside and stopped beside the entrance. Resting against the brick building, I bowed my head. My tears broke free, dripping off my face onto the concrete, making small wet spots where they landed.

Chapter Eleven
Searching

"Paige," Nathan said.

I lifted my eyes to the anxiousness in his. He reached for me, but I raised my palm, halting him. My purse and jacket dangled from his hand. He looked at me in confusion.

"Not here." I sniffed and swiped a hand across my wet cheeks. A group of people walked by and a few gawked, probably thinking we were having a fight. "Take me home." I took my jacket and purse from him and headed toward the truck.

"Please tell me why you're so upset," he said. "I heard what Tree asked you, but I don't know anything else, and it's killing me." He leaned forward to see my face.

I slipped my jacket on and choked back a sob. "I don't want to talk right now."

"Paige." He was on the verge of begging; I could hear it in his voice.

"Wait until we get home,"my voice cracked.

He didn't say another word, but I could tell by his quick gestures and how fast he drove, it bothered him. I didn't say anything when we stepped inside the house, or when I put my jacket away. All I could think about was my fear of him knowing something about my father and not sharing it with me.

What if he'd known all along, but pretended like he didn't? How would I be able to handle that? I didn't think I could. I mean, to me that would be just as bad as cheating. I knew though, Nathan would never betray me. At least, I thought I knew.

"What do you know about my father?" I demanded when he opened his mouth to speak.

His eyebrows knitted. "Nothing, except for what you told me. Why?" He seemed bewildered by my question.

I hung my head and breathed out all my tension. *Thank God.*

"Why?" he asked again, taking my shoulders into his hands.

"There was a dark spirit in the restroom with me," I said to the floor.

He dropped his hands. "What?"

"She trapped me." I thought about how close I came to dying and shivered. "She said Anwar knows about my father and that you might too."

He steered me to the couch, and we sat.

"I swear to you, Paige, I don't know anything about your father." He looked desperate, like he was afraid I wouldn't believe him.

I held his hand to let him know that wasn't the case. "I believe you and know you'd never lie to me. But what if Anwar knows something about him?"

"Why would Anwar know?" he wondered.

"I have to tell you everything she told me, so you can understand why she said that."

He squeezed my hand and nodded.

I began to tell him what she said, but when I got to the killing me part, he jumped up in a fit of rage and paced the floor, startling me with his quick gesture.

"Let me get this straight. She said if you don't promise to give her the ring in six weeks, she's going to hunt you down and *kill* you?" His words were flames shooting out of his mouth, like a pissed off dragon.

I nodded. "She also said if I say yes, but then change my mind when I become immortal, she'll shackle me and take me away from those I love."

He stopped in front of me, hands on his hips. "What does she look like again?"

"It doesn't matter," I said. "You won't be able to find her."

He jabbed his chest with his finger, his voice raised. "I've been tracking dark spirits for a very long time. I think I can find her."

"Okay." I lifted my hands in surrender. "So you find her and cast her out, but then what? She'll just find another human to possess."

His face fell, and for the first time in my life, I hated to be right. He ran his hand through his hair. "Yes. She'd be out of the body for a while, until she regained her energy, but who knows how long that would take? And besides, she could switch bodies right now, if there's an available vessel nearby," he rambled to himself.

"They can switch bodies without being cast out?" The shock rose in my voice.

He nodded. "But they have to be near an able human vessel. Remember, it's hard for the young ones to acclimate, so they don't reside in one for a long period of time. What they do is they'll leave the vessel they're in, jump into another one, and stay in it until it becomes uncomfortable, or reenter the same vessel later."

"The girl in the restroom must be young because her eyes didn't glow like Matt's."

"She is, but she sounds cocky, and that concerns me." He crossed his arms over his chest, hints of anger etched on his face. "Tell me everything she said."

I told him the rest, and after I finished, he sat beside me.

"Do you think she was telling the truth about my father? Was he chosen to be immortal and decided not to?" My eyes were wide, brimming with tears. The thought of my father having the opportunity to be immortal and not taking it deeply disturbed me. If he had chosen immortality, he'd still be here with me and my mom, and we would have been the family I'd longed for. Why didn't he want to be with us or with me? What was wrong with me? Maybe Ashley was right. Maybe he didn't love me enough to want to be around.

"I don't know," he whispered, staring at me, lost in thought. He glanced away, then back at me. He had a troubled expression on his face. Abruptly, he rose.

"Where are you going?"

"I'm going to get my phone and call Anwar," he said. "There's no reason for you to go through this. If Anwar knows something, he's going to tell me."

He disappeared.

A few minutes later, I heard the faint sound of his voice from upstairs. I couldn't really hear him though, and proceeded to go to him, but then he appeared in front of me.

"He didn't answer his phone, so I had to leave a message." He tossed his phone on the coffee table in annoyance. It made a loud, plastic sound. "It figures. When I really want to talk to him, he doesn't answer his phone."

"What if he's in trouble," I said, imagining him being tortured.

"Anwar is a clever guy." He paused and looked at me. "I'm not leaving you, Paige." His voice was firm, his face hard. "So don't even entertain the thought."

I looked away, and then a thought occurred to me.

"I know you two are immortal, but can you still die? Fictional vampires are immortal, but yet sunlight and fire can kill them."

"There's only one way we know of. It's being completely bled out."

I recoiled at the mental picture. The whole blood thing didn't settle with me, and I had no desire to think about it, or what I had to go through to become immortal, which was basically the same thing. So I focused my thoughts on what the dark spirit had said to me about my father.

What did my father know about the ring? Did he know anything? I needed to find out, and the first place to start looking was here in the house. I'd already searched through it years ago, but with Nathan's help, maybe he'd find something I'd missed.

Yeah, that would work. I mean, there was no harm in trying, right? I could throw some sweats on and search until I got tired, giving myself a head start.

"I think we should start searching the house, but we should change our clothes first." I headed for the stairs, but Nathan caught the crook of my elbow, stopping me.

"I won't let her hurt you." His voice was rough. "I'll make her suffer if she tries to touch one hair on your head." His eyes blazed with a fury of protectiveness. "I've made a huge mistake tonight, one which could have cost you your life. But I will *not* make the same mistake again."

I swallowed against the guilty lump in my throat. "It was my fault. You wanted to walk me to the restroom, but I allowed my stubbornness to get in the way. So don't put the blame on yourself."

He shook his head in disagreement. I couldn't stand seeing him being so hard on himself, so I stood on my tiptoes and gave him a soft kiss. His reaction was immediate. He pressed his lips to mine, and my heart raced from its intensity. It was deep and passionate, and during those few moments, all fear and time were lost. I didn't want it to end, but we knew it had to. I cursed the dark spirits for that and for everything else as well. We separated and stood there, catching our breaths. He bent his head and peeked at me. His eyes were bright with the same desire swimming inside me. He saw it on my face. The corner of his mouth turned into a crooked smile. He was so damned cute, I couldn't help but smile.

"As much as I detest saying this, I think we should refrain from temptation for a while," he said, his chest still heaving.

"I think you're right," I agreed, and then flashed him a teasing smile. "I guess I won't be kissing you for a while then."

He snatched my hand and pulled me into his arms. "Now, we don't have to take it to extremes. We just have to be careful not allow our feelings for each other to distract us from what needs to be done." He kissed my forehead and hugged me. "So, where do you want to start looking first?"

I thought about all the crap we were going to have to go through and became overwhelmed. Somehow, when I went through it years ago it didn't seem like the huge undertaking it did now, and I wondered why. I decided it had to be in the matter of perspective, in how we looked at things. The key to it was to not stress out, and to take it in baby steps, one box and tote at a time.

"I think we should try to put a dent in the basement tonight, but be prepared to get dirty because it's filthy down there."

A daring grin formed on his face. "I'll race you upstairs."

I laughed. "Yeah, right."

"Better yet"–he picked me up and slung me over his shoulder–"I'll race upstairs with you."

I continued to laugh and covered my face in fear he would run into a wall at the rate of speed he could go. But it seemed like he didn't even move, so when he set me down, I was baffled we were in my room.

"That's crazy." I pushed my hair off my face. "I didn't even feel you move."

"That's one of the many perks of being immortal," he said, reaching into his overnight bag for a T-shirt. He pulled a gray one out and took off what he was wearing. I averted my eyes from his muscular arms and chest, and tried to think of something else before my desires took a hold of me.

I went to the dresser to get my sweats. "Not that I wanted you to, but why didn't you hit Matt before Tree did?"

He stood in the doorway. "Because I was too preoccupied with thoughts of you. And to be honest, I didn't realize what he said until Tree tackled him."

"What happened to Matt anyway? I didn't see him in the club after Carrie and I came out of the restroom." I didn't care, really. But I was curious about it and wondered how he would be on Monday at school. I did have history class with him, and he always sat next to me. I wondered if he'd even talk to me or if he would try to make up with Carrie.

"The security guards took him to the back room and banished him from the club for six months." He leaned his hand on the door frame and rested his cheek on his arm, looking at me.

"What?" I hugged my sweats to my chest, suddenly feeling shy.

"Nothing." He smiled. "I just love watching you."

I dropped my eyes, my face flushing. "Well, I have to change so-- "

"I'll meet you downstairs," he said, then vanished.

***

The concrete basement, used for storage, smelled like mildew and boiled cabbage. We spent a few hours going through boxes, and I screamed a couple times when a spider crawled past. Nathan laughed and smashed it with his hand. He thought my fear of spiders was funny and told me I should envision them wearing a top hat, then maybe I wouldn't be afraid of them. I threw him a look like he was out of his mind, and he laughed again.

As I searched through a box of dishes, being careful not to clink them too hard, Nathan stood from a big box of Christmas stuff and stretched. I put the dishes back in the box and closed the lid. We were both getting tired, and I wanted to call it a night. I brushed myself off, feeling gritty.

"I think I'm going to take a shower and go to bed," I told him, depressed we hadn't found anything, and I wondered if we ever would.

Nathan wiped his hands on his jeans. "Sounds like a good idea."

He followed me out of the basement, but when I turned to go upstairs, he gently took my arm.

"Try not to worry. We'll find something. I promise," he said.

"And if we don't?" I asked, my voice full of doubt. "Then what do we do?"

He tucked a lock of hair behind my ear. "We keep searching until we do. The answers about your father and what he knew are out there. And if we don't find it in this house, we'll look somewhere else."

I tried to smile, but couldn't. I noticed the concern in his eyes, but didn't say anything. Instead, I went up the stairs. I didn't know what to think, and all I wanted to do was go to sleep to escape from it all. So after I took my shower, I crawled into bed, allowing the Sandman to take me to another place.

Chapter Twelve
Frustration

I awoke at three in the afternoon to Nathan's voice shouting downstairs. Kicking the covers off, I hopped out of bed, wondering whom he was shouting at, and lingered in the hallway to listen.

"I can't believe you didn't tell me this," he said, seething. He paused before shouting again. "I don't give a *damn* about your reasons, Anwar. You should have told me."

It appeared Anwar did know something about my father, which meant the dark spirit must have been telling me at least some truths.

My mouth filled with salty saliva, and my stomach rolled with nausea.

"I don't care if you wanted to wait until you got here to tell her. You have no *fucking* idea what it's doing to her."

Wow. I'd never heard him use the eff word before. *He must be pissed.*

"And you have no *fucking* idea what it's doing to *me* seeing her like this." There was another pause. "I *doubt* I'll be able to see your motives behind this." His tone dropped an octave, and then there was silence. I chewed on my fingernail until he spoke again. "Yes, I trust you, but I need to know everything you know *right* now," he demanded. I could hear him moving about in the kitchen. A chair banged against the tile, and he started shouting again. "What's that supposed to *fucking* mean? *I'm* too close to her for you to tell me the rest of it."

What did that mean, and why would it make a difference? I didn't get it. All he had to do was tell Nathan to make our life a little easier. Any bit of information would help us, but it was obvious he wasn't going to tell him.

I leaned against the wall, tasting the sour bile rising in my throat.

"I have to trust you on it? That's a bunch of *horseshit.* Do you *realize* the magnitude of sorrow and pain she's in and how helpless I feel because I *can't* do anything about it?" His voice shook with anger and frustration.

I thought about him hurting because of me and felt a sharp stab of guilt. If I could, I'd push him away. But I knew I couldn't do that, or bear the thought of him not being in my life. I hated being selfish and felt like crap for it. Maybe I should at least give it a try and think of him instead of my selfishness.

"I don't think you do understand. She found out, not from *you,* but from a dark spirit, her father had been marked for immortality and didn't accept it!"

That did it. I ran to the bathroom, flipped the toilet seat up and hurled, thankful I had put my hair in a braid last night. I couldn't hear the rest of the conversation through the retching noises I made, but not too long after, Nathan stood by my side. I tried to tell him to go away, but gagged instead. I stuck my head back in the toilet bowl, heaving one last time, my ears burning from embarrassment.

"Are you okay?" he asked, kneeling beside me.

"Yeah, sure." I went to the sink to brush my teeth and thought about my selfishness while he stood behind me and placed his palm on my forehead. He didn't need to go through this. What he needed to do was go get Anwar.

His voice was low. "I'm sorry if I woke you." He dropped his hand and stepped aside. His presence reeked of tension and anger–all because of me.

I straightened my back and turned. "No, I'm sorry."

His face went blank like he couldn't comprehend my words.

"I'm sorry for putting you through this," I continued. "And I think maybe you should leave." I grasped my shaking hands behind my back. "I also think you should go get Anwar before I end up like my father."

The space between his eyes wrinkled, and he bit his top lip. I turned when I saw the sadness enter his eyes. I washed my face with my chest pressed into the marble sink, forcing pressure against the fisted pain, threatening to knock me to the floor.

"Paige." His voice sounded strangled. He cleared his throat. "Do you really want me to leave you?"

I didn't move, knowing the look on his face would demolish me.

"No, but I hate causing you so much pain, and it's selfish of me to keep you here."

He turned me around and held my shoulders in his hands. I continued to stare at the floor.

"Please look at me." My gaze slowly lifted to his, and his eyes were raw with emotion. "I don't want you to feel sorry, or shameful for allowing me to see what you've kept walled inside you for so long. And you're not being selfish. If I didn't want to be with you, I wouldn't be."

"I never want you to leave me," I said, still feeling bad. "But I *hate* seeing you hurting because of me."

"Baby, don't you understand? *Your* pain is *my* pain. Just like *my* pain is *your* pain. That's just part of being in love." His hands moved to the back of my neck, his fingers lightly stroking it, setting off a wave of tingling sensations across my skin.

I nodded and smiled at the fact he called me baby again.

"I love you and want to be with you forever." He kissed me. It was soft and sweet.

"I love you too," I said when our lips parted, and he kissed me again.

"How are you feeling?"

I shrugged. "Fine. It was just nerves. So, what did Anwar tell you?"

The anger he felt earlier flashed across his eyes.

"I'll tell you after you get dressed."

"Okay," I said, flushing the toilet.

"Do you think you can eat something?" He had a hesitant look on his face, like he wasn't sure if he should have asked me that.

"A toasted bagel with cream cheese sounds good. Oh, and some coffee."

"I'm on it," he said and disappeared.

***

I sat at the kitchen table drinking coffee, listening to Nathan tell me everything Anwar had said. When he confirmed, my father had been marked for immortality, a cold numbness fell upon me.

I felt nothing. Seriously. It was like I became detached or something.

Nathan continued with Anwar refusing to tell him why my father had chosen to stay mortal. He had his reasons for not telling us, but promised he would in person. He did tell Nathan my father knew about the ring, but had never mentioned to him if he knew where it was.

"Does he think my father was murdered?"

"Yes, he does." Nathan took a sip of his coffee, watching me closely.

"Does he know which dark spirit did it?" In my mind I made a vow. I would seek out the dark spirit and make it suffer for taking my father away from us.

"No," he said, staring into his mug as if he was reading tea leaves.

I went into the living room and sat on the couch, thinking about my father not taking immortality, wondering why he turned his back on the world and us. And it kicked me back into despair.

Nathan sat beside me and rubbed my shoulder. "What's wrong?"

"It doesn't make sense," I whispered, choking back the tears. "If my father had chosen immortality, he would still be with us."

"No, he wouldn't," Nathan firmly said. "He would've had to leave you, just like I had to with my family."

"But he could have found a way to make it work." I thought about all the possible options to consider. My options. Would I be able to find a way to keep the ones I loved in my life, even after five or ten years? I knew I would have to leave Astoria, but there had to be a way to keep my mom, Carrie, and Tree in my life.

"I thought the same way once, but found out the hard way the only option was to walk away."

"That's right." I looked at him, remembering what he had told me before. "You told your father. What happened?"

Nathan rested his forearms on his knees and blew out a lung full of air. He tilted his head and squinted me.

"It was a very selfish thing for me to do, to put such a burden on my father, but at the time I didn't see it that way. Anwar was against me telling him, but I did it anyway."

"Why did you tell your father instead of one of your brothers?"

"Because I knew he'd take my secret to his grave. But what I didn't realize at the time was what it would do to him."

"What do you mean?"

"My father had to suffer through watching his family grieve, knowing all along I was alive and well. He watched helplessly as my mother went into a deep depression where she didn't get up out of bed for weeks at a time.

"Can you imagine the turmoil he went through, knowing all he had to do to mend her heart was to tell her the truth about me? But his loyalty to me kept him from doing that."

I held my cheeks in my hands and frowned. "I don't think I can do that, Nathan."

"What?"

"Make my mom believe I'm dead. I know she's never around, but she lost my father, and I don't know what it would do to her if she thought I was dead too." I felt sick thinking about it.

"You really have no choice, Paige," he said, his expression pained. "Because if you don't take immortality, you will be dead. So either way, she's going to suffer."

"I think we should finish searching the basement." I stood, promising myself I'd find a way to spare my mom any pain.

Nathan nodded, understanding this conversation was over. We headed to the basement, in hope of finding something of value to us.

***

We spent most of the weekend searching the house, discovering nothing. On Sunday afternoon, Tree called me. He said he was still feeling like shit (his words exactly) about the other night. He apologized again, and I told him to forget about it. He then cheerfully informed me he was dating Carrie again. I was so excited for them. I mean, totally excited. I'd been waiting for Carrie to acknowledge her true feelings for Tree, for like forever. I even did a happy dance in the hallway, and then caught Nathan smiling at me from the living room. Flushing, I stopped and went back into the kitchen to finish my conversation with Tree, feeling like a dork.

Afterwards, I sat on Nathan's lap in the recliner and groaned. I had forgotten about school until Tree told me he'd see me there tomorrow. I usually didn't mind going, but now with Nathan in my life, I wanted to be with him instead.

"What's the matter?"

"I forgot I had school tomorrow until Tree reminded me." I groaned again.

"It'll go quick, and I'll take you every day and be there when you get out." He pulled me against him and scooted down in the recliner.

"You will?" I didn't expect him to do that, but it did make me feel a little better.

"Absolutely."

"We do have Good Friday off," I said, staring at the weird elongated finger shadows the trees outside were casting on the floor and along the walls. "But what are you going to do while I'm in school?"

He kissed my cheek. "I'll go home and do some research on your father." His soft lips moved to my neck. I closed my eyes, feeling a tingling sensation stir parts of my body.

"We can't do this," I breathed, even though I so wanted to.

"Sure we can. We've been working all weekend, so there would be no harm in it," he murmured against my skin.

"No, we can't, at least, not for seven days." I was too embarrassed to tell him I started my period this morning and tried to give him a subtle hint.

He stopped kissing my neck and looked at me. "Oh, you're on your--"

"Don't say it!" I screeched. "It's too gross to talk about, and I hate it."

He laughed. "Paige, it's a natural thing. You shouldn't be embarrassed or grossed out."

"Well, I am, and I don't want to talk about it."

"You know, when you become immortal, you won't have to deal with that anymore."

I raised my eyebrows. "Really?"

He smiled and nodded. "Really."

"That rocks." I grinned. "Maybe this might be my last one."

"If Anwar gets here soon, it will be."

If Anwar gets here. What if Anwar doesn't get here in time to turn me immortal, and I end up dead? What if he never comes? Then what would I do?

"What are you thinking about?"

"I'm wondering if Anwar will get here in time to turn me immortal, and I'm afraid I might die before that happens."

Nathan crushed me to his chest. "I won't let it."

"You can't be my constant shadow. And you have to face the fact there is a possibility I might die before he gets here. Unless, you turn me immortal right now."

"I can't, Paige," he said, sounding depressed.

"Are you willing to risk me dying by the hands of the dark spirits instead?" I didn't want to start an argument or make him feel bad, but what I said was the truth, and I wanted an answer. "Or die of some freak accident?" I added.

When he didn't respond, I squirmed off his lap and went upstairs to get my stuff ready for school tomorrow. My books and reports were on the floor in my room beside my computer desk. I shoved them in my backpack, thinking about what I just asked Nathan, while trying to put myself in his shoes.

If I were immortal, and he wasn't, would I risk the possibility of killing him myself? If I did risk it, and he died, what would that do to me?

I sat on the floor against my bed, feeling a crushing blow to my chest. I would never forgive myself if that were to happen.

On the other hand, would I be willing to risk his life until he was able to turn immortal? That was a hard question to answer, but if I believed Anwar would soon be here to change him, and in the meantime, protected him until then, I think I would risk it, knowing in my heart there would be no room for failure.

I peeled myself off the floor and found Nathan where I left him. He had his head on his knees with his hands clasped on top of it. He didn't look up until I said his name. When I saw the sorrow on his face, I felt another blow to my chest. I rushed to him and embraced him. I told him it was okay. I understood why he wouldn't do it, and if I were in his shoes I'd do the same thing. I knelt in front of him and rubbed the side of his face, telling him again it was all right.

"It's not," he moaned. "If I weren't so afraid of accidently killing you, I'd turn you right now." He closed his eyes and shook his head.

I kissed his cheek. "I love you and understand why you can't do it." I wanted to say more to make him feel better, but nothing came to mind.

He seized my hands, squeezing them, startling me with the urgency in his gesture. "I love you." A fierce determination entered his voice. "And I promise you, if Anwar isn't here in five weeks, you and I will go to Europe and find him."

"We will?" The heaviness in my shoulders lifted, and I dropped to my knees.

"Yes, but I want you to know from now on, I'll be hovering above you like a mother over her sick child. I'm aware I can't do it while you're in school, but you'll be around a lot of people, so you'll be safe. But I do need you to promise me one thing." Before I could respond, he grasped the top of my arms. "Please don't comprise your life by going off somewhere alone, and *always* surround yourself with a bunch of people."

"I promise. But you know, I do have history with Matt. Well, the 'old one,'" I clarified.

His face darkened.

"I know."

I jerked my head back. "How do you know?" I tried to recall if I ever mentioned it to him, but I couldn't remember. But then again, sometimes I couldn't even remember what day it was.

His hand moved to the side of my face. The darkness in his features faded into a soft smile. "The Lion's Den wasn't the first time I'd seen you."

"Really? When was the first time then?"

"Well, I tracked Matt here to Astoria, and one day when I was watching him, I saw you, and instantly lost my breath. Right then, you stole my heart.

"From then on, I couldn't help but watch you as well. I didn't know anything about your family, but what I did know was the 'old one' had a great interest in you, and I was determined to find out why. During that time was when I discovered you two had history class together."

I narrowed my eyes. "That night at The Lion's Den, were you watching me as well?"

He nodded.

"Did you jump off the platform like I thought I saw you do?"

"Yes, I did. I normally wouldn't have pulled a stunt like that in public, but I had to get to you fast and knew nobody was watching."

"You lied to me." It wasn't a question, or an accusation, just a simple statement with a teasing tone behind it.

He shook his head. "No, I didn't. If you can recall, I said it's impossible for a *human* to jump off the platform without seriously hurting themselves."

"Oh, yeah," I said, remembering now. "You did say that." Then I thought of that horrible week without him, and when he showed up at the bar. "Hey, that week we weren't together, were you watching me?"

A slow smile crept upon his lips. "Yes, and I'm not sorry for it either." He pulled me to my feet. "C'mon, let's go make supper."

I spent the rest of the night trying to prolong it as much as I could. My mom called and said she'd be here Friday for Easter. I told her Nathan would be joining us, and we would make Easter dinner so she could kick her feet up, which made her really happy (Mom didn't like to cook much). I wanted to ask her about my father, but was afraid she wouldn't come home if I did. And when bedtime came around, I blissfully drifted off to sleep in Nathan's arms while wondering if we'd find anything in the attic we still needed to search.

Chapter Thirteen
Confrontation

"What are you doing?" I asked Nathan when he took my backpack, slung it over his shoulder, and slipped his hand in mine.

We were in the school parking lot among other students who were getting out of their vehicles, chatting in small groups, heading toward the red brick building. Low and heavy clouds hovered in the gray sky. A fine, watery mist stung my eyes when a cool breeze smacked me in the face. I took the sleeve of my rain jacket and swiped at my cheeks.

He flashed me a silly grin. "I'm walking you to your locker."

There were people staring at us, others pointing. *Great.* The rumors about what happened at The Lion's Den must have already circulated. I ducked my head, allowing my hair to shield my face from the onlookers.

"You don't have to do that," I said, my cheeks flaming.

"Remember what I told you last night. I'm not letting you out of my sight until I know you're safe."

"But everybody is staring at us," I complained.

"So." He shrugged. "They're just curious and have the need to perpetuate a story in a dramatic form to suit their own agendas. It's just human nature. People love drama."

He was indifferent about the whole thing and didn't care what others thought. I on the other hand, did care and didn't like the feeling of being placed under a microscope.

We entered the building, smelling of bleach and cleaning products and walked down the busy corridors to my locker. Even in here, people were staring at us, except for the girls gawking at Nathan with their mouths wide open and seemed to not acknowledge my existence. Some of them were part of Ashley's group, and I wondered what they were thinking seeing Nathan with me.

"Hey! Nathan. Right?" Max said–a cute guy with dark, spiky hair and blue eyes, stopping us in the hallway. "Hey, Paige." He smiled, revealing the deep dimples in his cheeks.

"Hey, Max," I said, returning his smile. Max was a good guy.

He looked at Nathan. "That was awesome what you did the other night, when you threw Matt across the room. I was about to jump in and help Tree, but you beat me to it."

The corner of Nathan's mouth lifted. "He deserved it."

"Most definitely," Max said. "Anyway, see you two around."

We said bye and went to my locker–still under watchful eyes. I tried to ignore the stares while opening my locker. And then I heard our names being called above the chattering voices and laughter. Tree was heading our way, towering over everybody. Nathan and I waved, and I was happy to see Carrie with him, holding his hand. Nathan handed me my backpack. I took the stuff I didn't need out and stuck it in my locker.

"Are you going to class with us?" Carrie asked Nathan as I slammed the locker door shut. I so did not want to be here and seriously thought about ditching.

Nathan snaked his arms around me from behind. "No. I just wanted to walk Paige to her locker." His arms felt wonderful, and I found myself wishing we were home, still in bed where it was nice and warm and comfy.

"Have you two seen Matt around?" Tree asked, looking about.

"No," Nathan answered.

"Maybe he's too embarrassed to show his face," I said.

Carrie moved closer to us. "Have you noticed everybody is staring at us?"

I nodded and caught a couple girls doing just that. They quickly looked away, and then the bell rang.

"Carrie, you better get your stuff, or we'll be late for class," I said.

Tree tapped my arm. "I'll see you in an hour." He pecked Carrie on the lips before rushing off to his own class. "I'll see you later, Nathan," he called over his shoulder.

"See ya," Nathan said.

"Be right back." Carrie ran to her locker.

Nathan turned me around. "I'll see you soon." His warm lips touched mine, his tongue darting in my mouth. My entire chest fluttered.

"C'mon, Paige, we got to go." Carrie snatched my hand, pulling me away from Nathan.

She threw him a desperate look. "Sorry, Nathan, but if we're late, Mrs. Hong is going to rip us a new one."

Nathan laughed. "That's okay. I understand." His eyes fell on mine. "Bye, Paige."

Carrie continued pulling me down the hall. I waved good-bye to him before we turned the corner.

***

We made it to our seats right before Mrs. Hong entered the room. I caught Ashley shooting glances at me from over her shoulder. I unzipped my backpack, pretending like I hadn't noticed and pulled my biology book out.

"I have to go to the office to take care of some things," Mrs. Hong told us after marking off everybody in her book. "I trust you will behave. If you don't, there will be detention with me for as long as I see fit." She stood like a miniature general in front of the class. She pointed her finger at us, jerking it back and forth, like reprimanding a child. "Believe me. You do not want to have detention with me, because I'll put you to work." Her voice took on a stern and intimidating tone.

Some of the students shrank back in their seats, while others wouldn't even look at her, as if they were afraid she'd turn them to stone if they did. Unfazed, I opened my notebook and doodled in it, hoping Ashley wouldn't use this opportunity to belittle me.

Satisfied with the reaction she received, Mrs. Hong left.

Ashley twisted in her seat, zeroing in on my face, but I continued to act busy until she spoke.

"So, Paige, I heard that a fight broke out at The *Loser's* Den because of you. Jack (she refused to call him Tree) and some hot guy that I heard is your boyfriend."–she rolled her eyes, like that was impossible for me to have a hot boyfriend–"defended you against Matt. Is that true?"

"Yes, it's true," Carrie said.

Ashley glared at her. "I wasn't talking to you."

Carrie glared back. "Ask me if I care."

"Shut up you guys, or we're going to get into trouble," Jordan said, throwing anxious glances at the door.

Ignoring Jordan, I looked at Ashley. "It's true."

Ashley puckered her lips like she just sucked a lemon. "Poor little Paige, whose father is dead and whose mother is never around, seeking attention from the opposite sex to get the love she has never received from her parents."

That was a low blow, right to my gut. I glanced away to hide the hurt on my face.

"That's not true," Max told her. "I was there, and Paige wasn't nearby when the fight happened."

"Yeah," Carrie chimed in. "And what you just said was uncalled for."

I turned to Ashley. She had a scowl on her Barbie face. "I don't know why you have it in for me. I've never done anything to you, yet you spout these hurtful things at me." I'd never confronted Ashley before and it felt good.

"She's jealous of you," Samantha–who used to hang out with Ashley–said.

"Yeah right," Ashley scoffed. "Why would I be jealous of her? She's pathetic."

"You're jealous because she has true friends, and she's prettier than you." Samantha smiled at me. Her white teeth stood out against her olive skin, revealing their perfection.

Ashley gave her a dirty look. "Whatever."

I didn't think I was prettier than Ashley, but appreciated Samantha's comment and returned her smile.

"*Whatever!*" Max said in a snotty, raised voice, imitating Ashley.

Ashley faced him. "Shut Up!"

"No. You shut up, *pee pee,* pants!" I shouted at her, fed up with her bull crap.

Carrie squealed with laughter, and so did the other kids who remembered Ashley wetting herself in the third grade.

"That's right." Max leaned across his desk, laughing hysterically. "You pissed in your jeans and didn't say anything until the teacher noticed it." He waved his hand under his nose, scrunching his face. "You still smell like urine, Ashley."

"That's because she can't control her bladder, and she has to wear

Depends," Carrie said.

Everybody was laughing now, and Ashley's face turned blood red. She grabbed her stuff and marched out the room. I felt bad doing that to her, but she'd gone too far this time.

"That was a good one, Paige," Samantha said. "I'm so tired of her prima donna attitude and how she treats you."

At that moment Mrs. Hong came in. We immediately turned to our work, pretending to be studying. She glanced around the room, scrutinizing everybody, and then her gaze fell on Ashley's empty seat.

"Where's Ashley?" she demanded in a sharp voice.

Heads popped up to look at her.

"She had to go to the restroom and was afraid if she didn't, she'd have an accident in her pants," Carrie said.

The class erupted into laughter.

"Are you being smart with me?" She jerked a finger at Carrie.

"No, Mrs. Hong, she's not," I said. "Ashley really had to go. I heard she has a weak bladder."

With her hands on her hips, Mrs. Hong glowered at us as the laughter turned to snickers, but she didn't say anything and went to her desk to do some paperwork.

After class, I thanked Samantha and Max for sticking up for me. Max grinned and said Ashley needed a kick in the ass. He lifted his hand and made a fist, bumping knuckles with us before we headed to our next class.

When I entered English class, Tree had his foot on the seat, saving it for me. I told him what happened with Ashley, which pissed him off at first, but when I told him the rest of it, he busted out laughing.

"Man, if I was there I would have put the smack down on her ass." He slammed the palm of his hand on the desk.

"I just hope she leaves me alone now." I thought about what she said and felt like crying. I mean, what she said about my parents was true. I couldn't deny that.

"It's not true what she said," Tree said. "So don't you go believing it."

I looked up to a pair of brown sympathetic eyes and frowned.

The hour went by quickly, and before I left, I handed Mr. Russo my essay and headed to biology class, telling Tree I'd see him at lunch. But after a half hour of trying to listen to Mr. Decker's monotone voice drone on about homeostasis, I thought for sure lunch would never arrive. My mind began to wander, crippling me into thinking about things I'd been avoiding since that night at The Lion's Den. The tip of my pencil snapped when I thought about my father being murdered by a dark spirit and the dark spirit in the restroom threatening me. But thankfully, as murderous thoughts entered my mind, the bell rang. I hopped out of my seat, gave Mr. Decker my work, and then rushed through the crowd of people to my locker. I found Nathan waiting for me, and all the tension in my body lifted.

He smiled. "Hey, you." He was holding two black plastic containers. "I thought I'd surprise you with lunch." This was a surprise. A welcome and much needed one.

I stood on my tiptoes, feeling all eyes on me again–but didn't care this time and kissed him.

"I'm glad you did." I smiled back at him.

"Are you okay?" he asked, studying me.

"Yeah, sure." I turned to my locker and spun the combination.

"Hey, Nathan," Tree said behind me. "Are you going to eat lunch with us?" He sounded pleased, which touched my heart.

"That's the plan," Nathan told him.

"You should do this every day." Carrie sounded pleased as well. I grinned.

I shoved my history book into my backpack and closed the locker door. I turned, the grin still on my face. "Yeah, he should."

"Well, that can be arranged," Nathan said, beaming.

***

"That's not fair." Carrie pointed from across the table in the cafeteria at what Nathan and I were eating. "Tree and I have to eat cafeteria food, and you two are eating gourmet sandwiches."

"You can have half of my sandwich if you want," I offered.

She raised her hand, shaking her head. "No, that's okay. I'm just giving you shit."

"Hey, tell Nathan what happened in class," Tree said to Carrie and me.

I waved a hand at Carrie. "Go ahead and tell him."

Nathan raised a quizzical brow, then shifted his attention to Carrie. I noticed the tightness in his eyes when Carrie told him what Ashley said to me.

"Ever since Zack asked Paige out, Ashley has been rude to her," Carrie said.

I never thought about that before, but Carrie was right. It all started after Zack asked me out. But I still thought it was ridiculous for Ashley to be jealous of me. She had it made.

"Who is Zack?" Nathan asked, and I thought I heard an undertone of jealousy in his voice.

"Some cheese sucker," Tree said, shoving a bunch of fries into his mouth.

"I never went out with him and didn't really want to," I told him offhandedly.

Carrie then went off into that story and what Ashley had done, before finishing the one that happened this morning. I picked at my sandwich, feeling awful now.

"She's something else," Nathan said. "And I think Samantha is right about her being jealous of you."

"Me too," Carrie said, stealing fries off of Tree's tray, smothering them in ketchup.

I shrugged. "I don't know. It seems silly to me."

Nathan looked at Tree. "Can you point her out to me? Is she in the cafeteria?"

Tree glanced around, craning his neck until he spotted her across the room, in plain view. We followed his gaze and caught her looking at us. She quickly faced the other girls sitting at her table.

"That blonde girl over there, wearing the white sweater is Ashley."

"Do me a favor." Nathan leaned forward and lowered his voice. "Don't be too obvious, but tell me when she's looking this way again." There was a mischievous glint in his eyes. He licked his lips and positioned my shoulders toward him. I knew then what he was planning on doing and licked my lips as well.

"Oh, you're bad." Carrie giggled, catching on to Nathan's devious plan.

"She's sneaking peeks right now, but wait a minute," Tree said, watching Ashley.

Nathan angled his body to me, facing in Ashley's direction. He gently brushed my hair away from my face, making my heart sputter.

"That's good." Tree nodded. "She's starting to look more."

Carrie pretended to sneeze and watched Ashley through the curtain of her hair. "The whole table is starting to watch," she reported, shielding her face with her hand.

Tree drummed his fingers on the table. "Okay, now."

Nathan cradled my face in his hands, and his soft lips touched mine. His kisses were slow at first, but then they grew deeper and more passionate. I felt a barrier keeping his desires at bay though, and I knew why. But the outside world didn't know that, and to them I imagined it to be like watching a romantic scene in a movie.

"Omigod," Carrie whispered. "Everybody is staring at you, and Ashley is like totally jealous."

Nathan pulled back and gazed deeply into my face. "I love you," he said with such intense emotion that I lost my breath.

"I love you too," I said, breathlessly.

"Some of the girls at Ashley's table have their hands over their hearts and dreamy looks on their faces," Carrie squealed with delight.

"Dude, that was cool." Tree grinned.

"Normally I wouldn't display such affections in a room full of students, but this time I had to make an exception," Nathan said with a half-smile.

I took a sip of my Dr Pepper, feeling a sense of vindication. Carrie cupped her hands around her lips and mouthed the word "erotic" to me. She then trailed her tongue along her lips and made a silly face. I kicked her foot beneath the table and lifted the collar of my shirt over my mouth, stifling a giggle.

"What are you two laughing about?" Tree asked us.

Carrie bumped her shoulder against his arm. "Sorry, it's a private joke."

The bell rang, and I suddenly became nervous about the "old one."

"Have you two seen Matt today?" I asked.

Tree shook his head, but Carrie nodded, and we stared at her.

"He came up to me after second period, wanting to talk. I told him I didn't want to talk to him after what he said about you. He tried to explain to me why he said it, but I wouldn't listen and told him to leave me alone."

"If he gives you any shit, you better let me know." Tree threw their trash away and turned to Carrie. A dark expression entered his face. He wasn't playing around.

Carrie raised her eyebrows. "All right, but I think he's harmless."

Nathan touched my arm. "I'll see you in an hour."

I nodded and followed Carrie and Tree out the door, not wanting to leave him.

***

The classroom was buzzing with conversation when I got there. I took my regular seat in the back and placed my backpack on the empty seat beside me. My ears were ringing, but I didn't look up, even though I could feel his eyes on me. I unzipped my book bag.

"Paige, can I talk to you?"

I yanked my history book out and turned to him. He sat in the desk next to the aisle, leaning toward me, his right eye black from where Tree had hit him. Everybody seemed to be avoiding our area, but some were staring in our direction.

"I have nothing to say to you," I said, but then he turned his head, and for the first time since that night at The Lion's Den, I saw his eyes glow for a second. The hair on the back of my neck rose, reminding me I was conversing with an ancient dark spirit and not Matt.

And then something in me snapped. I was tired of this charade, pretending like I didn't know who he really was, and I was sick of his stupid games. I had enough. I wasn't playing anymore.

"I think you do," he said, analyzing my face.

I leaned across the aisle, closer to him, and stared fearlessly at him. "I know what you are, and I think it's pointless for me to continue pretending like I don't," I whispered.

He smiled. "I concur with you and actually prefer it that way."

My eyes widened in surprise that he admitted to it, but they didn't waver from his, and I asked him why he hadn't attempted to kill me yet.

"I thought Aosoth already told you why," he said, acting confused.

I gaped at him. "That's her name?" I couldn't believe he told me her name, and he knew what she had said to me about him. I wondered what else he knew.

"Yes." He appeared to be enjoying himself. "You see, I started the fight on purpose so she could be alone with you. Just like now, Mr. Harrin's time is being occupied with a phone call."

My eyes darted to the round clock above the teacher's desk, and I realized class should have started five minutes ago. As I looked around the room at the other students engaged in their own conversations, I noticed him observing me, like a specimen he couldn't quite figure out. He had his head tilted to the side, watching my every movement. It gave me the creeps.

"You started the fight on purpose?"

He nodded. "Indeed."

"What's your purpose in all this, and why am I still alive?" My voice was harsh and demanding. I wanted him to tell me. I was even prepared to shake it out of him if I had to. Then I remembered my promise to Nathan. Damn. But we were surrounded by a bunch of people, so he couldn't hurt me if it came down to it.

His eyes danced across my face. "Because I like you, and I'm curious to see what you can do once the change has been made. That is, if you're still alive." He smirked.

My temper flared. "This is a game to you?" I wanted to blacken his other eye, and imagined my fist smacking into it.

He shrugged. "If you want to look at it in that light, then yes. But it goes deeper, and I will not indulge you in those reasons at this time."

God, he was annoying. "I'm surprised you haven't mentioned about that *damned* ring. Your *girlfriend* seems to think I can find it. She even wants me to give it to her."

He made a disgusted sound with his mouth. "Her vanity overlooks the true nature of my feelings for her. And in the matter of the ring, I believe you're the key instrument on a grander scale in all of this. Who you are, and your lineage leaves no doubt in my mind, you're the one who will tie the knots to the strings Solomon had cut, leading me to my glory."

I laughed sarcastically at him. "I think you're delusional." I was about to say there was no way I would help him, but bit my tongue instead.

"Most humans are delusional," he said, looking like he smelled something foul. "Their minds were made weak, their eyes blind, as soon as they entered this world. But I'm not." He reached to touch my face, and I jerked back in my seat, glaring at him. His face softened, and he smiled. "I have to admit; I do miss your company."

Right then, Mr. Harrin shot through the door, looking frazzled. I glanced at Matt, wondering what he had done. He shrugged innocently. I turned my attention to the front and didn't look at Matt for the rest of the hour.

At the end of class, I handed my work in and rushed out the door before the "old one" had a chance to speak to me again. Nathan was waiting at my locker, happy to see me, but he became anxious when he saw my face. I wondered if I should tell him about my little confrontation with the "old one"and if he would be mad at me. I didn't know. But I had to quickly make up my mind. I could tell by the looks he shot at me he knew something was up.

Chapter Fourteen
Disagreement

"What happened?" Nathan asked. When I didn't respond, he gritted his teeth and growled. "Did he threaten you?"

I slipped my hand in his. "No, he didn't."

"Why do you have a horrified look?" He wanted answers, and I knew I wasn't getting out of this one. I decided to stall.

"Yay. The sun finally came out," I said when we stepped into the sunshine. I tilted my chin up, closing my eyes, feeling the warmth on my face. The grass was wet, though, and squished beneath our feet, making the sides of my shoes damp, a subtle reminder of how fast the weather could change here. Reaching down, I wiped the grass and dirt off my sneakers.

Nathan's voice rose, his fingers twitching between mine. "Are you going to answer my question?"

"I'm horrified because I was talking to a dark spirit, and it still scares me to know they can inhabit humans. But what's weird is when I'm talking to it, I don't think about it since it sounds like the human it's occupying. Except for the guy you cast out. Now that totally freaked me out," I rambled.

When we reached his truck, Nathan stepped around me and leaned against the passenger door. He crossed his arms over his chest and squinted at me.

"Why are you so nervous?"

I made a quick decision to play dumb. "What makes you think I'm nervous?"

"Because a minute ago you were speed talking and that's not like you," he said with a slight smile, busting me out. "What are you avoiding telling me?"

I let out a surrendering sigh. "Fine. I'll tell you on the way home."

He opened the passenger door. I hopped in trying to think of the best way to tell him and wondered what his reaction would be. When he started the truck–without saying a word–and pulled out of the parking lot, I could sense his impatience growing with the long silence between us. I stared out the window, watching an orange VW bus drive by.

"I told the 'old one' I know what he is and there's no need to keep pretending like I don't," I blurted.

He was gripping the steering wheel. "Were you alone with him?"

"No, I wasn't. We were in class when this happened." Nathan instantly relaxed and let out a slow breath, as if he was holding it the whole time. "I promised you I would keep myself safe. I'm not going to break that promise."

"I just thought maybe he cornered you," he muttered, looking straight ahead. "But why did you say that to him?"

I smacked my thighs with my fists. "Because I'm tired of these games, Nathan."

"What do you mean?"

"He knows I'm marked for immortality, and I know what he is," I said in a shrill voice. "So why keep pretending like we don't know?"

Nathan thought about it. "I guess I see your point." He stopped at a red light and looked at me. "What did he say?"

I lifted my shoulders and flipped my palms up. "He said he prefers it that way."

"I bet he does," he grumbled, distrustfully, white knuckling the steering wheel.

"Why would you say that?" I thought it was a good thing.

He stared at the car in front of us with a savage look on his face. "Because he wants to get inside your head, Paige, and I don't like it."

"But that would have been silly if he acted like he didn't know what I was talking about when I told him I knew who he was," I said.

Nathan didn't say anything the rest of the way home, and I stubbornly refused to speak after that. Instead, I stared out the side window and watched the white lines on the road flash by, thinking he had no reason to be upset. Yeah he had a lot of experience dealing with the dark spirits, but

I'd know if the "old one" were trying to mess with my head, and I felt like Nathan wasn't giving me enough credit. I wasn't a stupid girl.

"I'm sorry if I appear to be unreasonable," Nathan said, turning the ignition off. He was looking at me, but I continued to stare out the window. He touched my arm. "Paige, please don't give me the silent treatment."

"You hurt my feelings, you know. It's like you don't trust my judgment." I watched a tan rabbit hop into the forest and had the sudden urge to follow it, thinking of Wonderland.

"I didn't mean to hurt your feelings, and I do trust your judgment …" He trailed off, then continued. "But I think you don't realize how deceitful they really are."

I turned to him. The expression on his face was urging me to try and understand where he was coming from, that he never meant to hurt me, which I knew he wouldn't, but my feelings were still bruised.

"I think I do know because of what he told me." I stepped out of the truck before he could reply. When I closed the door, he took my hand.

"What did he say to you?"

As we walked toward the house, I began to tell him. He quietly listened until I reached the part where the fight was started on purpose so Aosoth could talk to me.

"Wait a minute." He held his hand up. "He told you her name is Aosoth?"

"Yeah, why? Do you know who she is?"

He hung his head and peeked at me, nodding. "Remember when I told you sometimes dark spirits like to portray themselves as demons to frighten and toy with humans?"

"Yeah, you said there's no such thing as demons. It's actually a dark spirit, but humans call them demons because of their religion."

"Right. Well, they also like to adopt names of demons to fit their identity and sometimes create them, to become historical." He paused and ran a hand through his hair. "The name Aosoth represents passion and death."

I unlocked the door and went inside, my blood running cold.

"What do you know about her?"

"She'll stop at nothing to get what she wants, and doesn't think twice about killing somebody if it'll serve her purpose. She does have a flaw, though, which is her wicked narcissism. She becomes so self involved she ends up making foolish mistakes."

"I just don't understand why she would think I won't be immortal for six weeks," I said.

"Because she knows I won't do it and is probably keeping Anwar occupied so he'll stay away from you." He sat on the edge of the couch, resting his elbows on his knees, hunching his shoulders. "What else did he say?" He sounded tired.

I sat on the coffee table in front of him and told him the rest. But then right in the middle of him talking about the "old one's" contempt for humanity, I remembered the last part.

"Oh, and he tried to touch me, but I ducked his touch and glared at him." I grinned, proud of myself for my quick reaction, until I noticed Nathan's eyes turning hard. *Uh-oh.*

"What do you mean?" His voice rumbled from deep within his chest.

I hesitated, but when he raised his eyebrows, I knew I had to finish what I started.

"He reached out like this"–I stuck my hand out toward his face, like I was going to touch it–"and when I pulled back, he admitted he misses my company."

A blaze of anger whipped across his eyes, and he wiped a hand over his face. "I don't want you talking to him anymore." A blurry streak went by me, and he paced the room. "I realize you have class together, but it's obvious he's fond of you, to what extent, I don't know. So I'm asking you not to engage in further conversation with that *monster*."

I looked at him as if he had lost his mind. "Why? I'm perfectly capable of keeping my distance. Besides, I want to ask him who he is because maybe that will help us." I couldn't believe I didn't ask him that and was kicking myself for it now.

He stopped pacing and stared at me. His face was solid as stone, cast in frustration.

"What?"

"Please don't."

"But he told me about Aosoth, and now we know who she is. Don't you think that's helpful to us?" I didn't want to get into an argument, but I thought this was a chance I should take. I'm sure I could find out more information if I were to talk to him some more.

"Listen to me." He took a deep breath to calm himself. "I admit what he said is beneficial to us, but why would he tell you that?"

I shrugged.

"Because he knows you're going to tell me, and he has a reason behind it. You see, you have to start thinking"–he jabbed his finger on his temple–"like them instead of allowing your human to get in the way of your decision making."

"But I want to know his reasons, and if I play him at his own game I can find out."

He blew air out his nose, shook his head, and looked at me. "Do you trust me?"

"Of course," I said, as if that were a silly question for him to ask.

"Then please let it go. Don't talk to him anymore."

I threw my hands in the air. "Fine." I was done with this conversation, knowing this would only lead to a pissing match.

He appeared in front of me, making my shoulders jump back. I could tell by the discontent on his face; he wasn't satisfied with my answer.

"I mean it, Paige. He has his own agenda behind all of this, and you need to stay clear of him." He tried skirting around the fact he just slammed his foot down, but I could hear it in his tone, see it in his eyes. What he really meant to say was, "You *will* stay clear of him."

He stepped back when I abruptly stood up, and followed me into the kitchen. I opened the cupboard and grabbed the coffee canister and filter.

"I don't mean to be overbearing," he said above the sound of water pouring into the coffee pot. "But I need to know you will not talk to him."

I poured the water into the coffee maker, then scooped grounds into the filter, biting my tongue, afraid if I opened my mouth, I might say something rude.

"Paige."

I shoved the coffee pot under the filter holder. The bottom of it made a loud clunking noise against the burning plate. Clicking the button on, I faced him. He stood there with his legs spread apart, hands on his hips, waiting for my reply.

"I told you I won't talk to him. What else do you want me to say?"

"Why are you mad?"

"I'm not mad. I'm irritated because I disagree with you, but I will honor your request and not talk to him. Unless, Mr. Harrin makes us do a project together."

He took my hand, and drew me into an embrace. I melted against him and breathed him in, which instantly took away my irritability.

"I just want you to be safe," he said.

"I know, but let's talk about something else, like what did you do today?"

He pulled back, but kept his arms around me. "I do have some good news."

"You do?" I could feel the excitement and hope surfacing on my face.

"I spoke to Anwar, and he promised he'll be here within three weeks."

I leaned my head on his chest. "Thank God."

The aroma of fresh coffee filled the kitchen. I reluctantly tore myself away from him to get us some. We still had to search the attic, and I needed a jolt of caffeine before I could attempt a project like that.

"Did you find anything out about the ring or my father?" I asked, pouring coffee into two mugs. I was starting to doubt my father had actually known where it was.

Nathan made an appreciative sound when I handed him his coffee. "No, and personally I don't think the ring exists because it's been sought after for thousands of years, and nobody has found it."

"Have you ever seen *The Lord of The Rings*?"

He nodded while taking a sip of his coffee. "Yes, I know. This ring reminds you of that movie, but unfortunately this is real. Anybody can look up The Seal of Solomon on the internet, and see for themselves the legend behind it. So it's realistic to believe the possibility of its existence, where Tolkien's story is pure fantasy, an excellent one, but not real."

"Well, even if the ring doesn't exist, I think we should start looking in the attic to see if we can find anything," I said, setting my mug on the counter.

"I agree." He took one last swig of coffee and followed me up to the attic.

***

The next couple of hours went by quickly due to us finding stuff from my childhood and laughing about it, like my Indian costume I wore for my second grade Thanksgiving play.

"That's so cute." Nathan held it up. "I bet you can still fit into it."

"Ha, ha. Very funny," I said when he started laughing. I kneeled next to him and dug through the box. It was full of old coloring books and childhood projects.

He looked at me when I pulled a picture out and laughed.

"What did you find?"

It was a picture of that same Thanksgiving play with all the kids lined up on the stage. Carrie and I were one of the kids in the front row, and she was dressed like an Indian too. Tree was the Indian chief, tall and proud in the back, above everybody. Brayden was standing in front of Tree, a proud Indian himself.

I handed him the picture. "Guess which one is me, Carrie, and Tree," I said, still laughing.

"Here you are." He pointed, spotting me right away. "And is this Carrie?" He tapped his finger on her face.

"Yeah, she used to have long hair like me and hated it. So in eighth grade she wacked it off to her shoulders and had been wearing it like that ever since."

He turned his attention back to the picture and laughed.

"The chief is definitely Tree."

"That's right. You can't really miss him since he's the tallest and sometimes carries that goofy look on his face when he's being silly. Oh, and here's Brayden." I pointed to the cute dark-haired kid with the green eyes.

"That's Brayden, huh?" His forehead creased.

"Yeah. He's cute, but not as cute as you." I pinched his leg and winked at him.

He pursed his lips and stared at the picture for a long moment, deep in thought. The expression on his face appeared distant, almost sad.

"What are you thinking?"

He peeked at me. "I know this is absurd, but I'm envious of your relationship with Brayden." He looked almost apologetic, which didn't make sense to me.

I blinked. "Why?"

"Because the two of you have a history together."

"That's true, but all four of us have a history together. My mom used to babysit them and that's how we became our own little family."

He put the picture back in the box. "I think the relationship you have with Tree and Carrie is marvelous. Not many people in this world have friends like them or like you. I just wish I could have been part of that and have those memories to share with you."

I rose and moved behind him, locking my arms around his shoulders. "I understand, but you and I are already creating some pretty amazing memories."

My stomach growled, rescuing Nathan from this awkward moment.

He chuckled. "I think it's time for supper."

We went downstairs and made chicken fajitas–he cut up the vegetables and chicken, and I cooked them. Afterwards, we went back to the attic for an hour. We didn't find anything helpful, but there was still plenty of stuff to go through, so our hope didn't falter.

We spent the rest of the evening cleaning ourselves up and watching a show about prophecies on the History Channel. I had my head in Nathan's lap. His fingers drifted to the side of my face, lightly rubbing it. I closed my eyes, and my thoughts scattered, breaking free from their daily routine. Images of my life kept flashing, until they settled on Nathan and me.

I was now falling into a gorgeous dream of us being on a white sandy beach. All my worries and what would happen tomorrow when I saw Matt didn't exist here. And the last thing I remembered was Nathan's feathery touch on the apple of my cheeks, and his distant voice saying something about my premonitions.

Chapter Fifteen
Mystery

When my alarm clock went off the next morning, screaming in my ear, I groaned and smacked it, then drifted back to sleep.

Nathan and I were somewhere in Europe, walking across an old stone bridge, blissfully happy. The sky was gray, and there were quacking ducks in the river below us. We stopped in the middle of the bridge. He took my hand and bent on one knee. He opened his mouth to say something, but then a loud beeping noise came out. I awoke with a start, heart pounding.

"Damn alarm." I switched it off.

Nathan sat up and yawned. "What's wrong?"

I looked at him through bleary eyes. "I was dreaming we were in Europe, and I didn't want to wake up."

"One day we'll be there, love," he said in a British accent. "And it'll be smashing."

I giggled and covered my face, shielding it from the bright, gray light streaming through the gap between the curtain directly at me. I wondered how long he stayed in Europe and all the things he'd seen, so I asked.

"I've lived there most of my immortal life," he said. "And I've seen almost everything."

I rubbed the sleep out of my eyes and squinted at him. "Like what?"

He scratched his head and yawned. "I've seen Notre Dame Cathedral, the Roman Coliseum, Stonehenge, and so forth."

"Now I'm jealous." I pouted.

He leaned me across his lap, and although he had pillow creases across his cheeks and looked like a four-year-old who just woke up from a long nap, he grinned. "There's no need for you to be jealous, because I'm going to take you to all the places I've been, and we'll explore new places together."

I smiled, but then a thought occurred to me and it faded.

"Are you okay?"

I got up and remained quiet for a minute before I asked, "Did you have a companion with you?"

He stepped out of bed and stretched. I averted my gaze, only to find him standing in front of me, making me jump.

"There's never been anybody before you, if that's what you're hinting at. And I've only been in love once–with you." He softly kissed me, making my heart skip several beats. "I have some really good friends," he continued, "but I've spent most of my time alone, exploring, learning new things, tracking, observing dark spirits."

I placed my hand on his bare muscular chest, and every fiber in my being longed for him. I dropped my hand and turned away, busying myself by gathering my clothes, feeling the hot blood pooling in my cheeks. When I rushed by him, heading to the bathroom, he stopped me and brushed a finger down my cheek. I looked up. His eyes were bright, which made me crave him even more.

"Nathan, you know we can't do this until I'm over the …" I didn't want to say or think about the nasty thing I was on.

"I know." He brushed his finger on my cheek again. "But when I touch your red cheek, it's almost like I can touch the fire burning inside us now."

"Okay, well…" I stammered. "I'm going to get dressed and stuff." I rushed out the room straight into the bathroom, immediately splashing cold water on my face. In my mind I chanted: *grandmother, grandmother, grandmother*, hoping it would work for me like I heard it worked for guys who wanted to get rid of their boner. I felt like a dork doing it, but a minute later my breathing went back to normal, and I was able to finish getting ready, all the while wondering how this day would turn out.

***

"I wanted to tell you," Nathan said on the way to school. "I think I figured out why you have your premonitions and why you get them in an audio form."

"Really? I thought I heard you say something about it last night, but I fell asleep and forgot to ask you about it earlier."

"That's understandable considering the circumstances," he purred.

I shoved his arm. "Stop it."

He laughed. "I think it's your spirit guide talking to you."

"I don't know." I shook my head. "Why would he give me cryptic messages? Unless, he was once a troll, who used to live under a bridge and wouldn't allow people to pass until they solved his riddles." I grinned at him.

"I get the sarcasm, Paige, but I'm serious. Maybe it comes to you that way to prepare you for the life you're soon going to enter. It's teaching you to use your mind, so you can figure complex things out."

"I think you're grasping at straws here." I yawned, not wanting to talk about this.

"I think if you started tuning yourself into it," he said, ignoring my comment, "you'd be able to connect with your guide more."

"I think I have more important things to apply my energy to right now, but I appreciate your thoughts on it." I could hear the snottiness in my voice and instantly felt bad.

He didn't say anything, which made me feel even worse.

"I hope I didn't hurt your feelings," I quickly said, afraid I had. "It's just the voice I hear is a sore spot with me, and I don't want to deal with it right now."

He parked beside a row of trees, at the far end of the school's parking lot and turned to me. If I had hurt his feelings, it didn't show. His eyes were filled with nothing but gentleness.

"It's okay. I understand. I just wanted to share my thoughts with you on it."

I laced my fingers with his. "I do appreciate it, and I want you to always share your thoughts with me, even if we end up disagreeing. And I'm sure you want the same from me too."

He raised my hand to his lips and kissed it. "Absolutely."

"Now, I'm going to get this day over with and avoid talking to the 'old one,' even though I really want to, but I understand your concern."

"Believe me, I know what I'm talking about."

I dropped my eyes and turned to open the door, but he took my arm before I could grasp the handle.

"I love you." There was a fierceness in his voice.

I looked at him and became breathless when I saw the devotion on his face.

Was it possible to keep falling in love with the same person every day? Because it seemed each day I spent with him, I fell deeper in love.

"I love you, too," I said, hearing the fervent emotion in my own voice.

A slow sexy smile formed on his lips, muddling my thoughts. He stepped out of the truck and opened my door, taking my hand. And for the rest of this short week, this was how I started out each school day, with Nathan holding my hand, walking me to my locker.

When lunch time came around, Nathan was at my locker, holding two plastic containers in his hands. We ate with Tree and Carrie who were always happy to see him, and Carrie told him about Ashley not saying a word to us while I fretted over next hour with the "old one." I wasn't sure how I would handle the situation, or if I'd be able to clamp my mouth against my own curiosities, but I had to try.

When I got to history class, the "old one" wasn't there, and I overheard Steve saying Matt had the flu pretty bad. I leaned back in my seat and breathed out all my tension, thinking how pleased Nathan would be with this information. I couldn't wait to give him the news and found myself becoming more and more antsy as the minutes ticked by. Finally, the bell rang. I jumped out of my seat, snatched my backpack, and hurried to my locker.

"Guess what." I said, swinging our hands in the air on the way to his truck, thinking what a good day this had been. A whistle was being blown, and I could hear people clapping. Baseball practice, I imagined. It was about that time for spring training. I wasn't much into sports, although baseball was fun to play.

Nathan looked at me, and by the smile in his eyes, my mood seemed to be rubbing off on him.

I watched an airplane fly through the swirling clouds in the gray sky, and cheerfully told him what Steve had said. His fingers tightened around mine, and we stopped walking. He looked like a man who was just told he had terminal cancer.

My stomach dropped. "What is it?"

"If Matt is really sick, the 'old one' has vacated his vessel, and taken over another one." He rubbed the side of his neck and moved his head around. "This isn't good, Paige, and I need you to be on guard at all times."

"But what if he's lurking around here?" I frantically looked about.

"They can only lurk in places that suits their own energy, which puts a lot of restrictions on them, and one of the reasons why they love being in the flesh because they can go wherever they want."

"But I don't understand. If they can only lurk in certain areas, how can they find a vessel?" My voice came out all panicky, and I could feel the horror on my face.

"If there are soulless bodies nearby, spirits can jump in them. Or if people call to them, evoking the same energy, they can enter that area. But truthfully, most soulless humans vibrate an energy similar to dark spirits, so they can easily find their vessels."

There was a group of kids across the parking lot talking, and I suddenly became envious of their simple life. Now I knew why some people say ignorance was bliss. But then again, I was the type of person who wanted to know the truth, even if it would hurt me.

But why couldn't I have just one good day? Was that too much to ask?

When we reached his truck, he opened the door. "I'm sorry I ruined your mood." He sounded like I felt–glum.

"That's okay. I need to know this stuff." I hopped in and slid down the seat, pulling the hood of my jacket over my head.

"What are you thinking?" Nathan asked, pulling out of the parking lot.

"I just want to have a normal day without all these worries," I mumbled. "And right now, I want to disappear from it all."

"Would it help if we did normal things tonight and not talk about it?"

I lifted my hands and dropped them heavily into my lap. "We have to search the attic."

"That can wait until tomorrow." There was an appeasing tone in his soft voice.

"Okay, but did you find out anything today?"

"I spoke to Anwar about Aosoth, and he said she likes to move around a lot, which makes it difficult to catch her. But I did track down the girl she had taken over that night at The Lion's Den."

I flipped my hood off, shocked he found her. "You did?"

He nodded. "She was at the gym, but Aosoth was no longer inside of her."

I dropped my eyes and fiddled with my fingers. *That sucks.*

"There's more," he said. "When your father was born, a maid in a motel outside of Phoenix discovered him abandoned in one of the rooms."

I slapped a hand over my heart and could hardly breathe. I wasn't expecting this.

"Do you want me to continue, because this can wait?" He looked concerned, like I might fall to pieces, which was debatable at this point.

"Please do," I whispered. "I–I want to hear this."

"I called in a favor to a friend of mine, and he got word the maid is Hispanic. He located her, and she told him a young girl checked in with an older man, and they stayed holed up in the motel room for a few days. They wouldn't allow her in to clean the room, but they requested more towels and linen." He took a deep breath and continued. "After the third day, she discovered the door was ajar and heard a baby crying. When she went inside, she found a pile of bloody towels and linen. The baby was wrapped in a white bed sheet and placed in a beer crate. There was a note, written in block letters, pinned to the sheet saying to 'take care of him because he's special.'"

I suddenly realized we were home, and my face was wet.

"Does she know their names?" my voice cracked.

He shook his head, closely watching me.

"What did they look like?" A rush of anxiety poured through my veins.

"She told him the girl was short and pretty with fiery red hair."

"And the guy?" My heart was pounding painfully.

Nathan placed his hand on my shoulder. "You need to calm down. Your heart is racing, and you look like you're going to faint. Maybe we should finish this conversation later."

I took a couple of deep breaths. "What did the guy look like?" I persisted, not caring my hands were shaking, my heart still pounding, and everything seemed to be moving away from me. It was as if somebody forcefully shoved my chest, wheeling me out of the atmosphere.

"She described an older version of Matt," he said against his better judgment.

I sucked in a sharp breath and stuck my head between my knees, desperately trying to get air into my lungs. The more I tried, the tighter my chest became. Nathan was beside me in a flash, practically ripping the door off. His hand went to the center of my back, rubbing it in slow circles.

"Try to match your breaths with the movement of my hand," he instructed.

I tried, but all I could think about was the possibility my father had been conceived by a human possessed by a dark spirit, maybe by the "old one." And then I wondered if his interest in me might be because in a weird kind of way I was his granddaughter. A dark, haunting feeling sucked me into a spinning black hole. I wondered feebly if I gave into it, where it would take me?

"You need to *concentrate,* Paige," Nathan demanded when I closed my eyes. "Listen to my breaths," he said next to my ear, breathing loud enough for me to hear. "Don't think of anything else, but how to breathe correctly."

I did what he said, latching onto each one of his breaths with forced concentration, and eventually was able to pull out of it. Nathan tilted his sweaty face to the cloudy sky and blew out a sigh of relief, then dropped his head into my lap. I ran my fingers through his hair, and we stayed like that for a while, listening to the chirping birds and a dog barking in the distance.

"I'm taking you inside," he finally said, scooping me into his arms. "You're in no shape to be walking." I didn't argue and clung to his neck.

Once inside, he placed me on the couch and sat on the floor beside me.

"I'm sorry I scared you," I said.

"There's no need to be sorry." He took my hand and held it. "It's not your fault. But I think we should drop it for tonight."

I wondered if I'd be able to handle asking him what I had thought about earlier. I inhaled and exhaled a few times, thinking I could, but he frowned at me.

"Forget about it, Paige."

"I'm okay. I think I can handle it."

He shook his head.

"Please. Just one question, and I won't ask anything else tonight?"

He groaned. "What is it?"

"Do you think a dark spirit possessed the human who got my grandmother impregnated? And do you think it was the 'old one'?"

He narrowed his eyes. "That's two questions."

"So. Just answer them, and I won't mention it again tonight," I bargained.

"Yes, and quite possible," he said, and when I opened my mouth, he stuck his finger on my lips. "No more questions."

***

"Last night was nice, watching sitcoms on tv, and the documentary on elephants was interesting. Don't you think?" Nathan was trying to deter me from the questions I'd been itching to ask him since yesterday, and even though he knew me better than that, it didn't stop him from trying to talk about something else.

I stared out the windshield, watching the wipers move rapidly across it from the sheeting rain. Several bolts of red and blue lightning webbed across the dark sky. A loud cracking noise erupted above us, making me jump, but it didn't break my determination.

"If a dark spirit is in a human during the conception of a child, can his darkness enter that child?"

The corner of his mouth curled. "You're relentless."

"Well, I want to know."

"No," he said. "A dark spirit is dark because it chose to be; it's not an inherited trait."

I scratched my head. "I don't understand any of this."

His eyes turned thoughtful. "It's a mystery and probably won't get solved until after you become immortal."

"Why is that?"

"Because we already have a lot to deal with right now."

"That's true," I admitted. "But when I become immortal I want to see if we can find my grandmother. In fact, we *must* find her," I stressed, afraid we wouldn't. I wanted to meet her, even though she had abandoned my father.

"We will," he promised, pulling into the school parking lot.

I slapped a hand on my leg. "I'm going to get through today and tomorrow, and we're going to have a good time during this three-day weekend. You'll meet my mom and everything will be great." I was determined to move forward and not get caught up in misery or be scared about the "old one" possibly residing in another human.

"Sounds like a wonderful plan," Nathan said, smiling.

***

The next two days at school turned out fine. Ashley didn't talk to me, Matt was still sick, and not once did my ears ring. I was beginning to feel halfway normal. That was until Thursday afternoon when Nathan and I were at the grocery store getting food for Easter dinner.

At first we were having fun, acting like a silly married couple. He took charge of pushing the cart while I tossed food into it. But when I threw a frozen pie in the cart, he picked it up in disapproval.

"What is this?" He waved it in the air with a shocked look on his face.

"Why, honey, it looks like a frozen apple pie," I teased.

A young mother with her cooing baby in the grocery cart wheeled by us and snickered.

A tight, playful smile formed on his lips, and he batted his eyes. "Pop tart. Love muffin. The sweetest desire of my loins"–he covered his crotch with the pie box and swirled his hips around, making me laugh–"I'm well aware of that, but this simply will not do. Our pastry needs to be homemade, not from a store, and *certainly* not frozen."

I tightened my lips in an attempt to keep a straight face.

Lifting my eyebrows, I said, "Are *you* going to make it then?"

He stared at the ceiling and moved his head around as if he was watching a fly, then his gaze shifted on me. He innocently pointed at himself. "Are you talking to me?"

"Give me that," I said when he laughed, snatching the box from him. "We'll make it together." I opened the freezer door to put the pie back, wincing from the blast of cold air, and then the ghostly voice spoke:

"Tragedy strikes to the least expected, but they will reunite, and a new life begins."

I dropped the box and it smacked the floor. I stared at it, but not really seeing it. All I could think about through the zinging noise in my head was the word *tragedy.*

"Paige." Nathan picked up the box and stuck it in the freezer. He lifted my chin. My eyes shifted to his. "What is it? Did you have a premonition?" he murmured.

I nodded, feeling a sludge of sickness slosh inside my belly.

"C'mon, I think we have everything," he said, rubbing my shoulder.

As Nathan paid for our groceries, I stood in a daze, replaying the premonition in my mind. I could feel his eyes worrying over me, and his anxiousness when the receipt machine jammed, and we had to wait for the cashier to fix it. I continued to concentrate on the premonition, determined to figure it out. But I soon snapped out of it when a tantrum-throwing toddler started screaming at the top of his lungs. He ran by me, knocking me over. Nathan caught my arm before I fell face first on the concrete.

"I'm sorry," the mother apologized, chasing after him.

I turned to Nathan, my arm still in his grasp and smiled gratefully at him.

"Thank you."

"Anytime," he said, reminding me of the first night we met, flipping my stomach.

A few minutes later, as we were crossing the parking lot, the cart wheeling noisily over the rocky asphalt, I told Nathan I'd tell him about my premonition on the way home. For some reason, I had an unsettling feeling in my gut, and wanted to get out of there as quickly as possible. My hasty behavior made him nervous. He told me to get in the truck, but before I made it to the door, a high-pitched ringing sounded in my ears, and that was when I saw her coming.

Chapter Sixteen
Information

She was a tall blonde, wearing skinny jeans tucked in Ugg boots and a brown suede jacket that grazed her hips. *Playboy material,* I thought, and so did a couple young guys walking to their car. They stared at her like two horny dogs waiting to pounce on the bitch strolling by. But when the squeal of a car alarm went off, they jumped and turned the other way.

As she approached us, Nathan pushed me behind him and stood in a protective stance. I peeked around his side and saw the menacing sneer on her beautiful face. There were people in the parking lot coming and going, but they were too caught up in their own dealings to show any interest in ours.

"The notorious Nathan Caswell. What a pleasure to finally meet you," she said in a surgery, sweet voice. "My sisters and some of my brothers were right. You are a hottie. But I have to say, there are quite a few who would like to see you suffer." Her eyes darted to me and a beam of light swiped across them. I shrank behind Nathan, now knowing this was Aosoth.

Nathan swept his arm back, further shielding me. "Stay away from her," he warned, his voice deep and dangerous.

She leaned to the side to get a better look at me, then fixed her gaze on Nathan. "I could easily make it happen by ripping her throat out." She paused, her expression turning dark. "Or better yet, I could round up some of my brothers and make you sit and watch while we tear her from limb to limb."

A squeak escaped my lips, and I covered my mouth. Nathan's hands clenched into fists, and the thought of passion and death entered my mind.

"If any one of you touches her, I will personally create a hell for each and everyone involved, mercilessly inflicting agonizing pain upon you like you've never imagined!" His words were not a threat, but a promise, leaving no doubt in my mind he'd keep.

Her face twitched uneasily. "Yes, there is a brutality in you that runs deep. I see it in your eyes, and you wouldn't think twice about unleashing it for the one behind you." She hesitated for a minute; fear flickering across her eyes, but then she threw her head back and shrieked with laughter. I winced. "Nathan Caswell finally has a weakness."

"Shut up!" I yelled, now more angry than scared. I wanted to slap that taunting smile off her face and attempted to step around Nathan, but his arm flew out again, pushing me back.

Aosoth bent over with her hands out like she wanted to pinch me and wiggled her fingers. She looked amused, which was unsettling. "You're a feisty little thing." She straightened her back, still staring at me, her eyes turning cold. "I want to know if you have any information about the ring, and if you're going to give it to me."

"She'll tell you when her six weeks are up," Nathan angrily spat at her.

She whipped her head around, her face twisting into a grotesque mask. "I wasn't asking you," her hate hurled at him. "And if it wasn't for the 'old one,' I would have forced an answer out of her that night."

"What's that supposed to mean?" I recalled that night when I asked her if I could think about my answer, and how scared I was when she pondered it. I then realized it was all an act, just to screw with me. I mean, the "old one" told me he started the fight on purpose so she could talk to me. Therefore, what she said in the restroom had already been preplanned by the "old one." So it was because of him I was alive and given the time to do research on my father. But he had to know from hanging out with me for all those months, I wouldn't give them the ring. His motives made no sense to me.

"He's fond of you," Nathan said before she could answer me. "But we both know he's more fond of her."

"Don't take me for a fool. He has his sights on this one"–she pointed at me in disgust– "that's why she's still alive and because some of us are too coward to cross you,"she squawked at Nathan.

"He is fond of you," I told her, following Nathan's lead. "The other day in history class he told me if it wasn't for Aosoth, he wouldn't have been able to pull off what he did at The Lion's Den that night."

She gaped at me. "He told you my name?"

I faked a smile. "I think he has a sweet spot for you."

"Well," she said with a smug look, "I am good at what I do, and I've never been cast out."

"That's probably one of the reasons he respects you," Nathan pointed out.

She suddenly became giddy, twirling in circles with her arms out, confirming to me how stupid and nutty she was. But then she stopped and turned to us. "Tell me about the ring," she demanded. "He'll want to know."

"We haven't found anything yet," Nathan answered.

She waved a hand in the air like she was shooing a fly, clearly in a much better mood. But then she drew closer, and Nathan's arm flew back in front of me.

"You'll find the ring," she told me, her baby blues tunneling into mine. "Unless, I have to kill you before then." She clapped her hands together. "Anyway, you don't have to give me your answer now, so I shall be off." She paused and smirked at Nathan. "Don't bother tracking this human down like you did with the other one. I'll be out of it by the time you do." She pivoted and strutted across the parking lot to a tall dark-skinned guy waiting for her. She placed her arm around his waist, and he looked over his shoulder at us with damning eyes.

Nathan stared at him, delivering a threatening message through the murderous expression on his face. "Get in the truck, Paige. I'll put the cart away."

As we headed home, I watched the lightning flickering behind the dark clouds, turning them pinkish. Fat rain drops splattered the windshield, causing the automatic wipers to come on. I sat back trying to reel in my scattered thoughts so I could deal with each one individually. But before I could figure which to focus on, Nathan chose for me.

"What was your premonition about?"

"Don't you want to talk about what just happened with Aosoth?" His ears were red, and I thought maybe it wasn't such a good idea to talk about her after all. "Maybe we shou--"

"There's nothing to talk about," he said through clenched teeth. "She has no qualms about killing you if she sees fit to, and I'm *not* going to allow it to happen."

I shuddered and hugged myself to hide it and noticed Nathan denting the steering wheel with his tight grip. I decided to change the subject before he broke it. "Why are some of them afraid of you?"

He slowed to allow an elderly man pull out in front of him. The man raised his hand in thanks. Nathan returned the gesture and looked at me.

"I'm a loner, Paige. Or was before you. When I became immortal, I made it my prime objective to be a thorn in their side by spending most of my energy tracking, observing, and disrupting their plans. The ones who are afraid of me know I can be just as callous as they are. I've caused some of them tremendous amounts of pain to obtain the answers I needed. I'm not proud of it, but neither are the soldiers in war who have to do unspeakable things in order to protect their country."

"So you do have a brutality within you like she said?"

"Yes, but I've kept it tethered, and never once had the cord ever been broken. However, it almost snapped that night in the parking lot."

I gulped, remembering how petrified I was and could still hear the freaky guy's voice speaking Latin inside my head. It seemed like it happened a thousand years ago when really it hadn't been.

"Aosoth obviously knows my history, and she's right," he said. "I wouldn't think twice about giving into that side of me if somebody were to hurt you."

I didn't respond, and thought I'd be dead right now if it wasn't for Nathan. My heart skipped several beats when it occurred to me he loved me so much, he'd move heaven and earth to protect me.

"Now tell me about the premonition you had."

I really didn't want to. What I wanted to talk about was how did Aosoth knew Nathan had tracked down the other vessel, and who was that guy with her? But it seemed pointless to bring up. I mean, dark spirits were tricksters, and the guy with her had to be a soulless human, a backup maybe, or something for her to play with. So I repeated the premonition to Nathan, sounding and feeling ominous.

Nathan parked the truck in front of my house and at the same time a loud boom erupted from the sky, releasing a steady stream of rain. He reached behind his seat for an umbrella, telling me to stay there. When he opened my door, he held it over me, making sure I wasn't getting wet.

"I think it's talking about your grandpa or your mom," he said, as we picked up the groceries.

I froze with the bags in my hands, my stomach knotting up.

"What?" My mind went totally blank for a second.

"C'mon, we need to get inside," he said above the sound of the pouring rain.

We hurried across the lawn. I noticed Mr. Kitty wasn't on the porch and wondered where he went, but before I could look about, Nathan nudged me inside. I immediately headed to the kitchen. I dropped the groceries on the table, then took the ones from Nathan so he could put the umbrella in its stand beside the front door. My chest felt empty and cold. When he entered the kitchen, he embraced me.

"Try not to worry." His voice was soft next to my ear. "I could be wrong."

I pulled back to look at him.

"But what did you mean by it?"

"What I meant was your mom has been estranged from her father for a long time now, and maybe something is going to happen to bring them together and a new life will begin for them."

I thought about it for a minute. "But we don't even know if he's still alive."

"Maybe that's what it meant when it said to the least expected."

"I don't know." I held my cheeks in my hands, confused.

He leveled his eyes with mine. "Try not to worry. Your mom is going to be here tomorrow. Maybe she'll surprise you with information about your grandfather. In the meantime, we have a lot of work to do before she arrives. We also need to finish looking in the attic."

"You're right," I said, even though I couldn't shake off this sickening feeling I had in the pit of my stomach. "We should get busy then."

***

"This sucks," I complained after we went through the last box in the attic. I stood, swiping a cobweb out of my way and screamed when I thought I saw a spider crawling on my fingers. Rubbing my hand against my jeans, I jumped around.

Nathan shook his head, laughing to himself like he couldn't believe how ridiculous I was being. I think he was even slightly annoyed, but I didn't care because spiders were creepy and I didn't like them.

"You're fine, Paige. There wasn't a spider in it."

"How do you know?" I screeched, flinging my arms in the air.

"Because it was a cobweb."

"Maybe Aosoth was wrong about my father." I roughly swiped my hand across my cheek, feeling like something just crawled on it.

"You need to get over your fear of spiders or the dark spirits might use it to their advantage," Nathan said, smacking the dirt off his hands.

I rolled my eyes. "Nu-huh."

He peeked at me from beneath his lashes, his lips curving into an ornery smile. I took a couple cautious steps back, recognizing the devious look on his face. And then the next thing I knew, he had me slung over his shoulder.

"They're going to put you in a big box full of spiders," he teased.

"No. They're. Not," I half screamed and laughed.

He flipped me upside down, acting like he was going to lower me into a box. I grabbed his legs, pushing my body weight against his. He tripped backwards, knocking a metal cabinet over, and then swiftly lifted me to my feet, right before the cabinet fell to the floor with a loud bang. I latched onto his arm and flinched.

"Are you all right?" He glanced at the cabinet, then at me. "I'm sorry."

"That's okay," I said, amazed he knocked it over. "I don't even know why this cabinet is up here. It must have taken at least two guys to haul it."

Nathan was staring at the floor where the cabinet used to be. I stepped beside him and followed his gaze but didn't see anything except for a knot hole in the wooden plank floor. He moved to it and knelt. As I took a closer look, I noticed it was a shorter piece of wood flushed in between with the rest of the planks.

"What are you doing?" I bent next to him as he hooked his pinky in the hole and gasped when he lifted it. He set the plank aside and got on his hands and knees to look inside.

"I think it's a secret compartment," he said.

"Why do you think that?" My heart pounded nervously against my chest as I wondered if we finally found something.

"Because for one, there's no installation, and for another"–he reached his hand inside and pulled out what looked like a brown leather journal–"because of this." He grinned.

"Holy crap!" I snatched the journal from him. "Is there anything else in there?"

He checked again. "No, just that."

I watched him put the cabinet back while I brushed the dirt off the journal and found myself struggling with whether to open it or not. I knew I had to, but did I really want to know what was written inside it? The curious part of me did, but the other part of me was terrified.

I sat on a crate with the journal in my lap and stared at it, wondering why Mom would hide this from me. What did she know? I guess I was wrong about her being uninventive.

Nathan sat beside me. "Are you going to open it?"

"I'm afraid of what's written inside," I said apprehensively.

"It's okay. Whatever is in it, we'll deal with it together."

"Do you think we should move everything out of the attic and see if there's anything else under the floor?" I really didn't want to and became overwhelmed just thinking about it, but if we had to I would.

He shook his head. "I don't think it's necessary. We moved everything we went through, except for the metal cabinet."

I hung my head, causing my hair to fall forward, curtaining my face. I stared at the journal, telling myself I could do this, fingering the leather cord around it, but I still wasn't able to untie it.

Nathan tucked a lock of hair behind my ear and leaned forward. "Do you want me to open it?" His expression was sympathetic.

I handed him the journal and watched with bated breath as he unwounded the cord and opened it. His eyes skimmed across the pages, his face becoming more and more intrigued. I couldn't take the suspense any longer.

"What does it say?" I leaned closer and saw the words "Qumran caves."

"This is interesting," he said and continued to read. "He wrote the Israeli Antiquities Authority was in the Judean Desert looking for scrolls. He also mentioned the Qumran caves. He speculates a couple of Arab kids came across a cave in one of the barren hills and found some historic treasures they sold in the black market. He thinks one of them was the ring."

"Why would he think that? And why would he be able to figure this out and not the immortals or the dark spirits?" It didn't make sense. I mean, seriously, people have been searching for it for thousands of years, yet my father–a simple human–came up with this possibility.

Nathan lifted his eyes to mine. "Have you ever searched and searched for something and couldn't find it, yet somebody else was able to with no problem?"

"Yeah," I said, getting his point. "Like when I couldn't find my keys the other day and you found them."

"Exactly," he said. "And your father must have done some extensive research in order to come to the answer. He probably even faked his own identity in order to obtain the information he has in this book. Frankly, I think your father was quite clever."

I smiled. "I think so too. But why would the kids sell the ring when they could have used it to control the dark spirits?"

"They probably didn't realize what they had, and there's more to it than just wearing the ring. You have to know how to use it in order for it to work, like what incantations to use." He fanned the pages, revealing blank paper, making me realize my father didn't get to finish what he had set out to do.

"Do you think any of this can help us?"

Nathan went back to reading the journal, too captivated to acknowledge my question. I leaned next to him, trying to read what he was reading, but I couldn't understand it. My father's sloppy penmanship wasn't easy to read and appeared to be written in a frenzy. There were a lot of scattered notes and references that made my head spin in complete disarray.

"What are the Essenes?" I asked when that word caught my attention.

He remained quiet.

I elbowed his side. "Hey, are you going to answer me, or should I leave you alone?"

He closed the journal and wound the leather cord around it.

"Sorry," he said and shook it in the air. "But I could easily get lost in this."

I lifted my eyebrows and nodded. "I see that. I'm just glad you can understand it because I don't."

"Do you mind if I hang onto this and read it later?"

"No, I don't mind, but I'd like for you to answer my question."

He looked down, scratched his head, and tilted his face to me, half smiling. "Um, what was it you asked me?"

"About the Essenes," I reminded him.

"Oh, right," he said, now remembering. "They were a Jewish sect who lived in Qumran, secluded from the general population. They lived in piety and believed in the absence of personal property and money. They had a strict observance of the Sabbath and devoted themselves to charity and studying the books of the elders. They also preserved secrets. Your father thinks they had the ring, along with other treasures, but they hid them in the caves, during the great revolt against the Romans."

"Why would they have this stuff if they didn't believe in personal property?"

"Because they believed the angels chose them to protect it."

"Interesting," I murmured, staring off into space.

He stood. "Yes, it is. They use to pray daily to the angels and were supposedly attuned to them."

I followed him down the stairs as he went on about the Essenes developing the field of angelology and how their beliefs were deeply rooted into mysticism. I imagined them in simple white garments and sandals, living out in the desert with no air conditioning or running water, and realized how domesticated and spoiled we as people have become. We used to live out there in the elements without a problem, but now, a lot of us would probably die if we had to. I thought, the human race was now equivalent to a house cat and chuckled to myself.

"What's so funny?" he asked. I told him, and he laughed. "That's good, Paige, and so true. You know, I grew up using an outhouse, and we had no electricity. We also hunted and fished for most of our food."

I lifted my hair into a ponytail and wiped the sweat off the back of my neck, trying to imagine Nathan living that kind of life.

"I keep forgetting how old you really are and how you grew up. I bet it was wonderful, but inconvenient at the same time." I thought about having to go outside to use an outhouse in the cold or rain. Now that would totally suck ass.

"It was wonderful, and how we lived was a normal way of life, nobody thought differently of it, and something catastrophic had to happen in order for us to have a sense of inconvenience."

"Yeah, well, I'm glad you know how to live that way just in case a time comes when we might have to, because I wouldn't know what to do."

He placed his hand on my cheek. "You don't ever have to worry. I'll always take care of you." The fervent emotion in his eyes left no doubt in his words.

I turned my face and kissed his hand. "I'm going to go take a shower."

"Okay, I'll take one after you, and afterwards we'll see about supper and getting things together for your mom's arrival tomorrow."

"All right." I bounced on my tiptoes and gave him a quick kiss.

When I was in my room, getting my stuff to take into the bathroom, I decided to confront Mom about my father and wouldn't let her leave until she gave me some answers. She wasn't going to shut me out, not this time.

Chapter Seventeen
Mom's Answers

"Hi, Mom." I jogged to her as she stepped out of her new Ford Fusion Hybrid. "Nice car. I love the silver color." I checked out her navigation system and slick black interior, then grabbed her bag from the backseat.

She smiled and gave me a warm hug. "Thanks, sweetheart." She turned to the vehicle. "I was due for a trade-up and fell in love with this one. It gets great mileage and is good for the environment."

"Well, you deserve it with how hard you work." I grinned, happy to see her.

She patted my cheek. "You're such a good daughter." She paused and sighed. "I can't believe you're going to be eighteen soon. It makes me feel old."

I laughed. "You're not old Mom, and the gold highlights you put in your hair make you look young." I was happy to see she did something unpredictable for a change.

Blushing, she ran her fingers through her shoulder length brown hair. "I did this on a whim and wasn't sure if I liked it, but I think it's growing on me."

"It looks great. I bet you could pass for my older sister." Her blush deepened, and I wondered if that was one of the qualities endeared her to my father.

"Is that Nathan's truck?" She pointed to the street.

"Yeah, it is. He wanted to give us a minute, so he stayed in the house."

"Very nice. Did his parents buy it for him?"

"No, Mom." I frowned, thinking here we go with the questions, and was glad I already prepared for it. "His parents died in a car accident a few years ago."

Her hand flew to her chest, and her mouth widened in horror. "How tragic that must have been for him."

I gave her a sad face and nodded.

"Does he live with relatives now?"

"No, Mom, he's nineteen." I slung her bag over my shoulder. "And to answer your next question. He made money from the land he sold."

She tilted her chin down and had one of her *mom* looks. "That's fine, Paige, but is he in college?"

She was big on education and wasn't impressed about him being rich. I should have realized she didn't care about the size of a person's bank account. What mattered to her was getting a degree and becoming an asset to this world. *If only she knew how much of an asset he really was.*

"Yeah, he's in college. He's majoring in history and finished this semester early."

Her shoulders relaxed. "That makes me feel better." She looked up at the sky where the sun was poking out of the gray clouds, and then something caught her eye on the side of the house. "Do we have a cat now?"

I followed her gaze and saw Mr. Kitty lying in the grass watching us.

"Kind of." I shrugged. "He's been hanging around here. I call him Mr. Kitty."

"He looks like the stray cat your father and I had when you were four. Do you remember him?"

I pretended to think hard and shook my head.

As we were climbing the steps to the porch, Nathan came out. Mom's jaw dropped. He shook her hand, and she smiled shyly at him.

In that moment, she looked so young and unscathed by the world. My mind automatically took a mental picture of her. The beauty and childlike innocence in it brought a soft smile to my face. My mom truly had a beautiful spirit.

He gave her a warm smile. "Please to meet you, Mrs. Reed."

"Call me Marissa. Mrs. Reed makes me feel old," she said, already charmed by him.

Nathan took her bag from me. When he turned his back, she pointed at him and made an okay sign with her fingers. I grinned and followed her into the house, happy she finally got to meet Nathan.

"I have something for you, Paige." She sat in the recliner and dug through her purse. She pulled out a small white box and handed it to me.

"You didn't have to get me anything." I sat on the couch beside Nathan, his arm draped over my shoulders.

"I know, but it had your name written all over it."

I lifted the lid to a pair of silver knotted Celtic stud earrings.

"I love them!" I said. "Thanks, Mom." I put them on. "How do they look?" I gathered my hair into a ponytail.

"They look beautiful on you," Nathan said, smiling.

"He's right. They do. But where's the Celtic ring you always wear?" Mom asked, eyeing my right hand.

"I lost it down the drain a couple months ago," I said, my face falling.

"I'm sorry, honey," she said. "I know how much you loved that ring."

I touched the finger where it once was. "I was sick for days."

Nathan looked at me. "What did it look like?"

I touched my earlobe and poked it out. "Like these earrings."

Mom's eyes fell on Nathan. "Paige has always had an affinity with anything Celtic."

"Really? I didn't know." He sounded fascinated and angled his body toward Mom.

"Even when she was a baby," she went on. "I remember this one night I was flipping through TV stations when she was being fussy, and I couldn't calm her down. Well, I paused on a program playing Celtic music, and Paige instantly stopped crying." She snapped her fingers and laughed. "I thought I had found the Holy Grail because she was such a fussy baby."

"Mom!" I said, my cheeks warming. Nathan squeezed my shoulder. I'd never told Nathan this stuff about me and now wished I had.

She arched a brow. "You *were*. Anyway, the next day I went out and bought some Celtic music and used it whenever she became inconsolable."

"Interesting," Nathan said with a crooked smile.

"Do you know she plays the tin whistle?" Mom's eyes skipped playfully to me.

Nathan turned to me in astonishment. My face was flaming now.

"She even taught herself how to do those Irish and Scottish dances," she said, not waiting for his reply. "And she does it quite well."

"Okay, Mom. Enough about me. How was your Vegas trip?" I asked, hoping to get the conversation off myself. *Please* talk about something else, I silently begged.

"Hold on a minute." Nathan flipped his palm out. "I would very much like to hear you play the tin whistle for us."

"Are you serious?" I made a face at him.

"Absolutely." His adoring eyes taunted me.

"Yes, Paige, please play for us. I haven't heard you in years." Mom was enjoying herself, and even though she kept embarrassing me, I was glad to have her here.

"But that's just it," I argued. "I haven't played in years and probably suck now."

She waved a hand in the air. "You're just like your fath--" She stopped, and I saw the sadness in her eyes before she looked away. My heart slipped. Nathan took my hand, letting me know he saw it too. But then she cleared her throat and continued. "You're way too modest."

"Okay, but don't laugh if I make a mistake." I wanted to make her happy and headed for the stairs to get it.

"We won't," she called.

Once in my room, I sat on the bed and held my head in my hands. The sadness I saw in her eyes made me realize how much my questions were going to hurt her. But I had no other choice. I had to know what she knew about my father.

I glanced at the journal on the night stand and thought about Nathan spending half the night reading and pondering it. He came to the conclusion the ring did exist, and my father would have found it if he were still alive. He believed an innocent person owned the ring and probably had it tucked away somewhere.

"I think we can find it," he told me over breakfast this morning, his voice ringing with excitement.

"Why do you think that?" I took a sip of my coffee, feeling my own excitement bubbling inside me. If he was right, we could find the ring, destroy it, and that would be the end of it.

"Because your father was a genius, and we can follow his lead. I know it's been almost fourteen years since he wrote this, but we can start where he left off, find out where it was sold, and who bought it." He was practically jumping out of his seat with enthusiasm.

I didn't know whether to cry or laugh, so I stared at the ceiling and did both.

He took my face into his hands. "We need to wait until you become immortal before we do this because it will be dangerous, especially if Aosoth finds out. So we can't breathe a word of it to anybody."

"Even Anwar?" Surely, he'd want his longtime friend to know.

"Anwar is family, but I don't want him to know about your father's journal." His voice sounded tight, angry even.

"Why?" I asked in complete shock.

He ran a hand through his hair and gritted his teeth. "Because he withheld information about your father from me, which caused you great pain. And this ring has nothing to do with him. It has to do with you. With us."

I slipped my hand into his. "You shouldn't hold a grudge toward him."

Nathan's voice floated up the stairs, interrupting my thoughts.

"We're atrophying down here, Paige."

I hopped to my feet, hearing Mom's laughter, and got my whistle. I followed her laughter down to the living room, loving the sound.

"Nathan was telling me stories about growing up on a farm and some of them are just hilarious," she said, slapping her knee.

They were smiling. It touched me to see them having a good time together, but I felt a hollow space where my father should be and thought if he were here, everything would be perfect. I dropped my eyes to the whistle and turned it in my hands, swallowing against the lump forming in my throat.

Nathan stuck his hand out. When I lifted my gaze to him, his expression was silently telling me he understood. I placed my hand in his and sat next to him. I took a deep breath and rested my lips on the tip of the whistle, my fingers on the holes. Slowly, I blew air into it and moved my fingers up and down, deciding to play a melody for my father. I closed my eyes, allowing the music to take me to another place.

I was now with my father, standing among a group of lush emerald green hills. In the distance was an old stone cottage with a thatched roof and smoke snaking out of its chimney. The breathy music echoed off the hills, and a white mist rose from the ground. My father faced me and held onto my arms. An urgency sparked in his eyes. I squinted at him, not understanding why he looked so worried or how I arrived here.

"I don't have much time, but I promise I'll see you again," he said.

"No, Daddy, don't go," I begged.

He glanced at the rising mist. "You *must* listen to me," he said with an intensity that made my mouth dry and palms sweat. "There are still hard times ahead of you, but you have to find the strength within yourself to get through it and stay alive."

"But I'm tired of dealing with all these emotions. I don't think I can handle much more of it," I whined.

"Yes, you can, and you'll have Nathan to help you through it," he said in a rush, the mist now to my knees. He looked exactly like he did in those pictures I had of him.

"I miss you so much." I wept, and pounded my chest with my fist. "You should be here, and you're not. Why did you leave me, Daddy?"

"You'll always be my peanut girl." He tenderly brushed a lock of hair off my cheek. "I love you so very much, but that emptiness inside of you is from a lack of understanding."

"But if you love me, why did you leave me?" I asked. "Please help me try to understand, because I don't."

He embraced me. "I have to go," he whispered in my ear.

"Nooooo!" I clung to him. "You haven't answered my question." But then he disappeared, and I was clinging to air.

"I chose to stay mortal because I didn't want to live on earth without your mother and you," his disembodied voice told me. "Stay strong, Paige. Thank Nathan for taking care of my little girl for me. I love you and will see you again."

The song ended. I opened my teary eyes and dropped the whistle into my lap. I slouched forward, tucking my chin against my chest, silently crying.

Somehow, I was able to visit with my father, and now he was gone. Again. And even though I now knew he did love me, it didn't take away the ache inside of me. In fact, the pain seemed worse, like alcohol being poured into an open wound. Maybe because part of me still didn't believe he truly loved me. I mean, if he was able to visit with me, why hadn't he before? And what was with the hard times ahead of me? Wasn't this hard enough? I didn't know what to think. All I knew was, I missed him more than ever and needed answers from Mom.

"What's wrong, honey?" Mom asked as Nathan pulled me into his arms.

"You did a perfect job. Why are you crying?"

"She's crying because she played that song for her father," he quietly told her.

"Is that true?"

"Yes." I sniffed, wiping my face with the sleeve of my shirt.

"Wow. You really do belong together for him to know that. I could already tell when I first saw you two, and how you look at each other, but this confirms it," she said.

"I'm going to take a walk." Nathan kissed my cheek. "I'll be nearby if you need me," he whispered in my ear.

Mom stood when Nathan did, looking worried.

"You don't have to go." She gestured for him to sit back down.

"I'm going to get some fresh air," he told her. "Paige needs to talk to you alone."

"I miss Dad, Mom," I said when Nathan stepped outside. "And I want to apologize ahead of time for bringing this up. I hope this doesn't ruin your weekend, but I must confront you on this."

"I miss him too, but we can talk about this later. I need to go see Caroline and Tori." She acted like a caged animal, looking for a way to escape, but I wouldn't let her.

"They can wait. This is more important." I rose from the couch to let her know I wasn't backing down. "Why have you kept memories of my father from me?"

"I don't want to talk about this." She snatched her purse.

"No! We will talk about this because I need answers!" I hollered at her for the first time in my life and hated every last bit of it.

She dropped her purse on the coffee table and turned. Her face lost its color and beyond her eyes I saw a tormented soul. I almost told her to forget about it, but stood my ground instead and kept the determination on my face.

"Your father was the love of my life," she said, blinking the tears back. "I know it's selfish of me to keep the memory of him away from you, but I can't deal with it."

"But he's *my* father, and I have the right to know everything about him. Do you realize I have a huge gap inside myself because he's not around, and I know very little about him?"

She looked up, and the tears slid down her cheeks. "I ache for him every single minute of the day." Her gaze fell on mine. My own eyes welled with tears. "When he died, a piece of me died with him," her voice shook. "I'm sorry you have a gap inside of you, but imagine if you lost Nathan, what that would feel like."

I did, and grabbed my stomach as if the wind had been knocked out of me. The very thought of Nathan dying made my heart shudder in agony. I totally understood her now.

She pointed at me. "That's how I feel every time I think about him, and I can't afford to go through life feeling that way."

"Is that why you stay away from me because I remind you of him?" It had to be.

My question stunned her. She blinked a couple times, and brushed the tears off her face. I could tell by the guilt on her face I was right.

"I love you, and I realize I'm not like most mothers, but you're right, and I'm so sorry."

She cried again, breaking my heart. "I … I… I see a lot of him in you. The older you get, the more you remind me of him. It hurts me too much to be around you for a long period of time." She buried her face in her hands and sobbed.

I embraced her and cried against her shoulder. We stayed like that for several long moments, locked in sorrow, just like we had the day my father died.

"I do love you more than anybody." She dropped her arms and stepped back. "But I'm also angry at your father for leaving me."

"I know what you mean." I got a couple tissues from the end table and handed her one. "And I understand your reasons behind all of this, but I need answers."

"What do you want to know?" She blew her nose.

"I found a journal of his, and I want to know why you hid it from me."

"I don't know what you're talking about," she said, mystified. "I remember seeing him with a journal, but after he bought this house, I never saw the journal again."

"He bought this house?" I squeaked.

She nodded. "He wanted you to grow up in a small town and have a good childhood." She swallowed and sniffed, then continued in a small voice. "He died before we moved in."

"So, he hid the journal then?" I said more to myself than to her.

"It appears so," she murmured.

"Do you want to see it?"

Crap! I shouldn't have said that.

Her eyes widened in panic. "No. I don't."

I released the air from my lungs. "Did he act weird before he died or mentioned a ring at all?"

She picked up her purse and let out a tired sigh. "He didn't mention a ring, but he would leave for a couple days because of his job. He did do some research on religion and witchcraft. I was concerned about it until he assured me it was out of curiosity."

"Witchcraft?" I blurted, my brain shifting out of place.

"Yes. It scared me at first, but then he explained it to me. There's white magic and black magic. It's actually interesting."

"Did he ever use it?" I asked, still astounded at this piece of information.

"No, not that I'm aware of."

"Did you ever see a tall black guy around?"

"Yes, there was a couple times when a very tall and bald black man came to our house." She headed for the door, showing no interest in my odd questions. I moved aside, but before she opened it, she hugged me. "I hope you know I do love you, and I'm sorry I haven't been there for you, but now you know why."

"I love you too, Mom, and I do understand now. It's okay. I just thought you didn't like me." Another batch of tears welled in my eyes.

"Oh, honey." She reached out and rubbed my cheek. "I'm so sorry you thought that, but it's not true. You're a beautiful person. How could anybody not like you?"

I stared at my feet and shrugged.

"I not only like you, I love you." She hugged me again.

"I love you too." I didn't want her to go, but understood why she had to. I wondered though, if I had looked more like her than my father, if things would have been different between us.

She released me and placed her hand on the door knob. "I'll be back later."

"Okay. Tell them I said hi."

"I will," she said, opening the door. "And by the way, Nathan is a keeper. I really like him."

"So do I." I smiled as she went out the door.

Chapter Eighteen
Devastation

"I guess you were right about my father not taking immortality," I told Nathan while loading the dishwasher. "And I really can't blame him for it, but it still makes me sad." I pushed the dish rack back inside a little too hard, causing the dishes to rattle and clink.

"Of course it does. You love your father, and it's natural for you to feel the way you do." He was leaning against the counter, watching me. "Do you realize this explains the premonition you had when you were four?"

I stood rooted to the floor and stared as what he said sunk in. I replayed that premonition in my head, and I could feel the pieces of the puzzle finally snapping into place.

"You're right," I said and repeated it out loud. "He's going to leave you because he loves you, and it's his choice." I sat and rested my elbow on the kitchen table, holding my head in my hand. "He chose to stay mortal because he couldn't bear living in this world without Mom and me. And he probably thought when he did die, we would eventually join him. But if he became immortal, he'd have to exist without us." Talking to Nathan about this was making me feel a little bit better about it.

"That's right, and I have to be honest with you." Nathan pulled a chair out, scraping it against the floor, and sat next to me. "I would have done the same thing if I were in his shoes."

"You would?"

"Without a doubt," he said earnestly. "There is no way I'd want to live without you, and I'm thinking that's how your father felt about your mom."

"They really do love each other," I said. "I just wish Mom would find a way to deal with her loss. It hurts me to see her so sad." I ran my fingers through my hair. "And I have an idea of how she feels."

He held my hand. "Me too. That whole week without you was pure hell."

I looked at our hands and remembered what my father had told me to tell him. I told him everything else, but this somehow slipped my mind. I wiggled my fingers between his.

"I just remembered something."

"What's that?"

"My father told me to thank you for taking care of his little girl."

He lifted my hand to his lips and kissed it. "My pleasure." He paused and looked toward the living room. "I think your mom is home."

I glanced at the clock on the microwave, amazed at how time flew by. She'd been gone for almost five hours, but it felt like she just left.

Several loud bangs came from the front door, startling me. My head automatically turned in that direction, and I saw a blurry version of Nathan, zipping out of the kitchen. I stood to follow him, and my chest felt like somebody placed a huge ice cube inside it, raising goose bumps on my arms. Everything around me expanded and contracted in slow motion, and when I stepped forward, my feet felt like they were in quicksand. Nathan called to me when I edged toward the hallway.

"Stay there, Paige."

I stopped when I heard his troubled voice and held onto the wall. The sound of the door closing punched through my gut, causing me to hold my stomach, as if I had a bellyache. My mind raced with questions: Who was at the door? What did they want? Was Mom okay? I shook my head to clear it, telling myself she was with her friends, having a good time.

But then I thought about the premonition I had yesterday and what my father had told me today. Another blow to the gut knocked me on my hands and knees. My forehead pressed against the cold tile, and my body quivered. I pushed myself into a sitting position and hugged my knees to my chest.

Was this really happening? Or was I being melodramatic? With everything that had happened in these past few weeks, it would be understandable for me to respond this way. But why did Nathan sound so upset?

Maybe I imagined him sounding that way; I tried to rationalize, while nervously exhaling. I rested my cheek on my knees and rocked, repeating in my head I was just being paranoid, shutting all other thoughts out but that one.

I really didn't know how long I sat waiting for Nathan, but when I heard the door open and close, it felt like he'd been gone for hours. I remained on the floor, though, in a perpetual state of rocking. I didn't even look up when he entered the kitchen and got on his knees in front of me.

"I need to talk to you, Paige." His voice rattled with emotion. He cleared his throat. "Your mom--"

I slapped my hands on my ears, violently shaking my head. "Noooo! Don't say it!" I cried, the tears already flowing. He reached for me, but I jumped to my feet, and marched through the house, calling for my mom.

"She's not here, Paige," his voice cracked. He went to take my hand, but I jerked it away and ran upstairs to her room.

"Mom!… Mom!… This isn't funny," I yelled between strangled sobs, running through each room, checking the closets and bathtub as well. She wasn't there. I ran downstairs, still calling for her. Where in the hell was she?

"Please, Paige, listen to me," Nathan's voice choked behind me when I ran to the front door. "A police officer and Carrie's mom was at the door. They wanted to talk to you, but I insisted they talk to me instead. They told me your mom was in a car accident, and she--"

I turned and pointed at him, refusing to allow his tearful eyes get to me. "I don't want to hear it. She's fine." I spun, wrenched the door open, and ran into the cool night. "Mom!… Mom! …where are you?"

The bright moon illuminated everything around me. I stopped in the middle of the street, mildly aware of a hooting owl in the distance and cupped my hands around my mouth. "MOOOOOOM!" I screamed, throwing my hands in the air and dropping them to my knees, sobbing.

Nathan held my shoulders. "Paige. Baby, please. She's gone."

I twisted my shoulders out of his grip and ran toward the forest, thinking maybe her car broke down, and she took a shortcut through the forest instead of walking the long stretch of road, but he grabbed me and picked me up. He felt cold, and his body was shaking, but I refused to give in. My mom told me she'd be back later, so she had to be out there.

"Put me down!" I pounded on his back with my fists. "She might be lost in the forest. I need to find her," I sobbed. "*Please,* Nathan, she's *my* mom."

She *has* to be out there.

"I can't allow you to do that. It's too dangerous," he said.

"I don't care!" I half shouted. "She said she'd be back. I need to find her."

We were in the house now. He sat on the edge of the couch and pulled me down into his lap, still holding onto me. He sniffed a couple times and moved his hand across his face.

"I need to find her," I repeated, sobbing silently on his shoulder.

With his hand on the back of my head he rocked me. "I'm so sorry," he whispered.

My fingers went to my earlobes, and I touched the earrings she had given me today. None of this seemed real, and I couldn't grasp my mom no longer existed in this world. I mean, she'd been here today, in this house, and now she'd never walk through the front door again. How could that be? Her bag still sat on the floor, next to the stairs, waiting for her to take it to her room, proof of her existence. But now she was gone and with my father …

"*Oh, God!*" I wailed, clinging tighter to Nathan's shoulders. "*They will reunite, and a new life will begin.*" I covered my mouth, stifling the sobs.

"I know, baby. I know," he hushed, still rocking me.

Suddenly, the phone rang with an urgency that bounced around us.

"Don't leave me," I said when I felt his body jerk.

His arms tightened. "I'll never leave you."

I rested my wet cheek on his shoulder as the phone continued to ring. The answering machine finally clicked on, and I heard my own cheerful voice saying to leave a message. It beeped loudly, and Carrie's sobs filled the room. Fresh tears poured down my face.

"Paige. I'm … I'm." She broke off, crying again.

"We're sorry," Tree croaked. "If you need anything let us know." He paused. "My mom just started her night shift at the hospital when she saw them bring your mom in. She identified her right away and … "

They were both crying, and I whimpered on Nathan's shoulder.

"My mom and I stopped by your house," Carrie's scratchy voice said. "I'm sure Nathan told you. She called Brayden's mom. They'll be here Monday for the-- "

"I just got off the phone with Brayden," Tree said. "He's going to call you any minute. He's devastated. We all are. We love you, Paige, and we're here for you."

I could hear Carrie bawling in the background as Tree hung up the phone.

"The funeral is Monday," Nathan said. "Carrie's mom knows the director. I spoke to him on the phone when you were in the house. I told him the sooner the better."

"But I don't know what to do." I coughed and sniffed at the same time.

He rubbed my back. "You don't have to worry. I'll take care of everything."

Just then, the phone rang, and after the beep, Brayden's husky voice came on the answering machine. I felt Nathan's arms twitched around me, and for some reason, Brayden's voice tugged at my heart.

"Hey, Paige, I heard what happened, and I'm sorry you have to go through this." A long silence followed, and I thought maybe the phone line disconnected until I heard a weird noise come out of his mouth. And then he blew a deep "ah" sound out. "Sorry," he said in a rough voice. "I… I wish I was there with you. When I heard what happened, I grabbed my stuff and hopped in my car to go to you, but my mom stopped me because she wants us to go together. We'll be there Monday morning. I miss you like crazy, Paige, and I love you. See you in a few days."

"I'm going to go to the bathroom," I mumbled, not knowing what to think about seeing Brayden after two years of him being gone.

But right now I didn't care. All I wanted was for this horrible nightmare to end. All I wanted was… my mommy back.

Nathan held my face in front of him. "We will get through this," he vehemently asserted. His eyes were red and glassy, thick with emotion.

I dropped my gaze and wormed myself off his lap, not wanting to hear about it. Nathan didn't say a word or moved when I dragged my feet up the stairs, avoiding looking at Mom's bag.

I didn't want to hear things would get better and as each day passed it would get easier for me. My mom was gone, and I'd never get to see her again. And so help me, if somebody says it was God's plan to call her home, I'd rip their head off. I didn't care. I didn't care about anything right now.

Somehow, I found my way into her bed, barely recalling being in the bathroom. Heavy curtains hung over her windows. I welcomed the darkness, hoping I would fall into it so I'd never have to feel this insurmountable grief and despair again.

I crawled into the center of the bed and pulled a blanket over my shivering body. The cover didn't provide enough warmth, but instead of getting another one, I curled into a fetal position and shook uncontrollably. The bed bounced and squeaked when Nathan climbed in. He curled his body around mine, spooning me.

"You're so cold," he murmured, pulling another blanket over us.

"What happened?" I asked in a feeble, tired voice.

He moved his hand gently along the side of my face, pushing my hair back. "Are you sure you want to hear this now?" I could tell by his tone he didn't think it was a good idea.

"My eyeballs feel like somebody took sandpaper to them, and I don't think I can cry any more tonight. Besides, I need to know."

He let out a slow, unsteady breath. "On the way home, a deer ran in front of her. She swerved to miss it and flipped the car several times. It went off the road and smashed into a tree. She died instantly." He kept it short and to the point, probably to spare me the agony of having to endure all the details.

My eyes closed to the vision of her driving down a dark, desolate road, listening to her radio. I could see a deer darting out in front of her, and her car swerving to the right, then flipping several times. A scream bellowed out of me:

"MOOOOM!" I reached for her, but then realized when Nathan held me tight against him, I was doing it for real. My body jerked as dry sobs seized it. "Wh-why did she have to die?"

"I don't know, baby." His voice was low and woeful. "But I'll help you through this." He nestled his chin into the crook of my neck. "You're not alone. You're not alone," he whispered, and began humming a Celtic song I think he made up in a desperate attempt to soothe me.

The ghost of Mercy must have shown up and taken pity upon me since that was the last thing I remembered before falling into an oblivious sleep.

***

During the next three days, I went through the motions of what I had to do in order to close the book on Mom's short life. Nathan remained by my side, reminding me to do simple tasks, such as taking a shower and brushing my teeth. I took no interest in any of it and spoke only when required to. Even when Carrie's and Tree's mom came over to give their support, I was incoherent.

They brought food and sat with me for hours while I stayed balled up in the corner of the couch, hugging the blanket Nathan wrapped around me, staring off into space. Nothing seemed real or made sense in this thick fog that distorted everything around me. And when I heard my name being called, I'd glance at the person saying it, and tried to focus on the movement of their lips, but couldn't comprehend what they were saying. Their words became foreign to me, but their touch broke through the numbness, pulling me back into my skin, and I'd collapse in their arms.

"You've always been like a second daughter to us." I thought I heard their tearful voices say. But it was competing against the humming and whimpering noises reverberating from my chest, so I wasn't sure. They left shortly after, and I dragged myself back into Mom's bed, ignoring Nathan's plea to eat something.

When Carrie and Tree came, I refused to see them, knowing if I saw their distraught faces, it would bring me to my knees. There was no way I could bear to see some of my own pain reflected in their eyes. So I stayed in Mom's bed in a state of disbelief, while Nathan spoke to them downstairs. I tried to grasp at the reality, that I'd never see Mom again. Tomorrow, her body would be turned to ashes, and eventually cast into the sea where my father's ashes had been placed. But acceptance was far out of my reach.

"How can this be?" I moaned to myself. "This time yesterday she was here, but now she's gone. Why? I don't understand … I don't understand … I DON"T UNDERSTAND!" I seized a pillow and sent it hurtling across the room on top of Mom's dresser, smashing into the trinkets and empty glass perfume bottles. Without thought, I hopped out of bed, hearing thundering footsteps coming up the stairs, and snatched a vase off the night stand. I lifted it and forcefully brought it down on the night stand, shattering it.

"*Omigod,* Paige!" Carrie screeched after Nathan busted down the locked door and seized my wrist, raising it above my head. The look on his face was a combination of horror and anguish.

"I'll get a towel," Tree said in the hallway.

I shook my hand in Nathan's grasp. "Why can't I feel anything?" I cried, eyeing the blood trickling over his hand and down my arm. I dropped to the floor, bringing him with me. "Why did my mom get taken away from me? Wasn't my father enough?" I sobbed, and glanced at Carrie. She slid her back down the wall, burying her face in her hands, sobbing along with me.

I didn't want her or Tree to see me like this–to feel my pain. But everything happened so fast, like I had no self control. My emotions not only took me as its prisoner, but those I loved as well. It wasn't fair.

"There's a reason for all of this," Nathan murmured, his eyes gleaming with tears. Tree handed him a towel and stepped back. I looked up at him. Tears were rolling down his face. A sob escaped my lips. "It's not deep," Nathan said, wrapping the towel around my hand. "But we need to clean it out." He embraced me.

"I can't deal with this anymore," I said between sobs. "This is too overwhelming, and it's killing me."

"No, Paige, you *can't* allow this to destroy the life inside you," Nathan's tearful voice whispered. "Remember what your father said. You *must* be strong and get through this."

Carrie and Tree crawled over to me, and encircled their arms around us.

"We'll help you, Paige," Tree said, his voice hoarse with emotion.

"We'll always be at your side," Carrie cried.

I wanted to ease their minds and tell them I'd be okay, but I couldn't. I mean, honestly, throughout this past month, I'd been nothing but a blubbering mess due to my spirit being stripped from the armor that had been protecting it since my father died. And now I was defenseless and losing my will to fight. I knew it, but didn't want them to know. The last thing I wanted was to cause them more pain. So I pretended to make an effort to get through this when really I could feel myself shutting down.

***

The morning of the funeral turned into a big blur, like looking through a pair of prescription glasses you didn't need. My head ached, and my stomach churned. But then I saw Brayden, and somehow, seeing him sparked what life I still had inside me, and the blurriness faded.

Both he and his mom were late. I didn't see him until he marched up the aisle and stood on the pulpit. I was sitting in the front pew with Nathan, wearing round black sunglasses, surprised to see him brazenly standing before a church full of people without breaking a sweat.

He had grown since the last time I'd seen him and looked to be as tall as six feet. His black, short sleeve T-shirt, hugged his tan muscular arms, and when I looked at him before he began his speech, our eyes connected. Of course he probably didn't know I was looking directly at him since I had my sunglasses on, but when he looked at me, something flickered in his eyes. Nathan must had seen it too because he hugged me closer to him. Brayden's gaze shifted on Nathan, and Nathan stared at him until he looked away and turned his attention to the people waiting for him to speak.

After the service, all the hugs, and everything else that went along with it, I saw Brayden plowing through the crowd of people–heading toward another room where food was set out–to get to me. Tree and Carrie were following close behind. When they reached us by the front entrance, Nathan let go of my hand and stepped aside to talk to Tree.

"Paige," Brayden said, taking my hand. Nathan's eyes were glued on Brayden's hand in mine, and he had a hard look on his face. "I want you to know, I won't leave Astoria until you're okay." I saw that flicker in his eyes again and was able to identify it this time. Love.

I pulled my hand away–even though it felt normal to hold it–and stepped back. He glanced over my head, and clutched my arm, moving me toward him. I knew by the look on his face what he wanted to say and wished he could save it for another time.

"You left me, and I'm in love with Nathan," I said, hearing the exhaustion in my voice. "I appreciate you being here and what you said about Mom, but I belong with Nathan." I couldn't help but think how good he looked with his short black hair, messy on top. And somehow, through all my grief, my stomach dipped, stirring emotions that could have been his, but would never surface because what I felt for Nathan surpassed them.

"Not true," he objected. "I can help you through this better than *he* can because we've known each other since we were toddlers." His hand moved down into mine, once again holding it. "I know you better than he does."

I hung my head and sighed. "No, you don't, Brayden. You may think you do, but don't. There are things about me only Nathan knows."

He lifted my chin so I had to look at him. "Does he know how silly you get when you've had too much caffeine? Was he there when you fell from a tree when you were nine and thought you broke your leg? He wasn't, but I was, and I carried you all the way home. Was he your first kiss?"

His lack of sensitivity aggravated me. This was the last thing I needed right now, and he should know that. I removed my hand from his, squared my shoulders, and threw him a curve ball:

"You may be my first kiss, but Nathan was my first…" I stopped, not needing to go any further, and watched all the color drain from his face. He staggered backwards, covering his mouth, and the hurt I saw on his face caused my heart to twist in pain. I spun to leave and bumped into Nathan. He had heard everything. I could tell by the dark warning look he aimed at Brayden.

"Brayden. Dude, chill out," Tree said, bracing Brayden against the wall when he tried to lunge at Nathan. Brayden's blood-red face and flaring nostrils shocked me. I'd never seen him this mad before. "You knew they were together," Tree told him.

Nathan pushed me behind him, which fueled Brayden's anger even more. I jerked my head around, thankful nobody could see us behind the short wall that blocked us from their view. Carrie stepped beside Tree to help calm Brayden.

"How dare you push her behind you," Brayden spat at Nathan. "I'd never hurt her."

"Shut up, Brayden," Carrie said. "Paige has been through enough already."

"You can't keep me away from her," Brayden continued, struggling against Tree.

"Try me," Nathan said. "If you continue to disregard her feelings like you just did now, knowing she's in a fragile state, I'll-- "

I ran outside, not able to take it anymore. Today was one of the worst days of my life, and I never expected Brayden to behave in this way. He was supposed to be like Tree and Carrie, not like this. He acted like he had dibs on me, and used the bond we shared as leverage. How could he do that to me at a time like this? And yeah, he knew things about me, Nathan hadn't discovered yet, but so what? Those were petty things compared to what Nathan knew.

My ears were ringing, and I spotted her right away, standing next to a black SUV. It was the same blonde who approached us in the parking lot at the grocery store. *Aosoth must have decided to stay inside that vessel after all.* She waved, and a strong urge to beat the crap out of her engulfed me. I didn't know what came over me, but I took off running with the intent of doing just that, staring at her cruel smile head on.

"Paige! No!" Nathan yelled. I felt his strong arms around my waist, and he swung me in the air away from her. "She'll kill you!"

A dark and taunting laugh echoed around us.

"No, she won't." I kicked my feet in the air and pushed my body forward, wind-milling my arms. "She wants that damned ring too badly to kill me right now." I wanted to pound her face into the asphalt and submerge it into the puddles of water that were left from this morning's rain. She had some nerve to show up here, and I had enough of her threats.

He turned his back on Aosoth, and dropped me to my feet. I dashed to get around him, but he seized my arms. *Damn it!* I just wanted to hit her once.

"Listen to me," he stressed, slightly shaking me. "You will get your chance, but not now."

Angry, hot tears escaped my eyes as the rational part of my brain took over. He was right. This wasn't the time or place to be doing this. But when would that be? When I turned immortal? I found myself not caring again, and the heaviness in my heart reawakened in full force, sparing me no leniency.

I slapped a hand over my chest, curling my shoulders over, swallowing hard as the searing pain moved to my face. "Take me home," I whispered.

Nathan's eyes moved anxiously across my face. He glanced over his shoulder and back at me. "She's gone"–he took my hand–"C'mon, I'll get you home as quickly as possible."

I concentrated on the warmth of his hand in mine and moving my feet forward. I noticed a red lollipop stuck to the ground and imagined the kid who must have dropped it, in an attempt to distract myself from the extreme weakness coming over me. But my attempt was futile, and the ground spun. I stumbled forward and closed my eyes, no longer able to fight the darkness that was reaching for me.

"Paige!… Paige!…" Nathan's panicked voice called out in the far distance. And then the darkness snatched me away from him.

Chapter Nineteen
Brayden's Promise

"I'm really worried about her." Nathan sounded weary outside Mom's bedroom. "She's been in and out for more than four days." He paused, and I realized he must be talking on the phone since I only heard him. "Yes, I had a doctor examine her. He said she passed out because of the trauma she's going through and not eating when she should be."

I touched my forehead, trying to recall a doctor checking on me. My mind shifted on a vague memory of a man lifting my eyelids and flashing a bright light in them, but I couldn't remember anything else.

Nathan coughed, and his voice became unsteady. "The only time she shows any life is when she gets up to use the bathroom, and I'm able to catch her long enough to feed her some soup, but even that is a challenge." The floor creaked outside the door, and I thought about him trying to feed me.

It seemed like a distant dream, him sitting me against the headboard and putting a spoon to my mouth. I think I even batted his hand away a few times, knocking the spoon across the room. I cringed at how horrible I must have been.

Nathan spoke again, but this time his voice sounded tearful, ripping my insides. "I need your help because I don't know what else to do, and I'm afraid I'm losing her." He paused and when he spoke again, I heard some relief in his voice. "You did? It'll be here tomorrow?" He took a deep breath and exhaled. "Thank you. I think that will help tremendously. But why didn't you tell me this before?" He sighed heavily. "You know what. I don't care. If this helps Paige then--"

Silence.

"That's excellent news. I'll see you then. Bye."

I lifted my hand off my forehead and stared at the band-aid beneath the dull light of the bedside lamp. And then everything came back to me in a rush. I sat up and hollered for Nathan. In a matter of seconds, he had me in his arms.

"Shhhhh, I'm here. It's all right," he soothed.

"I'm sorry for putting you through this," I said.

His eyes were rimmed in red. I placed my hand on his cheek, and he covered it with his hand. I hated I had caused him so much sadness.

"You don't need to be sorry or feel guilty." He moved my hand to his lips and kissed it. "You've been through too much lately. I just wish I can alleviate your suffering, and it torments me when I can't."

I tilted my head to the side and stared into his eyes. "Thank you for everything you've done for me." The universe mustn't totally hate me because I had Nathan.

His expression was an emotional intensity of fierce love that made my stomach do a gigantic somersault. I could feel the whip marks on my soul starting to heal, scabbing over with hope, letting me know I'd pull through this.

"Baby, you don't need to thank me. I love you. You mean more to me than anything. There's nothing I would not do for you."

I pulled him into my arms. "I love you too."

He held me, and we stayed that way for a while. The warmth of his arms around me felt good. I was beginning to experience a small part of the world again, and even though my heart ached for my mom and the vacant gaps still resided inside, I was coming to terms with it. It was clear to me if I were to lie down and die, eventually Nathan would too, and I wouldn't let that happen. I must find the strength within me to understand and overcome this emotional baggage of my mortal life in order to move on into my immortal life. Like my father said, I had to be strong and not give up.

"Paige," Nathan said, breaking the silence. "I think you should eat."

As soon as he said that my stomach growled in agreement and for the first time in like forever, I giggled. Nathan pulled us on the bed and covered his face. When he didn't move, I raised myself on my elbow and looked at him.

"Are you all right?"

He dropped his hands, revealing a cheerful smile.

"You don't know how good it feels for me to hear you laugh."

"I think I'm going to be okay," I told him, wiping a tear off his face. "I just wish I knew what brought me out of it. One minute I was dead to the world and the next I heard you talking on the phone."

He sat up. "These are happy tears." He showed me his wet fingers, and stepped out of bed. I followed him with the intention of taking a shower. "And to answer your question, the doctor told me there was a possibility you would snap out of it. He said sometimes when a person becomes traumatized, the mind shuts down and the person goes into a comatose state. It's the mind's way to protect a body from harm until the person is able to cope with things."

My body swayed sideways, and Nathan steadied me. I took a couple more steps and swayed again. My legs felt all rubbery. What the hell?

"Why can't I walk straight?" I asked when he cupped his hands on my shoulders.

"Because all you've had in almost a week are liquids." He lifted me in his arms. "I need to feed you some real food."

"But I need a shower," I argued. "I look like crap."

He smiled. "You look beautiful. You can take a shower after you get some food in your belly."

I held onto his neck and closed my eyes until I felt him carefully placing me in a chair. I squinted against the bright kitchen light, still amazed at how quick he was. My gaze fell on a sink full of dirty dishes and coffee mugs crowding the counter, a reminder of how long I'd been out of it.

Nathan flashed me a guilty look. "I'm sorry about the mess. I'll clean it up later."

I narrowed my eyes. "Nathan, you don't need to apologize. I mean, you had a lot on your shoulders dealing with the aftermath of everything, so don't worry about the dishes."

He opened the refrigerator and pulled out a glass casserole pan. "Well, quite a few people had stopped by to see how you were doing." He set it on the counter and got a couple bowls and forks. "How does crab pasta salad sound? It has huge chunks of fresh crab meat. I think Carrie's mom made it."

"Sounds great," I said. "I've tried it before, and it's yummy." I glanced at the microwave and was instantly brought back to the last time I sat here in this exact position. A sharp pain stabbed through my heart, causing it to shudder and ache. I rested my forehead on the edge of the Formica table, staving off tears. The sound of a chair scooting next to me filled the room.

"Paige?"

"Being in the kitchen like this reminds me of that night," I mumbled.

He placed his arm around my shoulders and leaned his head next to mine. "I'm sorry, but there are going to be things that will trigger reminders of that night and of your mom."

I lifted my head. "I know, but it's hard, and a part of me is still having a difficult time believing she's gone. I feel like she's away at work or bailed on me, and that's why she's not here. It makes it easier for me to deal with it." I sighed. "Is it terrible of me to think that way?" I scanned his face for any hints of disapproval, but saw empathy instead.

"Not at all," he said. "It's a harmless way to cope, but I have to be up front with you about something."

I stared at him. His expression showed no reason to be alarmed.

"There are still physical things we need to deal with, like her will and ashes," he said.

"She had a will?" That shouldn't have surprised me, but it did.

He nodded. "She also had a life insurance policy."

A sudden overwhelming, crushing feeling came over me.

"But I don't--"

He placed his finger on my lips. "Don't worry. I'll help you through it." He kissed me. "It'll be okay."

I didn't say anything because I was too busy trying not to cry.

"Let me get you some food." He pushed away from the table and rose.

I stared at my hands in my lap. "I'm not hungry now."

"You're going to eat, Paige. If you don't, I'll take you to the hospital where they'll stick a needle in your arm and feed you intravenously."

I looked up to a stubbornness in his face that told me he wasn't playing around. He picked up a bowl and fork and waved it in the air in question, his eyebrows raised.

"Fine, but don't give me too much." I watched him scoop large amounts of pasta and crab meat into a bowl, and I pointed at it. "That's yours, right?" He grinned and shook his head, piling more in. "Nathan, I can't eat all of that!"

He stuck the bowl and fork in front of me. "Yes, you can."

Grabbing the fork, I stabbed at the food. "Whatever." But as soon as I took a bite, I became ravenous and shoveled it into my mouth.

"See, I told you." He sounded pleased. "But you should really chew your food instead of inhaling it," he joked.

"Shut up," my distorted voice said. I heard him softly laugh, and the clinking sound of ice cubes being thrown into a glass. He popped open a can and a hissing sound came out of it.

"Dr Pepper." He set the glass on the table and sat to eat with me.

I took a deep drink. It tasted so good that I drank the whole thing in no time. I set the glass down and went back to my food.

A few minutes later I pushed the empty bowl aside and scooted down in the chair, baffled I had eaten the whole thing. My hands went to my full belly, and I let out a long, satisfying sigh.

"You're right," Nathan said, still eating. "This is yummy."

"Yeah, if I lived at Carrie's house, I'd probably weigh like two hundred pounds." I took my bowl and glass and placed it on the counter.

"I doubt it. You eat like a bird, except for tonight." He flashed me a humorous grin, and I threw a towel at him.

"Can you call Carrie and Tree and invite them over while I take a shower?" It was only a little after six, and I really wanted them to see I was doing better. "I'd like to see them tonight."

Nathan set his dishes beside mine and leaned his hand on the edge of the counter. "Sure, but what about Brayden?" I could tell by the tone of his voice he had a strong dislike toward Brayden, but he kept his face impartial. "He wants to see you."

"What about Brayden? Isn't he back home?"

His face darkened. "No. He won't leave Tree's house until he sees you're okay. And if you're wondering, he hasn't been around because he's still sore at me for confronting him at your mom's funeral."

I slipped my hand in his, lacing our fingers. "I know he pissed you off, but he's one of my best friends, and I'm going to have to invite him over."

He gazed into my face. I became breathless at how his eyes seemed to peer straight into my soul. My stomach flipped, reconfirming I was going to be okay.

"He's in love with you, Paige. I saw it in the way he looks at you. He's one of your best friends, and I would never want to compromise that friendship, but your well-being comes first above anything else." He ran a hand through his hair and exhaled sharply. His voice became tight, almost dangerous. "And if he threatens that, like he did before, I'm going to be in his face."

"I can handle Brayden," I firmly said. "So have them come over in an hour, and I'll deal with him myself." I left the room before he could reply.

***

An hour later, the voices of all the people who mattered most to me in this world drifted from downstairs. I zipped up my black hoodie and wiped my sweaty palms on my matching sweat capris, wondering why I was so nervous.

Could it be because Brayden was here? No. I wasn't in love with him. I mean, I did love him, but I was in love with Nathan, and Brayden needed to accept that. I had to admit, though, I did have feelings for Brayden that went beyond friendship, but they paled in comparison to my feelings toward Nathan.

"You can do this," I whispered.

The image of the look on Brayden's face when I told him about Nathan being my first entered my mind, and I recoiled against it. I hated hurting him and was actually surprised at how much it did hurt him, but I had no choice. He needed to know Nathan and I belonged together, and I would remind him again if I had to. I squared my shoulders and marched out my room.

"Paige!" Carrie ran to me and threw her arms around my shoulders. "How are you doing? I've missed you. It's so weird being at school without you, which by the way, you don't have to worry about your grades," she rattled on.

Nathan and Tree were standing in the middle of the living room, beaming. I glanced at Brayden. He was standing beside Tree. He smiled, but the look in his eyes went deeper than his smile.

Carrie dropped her arms, her face full of reassurance. "My mom had a talk with your teachers, and they told her you already did all your assignments for this last semester, and you're going to graduate."

"That's good to hear." Her mom's thoughtfulness touched my heart, and I had to swallow back the tears when I thought about her always treating me like a second daughter.

"I can't believe you finished all of your work for the year," Carrie said, impressed.

"How are you doing?" Tree asked, hugging me before I could respond to Carrie. "We were so worried about you."

I forced a smile. "I'm doing better. It's still hard, but I'll be okay. And I appreciate what all of you has done for me. I'm sorry you had to see me like that." I looked down, staring at the floor. Tree bent his face in front of mine. I turned away, but he stuck his face in front of mine again, giving me his famous goofy look. I laughed.

"Now, isn't that better than feeling sorry for something you shouldn't feel sorry about?" he asked.

"Yeah. The look you just gave me reminds me of the picture Nathan and I found in the attic," I said.

"Which picture is that?" Carrie asked, sitting on the love seat. Tree sat beside her, taking her hand. They looked so cute together.

"Remember our second grade Thanksgiving play?"

Brayden looked at me in surprise. "You have a picture of that?"

I nodded. "I couldn't stop laughing when I found it. Remember, Carrie had long hair then?" The memories we shared surfaced on their faces.

"Oh, God," Carrie moaned, covering her face. "And Nathan saw that?"

All of us laughed.

"You and Paige were so cute in your pigtail braids." Nathan wrapped his arm around my waist. I looked at Brayden, and he was staring at the front door, deep in thought.

"I agree." Tree grinned.

"Can I talk to you, Paige?" Brayden opened the door.

"Sure." I followed him outside.

The sky was swathed in beautiful pink and orange colors, but the air smelled like a wet dog, causing me to wrinkle my nose.

He opened his mouth, but then closed it, looking past me. "Do you know there's a cat lying on your porch?"

I turned. "Oh, that's Mr. Kitty. He's been hanging around here for a while."

He tilted his head to the side, his green eyes jumping with laughter. "Mr. Kitty? Couldn't you come up with a better name than that?"

I shrugged. "That name suits him." I thought it was perfect.

He curled his fingers on his lips, snickering.

"Shut up." I shoved his waist, pushing him backwards.

He took my wrist and held onto it. "I saw a cat a lot like that outside our garage before we left, and if he's still there when I get home, I'm going to give him a better name than *Mr. Kitty.*" He lowered his voice in a mocking tone when he said "Mr. Kitty."

Against my will, my stomach dipped when my eyes fell on his lips, and the memory of our long make out sessions entered my mind. I dropped them to his hand still holding my wrist, and remembered a time when he had grabbed me like this, and took me into his arms, kissing me. I pulled my wrist away and rubbed it. It felt warm, just like my cheeks, and I knew I felt this way because of our past.

"Paige," he said. "I'm sorry how I acted the last time we saw each other. That was wrong of me to do."

"Apology, accepted," I said, unable to look away from him. His sincerity evoked a trove of old feelings I didn't want to feel.

"I mean it. I am sorry." He ran his fingers down the length of my face. "You're so beautiful," he half-whispered. "I should have never left you."

I took a step back. "Don't do that. I'm with Nathan now."

He looked away into the street while I nervously moved my zipper up and down on my hoodie. He closed his eyes and stuck his palm to his forehead. For a second I thought he was going to cry. I chewed on my lip, feeling guilty, but then he abruptly turned to me. My fingers froze on my zipper when I saw the eager passion in his face.

He stepped forward and lightly gripped my arm. "I'm in love with you, Paige, and I have no doubt in my mind that we belong together. I know you're with Nathan, but you belong with me."

I removed his hand from my arm. "Listen to me," I said. "I will always love you, but I'm in love with Nathan."

"No, Paige." He placed his hands on my arms. "You're wrong, You just don't see it yet because you're infatuated with Nathan and--"

"What Nathan and I have goes *beyond* infatuation," I said, breaking free from his hands. "There are no words to describe the bond and love we have for each other."

He raised his eyebrows and made a vibrating sound with his lips, like he was doing a raspberry. "Bond?" He let out a humorless laugh. "How long have you known each other?" He crossed his arms and looked down his nose at me, reminding me of Mr. Harrin, pissing me off.

I stuck my hands on my hips. "That doesn't matter," I fired back. "When

I first looked into his eyes, I knew he was the one." I could feel the heat rising up my neck. The last thing I wanted was to part ways like this. I smashed my lips together to prevent myself from shouting at him.

He rolled his eyes in disgust. "Just because he had his *cock* inside of you doesn't mean he's the *'one'?*" He yelled, waving his fingers in the air, raising his eyebrows again.

A loud crash came from inside the house, and we jerked our heads toward the door.

"Brayden!" I yelled back, mortified. "That was rude!" I couldn't believe what just came out of his mouth. It was like the rudest thing anybody had ever said to me. He even trumped Ashley with that remark.

He lowered his voice. "I'm sorry, but it frustrates me because you're so blind."

I pointed a finger at him. "You're the one who's blind." My face felt hot.

He shook his head and jerked his hands in the air. "No. I'm. Not. And if I have to wait until you realize you and me"–he moved his finger back and forth between us–"are meant to be together, then I will."

"Well then you're going to grow to be a lonely old man," I replied. "Because I'm going to be with Nathan forever." I glared at him.

His face softened, and he touched my cheek. "I don't believe that, not for one second. I saw the way you looked at me earlier, which tells me differently than what you're saying now."

I pushed his hand off me. "I do love you, Brayden, but those feelings you saw in my face stem from what we once had, and they're *nothing* compared to my feelings for Nathan. You need to accept it and move on."

"I'm never going to give up on us, Paige. I might have a girl here and there, but you're the one I'm going to be with."

Irritated, I turned away.

God, he was thickheaded.

But then I felt his hand clamp my arm, turning me around, pulling me to him. I yanked my arm back, but he had a strong grip. He pushed my hoodie off my shoulder, exposing my naked breast through the lace tank.

His voice was husky, his eyes on my breast. "I bet if I touch you like I used to, you'd realize I'm right about us." His hand drifted to my breast, fondling it. He moved his face down, his rapid breaths blowing across my lips.

"Brayden! Get your hands off me!" I screeched, fighting to get away, but his determination to prove his point caused him to tighten his grip, restricting blood flow.

And then I heard a loud bang, and Brayden went flying backwards. Nathan stepped in front of me. Carrie moved to my side while Tree went to Brayden.

Nathan pulled my zipper up and cupped my cheeks in his hands. "Are you okay?" His furious eyes were searching my face for the answer.

"I think so," I said, even though I was shaking.

"I'm not going to look at him," he said between clenched teeth. "Because if I do, I'm going to *kill* him." His voice had a deep, wrathful tone that worried me.

"I'm sorry, Paige." Carrie anxiously looked at me. "We shouldn't have brought him here, but you're all he talks about."

"I just don't under--" I stopped when Tree raised his voice at Brayden, telling him what he did was wrong.

"She belongs with me, not *him*!" Brayden hollered, shoving Tree back.

"Stop it, Brayden!" Carrie yelled, running to Tree's side. "It's over between you and Paige. She's with Nathan now."

Nathan's face was consumed with rage and agitation, and he was breathing rapidly through his nose. This wasn't good. I knew I had to do something in order to stop it. But then Brayden opened his mouth and it was too late for me to do anything.

"I've known and loved Paige way before *he* showed up, and I know she loves me too. I also know if she'd let me touch her like I used to and make love to her, she wouldn't be with him."

"Whoa," Tree and Carrie said in unison when Nathan suddenly appeared behind Brayden, pinning his arms behind his back.

"What the hell," Brayden said, not realizing what was happening. But when he twisted his head back and saw Nathan, he started fighting against him, swinging his body from side to side.

Tree and Carrie moved out of the way. I ran to them, afraid of what Nathan would do.

"You will not touch her," Nathan raged, forcing him forward.

"Fuck you," Brayden said, struggling to break free from Nathan's grasp. "I'll be back, and you won't be able to keep me away from her. And *that's* a promise."

Nathan tossed him off the top step in disgust, sending Brayden tumbling to the ground. Brayden hopped to his feet and Nathan was in his face. Brayden threw a punch, but Nathan caught his fist and powered Brayden to his knees. He slammed his foot against Brayden's chest, pushing him backwards, restraining him against the ground. I hurried to them, scared Nathan might crush Brayden's chest. When Nathan looked at me, the porch light caught his eyes and the brutality Aosoth had mentioned, flickered in them.

I shook my head, mouthing not to hurt him. He turned to Brayden.

"If you *ever* violate her again, I will forget you're her friend, and open the gates of hell upon you with my own vengeance," Nathan said furiously.

Brayden squirmed beneath him, his hands clawing at Nathan's iron foot.

"I'm not afraid of you. And I didn't violate Paige. If you weren't around, she would have let me touch her and liked it. Paige knows I'd never hurt her."

Nathan lifted his foot, shaking with rage. "Get him out of here before I seriously do some damage," he told Tree, and then took my arm.

Tree's face was frozen in shock. "Okay."

"I love you half-pint," Brayden called, sounding like his old self.

"Don't look at him, Paige," Nathan told me when I went to turn around. "That's what he wants."

But my heart wept for the Brayden I grew up with and love. I wanted to shake this craziness out of him and bring my old friend back to me. He was still inside there. I just heard it in his voice, and he would have never forced himself on me. I truly believed that.

"We need to take you home." I heard Tree say.

"This isn't the last time you'll see me!" Brayden hollered from across the lawn. "One day I'll come for her, and you won't be able to stop me! What Paige and I have cannot be broken, and she'll see the light and be in my arms instead of yours!"

I heard a deep rumble in Nathan's chest. A growl maybe. And then he flung the door open. When he slammed it behind us, the whole house shuddered in response to his rage. I touched my cold cheeks. They were soaking wet. Nathan sat on the couch, clenching his hands into fists, taking deep breaths. He hung his head and stared at the floor. I noticed his ears were beet red. When he looked up, his gaze went to my cheeks. He shook his head and jumped to his feet.

"I need to get out of here." His voice was thick with anger, and for a second I thought it had to do with me. "You stay here, and don't go outside," he ordered.

"Are you mad at me?" I hated the way my voice sounded, weak and pathetic.

He looked at me, the fury still visible in his eyes.

"No. I'm not mad at you. Why would you think that?"

I bit my lip, hearing the annoyance in his voice. I moved my hand across my cheek.

"Because I was crying."

"I'm not mad at you, Paige. I'm mad at him for putting you through this. The last thing you need right now is more heartache in your life, but he will not stop." He paced the room.

"He's not going to quit"–he jabbed a finger on his chest–"and *I* have a real problem with that." He paused in the middle of the room and shook, his hands balling into a fist. "When he forced himself on you, and I saw where his hand was ..." He blazed passed me. "I'm sorry, Paige, but I have to leave."

I turned to look at him, but saw the door close instead.

Chapter Twenty
Anwar

The clock ticked past midnight, and I wondered when Nathan would come home. After he left, I stood for the longest time staring at the door, knowing he was right about Brayden not quitting. I saw the willfulness in Brayden's eyes, and his strong belief that we belonged together, which caused him to touch me like he had. I didn't appreciate it at all, however, in my heart I knew he would never hurt me. I mean, growing up with Brayden and dating him, he had always made sure I was okay. But regardless of how I felt, he did violate me, and now we could no longer be friends. I held my stomach, feeling sick over this whole mess. I needed to talk to somebody.

I called Carrie.

Carrie and I spoke for a while. She told me she and Tree didn't blame Nathan for his actions toward Brayden, but what they didn't understand was how Nathan got behind Brayden. It was like he appeared out of thin air. I tried to sound nonchalant about it and told her he snuck up on him, but she disagreed. I quickly changed the subject and told her Nathan was so mad that he left. She took the bait and went on to tell me if she were in his shoes, she'd be pissed off too.

"I saw where Brayden's hand was and how you were trying to push him away," she told me. "Then I saw Nathan's face and thought he was going to kill him."

"I know," I said.

"I'll tell ya, Paige, I've never seen somebody so protective over another person like Nathan is with you."

"Do you think that's bad?"

"God, no. I think it's cool," she said without hesitation.

"Tree is like that with you," I informed her. "He told me once if Matt hurts you he'd beat his ass."

"He did?" I could hear the smile in her voice. "When did he say that?"

"When we were at The Lion's Den, the night we met Nathan."

"Really?" She sounded pleased.

"Yeah, so if anybody messes with you, Tree will beat his ass and so will I."

While we talked, I discovered a broken lamp on the floor and asked about it as I picked up the pieces, careful not to cut myself.

"Oh, when we were in the house, we heard Brayden's big mouth get louder and all three of us jumped to our feet. I think Tree was the one who knocked it over."

"That's okay. I didn't like that lamp anyway." I dropped it in the trash, and it thunked when it hit the bottom. "When is Brayden leaving?"

"Tomorrow morning. Tree is pissed off at him and wants him gone, but he's coming back," she warned. "He said sometime this summer."

I sat at the kitchen table and held my head in my hand, telling her she needed to seriously talk to him about me being with Nathan. *This was bad.*

"We have, Paige, but he won't listen. He seriously believes you two belong together, and right now we don't want anything to do with him. The least he can do is apologize to you for his behavior, and so far it doesn't appear like he intends to."

I groaned. "I know Brayden crossed the line tonight, but please keep trying. I don't want him to cause more trouble."

She agreed to keep trying, and we talked for a few more minutes before saying goodnight. I decided to go to bed and went upstairs. It felt weird not having Nathan here, and the emptiness in the house reflected the emptiness I felt when he wasn't around me. It was like he took part of me with him when he left. I wondered if it was healthy to feel this way. I'd heard of people being dependent upon each other, and I'd never wanted to become one of them, but now it seemed like I had.

What would I do if Nathan were no longer in my life? Would I lie down and die? Not if I were immortal. But then what would I do? I knew my happiness couldn't be wrapped around another person. But what would make me happy without him? Nothing, was my first thought, and just thinking about living a life without him turned my heart into pulp.

"You're hopeless, Paige," I mumbled to myself, turning over in my bed.

My room was dark except for the wedge of white moonlight streaming through the gap in the curtain. I stared at it in a daze, and then had the sudden urge to grab my whistle and go outside and play for the moon.

What a dork I am. But for some reason it felt like a natural thing to do, and it made me happy. I envisioned myself dancing around a bonfire in the woods, playing my whistle while the bright moon smiled down upon me and the earth sighed beneath my bare feet. And I was amazed at how much joy that vision brought me.

"Paige," Nathan's voice called from downstairs, making my heart skip a couple beats. "Paige," he said again, now in my room. The bed dipped, and his hand lightly brushed my hair away from my face. "Are you awake?"

I rolled to my side, facing him.

"I'm sorry I left you like that, but I had to burn off my anger."

"How did you do that?" I squinted at him in the darkness, and thought he smiled, but wasn't sure.

"I ran."

"Like Forrest Gump?" I heard the humor in my voice and it felt good.

He laughed. "Sort of, except I broke a few trees along the way."

"Maybe you should go to rehab for anger management," I joked.

He fell silent for a minute, and I thought maybe he took what I said the wrong way, but then he spoke. "I've never been like this before," he said, kicking off his shoes. "But when it comes to somebody hurting you, it infuriates me." He stood, and I heard the sound of his zipper go down and his pants dropping to the floor. He sat back on the bed, bouncing it, and took off his shirt. A warming sensation filled my solar plexus, but my body still felt too weak to act on it. I decided to focus on his voice instead of my hormones. He slipped into bed, and I felt his strong arms curl around me. "Does it bother you I feel that way?"

"No, it makes me feel safe."

He tightened his arms, hugging me. "I'll always keep you safe. You mean more to me than anything and why the beast within me emerges when it comes to your well-being."

"What are we going to do about Brayden?" I asked, and felt his body stiffen. "I spoke to Carrie tonight, and she warned me he's going to be back for me this summer."

"It's not going to happen." His words burned in an angry rush. "You'll be immortal and stronger than him when he shows up again. And if he continues to pursue you, he'll have to deal with me."

"Were you talking to Anwar earlier?" I asked in the middle of a yawn. It boggled my mind how tired I was when all I did for almost five days was sleep. But I felt exhausted, and my eyelids were heavy.

"Yes, and he told me something I've been meaning to tell you."

That caught my attention, and my lids perked up.

"What?"

"You're going to be getting a VCR tape tomorrow. It's coming Federal Express."

"What's on the tape?"

"Your father."

I bolted up, my eyes instantly filling with tears. "Are you serious?"

He pulled me back into his arms. "Yes, I am. Your father made the tape for you right before he died. He gave it to Anwar and made him promise to give it to you if you were marked for immortality. He wasn't sure if it would happen, but he had dreams about it, and felt compelled to do it."

"Has Anwar seen the tape?"

"No. He doesn't believe in invading somebody's privacy unless there's a good reason to."

"I'm scared," I blurted without realizing what I was saying. I wished I hadn't because I didn't want him to worry. I'd put him through enough already.

"Why is that?" His voice was gentle.

"Because I don't know what he's going to say or if I can handle it. I mean, I'm emotional right now just because my dad made a video for me. How will I be tomorrow when I see it?"

"I'll watch it with you if you want," he offered.

"Of course I want you to watch it with me." I paused, feeling nervous now. "Did Anwar say anything else to you?"

"Yes, he told me he'll be here sooner than he thought, but he wasn't sure when."

"Finally, some good news," I said, feeling the tension in my shoulders lifting.

We fell silent. The wind was howling outside, rattling the window. I rested my head on Nathan's chest, listening to the slow beating of his heart, thankful he was here with me.

"So, did you tell him about the journal?" I asked, breaking the silence.

"No, I didn't, Paige, and *we're* not going to either," he said in a sharp voice.

I kept quiet, knowing Anwar pissed Nathan off more with keeping this video from us.

"I'm sorry. That was rude of me." He paused. "Let's go to sleep. You need your rest. And don't worry about tomorrow. I'll be there with you, and we'll get through it."

I closed my eyes and saw myself back at the bonfire again, but this time Nathan was with me. We were dancing around the fiery pit, the huge orange flames dancing along with us.

"I'll always want you with me," I said in my dream. Or did I say it out loud? I wasn't sure, but I felt his warm lips on my temple.

"I'm yours forever," he whispered in my ear and smiled in my dream.

***

"Are you ready for this?" Nathan waved the tape at me.

It was early afternoon, and I just got off the phone with Carrie's mom who invited Nathan and me to her house tonight for a fish fry, along with Tree and his mom. I told her we'd be there around six and thanked her for everything she had done for me. She blew it off like it was nothing and told me she loved me, which brought tears to my eyes. I said the same before hanging up.

"We've been invited to Carrie's house for dinner tonight," I told Nathan, staring at the tape in his hand. "Tree and his mom will be there too."

He took my hand and led me into the living room, then closed the curtains and turned the TV and VCR/DVD player on. He popped the tape in and picked up the remote before sitting next to me.

My stomach rolled, and I groaned. "I don't know about this."

Nathan rubbed my shoulder. "It'll be okay."

I sat on the couch and held my face in my hands. My knees were bouncing, and I blew air through my fingers, then dropped them to my lap. "Okay, turn it on."

He pushed a button. The TV came on, and my father's hand was adjusting the camera.

When he sat back and smiled, a weird choking noise escaped my lips.

"Daddy." I covered my mouth and felt Nathan's hand on my leg. My father looked so young and still had the James Dean look going on, with his tousled auburn hair and white turtleneck sweater. "I miss you so much, Daddy," I cried inside my head.

"Hi, my little peanut girl," he said, and I exploded into tears. He had a silly smile on his handsome face and looked down, pausing for a minute before facing the camera. "I know you're probably too old for me to call you that now, but you'll always be my little peanut girl."

"I'll never be too old for that," I half cried and laughed. Nathan scooted closer and squeezed my leg.

"If you're watching this tape," he continued, "Then the dreams I've had of you being marked for immortality have come true, and I'm sorry the weight of the world is on your shoulders now." He shifted in his chair and took a deep breath. "I'm also sorry for not being there while you were growing up. But I assure you, in spirit, I'll always be with you and your mom."

I nodded and a sob escaped my lips when I noticed his own eyes were brimming with tears. He looked away and moved his fingers across them.

"I'm sorry if I'm upsetting you. It's not my intention here," he said to the camera. "There are some things you need to know. First and foremost, I didn't take immortality because I didn't want to lose the two loves of my life. I just couldn't do it, and if that's a selfish act on my part, so be it, and I'm sorry you had to suffer because of my decision. But one day your mother will be with me, and both of us will look after you."

Nathan pushed the pause button because I was sobbing in my hands. I got a Kleenex and wiped my nose, staring at my father's frozen image on the TV.

"Do you want to continue watching this?" His voice was soft and sympathetic.

I leaned forward and nodded. He pushed the button again.

"The second thing you need to know is I think you should choose immortality. I know eventually you'll have to leave your mother, unless you tell her, but that's your call. But I think this world needs you to help protect it. You need to be strong, Paige, even if the road you travel on gets lonely at times. I spoke to my friend Anwar, who is immortal, and he promised me he'd help and guide you through all of this. He saw you once and told me the oddest thing"–he moved his finger up and down at the camera and smiled–"He said there's a powerful light within you, and he can see energy vibrating around you."

I grabbed the remote and paused it, turning to Nathan.

"Can Anwar see energy?"

"Yes, he can. Remember he's from the jungles of Africa where they practice mysticism. He has an uncanny keen awareness of the energies in this world. He can also see people's auras."

"That's crazy. The more you talk about him, the more I can't wait to meet him. He sounds like an extraordinary person."

"He is," Nathan said as I restarted the tape.

"I think he's right," my father went on. "You need to take this opportunity. Another thing I want to mention before I go is a ring the dark spirits are after. Anwar told me he'd tell you about it so I didn't have to explain to you what it is or the importance of it. Some people don't even believe it exists, but I think it does, and if they haven't found it by the time you're watching this, then you need to find and destroy it." He stopped for a moment. A strange look came over his face, and he began to speak in a cryptic tone. "The way will be written within the boards in the dwelling of one's mind. The iron cap keeps your thoughts and ideas hidden from the eyes of the world."

"Holy crap!" I looked at Nathan, and he was grinning. "That's why I've been getting those damn premonitions, to prepare me for this and what's to come."

My father's voice went back to normal. "Follow my footsteps and finish it. I know you'll make me proud." He kissed his fingertips and touched the lense. "I'll forever love you and be with you in spirit. Be strong and never give up on yourself and what's been given to you. And most importantly, grow your mind so your intellect can be your shining light to guide you through this world and bring all truths to you." His hand went to the camera. Then the tape went blank.

Nathan ejected the tape from the VCR and opened the curtains, allowing the gray light to flood into the room while I sat, zoning into space, thinking about what my father said. He wanted me to become immortal and seemed to think I could find the ring, just like the dark spirits thought. But what if he was wrong? The last thing I wanted was to fail my father. I leaned forward and held my head in my hands as the doubts took hold of me.

"What's wrong?" Nathan asked, sitting beside me.

I lifted my face and dropped my hands. "My father has too much faith in me when it comes to finding the ring. I mean, what if I can't?"

He took my hand and rubbed it. "You know what I think?" I shook my head and stared into his dark blue eyes. They were so serious and honest. "I think you have abilities within you you're not aware of, and once you stop over-thinking things and trust in yourself, those abilities will start to flow through you."

"So you think I can find the ring as well?"

"I do," he said. "But only if you believe you can, because if you take a self defeatist approach to this, then you've already failed."

I sighed. "You're right. I need to change my thinking."

He stood. "I'll tell ya what. I have some books at my house that might interest you and ease your mind."

I pushed myself off the couch and got my purse and house keys. "Okay, let's go."

***

"How cool. I didn't know you had a Hummer," I said when he parked in front of his house.

Nathan grinned. "It's Anwar's."

"He's here?" My heart raced from the anticipation of finally getting to meet him, and then a tall, bald African guy appeared in front of the house, walking toward us. He carried himself with an air of intelligence and grace. Nathan opened my door and gave me his hand. I took it and stepped out of the truck, meeting the gentle smile on Anwar's face.

"Anwar, this is Paige." Nathan gestured to me proudly.

Anwar bowed and stuck his huge hand out. "Please to meet you," his deep, rich voice said with an accent much like the Watusi men I'd heard on the Discovery Channel. He looked like he was in his early twenties.

My hand disappeared into his when I shook it. "I'm pleased to finally meet you," I said. "I've heard great things about you."

His brown, soulful eyes reached the depths of mine when he said, "The pleasure is all mine." He was a handsome man, and I loved the sound of his voice.

Nathan took my hand, his face beaming. "When did you get here?"

"My arrival was an hour ago. I wanted to surprise you." Anwar ducked his head when he entered the house, and sat in the living room chair. He gestured for us to sit with him, folding his hands in his lap.

"This is a pleasant surprise," Nathan said. "We just finished watching the tape."

"Splendid." Anwar crossed his long legs, and for some reason I was waiting for him to ask me if I wanted to take the red pill or blue pill. "Did you learn anything of value?" His eyes fell on mine.

I said the first thing that came to mind. "He thinks I can find the ring."

He curled his finger beneath his chin and nodded. "I can see why he would think dat, but let me indulge you in a few things so you will understand why I withheld information from you, and why you have been through so much heartache lately," he said to me, and I realized I felt comfortable around him.

"Please do because I don't understand any of it." I sat back in Nathan's arms and waited for him to continue.

He put his palms together as if in prayer and held them to his lips, collecting his thoughts I suppose, but then he dropped them.

"Everything is made up of energy. Unfortunately most people's energy in dis world is contaminated by the harshness of others and their own lives. If they don't get rid of dis negative energy, their lives are only half lived. But if they face their demons, seek understanding and grow from it, a new world will open up to them." He paused to see if I was following him, and I nodded. "But the energy residing in the flesh is unique and different from other energies dat resides in the flesh as well, however, some are similar," he mentioned as an after thought.

"When you say energy, are you talking about a person's soul?" I asked, making sure I understood him correctly.

"Yes." He pointed at Nathan and me. "I have never encountered two energies dat compliment each other so well. It is quite astonishing to see."

"Then that explains why the first time I saw Nathan I felt this magnetic energy toward him," I said in awe. "But it goes deeper than that. I can't explain it."

"It's the same for me too," Nathan replied.

"Dat's correct," Anwar said. "But Nathaniel, your fierce love for Paige might harm her if you are not careful."

"What do you mean?" Nathan leaned forward.

"I mean, one day she might be in danger and the red dat you will see will obstruct your vision and mind, and it will distract you from the correct actions to take."

"Okay, I'll take your warning to heart," Nathan said, sounding disturbed.

I looked at Anwar. "How do you know all of this?"

Anwar pointed at us again. “I can see it in your energy field, and I can read body language.”

“So why did you keep the information about my father from us?” I asked.

“I was getting to dat,” he said with a gentle smile.

Nathan pulled me back into his arms.

“What you’ve been through recently had to be done in order to clear your energy, to teach you to be a stronger person. If I were to have told Nathaniel about your father, it would have hindered your growth. Do you understand?”

“I guess, but I still think it was wrong of you do,” I said, staring him in the face. He didn’t look sorry, which irked me.

“I agree with Paige,” Nathan replied, sounding perturbed. “You had no right to do that.”

“What is done is done,” Anwar said. “I cannot change it.”

Nathan stiffened. I glanced at him and noticed his ears were reddening. I decided to change the subject, to break the sudden tension between us.

“So how does my energy look now?”

He stared at me for a minute. “It looks good, but there are aches you need to overcome, and you are unsure of yourself. I also see a powerful light inside you.”

“You’re good.” I smiled, impressed and excited about him being like a living oracle I could talk to.

“I know these things from years of practice and freeing my mind from the restraints of others,” he said modestly.

“What about my premonitions?” I definitely wanted to know about them.

“Your spirit is attuned to the other world, and dat’s why you have them. The ‘old one’ knows dis and had told some of the dark spirits dat your flesh houses a remarkable energy. So when you do become immortal it is imperative you become acquainted with dat side of you and learn how to use it.” He paused in thought, and then said, “I would like to add dat our spirit is not one thing, it is multifaceted, and each one of us has the opportunity to create ourselves on how we want to become. We are autonomous. And each experience becomes a piece of our spirit, like mosaic art. So be cautious with each decision you make.”

I sat up, intrigued by what he was saying. “Do my premonitions come from a guide?"

"It comes from your guide and your higher self, the part of your spirit dat's connected to all things. It is its own living entity with tentacles dat reaches out into the universe and snatches information to bring back to you. It relays messages to you from your guide, and they are cryptic because it is teaching you a skill you are going to need in the future."

"That's a trip." My brain was totally fried now.

His warm eyes were fixed on mine. "After you become immortal, I will teach you how to harness and use the powers within you to your advantage. And on the matter of the dark spirits, there are things dat you must know, like where your boundaries lie, and what you can do about them, among other things."

"Like what?"

Anwar's attention shifted to Nathan.

"I already explained it to her," Nathan said, reading Anwar's face.

"Explain what?" I looked at them both.

"Dat you will not be as strong as Nathaniel. You gain strength as the years go by. Dat's why he cannot cast out an ancient spirit like I can because I am older. But you will be able to cast young ones out."

"Oh, he did tell me that, but what about Latin? I don't know Latin."

He tapped his finger on his forehead. "Dat is already embedded in your super-conscious mind, so fortunately you will know it when you become immortal. But the incantations you will need to learn, and we will teach them to you. We will also teach you how to fight, move, and think on a strategic level."

All three of us fell silent for a minute, and then I thought of something I'd been wanting to ask.

"The cat at my house, I call him Mr. Kitty, but what's his real name?"

"You call him Mr. Kitty?"Anwar snickered.

I threw my hands in the air, exasperated. "Not you too." He had a blank look on his face. "Brayden laughed about it as well," I said, feeling Nathan's body tense.

Interest flashed across Anwar's eyes. He uncrossed his legs and leaned forward. "Dis Brayden you speak of, what is his last name?"

My stomach dropped.

"Blackwater. Why?" My heart raced at the recognition in Anwar's face.

His eyes darted between Nathan and me. "He too has been marked for immortality."

Nathan's blur streaked to the center of the room. "You got to be *fuckin'* kidding me?"

"Are you sure about this?" I then remembered Brayden mentioning he had seen a similar cat at his house, and I wondered if this was for real.

Anwar watched Nathan pacing the floor, but then he looked at me. "I'm quite sure. A friend of mine will be approaching him shortly."

"This is just *great*," Nathan fumed.

"But how are you sure?" It was still hard for me to believe. I mean, *Brayden*?

"The cat's name is Zeruel, and he lets me know who is being marked."

"You communicate with him?" The shock I felt soared out of my voice.

"Yes, and he is very fond of you," he said with an endearing smile.

I grinned, but it quickly subsided with Nathan's continual rants.

Anwar frowned. "Nathaniel, please sit."

Nathan stopped in front of the fireplace. "You don't understand, Anwar. Brayden wants to claim Paige for himself and will not stop until he haves her. I wanted to kill him last night when he forced himself on her." His angry voice amplified around us.

"Brayden and I grew up together, and we dated," I explained to Anwar when I saw his confusion. "He moved to California two years ago, but we remained good friends. Last week he showed for Mom's funeral, and believes we were destined to be together. I've tried to tell him differently that I belong with Nathan, but he won't listen to reason. He won't even listen to our two close friends."

"I see." Anwar ran his finger across his bottom lip. "And when he finds out you are immortal as well, dat will cement his belief in you belonging with him."

Nathan ran a hand through his hair. "*Exactly!*" he seethed. "And this is going to present a real problem because he's relentless when it comes to Paige."

I held my hand out to Nathan. "Please sit with me."

He hung his head, groaned, and then sat next to me. I took his hand, hoping it would calm him. He relaxed a little, but I could feel the anger rolling off him.

"Your dealings with Brayden are your own. I cannot help you with dat," Anwar told us. "For some reason your fates are intertwined, and you are going to have to figure dat one out."

"Is it unusual for two people who grew up together to be marked for immortality?" I asked, knowing Brayden would accept immortality and wondered what he was going to do when he found out I was immortal as well.

Anwar was watching Nathan's hand gripping the arm of the couch. "Remember what I told you, Nathaniel, about seeing red." Nathan dropped his hand into his lap, turning it into a fist.

Anwar looked at me. "It is rare." He stood. "Come, I would like to show you some books dat will benefit you."

The rest of the afternoon was spent talking about the ring–Nathan and I didn't tell Anwar about the journal–and Anwar showing me some historical books on King Solomon's ring and on elemental magic. He reiterated about the powerful light within me and said in order to wield that power, I needed to become more attuned to it. I half listened to him–even though there were a trillion questions I wanted to ask–because I was still shocked about Brayden and nervous about the act of turning immortal. Nathan, on the other hand, didn't say much until Anwar asked me if I wanted him to turn me immortal tonight. I could tell by the way Nathan kept pushing his hands together, flexing the muscles in his arms, he was still upset.

As I watched his muscles flex, my mind drifted to another place. A place where those arms were wrapped around my body. I knew then what I wanted to do first and told Anwar we'd pick him up tomorrow afternoon to do it.

"What?" Nathan said, not pleased.

"It's okay Nathaniel. Dis can wait until tomorrow." Anwar threw me an understanding look.

I looked down, blushing.

"She should do it tonight," Nathan said, annoyed. He turned to me. "I know you're scared of the pain, but you'll be okay." He took a deep breath in an effort to calm himself, but his eyes were angry. "I actually want you to do it now."

I shook my head, and he rolled his eyes, looking the other way.

I reached up and nudged his chin so he had to look at me. "Do you trust me?"

"Listen to her, Nathaniel. I think she has a fine reason."

He crossed his arms over his chest. "What's the reason?"

I uncrossed them and took his hand. "It's a surprise. Believe me, it'll be worth it."

He scowled at me, but when I gave him an encouraging smile, he finally said. "All right. I hope it's a damned good one."

"Trust me. It is." I pulled him outside to the truck and said good-bye to Anwar.

Chapter Twenty One
Ambush

I had Nathan stop at a flower shop on the way to Carrie's house to buy a bouquet of colorful flowers and a box of chocolates for Carrie's and Tree's mom. The tiny shop smelled of fresh flowers and had a cozy atmosphere. I was admiring the cute little china sets on the shelf beside the counter while I waited for the heavyset lady with too much blue-eyeshadow, to prepare the flowers.

"Look at these. Aren't they cute?" I picked a little tea cup up to show Nathan.

He glanced at it, uninterested. "Yes," he muttered, still brooding.

I turned my back on him and drifted to the used cookbooks on the far wall. He followed with his hands in his pockets, his eyes on the floor. I sighed, feeling his temper getting to me, so when we were back in his truck, and the flowers were placed safely in the backseat, I faced him.

"You need to snap out of this crappy mood, or I'm going to Carrie's without you," I told him.

"You know it's too dangerous for you to be by yourself," he said.

I raised my eyebrows. "Are you going snap out of it?"

He stared out the windshield, his lips pressed together.

"Fine!" I reached for the handle on the truck, but he quickly snatched my hand. "Let. Go. Of. My. Hand," I said.

"I'm sorry, Paige." His eyes looked sad. I wanted to comfort him, but I was still angry. "I don't want you mad at me, and I want this to be a fun night with your friends."

"They're your friends too, ya know." I yanked my hand back and glared.

He frowned. "I know, and I don't mean to be an ass, but this whole Brayden thing bothers me."

"I understand," I said, "but let's try to forget about it tonight. Okay?" I gazed at him from beneath my lashes, hoping it would lure him into a better mood. "Please. For me."

That slow, sexy smile of his appeared, and a swarm of butterflies filled my chest. "Anything for you," he said.

I returned his smile and sat back, satisfied now. "Good. Now let's go have some fun with *our* friends."

***

"I really enjoyed myself tonight," Nathan said when we stepped onto my front porch. "They're good people, and Carrie's dad is a ball buster."

The moon was almost full. Its bright light cast enough light for me to see the happiness in his face. My eyes strayed down to his arms, chest. He turned to unlock the door, unaware of the hungry desire stirring inside me. I suddenly realized I should say something in response to what he just said.

"They are good people, and I love them all." I noticed something moving toward me from across the porch and smiled when I saw what it was. "Hi, Mr. Kitty. I mean, Zeruel." He rubbed against my leg, and I bent to pet him. "I want you to know I'm very fond of you too." I kissed his head. "I love you."

"Did you just kiss him?" Nathan laughed, opening the door.

"I did, and he's purring, so he must not mind it."

He shook his head, flashing me his sexy smile again, and that familiar fire inside my belly ignited. I stood, winked at Zeruel, and entered the house.

"You know, it's only a quarter past ten. We can still go to my house and have Anwar turn you immortal tonight," Nathan said, turning on lights. "I really would like for you to reconsider and do it tonight instead of tomorrow."

My back was turned to him, and I unbuttoned my white blouse, revealing my white lace bra. I ran my hand down my flat belly. My soft skin rose and fell beneath my hand.

"Are you listening to me, Paige?"

I turned, and his gaze immediately went to my chest. He looked up, and to my satisfaction, his eyes were bright with the same desire I felt.

"I want you to make love to me for the last time as a human, so it'll be fresh in my mind when we make love again as immortals," I said, the raspy part of my voice adding a sultry tone to my words. "I want to record it into memory, so I'll have it with me for eternity."

"Now I understand," he whispered, his bright eyes pouring into mine.

"Is that stupid?" My words came out breathy because of the way he was looking at me, with such love, passion, and yearning.

"No, it's beautiful. You're beautiful." His hand went to the back of my neck, and he gently pulled me to him. "I love you," his warm breath blew into my ear. My heart fluttered at the intense electricity between us. His hands moved to the side of my face, lifting it.

"I love you too," I whispered as he lowered his lips to mine.

His kisses were long and deep, but slow, like he wanted to savor each one. He moved his hands to my neck, my shoulders, pushing my blouse off. I lifted the bottom of his T-shirt, and he broke our kiss to take it off. He threw it across the room, then picked me up. I wrapped my legs around his waist and held his face in my hands, our mouths and tongues reconnecting. We were both breathing erratically, and when he pushed my back against the wall next to the stairs, kissing the side of my neck, a breathless moan escaped my lips. Every nerve ending in my body was like a live wire, and I longed for him to touch every inch of it.

"I want you." His voice was deep and primal.

"I'm yours," I breathed, already feeling an explosion building inside me.

We were suddenly in my room, and he positioned me on the bed, my backside on the edge of it. Within a minute, he was above me, his hand softly touching my body. I shivered, and when I moved my hand down his bare chest, he shivered as well. He pushed me farther up on the bed, and I raised my hands above my head, arching my back as he did things to my body that caused me to moan loudly and twitch beneath him.

A long while later, after I had my fun with Nathan, and he had his fun with me again, I fell into his arms. We were both panting, blissfully happy. It was well past one in the morning, and I thought this time tomorrow I'd no longer be human. The thought of the pain and the blood that would be drained out of me entered my mind, and my mouth filled with salty saliva. I curled an arm around my queasy stomach and forced that thought out of my mind. I didn't want it to ruin this wonderful moment and tried to think of something else. Thankfully, Nathan spoke, and I was able to focus my attention on him instead.

"That was beyond extraordinary. I just can't get enough of you." He hugged me to his side.

"I know exactly what you mean." I touched his smooth washboard stomach and was glad he wasn't hairy like most guys. Why I thought of that, I didn't know.

"Do you think other people feel this way?" He propped his pillow against the headboard and scooted up, bringing me with him. "I mean, I'm sure other people have great sex, but with us it's much more than that. It's not about the act of getting my rocks off. It's about making love and trying to physically express not only my desires for you, but what I feel that cannot be put into words. Am I making sense? I know I'm rambling, but I'm in awe of what we have together and what I feel for you."

The adorable look on his face made me forget how to speak for a second. He was so damn cute. I reached up and touched his cheek. "I hope other people feel this way or close to it," I said. "Otherwise, this world is much sadder than I thought. And you're making complete sense because it's the same for me. I'm so in love with you that when you're not around a part of me is gone with you."

His eyes locked onto mine. "Yes, it's the same for me too." He kissed my hand. "I want to marry you." He sounded serious, and his expression was filled with adoration, stunning me.

I didn't know what to say. I mean, this was the first time he ever mentioned marriage, so I had assumed we'd be together like we were for the rest of eternity. But the thought of marrying him, taking on his name, and sanctifying it in front of the people we love, blew me away. My throat tightened.

He pulled me up and cradled my face in his hands. "I mean it, Paige. I want to marry you, and I'm not saying this because of Brayden. I've known this since the first day you caught my eye. You're everything to me, and I want you to be my wife." His thumbs moved across my cheeks, brushing at the tears. "I know in this day and age marriage is just a piece of paper some people find unnecessary, but to me it's much more than that. It shouts to the world we are united in love, trust, friendship, and loyalty."

"I never knew you thought about this," I whispered.

He brushed his lips against mine, then our foreheads connected. "I've thought about it a lot, but there's never been a more perfect time to bring it up."

"So, are you proposing to me?" I wiped my wet cheeks with the back of my hand.

The corner of his mouth curled, and he had a mischievous look on his face that confused me. He shook his head.

I glanced down, feeling the heat in my face. What an idiot I was to presume he was proposing to me or working up to it. I was probably too young to get married anyway, but then again, people in the 1800s were married at a lot younger age than I, and had a couple kids by the time they were my age. And when you *knew* without a doubt you were with the right person, you should get married. But still, I wanted to crawl in a hole and disappear.

He tilted his chin down, his eyes on mine. "You deserve a proper proposal, one I intend to give you when the time is right. I just wanted you to know the type of future, I envision us having, and how incredibly in love I am with you."

The heat subsided from my face, and I couldn't help but give him a teasing smile. "Well, I guess you'll have to wait for my answer then."

He laughed and playfully rolled his eyes, sticking the palm of his hand to his forehead. "Oh, the agony of it all. I don't know if I'll be able to handle the anticipation of not knowing what your answer is going to be."

I smacked his arm, laughing along with him. "Shut up."

He grinned and pulled me into his arms, moving us on the pillows. I glanced at the clock and saw it was almost two in the morning.

"I think maybe we should try and sleep so we can get up at a decent hour tomorrow," I said, feeling my stomach churning.

"It'll be okay."

I didn't respond.

"I swear. You won't feel most of the pain."

"Most?" I gulped. I didn't like hearing that.

"It's not that bad." He leaned across me and switched the lamp off. "At first it feels like a bad paper cut, but then your body goes into shock and all you feel is something cold running off you, and then you drift off and black out."

"What will it be like afterwards?" I asked, not wanting to think about the pain.

"It'll be a whole different world. All your senses will be heightened exponentially. Your eyesight and hearing alone will astound you. Your mind will be sharper, and all the flaws in your skin will vanish. Not to mention, the agility, the strength, and swiftness you'll have in your body will astound you even more."

"It's almost hard to imagine I'm going to be like that."

Nathan yawned. "Soon you'll find out."

"Ten more hours," I muttered, hearing him breathing much slower now, and thought how unfair it was for him to be already asleep. But then I closed my eyes, and before I knew it, I too fell fast asleep.

***

"I'm going to stay in the truck while you get Anwar and the stuff you need to do this," I told Nathan when he parked in front of his house. "I don't feel so good." My stomach was in a knot, and I could taste the Lucky Charms I had earlier rising in my throat.

He kissed me. "I'll be back." He paused, his eyes fixed on my face. "You look paler than normal. Are you all right?" His hand went to my forehead, and he wiped the sweat off.

"I think I'm going to be sick," I moaned, holding my stomach.

"Try to think of something else, and I'll see if Anwar has an herb you can take to help you through this."

I nodded, staring at his anxious eyes. He kissed me again then vanished. I sat trying to focus on something else, but my mind kept shifting back onto the pain and blood. A wave of radiating heat pulsed through my body. I flung the door open, spewing Lucky Charms on the ground. *Ugh*, I hated throwing up. But at least it didn't come out my nose or get in my hair, I told myself. I got a mint from my purse and chewed it, sitting still for a minute to make sure the nausea subsided.

Finally, I was able to get out of the truck. I rubbed my stomach, breathing in the cool, damp, air. It had an earthy smell, the genesis of all smells. And as I stared at the gray sky, watching it growing darker by the second, a high-pitched ringing sounded in my ears.

"Paige," I heard Tree's voice call. My head snapped in the direction of his voice, confusion clouding my mind.

How did he know where Nathan lived? And why were my ears ringing?

I spotted him and Carrie right away, stepping out of the foggy black forest, like two ghostly apparitions. I noticed the smug look on Carrie's face, and my blood ran cold.

How in the hell did she get inside Carrie?

Tree waved to me. "Carrie wanted to surprise you and Nathan, so we parked down the road," he said.

They were getting closer now, and Carrie narrowed her eyes, like a cat getting ready to pounce on its prey. A rush of adrenaline coursed through my veins as fear exploded in my heart. I glanced over my shoulder and saw two guys–who looked like they belonged in prison–holding heavy chains and billy clubs dart inside the house.

"Who are they?" Tree asked. His eyes widened when he noticed me shaking. "What's going on?" His hand went to Carrie's arm, and she pushed him away as if he were an annoying dog jumping on her. He stumbled backwards, his boots scraping the ground, and fell.

A loud crashing noise came from the house and one of the front windows burst, spraying shards of glass all over the deck.

"Paige!" Nathan's frantic voice bellowed through the crashing noises erupting from the house.

Hearing his voice ripped through my heart, and the fear of never seeing him again devoured me. I knew I had to do something, so I did the first thing that came to mind. I ran to Tree.

"You need to get back to the car right now," I told him. "You're not safe here."

He scrambled to his feet, rubbing his back, his eyebrows knitting together in confusion. Carrie snatched my wrist, spinning me around. A beam of light swiped across her eyes. I jerked my hand to break free, but it was useless; she was too strong. A malicious sneer crossed her face, and she forced me to her.

"What is your decision?" she asked, her voice higher than normal.

"Carrie, let go of Paige. You're hurting her." Tree reached out to remove her hand from my wrist. She shoved him with her free hand, knocking him to the ground, much harder this time.

"Leave him alone," I said, and out the corner of my eye I saw Tree getting up. "Stay away, Tree. This isn't Carrie."

He looked at me in bewilderment, then jerked his head toward the house. "There are two more guys going inside the house." He pointed.

I tried to look, but Carrie jerked my arm so hard it felt like it went out of the socket. I yelped.

"What's your answer?" She was losing her patience.

"Get the hell out of here!" I yelled at Tree. He looked at the house again, then at me, torn about what to do. I could hear horrifying shrieks coming from the house, and Nathan's ferocious voice roaring throughout it.

Carrie reached to her back pocket and pulled out a sharp hunting knife. Her eyes turned small, and her mouth became even crueler. "I'm going to ask you one more time," she said, coldly between her teeth, raising the knife blade to my face. "What is your decision?"

I jerked my head back and glanced away and saw Matt running out of the foggy woods, straight for Tree. "Behind you Tree!" I hollered.

Tree turned, and Matt barreled into him. Tree fell backwards, and his head bounced off a log, knocking him out.

"You son-of-a-bitch!" I screamed and cried at the same time. "He has nothing to do with this!"

With a twisted smirk, Matt arrogantly wiped himself off. He casually walked to me and grabbed my other wrist. I looked at Carrie. On her face burned a delight that could only be evil. I knew then they were going to kill me. I screamed for them to let me go as they dragged me to a tree. I dropped my weight and tried to kick their feet out from under them, but they took hold of my armpits and swung my body against a tree. I thought about Nathan and me never being together again, but instead of crying and pleading for my life, I became angry.

How dare they do this to us!

"I have plans for you, Paige," Matt whispered. "I found the ring, and I'll be needing your assistance in finding the incantations." He glanced at Carrie who was dancing around with the knife in her hand laughing. He leaned closer to my ear. "Aosoth isn't aware of this, but soon she will be, however, I'll be out of the country by then." He lifted my hands above my head. "I'll be seeing you again." He pulled a leather cord out of his pocket and tied my wrists to the tree. The cord was so tight, my hands became numb.

I spat in his face. "Fuck you!" I glared at Carrie. "And fuck you too! You're nothing but a crazy, stupid, bitch!" Matt chuckled under his breath, and Carrie stared scornfully at me.

"Let me cut her throat," she hissed blackly, lifting the knife to my neck. I turned my head, feeling the blade press into my skin and heard a strange squeaking sound escape my lips.

"No," Matt snapped, removing her hand. "Stick to the plan."

She snatched my face and dug her sharp black nails into my cheeks. Her hot breath blew into my ear. "Vos ero pessum ire," she said in a dark, hateful voice, reminding me of the horrific dream I had. I squeezed my eyes shut, forcing angry, scared tears out.

"This will only hurt for a few minutes," Matt whispered into my ear.

I opened my eyes to a tenderness glowing in his, then a sharp pain seared down both my forearms. I screamed in agony, and a loud clap of thunder broke across the dark sky. The tree I was tied to shook violently, and Carrie twirled around with blood dripping off the knife, her head thrown back with her mouth opened wide in sadistic laughter.

I cried from the excruciating pain of my skin being laid open like a slaughtered animal, but then felt my body going into shock and quickly becoming weak, just like Nathan had said.

And then I heard a vicious, snarling animal running at us. I realized it was Nathan when I saw his face contorted into a mask beyond rage. Anwar was close behind him. His hand clamped onto Matt's throat before Matt had the chance to react.

I could feel myself disconnecting from my body, no longer aware of the pain. My eyes fell on Nathan lifting Carrie above his head, his wrathful voice saying and chanting things, I couldn't understand. With what I thought was my last breath, I told him not to hurt her, and hoped he had heard my weak voice.

I catapulted out of my body and found myself standing a couple yards away from them. I felt the same as when I had the out-of-body experience at The Lion's Den. I was free from my fleshly prison and felt wonderful. But then I saw Carrie on the ground gasping, unable to move, and Nathan rushing to my limp body.

"Paige! … No! … Please baby, hang on," he cried, ripping the cord off my wrists. My body fell forward into his arms. He was crying and shaking while he lowered me gingerly to the ground, my blood covering the front of him.

Anwar was chanting a Latin incantation, holding Matt by the neck, high above the ground. Matt stared defiantly at him without saying a word, and then a black ghostly thing with glowing eyes left the body. The spirit flew passed me, disappearing into the trees, swaying the branches in flight.

"Nathaniel, you must do it now!" Anwar yelled, tossing Matt aside and picking Carrie off the ground.

"I can't," Nathan's anguished voice told him.

Tree was awake now, rubbing the back of his head. His attention immediately snapped on Anwar holding Carrie by the throat. He jumped to his feet and ran to her.

Anwar stuck his hand out. "I'm trying to help her." Tree stopped when he caught the stern look on Anwar's face. Carrie writhed in his grasp, spouting what sounded like curses in Latin. "Nathaniel! Do it now! You're going to lose her forever if you don't!"

It was weird how I could see everything happening at once, and when I'd focused on one person, I'd end up beside them.

Now I stood beside Nathan, helplessly watching. His hands were planted on the ground beside my shoulders. Tears were dripping off his face onto my cheeks.

"I love you, Paige. Baby, please don't leave me." He grabbed the knife Carrie dropped, then everything stopped, like the universe had just pushed the pause button.

A bright white light encompassed me. I didn't know if it came from above or below me, but I was inside it, enfolded in the arms of peace and love.

"Paige." I heard my mother's voice behind me and felt a hand on my shoulder.

"Mom?" I turned to her and my father holding hands, smiling.

I threw my arms around them, laughing and crying at the same time. It felt so right, the three of us together, and the two huge gaps inside me finally became full again.

"Paige, honey, you need to go back," she said. "They need you, and you need them."

"Your mother is right," Dad said. "There's so much good you can do, and it would be a shame if you were to walk away from it."

My lip trembled. "But I'll never see you again, and I miss you two so much." I totally didn't want to leave them, especially since the three of us were now together. It was ironic though, that my father had chosen to leave us because it was the right thing for him to do, and now I was faced with the same dilemma.

Mom took my hand. "We'll always be with you, and I believe we'll see each other again. This isn't good-bye." She hugged me and somehow I knew she was right.

I could feel their love for me pouring from them, a warmth so overwhelming I covered my mouth to stifle a sob, realizing they had loved me all along. I still didn't want to leave, but knew in my heart I had to because being with them wasn't my destiny. Protecting humanity was. I had to go back.

"We love you very much," Dad said, hugging me as well.

"I'll forever love you two," I cried. "And I'll do the best I can to make things right."

"We have no doubts." Dad smiled, his eyes twinkling.

Mom glanced over her shoulder. "Gordon, we have to go."

I looked past her and saw the background was shimmering in a kaleidoscope of brilliant colors. They quickly embraced me, then disappeared, taking the white light with them.

"What are you doing?" Tree asked in horror when he saw Nathan gash a deep cut on his forearms. He ran to Nathan, but stopped when he heard Carrie's agonizing shrieks. He looked at us in turn, his face drenched in tears.

Nathan lay on top of me–careful not to press his full body weight down–and placed his forearms on mine, allowing his blood to seep into my open wounds. Carrie's body went limp in Anwar's arms. He put her down, then rushed to Nathan. Tree checked on Carrie before running to us, dropping to his knees beside Nathan.

"How long did you wait until her heart completely stopped?" Anwar asked Nathan.

"I don't know," Nathan half bawled. "But it has to work. It must work!"

"I don't understand," Tree cried, wrapping his arms around his head. "Paige is dead!" He wailed. He rested his forehead on the ground, his shoulders shaking.

"Wait," Anwar said, causing Tree to lift his head. "It's working."

"Wh-what's working?" Tree choked in frustration.

That silvery cord I had seen when I was out of my body at The Lion's Den appeared and was pulling me toward my body.

Nathan raised his face. "My God, I can hear her heartbeat, and it's strong."

"Nathaniel, you can break contact now. Her spirit is returning," Anwar told him.

"What the hell!" Tree half-shouted when he saw our wounds healing.

And at that very second, I slammed back into my body.

Chapter Twenty Two
Telling Secrets

The voices that surrounded me echoed inside my skull, along with other sounds, like hearts beating–two of them beating faster than normal–and things scurrying in the woods. I could feel two strong arms around my body, rocking me, and soft lips covering the side of my face in kisses.

"I am going to take care of the bodies," Anwar said. "You stay here and wait for Paige to wake up. Right now, she is discovering her keen sense of hearing."

"Okay," Nathan said, his voice filled with happiness. "If you don't concentrate on those sounds, you can block them out," he whispered in my ear. "I love you." He kissed the soft spot next to my ear, and I sighed in contentment. He felt it and squeezed me tighter against him.

"Paige!" Carrie's screaming voice rushed at me.

"It's okay, Carrie." Tree's voice was behind her. "She's alive, just not awake yet."

Carrie's sobs reverberated as her cold hands grabbed at me.

"Back off, Carrie," Nathan warned, his voice growling from deep within his chest.

"But … But … How?" she stammered. "I'm … I'm … So sorry." She continued to sob. "I… I would never hurt, Paige. I love her. You got to believe me. I don't know what happened. I felt pressure on my chest and blacked out."

"Come here, Carrie," Tree's gentle voice said.

"You got to believe me," Carrie's pleading voice cried.

"Carrie, I know you'd never intentionally hurt Paige," Nathan said, but then his voice acquired a disgusted edge. "But why would you invite a spirit inside you?"

"You invited a spirit inside you?" Tree asked, his voice raised in shock.

"I… I," she said between tears. "I don't know," she whined. "When Matt and I were hanging out one night at his house, he took out his Ouija board." She paused to cough. "He told me if I gave my permission to the spirits to work through me, we'd be able talk to them. That's all I know."

"How come you never told us?" Tree still sounded shocked.

"Because I didn't want you to know," she stated simply.

"It's an innocent mistake," Nathan told them, understanding the situation now. I stirred in his arms and felt his hand move softly down the length of my arm.

"Nathan,"my sluggish voice said.

"I'm here, baby." He kissed my cheek.

"Paige," Carrie said, crying again.

My eyes fluttered open to her moving toward me. Carrie's image magnified to bizarre proportions and jumped at me. I flinched and flipped my hand over my eyes, taking a couple deep breaths to calm my racing heart. That was freaky.

"Carrie, I need you to stay back," Nathan said, lifting his hand off of me.

"Why?"

"Yeah, why?" Tree's voice was filled with interest, and I could tell he knew something was up.

"Because Paige is seeing the world through different eyes now, and her mind needs to adjust to it," Nathan answered.

"You're not making sense," Carrie said, annoyed.

"I think I know," Tree replied. "But I want Nathan to tell us."

"I will once we're inside the house, and Paige can be a part of it."

"This is bullshit," Carrie said, suddenly angry. "You guys are holding out on me. Just because I made a stupid mistake doesn't mean you have to be a--"

"Carrie," I said, feeling my body getting stronger and stronger by the minute, but my hand remained over my eyes. "Please listen to Nathan. As for Tree, he has a hunch because one, he has a gift for reading people, and two, he saw what happened."

"Thank you, Paige," Tree said, cheerfully. "And welcome back."

"I'm so sorry, Paige." Carrie's voice was shaking. "I honestly don't know what happened. And you and Nathan are covered in blood, so it had to be bad. I don't even know where all that blood came from." She started crying again.

"It wasn't you doing it, so please stop crying." I peeked through my fingers, amazed at the clarity of my vision. I could see every tear on her face, and the bags forming under her eyes. It was incredible. I also smelled the blood on Nathan and me, which made my stomach churn.

"But what if it happens again?"

"Tree, lift Carrie's hair on the left side of her neck," Nathan told him. I decided to be brave and dropped my hand. They both had a weird look on their faces. "Go ahead," Nathan urged and lifted my hand to his lips, kissing it.

Tree did what Nathan said and sucked in a sharp breath. "What is that?" His wide eyes fell on us.

Carrie jerked her head back and slapped a hand over her neck. "What's on my neck?" she screeched.

"It looked like a three-dimensional spiral," Tree said. He looked at Carrie. "And it's the size of a dime." She screwed her face up and rubbed her fingers on it.

"Correct," Nathan said. "Humans who invite spirits in receive that mark after one of us casts the spirit out, so a spirit can never enter them again. It's a self-protection mark. So Carrie, you won't have to worry about it now."

"Does Matt have the mark too?" she asked, baffled.

Nathan shook his head and confusion crossed her face. "It doesn't work on people who are soulless."

"He doesn't have a soul?" she shrieked, horrified.

"That explains why he's such a dick," Tree muttered.

"There are people in this world who are soulless, Carrie." Nathan laughed, amused at Tree's comment. "And spirits can enter those vessels at will."

"Carrie, let me see the mark on your neck," I said. She scrambled to her feet. "Stay where you're at. I can see it from here." She gave me a funny look, but did what I said. She lifted her hair and tilted her head to show me.

"Cool. It looks like a birthmark." Tree was right. It was a three-dimensional spiral, conch-shell form.

"You need to tell us what's going on," Tree demanded.

I'd seen that stubborn look on his face many times, and knew we had to tell them.

"Yeah," Carrie said, sounding like a bratty kid. "And we want to know *now.*"

"It is okay, Nathaniel. They can come in the house." I heard Anwar say from inside, and knew Carrie and Tree couldn't hear him. I was really liking this bionic hearing, and was able to control it and block the sounds I didn't want to hear. It was easy.

I looked at Nathan, and he smiled. "I'm okay with it." But then I looked at my arms and realized what Carrie was talking about earlier. They were covered in dried blood, and Nathan's white T-shirt was drenched in it too. We looked like we'd committed a murder. "But we need to clean up first," I added.

"Don't get up too quickly," he whispered in my ear. "And keep in a stride with them while walking."

I nodded, and then his warm lips joined mine, soft and sweet. I shifted in his lap and looped my arms around his neck, kissing him harder, deeper. He responded with an eagerness that sent my pulse racing.

I had felt like this before with him, but never imagined it to be greater than what it was, however, the change in me enhanced everything, and for a second I forgot about Carrie and Tree. Until Tree cleared his throat.

Nathan broke our kiss, his bright eyes on mine. "I love you," he whispered.

"I love you too," I whispered back, moving my thumb across his lips, then rising to my feet. "I'm sorry," I said to Carrie and Tree, slipping my hand into Nathan's, noticing my body wanting to move faster. I pretended I was walking in thick mud. "I didn't mean to get carried away." I paused. They were totally gawking at us. "What? Why are you two staring at us?"

"Because your eyes are really bright," Tree said.

Carrie stuck her face in front of mine. "Why are they like that?"

"Well, to put it bluntly," I said. "It's because we're horny for each other."

"That's just wrong." Tree scrunched up his face. "You're like my sister, Paige, and I don't want to think about you getting horny and doing you know what."

"Come on, Tree. You know Nathan and I have had--"

"Stop! I don't want to hear it," he cut me off and stuck his fingers in his ears and said, "La, la, la."

"Erotic," Carrie murmured, and we laughed.

She seemed to be in a lot better mood now, probably because we were going to tell her our secret. And I knew once her and Tree found out, they would carry it to their graves like Nathan's father had.

When we walked across the deck, glass crunched beneath our feet. Two gaping holes where the windows once were, now had thick black plastic covering them. And then something occurred to me when we reached the front door, and I started laughing and crying at the same time. Everybody stopped, not understanding my bizarre outburst. I encircled my arms around Carrie in a bear hug.

"Owe, Paige. You're holding me too tight," she said, while I continued to laugh and cry on her shoulder.

"Sorry." I released her and saw tears in her eyes. Then I pulled Tree into my arms and hugged him too.

"Damn, Paige. You're going to crack my hip if you keep squeezing me like this." Tree laughed, not realizing I actually could if I were to use my full strength.

Dropping my arms, I smiled between tears. "I'm just so happy I don't have to say good-bye to you two." I glanced at Nathan, and he was beaming. He knew how much Carrie and Tree meant to me and how happy I was I could keep them in our life.

"Why would you say good-bye to us?" Carrie asked, sounding upset.

"Because," I said, walking inside the house, "of what we're going to tell you in a few minutes."

"Okay, I'm really nervous about this now." Carrie stopped to look around. "I love your place," she gushed to Nathan. "It's totally awesome!"

"Thanks," Nathan said, looking about. "I like it."

Anwar stepped into the room, and with an inviting smile, he gestured for them to sit. They sat on the couch, looking up at him as if he were a mythical god.

"Anwar, these are my friends, Carrie and Jack, but we call him Tree," I told him.

He bowed his head. "I have heard many great things about you two," he said, his warm eyes on them.

"Tree and Carrie, this is Anwar." I turned to him and smiled.

"Please to meet you," Carrie and Tree said in unison, awestruck.

Anwar pointed at them. "Your energies go well together," he said. "And I see much love there."

Carrie blushed, but Tree was staring at Anwar like a little kid meeting his idol for the first time. I'd never seen Tree fascinated by somebody like this before, and I couldn't help but smile, enjoying his reaction.

"Nathaniel, I will play host to these two while you and Paige get clean," Anwar said, looking at Nathan. "And then I must go for a few weeks to attend business."

My face crumbled. "But I don't want you to go. You need to start teaching me stuff." I didn't want to sound like a whiny child, but I could hear it in my voice.

He turned to me, his expression filled with affection, clearly touched by my words. "I will be back before you know it, little one. But in the meantime, your body needs to acclimate to the changes before we can proceed with your teachings. However, Nathaniel can teach you a few things in my absence. And from what I understand, you still have weeks of school left dat you must finish."

"True." I chewed on my lip. "But I already know I'm going to graduate. I just need to take the written finals." I was hoping he'd suggest for me to take some more time off, to get use to these changes.

He chuckled, reading right through me. "Your father would haunt me if I were to support your desire in dismissing your education, which I will not do. You need to finish the year out with your dear friends. Dis summer I will teach you what you need to know."

I let out a complacent sigh. "Fine."

Tree rolled his eyes. "Jeez, Paige, it's not the end of the world. I'm sure Nathan will take you to school and eat lunch with us like he did before."

Nathan placed his arm around my waist. "Absolutely," he said.

Carrie glared at me. "Yeah, you need to be at school with us."

"Okay, I'll go back to school tomorrow," I said, annoyed they were taking Anwar's side, even though I knew they were right. "Anyway," I continued, "Nathan and I will be right back. I can smell the blood on us, and it's making me sick."

"C'mon, Paige." Nathan took my hand and led me to his room. "I have a shirt you can wear until we get back to your house."

"Hurry back," Carrie called. "I'm dying to know what's going on."

***

"I can't believe this," Carrie tearfully said after we told her and Tree almost everything that happened after the first night I met Nathan. We left out the ring part because it was bad enough they now knew about the dark spirits, which could put them in danger if they weren't smart about it. But if they knew about the ring and my involvement, they'd want to help, and I couldn't risk their lives. I did, however, still needed to tell Nathan what the "old one" had said to me. "Tree and I are going to be old and decrepit while you and Nathan remain looking like you do now. That's not fair."

"Carrie," Tree said, trying to calm her down. "Brayden will be old too."

Nathan was standing between the two couches. I glanced at him, and he nodded.

"Um." I scratched my head, tilting it to the side.

Tree scrutinized my face, then blanched. "Brayden too?"

Carrie's eyes darted between us. "What?" She wiped her nose with the back of her hand and sniffed.

"Anwar told us yesterday Brayden has been marked for immortality as well," I said and winced, knowing she was going to have a fit.

"Brayden too!" She smacked her knee with her fist and slammed her back against the couch, burying her face in her hands, crying again.

"I can't believe it." Tree shook his head, draping an arm around Carrie. "Does Brayden know about you two being immortal as well?"

Nathan placed a box of Kleenex on the wooden coffee table in front of Carrie. "No, and we would like you two not to tell him or let him know what you know about him. You need to keep what we've told you a secret because it's not safe."

"Anwar already spoke to us about that and we will," Tree said. "But what if Brayden tells us?"

"It's your judgment call." Nathan shrugged. "We trust the two of you will do the right thing." He sat next to me, but when I stood, he took my wrist, giving me a where-are-you-going look. I glanced at Carrie still crying in her hands and understanding dawned on his face.

"Carrie," I said, sitting beside her. "It's going to be okay." I bumped shoulders with her until she dropped her hands.

"It's not okay, Paige. I'm going to be an old hag, and you're still going to be young and beautiful. And Brayden is going to stay young as well. It's not fair. Why can't we be immortal with you?"

I tenderly wiped her tears. "I don't know, but like we told you before, you have to be marked in order to be able to turn immortal. We can't willfully turn you. It doesn't work that way."

"I just thought of something." Tree moved to the edge of the couch with his legs spread apart, his face ghostly pale. "When Brayden finds out Paige is immortal too, he's going to see it as proof they belong together."

"Yes, we've already acknowledged that fact," Nathan answered with displeasure.

"You two don't understand," Tree said, a note of panic in his voice. "Something is going on with Brayden, and I've noticed a change in him."

"We all have," I said.

Carrie made an agreement sound while she grabbed a Kleenex. She blew her nose.

"Brayden was never like this before," Tree told Nathan. "But I've seen a strong determination in him when it comes to Paige. He seriously believes they belong together, and he hates you. He thinks you're taking advantage of her, even though we've told him otherwise, and he believes you're using her vulnerability to get what you want from her."

I looked at him. "But it's not true."

He rubbed his hands together, his grave eyes on mine. "We know, but that's what he thinks. He feels like Nathan has seduced you into thinking you two belong together."

"That's so *frickin'* stupid," I said under my breath, noticing Nathan clenching his hands in his lap.

"I know, but when he finds out you're immortal as well, he'll make it his mission to get you to see the truth as he sees it, and he won't stop until you're his."

"He's going to have to go through me before he gets to her," Nathan fumed. "My tolerance for that boy ended when he put his filthy hands on her, and he's damned lucky I didn't bash his head in."

"But," Carrie said, much calmer now. "Paige is stronger now, so she can fight him off."

"So is Brayden," Tree commented with a sour look.

"Brayden will always be stronger than me," I told them. "But Nathan is much older and stronger than him."

Nathan's ears were dark red, and I could hear the quickness in his breaths and heartbeat from across the room.

Tree held his hands up. "Wait a second. How old are you Nathan?"

Nathan took a deep breath, then released it. A whooshing sound flooded my ears. "I was born in 1837 and turned immortal in 1856," he answered.

"*Holy fuck*," Carrie said, clapping a hand on her mouth.

"Are you serious?" Tree's eyes were so big, I thought they were going to bust.

I laughed. "That was my same reaction when he told me."

"Were you in the Civil War?" Tree asked, which stunned me because I never thought to ask him that. Dang it. Why hadn't I thought of that? I was the one who loved history.

The corner of Nathan's mouth lifted, and I was thankful for this change in conversation.

"My brothers were. They fought with the German immigrants who were antislavery, and they were at Camp Jackson with General Lyon when they captured the local militia, who were pro-slavery. This happened on May 10, 1861. I wasn't a part of it in fear my brothers might recognize me, but I did what I could to protect them."

I was speechless. I had no idea about this part of his life and was in total wonderment of him. He had told me what it was like back then, but never mentioned this.

Carrie removed her hand. "Did they die?"

"No," Nathan replied. "But one of my brothers lost a leg and almost died from it."

"What did you do to protect your brothers?" I asked him.

"Well, besides tracking dark spirits, I gained the confidence of independent guerrilla bands. I discovered their tactics and used the knowledge to protect my brothers. I actually obtained quite a bit of useful information from Jesse Woodson."

"You're *shittin'* me?" Tree's jaw dropped, his eyes still huge. Carrie and I looked at each other, not getting why Tree was acting like this. "You knew Jesse James?"

"*What!*" Carrie and I screeched.

Nathan smiled, entertained by our reaction. "Yes, and he's not the Robin Hood some people claim him to be. He participated in terrible atrocities and after the war he used the tactics he learned and applied it to bank and train robberies."

Tree turned to me accusingly. "Did you know this about him?"

I playfully shot a dirty look at Nathan. "No."

Nathan laughed. "Well, I didn't know about you playing the tin whistle."

I went to him and smacked his knee. Grabbing my hand, he pulled me to him and bent me over his lap. He flashed me a silly grin and kissed me.

"Have you heard her play?" Carrie asked him.

"Yes, I have, and she plays beautifully." He shifted me into his arms, and I felt warm blood rushing to my face.

Carrie leaned forward as if this was the most fascinating conversation she'd ever had. "Have you seen her dance to that type of music?"

"Carrie." My cheeks were getting hotter. She made a face, enjoying my embarrassment.

Tree, on the other hand, was deep in thought, not paying attention to us.

"No," Nathan said. "But I plan to."

Carrie continued embarrassing me. "We used to play make-believe in the woods where Paige was the fairy, which is why Tree sometimes calls her that. I was the princess, Tree was the wizard, and Brayden was the knight. We would pretend an evil sorcerer had put a sleeping spell on all of us, except it didn't affect Paige. So in order for her to break the spell, she had to play her Celtic music and dance around us until the spell was broken."

"You guys were very imaginative," Nathan said, impressed.

"Well, our parents didn't believe in kids rotting their brains inside the house," Tree said. "Anyway, I want to know more about the Civil War."

"Give it a rest, Tree." Carrie rolled her eyes. "I'm sure he'll tell you more about it some other time. I want to know what these two can do." She looked at us in anticipation.

"I'm not sure. I haven't even tried it out yet," I said.

"Let's go see what you can do." Nathan stood and took my hand.

Chapter Twenty Three
Revelation

Tree punched the air after Nathan showed them how quick he was. "Awesome! You're like a superhero." He was grinning from ear to ear. I couldn't help but laugh.

"That explains how he got behind Brayden so quickly." Carrie narrowed her eyes at me and pursed her lips. "I knew there was something strange about it, but Paige told me you snuck behind him."

I shrugged. "I had to because you weren't supposed to know."

Nathan stepped in front of me. "Now you try it."

"But I don't know how." I felt stupid all of a sudden and didn't want to make a mistake in front of them. Carrie and Tree were looking at me expectantly, which made me feel even more nervous. I mean, what if I ran into a tree and knocked myself out? I'd never hear the end of it.

Nathan looked at me encouragingly. "Just think about where you want to go and move like you're going to run. It's that simple." He stepped aside.

I gave him a wary look, but when he mouthed "trust me" I took a deep breath and focused my attention on the trees ahead. I moved my body forward in a running stance, feeling my muscles quivering like an excited dog anticipating a walk.

I took off.

My hair flew back, and the damp, cool air brushed against my face as I ran deep into the woods. I dodged the trees and logs with no problem, feeling an elation I'd never known. It was almost as if I were flying inches above the ground, with no sound, like being in stealth mode.

My breath came out slow and steady, and my reflexes were quick. Each limb seemed to have a mind of its own, and the powerful strength in my muscles pushed me forward. They were alert and jacked up.

I leaped over a broken oak tree and found myself high in the air, above the tall trees, wind-milling my arms, tilting my head back, squealing with laughter. I fell to the earth, landing in a crouched position, my hands in a pile of wet muddy leaves. I spun, laughing hysterically while I breezed through the forest, heading to my waiting friends.

"Omigod, Paige."Carrie raised her hands. "You just disappeared into thin air, and now you're back. That totally whacks my brain."

"That was bitchin'," Tree said, grinning.

I was still laughing, tears streaming down my face. I tried to speak, but couldn't. My sides ached. I hugged my arms around them, trying to catch my breath. Finally, I was able to speak. "I felt like I was flying."

"It is exhilarating," Nathan admitted. "But Paige, try moving quickly without running."

"Okay." I moved behind Carrie and tapped her shoulder. She jumped and screamed.

"Boo!" I giggled.

She slapped my shoulder. "You scared the shit out of me."

Tree roared with laughter.

Carrie kicked his foot, but then joined in the mirth.

"Hey, Paige. Try doing this." Nathan jumped high in the air and did a somersault, landing on his feet with his hands on his hips, like Peter Pan.

"That's not fair you two and Brayden can do all of this," Carrie complained.

"Yes, but Carrie," Nathan said. "You're not chained to the earth for eternity like we are."

"Isn't there a way you can die though?" Tree wondered.

Nathan held a finger up. "Only one way we know of, which is being completely bled out."

I looked at Nathan. "How did you do the somersault thing?"

He bounced on the tip of his toes. "Watch me again." He bent his knees and leaped high in the air, doing another somersault, landing soundlessly on his feet. "You try it."

I did exactly what he did and felt the power of my leg muscles lift me off the ground, my arms reaching for the cloudy sky. The top of trees turned upside down when I did a flip. But when I landed on my feet, I slipped and fell on my butt. Laughter erupted around me.

Nathan pulled me into his arms, chuckling. "The landing part takes practice."

"That was too funny," Carrie said, but then paused. Her face went blank. "Oh, no." She looked at her watch.

"What?" I asked.

Tree turned her wrist to see the time. "Shit. Carrie, we have to go."

Carrie looked at me. "Mom just got a shipment of stuff in for her store, and we're supposed to be there right now to help her sort through it and put it into inventory. She's going to be pissed."

"We'll see you later." Tree took her hand, and they half ran down the dirt path toward the forest.

"Bye," Carrie yelled over her shoulder, disappearing into the trees.

When they left, I turned to Nathan and told him what the "old one" had told me.

He ran his fingers through his hair. "If it's true, we're going to have to get the ring from him."

"I can trick him," I said. "I mean, he's going to come back for me because he needs me to find the incantations, so I can play along until I get the ring from him."

"No, Paige," Nathan sternly said. "It's not safe. I will not risk you getting harmed again."

"You're probably right," I said, even though I was willing to try.

"I'll talk to Anwar about it tomorrow. I'm sure he'll come up with a solution, but for now let's forget about it. We both had a trying day, so let's relax and enjoy what's left of it."

We stood there for a while, holding each other, listening to the trees swaying in the wind, knowing in our hearts, this battle was far from over.

***

"Nathan," I called from the crack of the bathroom door, intentionally making my voice sound fearful. I adjusted the towel tighter around me, and glanced at the foggy mirror. I didn't have enough time to swipe my hand across it for one last look at myself. But I felt the damp condensation clinging to my face, and when I looked down, my skin glistened with it. I smiled, confident and self-assured.

I felt bolder than ever before because of this new improved body. The small stretch marks on my hips, caused by a growth spurt, were gone, and my breasts were a fuller B cup. My skin was flawless, like Nathan said it would be. Not to mention, every muscle in my body was tight, as if I spent all my spare time at the gym. It was awesome, and I couldn't wait to find out how it would feel to have Nathan's hands all over it.

I'm so bad.

"What's wrong?" Nathan stood in front of the door, his nervous eyes on mine.

I dropped my gaze and made an effort not to look at him. Instead, I opened the door wider, dropped the towel, and snaked my hand down my body. I looked at him when I heard a pleasing sound cluck from his throat. His eyes were bright and lustful. I pulled him into the bathroom and closed the door.

"I think we should conserve on water tonight," I told him, stepping into the shower.

"I think you're right," he said, stripping. I could hear his heart beating faster and the yearning in his voice. He stepped in next to me and placed his hands around my neck, tilting my face up. "You're the most gorgeous person I've ever seen."

I bent my head back, allowing the hot water to cascade down my hair, lightly spraying my face. I never knew happiness like this existed.

"No, Mr. Caswell." I rubbed his damp cheek, "I think you are."

A slow smile formed on his lips, then curved into a crooked one. He shook his head. And then his scorching lips were on mine. My tongue flicked and danced against his. I lightly bit his bottom lip, causing him to groan. I stepped back, bringing us under the gentle spray of water, while our mouths hungrily moved together in harmony, as if he was going off to war and this could be our last kiss.

Every nerve ending in my body hummed with pleasure beneath his touch, more sensitive than before I became immortal. It was as if the receptors were now wide open, sucking in each luxuriant feeling.

Time ran away from us, like it did when people were having fun together or engrossed in conversation, and before we knew it, it was well past midnight. We were lying in bed, tired, but glowing.

"I have something for you." Nathan reached in his overnight bag beside the bed.

"You do?" I wondered what it was and how long he had it.

"I was going to wait until your birthday to give this to you, but in a way it is your birthday since you were just born into immortality." He handed me a black velvet ring box.

"You didn't have to do this." I held the box in my hand and stared at it. It couldn't possibly be an engagement ring. Maybe it was a promise ring.

"I wanted to because it represents us. And to be honest, I really enjoyed buying this for you. So please open it and tell me what you think."

I opened the box and immediately became teary-eyed.

It was a silver Claddagh ring.

"Do you like it?" He studied my face, and then smiled when he saw the happy tears in my eyes.

"I love it." I kissed him. "Thank you so much. This means a lot to me." I slipped it on my right wedding finger and it fit perfectly. "But how did you know my size?"

"Your mom told me when you were upstairs getting your whistle."

"She knew about this?" More tears pushed out of my eyes at the thought of Mom having some part in this.

"She thought it was a brilliant idea and knew you would love it." He picked up my hand and rubbed his thumb across the ring. "Do you know what it means?"

"Of course I do, but I want you to tell me."

I watched his thumb touch each individual representation as he told it to me.

"The hands mean friendship and togetherness. The heart signifies love, and the crown stands for loyalty." He lifted my hand and kissed that finger. "Us, tied up into this clever, little ring."

I kissed him again. "This is the most wonderful gift anybody has ever given me. Thank you." I was touched by how much thought he had put into it.

"You're very welcome." He reached across me to turn the light off.

"Wait." I held my hand up to look at the ring one last time. "Okay, now you can turn the light off."

He switched the lamp off and settled back in bed. I sat up, looking around the dark room.

Well, to a human the room would be dark, but to my new eyes the room was bright with a light gray cast to it, and everything was colorless, like a black and white TV. It was cool I could see clearly in the dark, but I was perturbed by it. I lay back down and grunted.

"Don't you like to be able to see in the dark?"

"I do, but I love sleeping in a pitch dark room and now I'm wondering if I'll ever have a good night's sleep again."

"You'll adapt to it, and if worse comes to worst, we can always buy you one of those sleeping masks."

"I guess so." I closed my eyes in annoyance. I knew it was stupid to feel this way, but I couldn't help it. I cherished my sleep and the whole ritual of it, which included a pitch dark room.

"It'll be okay," his groggy voice said.

I pressed myself against him and sighed.

A few minutes later, Nathan fell asleep, and I lay there for a while listening to his shallow breathing. That was until I heard my name being softly called by a female voice.

"Nathan." I shook his arm. His lids flew open. "Don't say anything, just listen," I whispered.

The female said my name again. He looked at me, and we sat up when a white light filled the room.

"Paige," the female said yet again, now visible in the room. She was wearing a white cloak. Her long, fiery red hair framed her pretty, delicate face, beneath her hood.

"Grandmother?" I choked, not sure if I was correct.

She moved closer to the bed. Protectively, Nathan hugged his arms around me.

Her emerald eyes fell gently upon me. "Fear not, my child. I'm not here to harm you, but to help. I would've come sooner, but I was preoccupied."

"Are… Are you dead?" I stammered.

She glanced at her body. "My physical body has been dead for a while now, but that's not important. I need to inform you two on some things."

"What is it?" The urgency in her face disturbed me, and I held onto Nathan for comfort.

"Solomon's ring does exist, but it no longer holds its power."

"How do you know this?" Nathan asked, sounding skeptical.

"Because I had found it, but I don't have time to tell you how, only Paige's father was on the right track."

"So the power has been destroyed?" I felt a jolt of relief, but then her eyes dimmed, and I knew this wasn't going to be good. My stomach clenched.

"I tried to destroy the ring," she said, "but couldn't, and found the only way to turn it into a useless piece of costume jewelry was to transfer its power into another object."

"Where's the object?" Nathan asked, interested now.

She averted her eyes, and her shoulders slouched forward. I thought she was going to cry, and felt a thickness growing in my throat, but then her attention fell back on us, and her face was masked in regret. "You have your arms around it," her soft voice said.

A haunting chill ran up my spine, and a violent shudder went through me. Nathan squeezed his arms tighter around me and let out an unsettling groan.

"H-how?" I asked, thinking how wrong and unfair this was. Why me?

"When you were born, I snuck into your bedroom, and did it while you were asleep. I apologize for doing this to you, but at the time I thought it was the right thing to do since you come from an ancient line of witches."

Witches? I couldn't believe it, but then I recalled Mom telling me about my dad doing research on witchcraft. I still couldn't believe it though. I mean, I'd know if I were a witch, right?

"The 'old one' knows about Paige's bloodline doesn't he? That's why he's interested in her?" Nathan's voice was hard with anger.

She turned her attention on him. "He's interested in her for many reasons." She paused and folded her hands. "Please forgive me for my brevity, but my allotted time is coming to an end, and I must get to the point."

"Wait. Did he kill you?" I had to know.

She shook her head. "No. I don't think so, but I was struck from behind, so I don't know who did it."

"Does my father know about this, now that he's dead?"

"No, but I'll be visiting with him when I cross over to where he is, and I'll tell him then."

"Can we transfer this power out of Paige into something else?" Nathan asked. I noticed the light was starting to fade and felt a lump forming in my throat. I didn't want her to go.

She looked around the room, and her face turned anxious. "The power cannot be transferred from Paige, and as you know, the power is impotent without the incantations Solomon used to control the dark spirits. I wasn't able to look for the incantations, and I don't know where they are." She stopped, as if to catch her breath, and continued. "When the vessel the 'old one' had been dwelling in was sick, he took his leave and found another one. While he was in that vessel, by pure luck, he found the ring I had tossed into a gutter, at an antique store here in town and--"

"Carrie's mom's store," I gasped.

"Yes," she confirmed, "and now he's going to want you to find the incantations. That's one of the reasons why he wanted you to become immortal. You see, Solomon was a very wise magician, and not just anybody can find his incantations, even if they have the ring. The 'old one' is aware of this and knows you can find it for him.

"Now, there's the matter of Aosoth." She looked at Nathan. "She knows the 'old one' has the ring, and he tricked her. She's not happy about it. She wants that power for herself. So she's going to do the next best thing, which is forcing Paige into finding the incantations for her before the 'old one' gets a hold of Paige."

I could hear Nathan's breaths coming out faster, his heart keeping in time with it. *What the hell am I going to do?* The only thing I could do was go along with Aosoth or the "old one," find the incantations, and use it on them. That was my only option.

His voice came out harsh. "She will *not* get hold of Paige."

"Hold on a minute," I said. "I'm immortal, so she can't get hold of me. I'm stronger than her because she's younger." I totally forgot about that until now. *Ha, ha, the beeotch can't get me.*

Nathan frowned. "She's conniving, Paige, and I'm sure she'll find a way to take you down." I rested my forehead on his shoulder, feeling sick to my stomach. "Don't worry. I'm going to take care of her," he said, rubbing my cheek.

"I have to take my leave now," my grandmother said. She placed her fingers on her lips and blew a kiss at me. "Just a couple more things. The 'old one' is aware you hold a power, and he's starting to question why he doesn't feel any energy in the ring. What I'm trying to say is, if he realizes what I had done, and the light some of the dark spirits can see in you is actually the ring's power, your immortal life will be in grave danger. Especially, if others find out. So I suggest you two keep this knowledge to yourselves, and don't breathe a word of it beyond safe walls. And Nathan, I know you incapacitated Aosoth with your clever incantation before Anwar got a hold of her, and she's withering in pain right now. I also know about your savage capabilities, but be cautious. Aosoth will regain her energy, and there's no telling what she's going to do." She moved her hand in a circle, saying a few words I couldn't understand. Her image was shorting out, like a flickering light bulb, and that was the last thing I remembered.

Chapter Twenty Four
Friends Forever

"Absolutely not." Nathan's hands tightened on the steering wheel. We were heading to school, and I reminded him of my idea about going along with Aosoth or the "old one" on finding the incantations and using it on them.

"Why not? I think I can do it." Actually, I wasn't sure if I could, but he didn't need to know that. "It might be my only option," I added for good measure, knowing he was right, but I didn't see any other way out of it.

He smashed his lips together and glared out the windshield.

"You just became immortal, Paige," he said at last. "You're unskilled in your abilities and haven't even started your training. I can teach you some things, but that would only be enough to get you by until Anwar can begin preparing you." He was trying his best to stay calm, but what I had suggested unnerved him. He was worried now, and I silently berated myself for voicing my idea again. The last thing he needed was another splinter planted in his brain.

"You're right," I said, wanting his mind to be eased. His eyes flicked to mine, and they weren't convinced the white flag I held was genuine. I looked the other way, thinking about earlier this morning.

After my alarm clock had gone off, we immediately dove into a conversation about my grandmother's visit and what she'd told us. A while later, Nathan caught me crying in the kitchen.

I didn't want to cry, and tried not to, but my emotions overpowered me. All I could think about was this damned power I had inside me. I didn't want it, and there was nothing I could do to get rid of it. My own grandmother cursed me, even though she did it with good intentions. And, for an added frickin' bonus, I came from a long line of witches and might be a witch myself. And yeah, to be a witch like in the Harry Potter books would rock, but unfortunately this wasn't Hogwarts. Instead, this was the school of, "What the hell?"

What the hell was I going to do? What the hell was my life going to be like?

Nathan comforted me and made me realize what I could do with this power. It wasn't a curse, but a weapon to use to help protect humanity. And as he spoke, I remembered my promise to my parents–*I would do my best to make things right*–and I was determined to uphold that promise.

Afterwards, I asked him about what he'd done to Aosoth. He told me he'd created some of his own organic incantations and used one of them to incapacitate her, which in effect would prolong her agonizing pain. I then asked him what he was planning on doing to her. He said he wasn't sure yet, but promised to tell me everything before he executed the plan. I wasn't satisfied with his answer, but I knew he had a lot on his mind, so I let it go.

Now, Nathan was parking in the school parking lot. The bell was about to ring, but instead of hurrying to class, I reached out and touched his arm. I had a burning question I needed to ask him, a question that couldn't wait. It was a question that could come with a devastating answer. But I had to ask.

"Do you want to break up with me?" I stared at him, swallowing back the tears.

The skin between his eyes crinkled. "W-what?" He placed his hands on my shoulders. "No, Paige. Why would you ask me that? You mean more to me than anything. Did I do something to cause you to question my love for you?"

"No, but I wasn't sure if you wanted to be tied down to a burden like me, and I understand if you want to bail. I mean, what kind of life are you going to have with me?" If he did leave, I'd be grief-stricken, and my heart would never mend, but I'd continue on. I had to. There was no way I could blow off what had been given to me.

He cradled my face in his hands, his thumbs resting on my cheeks. "You're not a burden in my life, Paige. You're a gift bestowed upon me from the heavens. A gift I sometimes can't believe is mine." He kissed me, creating that funny feeling in my belly. "I'm madly in love with you, and the life we'll share together will be a good one."

"I have to go," I said, hearing the bell, grabbing my backpack. I scanned the school grounds. "Is it safe to run?"

He looked. "I don't see anybody, so you should be good."

I gave him a quick kiss. "I'll see you later."

"Okay," he said as I opened the door and ran toward the building with the elation I'd felt yesterday when I ran into the woods. "I'll see you at lunch." I heard him say before I stepped inside.

The halls were vacant, so I zipped to my class. I stopped in front of the door, hearing books opening and pencils scratching on paper. I also heard sighs and bodies moving against the wooden seats. Not to mention, twenty or so hearts beating at once, like kettledrums. I closed my eyes and focused on tuning those sounds out, thinking how I hated walking into a room filled with students. I took a deep breath and walked in.

Mrs. Hong was at her desk, marking off everybody in her book. When our eyes met, I mumbled I was sorry for being late and hung my head to avoid the stares, taking my seat in the back.

"I thought you decided not to come to school today," Carrie whispered while I pulled my biology book out of my backpack. She looked away when she saw Mrs. Hong walking toward my desk.

Mrs. Hong covered my hand with hers, and her stone-cold face melted into sympathy, shocking me. I never knew she had a soft side to her.

"I lost my mother at your age to a tragic accident as well, and I'm deeply sorry for your loss." Sincerity filled her dark eyes, and I stared at them, trapped in their warmth. I bit my lip and blinked back the tears.

"We're all sorry," Max called from across the room.

I looked at him, suddenly realizing the whole class was watching me and heard what our teacher had said. Heads nodded in response, including Ashley's.

I forced a weak smile and dropped my gaze, feeling tears trailing down my cheeks.

Mrs. Hong patted my hand. "If you need to talk, my ear is yours."

I nodded, unable to speak in fear my voice might crack. She went back to the front of the class. All eyes fell back on their work.

An hour later, when I entered English class, Tree was eagerly waiting for me, looking like he was going to explode. I shook my head and smiled at him. He lifted his eyebrows and flipped his palms up, giving me a "what" look. I took my seat next to him, blocking out the many conversations going around the room.

"Okay, what do you want to know?" I squinted at the goofy grin on his face.

"I've been thinking a lot about." He paused to evaluate the room, making sure nobody could hear us, then cupped his hand around his mouth. "You know," he whispered. "It's still hard for me to believe even though I know it's true, but I feel you both haven't told us everything, and I want to know. Carrie and I want to be a part of it, sort of like your sidekicks."

I burst out in laughter and the more I thought about what he said, the harder I laughed. My stomach began to cramp. I leaned forward, curling my arms around it. Some of my classmates turned to stare, but I continued to laugh until a scowl appeared on Tree's face.

"Why are you laughing? I'm serious. I think we can help you and Nathan if you let us."

"I'm laughing," I said, catching my breath, "because you have the superhero thing going on in your head. This isn't make-believe like when we were kids, and we're not superheros. *Dork.*"

He leaned over his desk, gripping the edge, tilting it forward, his face begging for me to consider what he just proposed. I shook my head and grinned.

"Come on, Paige. *Please.*"

I opened my notebook and wrote: *It's too dangerous. Besides, I'll be training all summer, and we're probably going to leave Astoria for a while.* I turned it so he could read my words.

He dropped the desk back down. A thudding sound amplified in my ears.

"Leave? Where are you going?"

Mr. Russo walked in and called the class to attention.

"Europe," I mouthed to him.

"Why?" he whispered.

"Many reasons," I said out the corner of my mouth, and he glowered at me. I settled in my seat, turning my attention on Mr. Russo, ignoring Tree's constant fidgeting throughout the rest of the hour.

"So, you're not even going to consider it?" Tree asked on my way to biology class.

We walked side by side up the stairs. Students were dodging Tree. He held onto my wrist to make sure they wouldn't knock me over, *like falling could hurt me now*. But it was sweet of him to do.

"Why didn't Carrie say anything to me about this?" I asked.

"Because she wanted me to and is still coming to terms with it."

We stopped outside my class, and I pulled him aside. "Listen to me. Besides Nathan, you and Carrie are the most important people in my life."

"We feel the same way about you and Nathan. That's why we want to help you."

I squeezed his hand. "I love you two, and if something were to happen to either one of you, I'd never forgive myself. I'm sorry, but the answer is no."

"But, Paige, it's our life. If we want to risk it then it's our choice." He thumped his fingers against his chest. "It's *our choice,*" he repeated, raising his eyebrows.

"Could you forgive yourself if one of the dark spirits slit Carrie's throat or harmed her in any way?"

He flinched, and I hoped that scenario knocked some sense into him.

"I get your point now," he grumbled, staring at his combat boots.

"Good. I'll see you in an hour."

"Okay," he said, sounding dejected. He turned away from me, and I watched him trudged down the hall with slumped shoulders.

***

Biology class whizzed by and before I knew it, all four of us were sitting in the cafeteria, and Tree was asking Nathan about the Civil War again.

"It was a very brutal war, Tree," Nathan said. "And I saw some horrific things."

"Like what?" Tree leaned into the table across from Nathan.

"I'll tell you one thing, but then I want you to drop it for now."

Carrie smacked Tree's arm. "You should leave Nathan alone about this."

Tree rubbed his arm, pretending like she had hurt him.

"I'm sorry, but I've always been fascinated by the Civil War. I just never shared it with you and Paige."

"That's okay," I said. "You two didn't know about my premonitions, and we didn't know about Carrie's dealings with the talking board." I flashed her a silly grin, and she stuck her tongue out at me, then a thought occurred to me. "Have you two seen Matt around?"

"I saw him earlier," Carrie said. "But he's keeping to himself like he did last week."

"Anyway." Tree turned his attention back on Nathan. "Tell me that one thing, and I'll leave you alone."

Nathan removed his arm from my shoulders and leaned forward, folding his hands on the table. "Have you heard of William 'Bloody Bill' Anderson?"

Tree stared into space and thought about it for a minute. "No, I don't think so."

"Have you heard of William Quantrill's independent guerrilla band?"

"Yeah. Wasn't Jesse James a part of it?"

"That's right and so was Anderson, but eventually he broke away from Quantrill's band and formed his own."

Carrie scrunched up her face. "Why did they call him 'Bloody Bill'?"

"Because he did unimaginable things to people," Nathan said, "and I've seen scalps of people he had slain tied to the bridle and saddle of his horse."

Carrie and I covered our mouths while Tree's hung wide open.

"Are you serious?" Carrie's muffled voice asked from behind her hand.

"Yes. It's a vision branded in my mind for eternity and one I prefer not to revisit." Nathan sat back, placing his arm around my shoulders.

Tree looked down, his cheeks pink. "Sorry."

"It's fine, Tree. Maybe one day I'll tell you everything about it, and what I did during that time. But right now I'm not in that frame of mind to do it just yet."

Tree picked up his Coke can and stared blankly into it. "I understand."

"Okay, change the subject," Carrie said with a mouth full of greasy pizza.

I glanced at my ring finger. "I forgot to show you this." I stood and leaned across the table, thrusting my hand out so they could see my ring. "Nathan gave this to me last night. It means friendship, love, and loyalty."

"Cool, Paige." Carrie smiled.

Tree took a huge bite of his brownie and made an agreeable sound.

"You know," Carrie said, pointing at my hand. "That ring also represents us as well."

"She's right." Tree said. "All four of us are family, and you will have our friendship, love, and loyalty forever."

"You have ours as well," Nathan told them.

"Forever." I said, resting my head on Nathan's chest, and as I watched Carrie kiss Tree and saw how happy they were together, I knew my decision to tell him no was the right one. And with what I knew now, there was no way I would allow them to get involved in any of this.

"What are you thinking?" Nathan whispered. His warm breath brushed against my ear, making my whole body tingle.

"I was thinking they have a life of togetherness ahead of them. A life filled with children and grandchildren," I said in a low voice.

"What are you two whispering about?" Carrie asked.

I grinned. "I was telling him you and Tree have a long life together ahead of you, filled with children and grandchildren."

Her expression turned doubtful. "I don't know if I want to have children."

"Really?" Tree turned to her in surprise.

Carrie shrugged. "I'm not sure about it yet."

"Oh, come on, Carrie," I pressed. "It would be cute having a couple little Power Rangers with Mohawks running around."

All four of us laughed at the mental visual.

"Yeah. Right." She rolled her eyes and then tilted her head to the side, her gaze on Nathan and me. "I know this is a stupid question, but you can't have kids, huh?"

"Nope," I said. "To be honest, I never wanted any."

Tree placed his arm around Carrie. "Well, I don't know what's going to happen, but I'm sure it'll be great because Carrie and I will be together."

"You two are such a cute couple," I gushed when Tree kissed Carrie on the cheek. Then I thought about Brayden, wondering if he regretted what he had done to me and if he would apologize to try to make things right between us. Or if he'd continue to pursue me. If he did, I'd have to find a way to get it through his thick head we didn't belong together. But hopefully, I wouldn't have to do that.

The bell rang, and as we gathered our stuff, I glanced at Carrie and Tree and knew we would always be in each other's life. And when I went to say good-bye to Nathan, and saw the fierce love in his eyes, my stomach flipped.

He pulled me into his warm embrace and slowly kissed me, stealing my breath. If any two people were ever made for each other, I think we were. As a team we would fight to protect humanity against the darkness planning to engulf it.

Yesterday my mortal life had ended, and now my immortal life begins. With Nathan by my side, there were three words I wanted to say to the dark spirits: *Bring it on.*

Preview:

DARK SPIRITS

Here's a sneak peek at Dark Spirits the captivating sequel to Beyond the Eyes.

DARK SPIRITS

Chapter One
Ayperos

I opened the brass urn and scattered my mother's ashes over the Pacific Ocean. They sailed through the gentle breeze, into the boundless sea, like magical dust trailing behind a fairy heading for home.

My bare feet gripped the craggy rock where I stood above the shoreline. In the fiery evening sky, a group of pelicans soared gracefully above the water. One by one, they dove into the water, creating splashing sounds that echoed in my immortal ears.

Wiping the tears from my eyes, I bent down. My dark red hair fell in a curtain around my face. I tucked it behind my ears as I shoved the urn into my backpack. From the side pocket, I retrieved my tin whistle. Mom always loved when I played for her, so I would play her a song now.

The tip of the whistle rested comfortably between my lips. I placed my fingers on top of the holes, but then hesitated as the sound of a barking dog reached my ears. I glanced over my shoulder. A black lab ran past me, followed by a handful of runners in matching orange and white track uniforms. All eyes were trained on the dog, except for a dirty blond-haired guy who appeared to be around my age. His gaze latched onto my white gauze sundress, then rested on my bronze chest. He smiled and winked when my hand went to the crocheted spaghetti straps, tugging it back to pull my breast firmly into the V cut of my empire waist. He winked again, and I turned to the ocean.

I had hoped for some solitude on Cannon Beach and thought with it being the end of August and late in the evening that would be possible. I had considered Nathan's suggestion on renting a speed boat to release Mom's ashes farther into the sea, but this spot was where Mom had released my father's ashes when I was four, fourteen years before. Therefore, I'd do the same for her, regardless if I were to become a spectacle for all to gawk at.

Nathan stood below me, staring at the guy's back, burning a hole into it. And even though he had given me immortality five months before, he still remained overprotective. He looked up, his deep blues locking onto mine, their hardness melting into molten liquid. I licked my lips, feeling the warmth Nathan only shared with me. It never ceased to amaze me how he always took my breath away. My gaze fell onto his khaki pants, rolled to his knees, the surf lapping at his tan shins, then to his muscular arms, and short brown hair with the blond-tipped spikes.

"It's okay, Paige," Tree said on the other side of me, diverting my attention. He had his arm around Carrie's waist, and when I looked at him, he jerked his head, his perfectly straight black Mohawk pointing in the direction the runners had gone. "You can play now."

I took a deep breath and resumed my position, slowly blowing air into the whistle. I closed my eyes, allowing the breathy music to unfold into the eternal abyss where pleasant dreams and happiness resided. This Celtic song would reach those boundaries, straight to my mom. I believed that because I had seen and conversed with her and my father before I had turned immortal. And somehow, I could feel her presence now, her soft hand on my shoulder.

"It's lovely, Paige, but you must stop. They're coming," Mom whispered into my ear, surprising me. I glanced at Nathan. He nodded toward Haystack Rock, a basalt monolith two-hundred and thirty-five feet high, jutting out of the ocean. I stopped playing, and followed his gaze to the rock.

"What is it?" Tree asked, reaching into his baggy camouflage pocket, squinting in the direction we were staring at.

A man clad in black jerked his head from the binoculars he held, then inched his way behind the rock, disappearing from sight.

"I think there was a man watching us," Carrie said, pointing in that direction, slipping her sunglasses in the front bib of her red plaid capri overalls. Tree opened her hand and stuck something in it. It was a small, black canister. Pepper Spray.

I silently chastised myself for allowing them to come here with me, knowing the dark spirits either wanted to torture me, kidnap me for Aosoth, or use me as a bargaining chip. I mean, Aosoth was a heartless female dark spirit who had wanted me to find Solomon's ring, then give it to her. But now that "the old" had found the ring, she was going to want me to find Solomon's incantations for her since the ring was impotent without it. And even though Tree and Carrie knew about me becoming immortal, they didn't know much else.

The wind began to pick up, swirling my hair and dress about. The surf softly roared as the low tides sloshed against the rocks, slowly gaining momentum. When I spotted ten Goth-looking people headed our way, I snatched my backpack, slung it over my shoulder, and stuck the whistle in the side pocket. Jumping down, I took Nathan's hand, feeling wet sand squish between my toes.

"What do you think we should do?" I asked him.

"Do about what?" Carrie asked, moving next to me. "It looks like that guy left," she added, focusing on Haystack Rock.

I pointed to our left. "There are ten people walking toward us, and they could be dark spirits."

Both Carrie and Tree squinted in that direction, but their human vision was too weak to see, and the darkening sky didn't help either.

Tree frowned. "But I thought your ears ring when they're around."

"They do, but they have to be within a certain radius in order for that to happen," I told him. "That's why they've been keeping a certain distance, so Nathan and I won't detect them."

"I think I see them now," Carrie said, staring off into that direction, poking her chin out, still squinting. "It looks like they're walking shoulder to shoulder, in a straight line."

"They are," Nathan said with a sigh. He let go of my hand and turned to us. "Okay, this is what we're going to do. Tree and Carrie, stay behind Paige and me." He glanced down at their hands and nodded in approval. "I see you both have pepper spray. Smart thinking. Keep that hand in your pocket, but don't let go of the pepper spray. I'm going to try to handle this on my own and--"

"Handle it on your own?" I said, dropping my backpack in irritation. There was no way I'd stand back and allow him to handle this on his own. I didn't spend my whole damn summer training with Anwar and him on a deserted island in the Baltic sea to stand here and do nothing.

"Uh-oh. I know that tone of voice," Tree said with a half-smile, looking at Nathan. "You just pissed Paige off."

"I can really see them now," Carrie said, sounding nervous. "They look like vampires or something." She turned to Nathan. "Paige isn't a helpless mortal anymore, Nathan. I get you want to protect her, but she can kick some ass now, so cut her some slack." She hooked her arm through mine and hugged it. "Paige can be my bodyguard any day."

"Thank you, Carrie," I said, smiling, hearing Tree chuckling under his breath, surprised at how lax he was considering our current situation.

Nathan ran a hand through his hair and took a step closer to us. "Look. I agree whole-heartedly with you, Carrie. However, you don't know the whole situation and--"

"I knew you two were holding out on us," Tree said, raising his eyebrows. "And I think you should tell Carrie and me what's going on."

My ears began to ring, and I pushed Carrie behind me.

"We don't have time," Nathan said in a rush, looking over his shoulder. "There are too many of them, and if things get ugly, I'm going to have to kill them." He took my hand, and we turned our backs on them. "Remember to keep the pepper spray ready," he whispered over his shoulder as the group approached us. I could hear Carrie's heart racing, and again wished I had never allowed them to talk me into coming here with me. I should have known it wasn't safe for them to be around me in a less populated area.

The group stopped short a half a yard away from us. There were six males and four females. All of them looked to be in their early twenties. I recognized the guy at the end on the far left. The binoculars now hung from his neck. He gave me a smug look. I drew myself up, shoulders back, refusing to allow him to intimidate me.

Soft giggles erupted from the girls, grouped together to my right. The platinum blonde one with the short, spiky hairstyle, pursed her black lips when my gaze fell upon her. Her brown eyes had flecks of gold in them, and they were heavily lined in black. They swelled in cockiness, followed by a twisted smile. Then a yellow laser beam of light swiped across her irises.

She was a young dark spirit, which meant I could cast her out.

Good.

I didn't like her attitude.

The guy in the middle with the shiny, long black hair, stepped forward. Nathan took half a step in front of me, spreading his legs, positioning his body into a protective stance. I didn't budge. I mean, honestly, Nathan was much stronger and experienced than I was, so I decided to hang back and would make a move only if I had to.

The guy's startling blue eyes took in Nathan's position with caution. He slowly raised his hands. "I have no quarrel with you," he said. "My name is Ayperos, and I'm just here to deliver a message to you."

"And what message might that be?" Nathan said in a stiff voice.

Ayperos' eyes slid off of Nathan, and onto me. A beam of light swiped across them, but the beam was much larger than normal. I then realized he had to be an older dark spirit. Not as old as the "old one" whose eyes completely glowed, but old enough. I wondered if Nathan would be able to cast him out if he had to. I didn't think so since Nathan was too young an immortal to cast an old one out. It sucked because Nathan was a hundred and seventy-five years old, and you'd think he'd be able to do it. But no, it didn't work that way. Now, if Anwar were here, he could, but he had left town a couple days before.

"Aosoth is regaining her energy, and she has allies who will help her get what she wants, which is you, Paige," Ayperos said. He reluctantly looked away from me to address Nathan. "The 'old one' wanted me to relay that message to you."

"Why would the 'old one' do that?" I asked, not getting why he'd care, but then the answer came to me. If Aosoth were to get a hold of me first, it could jeopardize his plan to use me to find Solomon's incantations for him. But then again, why would he screw around, giving Aosoth the opportunity to nab me before him? It didn't make sense.

Ayperos' gaze fell back on me, and he stared for an uncomfortable moment until Tree cleared his throat behind Nathan. I had almost forgotten Tree and Carrie were behind us. I glanced at Tree, and his eyes shifted to Ayperos, then to me. I knew Tree well enough to know what he was silently saying. This guy was attracted to me, which sent chills across my body.

"The 'old one' was right," Ayperos said more to himself than to us. "You are more beautiful than your grandmother Kora."

I gaped at him because I never knew what my grandmother's name was until now. A soft smile crossed his handsome face, and he nodded at the same time Nathan took a step forward, standing nose to nose with him.

"You need to back off," Nathan said between clenched teeth. He shoved Ayperos' chest. Ayperos stumbled backwards, his arms flailing. He collapsed against a tall, lanky dark-haired guy who had a thin chain attached to his nose ring all the way to his ear. It flapped against his cheek when he caught Ayperos and lifted him to his feet, pushing him forward. The group advanced on us, and I took a step forward. Ayperos raised his fist above his shoulder. The group stopped. He brushed his pinstripe bondage shirt, and wiped his hands on his black jeans.

He glared at Nathan. "Like I said, I have no quarrel with you." He paused, and his angular face contorted into a hideous mask of righteous evil. The laser beam of light swiped across his eyes again. "At least, not yet."

"Then get on with it," Nathan barked, unfazed by Ayperos' obvious threat.

"To answer Paige's earlier question." Ayperos' eyes flicked to mine, and I swear they softened at that very moment. "I was once one of the 'old one's' commanders, and he trusts me."

"But why would he want to warn me?" I asked. I could hear the sea crashing against the rocks in violent waves, and the temperature was dropping. My arms were cold, so I hugged them to my body. Nathan moved closer to me and wrapped his arm around my shoulders. Tree and Carrie stepped beside me. I noticed Carrie still kept her hand in her pocket, which gave me comfort.

His soft smile returned, produced this time by affection, which he defiantly displayed in front of Nathan through his words. "It's all part of the plan, Paige. And the 'old one' fancies you." He looked at Carrie, and inclined his head toward her. "He likes you too and really enjoyed your long make out sessions." His quick eyes went to Tree, and he smirked.

"You son-of-a-bitch," Tree said, shielding Carrie who made a squeaking sound. I glanced at her. She looked pale.

"Stay back, Tree," Nathan said, stepping in front of him, pushing the hand holding his pepper spray back. "He's just razing you."

Ayperos laughed and so did his group. "Well, I can also say this," he said between laughter. He pointed at Nathan and Tree. "He doesn't like you two." He swayed his finger to Tree, as if in a drunken daze. "And the reason why you're still alive is because of Carrie. But if you ever lose her favor"–he spread his arms out, palms up–"you're fair game." He bowed his head, then turned to his group. "Our business is done here. Let's go have some fun."

"Wait!" I said. I didn't want him to leave without answering a question I'd been wondering about.

Ayperos slowly pivoted. "Yes, Paige."

"What's the 'old one's' name?"

He gave me a conspiratorial smile. "That my dear will be revealed to you by the 'old one' himself." He tilted his head to the side in mocking thought. "Not even Anwar, the six-hundred-year-old African knows his name." He raised his hands and shook them in the air, puckering his lips. "Wooooo, the Almighty Anwar, whom you think so highly of." He pointed a sharp finger at us. "Let me tell you something about Anwar," he said, his eyes turning cold, his lips tight on each word he spoke. "He has his own agenda, and eventually you'll find out what it is. He's not as noble as you think." Snorting and snickering broke free behind him, and half of the group were nodding in agreement. And then they left, leaving the four of us in stunned silence.

About the Author

REBEKKAH FORD grew up in a family that dealt with the paranormal. Her parents' Charles and Geri Wilhelm were the Directors of the UFO Investigators League in Fairfield, Ohio, back in the 1970s. They also investigated ghost hauntings and Bigfoot sightings in addition to UFO's. Growing up in this type of environment and having the passion for writing is what drove Rebekkah at an early age to write stories dealing with the paranormal. At one point in her life, she thought she wanted to be a journalist, and although she enjoyed writing articles, she quickly discovered her real passion was writing fiction. Her fascination with the paranormal is what led her to write the 'Beyond the Eyes' series. Visit her online and read her blog at http://themusingwriter.blogspot.com

13807338R00171

Made in the USA
Charleston, SC
02 August 2012